MARK J. SUDDABY – Born in England, in the year of Apollo 13 and Luna 17, Mark grew up sitting in front of the telly, in paisley pyjamas, staring wide-eyed as *Doctor Who* (Tom Baker), *Space 1999*, and *Blake's 7* romped across wobbly sets in garish outfits and big hair. Mark grew up in a large family which conversely meant playing alone, constrained only by a boundless imagination.

At sixteen, realising that he was unlikely to become an actual space hero, Mark joined the Army. After a career bookended by Sandhurst and War College – gaining a Masters in Defence and Strategic Studies along the way – Mark left the military after 25 years, having reached the dizzying heights of the sixth floor of the Ministry of Defence, where he worked as a staff officer, preparing papers for senior officers and wishing he was anywhere else in the universe.

Mark now lives in the West Country where he is endlessly fascinated by technological advances, philosophical questions, geopolitics, the universe, and wondering what it would be like, if…

For Tracy
for seeing it through
(and for her psychologist's gaze)

MARK J. SUDDABY

ECHOES OF A LOST EARTH
PART TWO

AUSTIN MACAULEY PUBLISHERS™
LONDON • CAMBRIDGE • NEW YORK • SHARJAH

A CIP catalogue record for this title is available from the British Library.

ISBN 9781398490253 (Paperback)
ISBN 9781398490260 (Hardback)
ISBN 9781398490277 (ePub e-book)

www.austinmacauley.com

First Published 2023
Austin Macauley Publishers Ltd®
1 Canada Square
Canary Wharf
London
E14 5AA

The kernel for this story first evolved out of a series of threat-based lectures on climate change and energy security given at the UK Defence Academy, back in 2007. It has taken this long to go from writing that first draft, to publication, because I was never quite certain of my skill to tell the story. It's easy to compare with authors of renown and find yourself lacking; it's harder to put it all on the line anyway. But I'm older now, wiser, I hope, and more able to bite the bullet and put myself out there, warts 'n' all.

The themes, the ideas, the interplays, were all born back then, and yet they resonate with today's world far more than that of a decade ago. Watching the news and seeing disturbingly similar events play out in the real; I mean...

So first, I should acknowledge UK Defence and the British Army for their unwitting role in the curation of this tale from spark to fleshed-out, two-part novel. Without their investment in me, in my training and education – some of the best in the world – this story would not exist. And nor would I, as the person I am today.

Next, to John Jarrold for his professional advice, notes, thoughts and kind encouragement. And Gollancz, and just for what they said.

Then it descends into a litany (in a good way) of the people, of friends, who took the time to read my early (eye-peeling) drafts and offer their diplomatic thoughts and suggestions. Friends such as Tracy, Susie, Rich, Britt, Mark, Marcie, Gareth, Adrian, Matt; the list goes on. And those that continue to encourage me today to be better, do more; who keep me motivated and learning. To them all, I owe a huge debt. Any errors, though, are my own.

And last, to Austin Macauley Publishers, who took a punt. Without you, well… I am indebted to all those personally and professionally that spied the author and drew him into the daylight.

Thank you all. I hope that you, dear reader, enjoy reading *Echoes of a Lost Earth* as much as I have enjoyed writing it.

MARK SUDDABY
July 2022

Table of Contents

Völuspá

"The Wise Woman's Prophecy"

56. *In anger smites | Thor, the warder of Midgård*
Forth from their homes | must all men flee;
Nine paces fares | the son of Fjörgyn,
And, slain by the serpent, | fearless he sinks.

57. *The sun turns black, | Earth sinks in the sea,*
The hot stars down | from heaven are whirled;
Fierce grows the steam | and the life-feeding flame,
Till fire leaps high | about heaven itself.

58. *Now Garm howls loud | before Gnipahellir,*
The fetters will burst, | and the wolf run free;
Much do I know, | and more can see
Of the fate of the gods, | the mighty in fight.

59. *Now do I see | the Earth anew*
Rise all green | from the waves again;
The cataracts fall, | and the eagle flies,
And fish he catches | beneath the cliffs.

Book III
They Used to Call it: M.A.D.

| *war* |

And war is *coming* | *It stalks the minds of those with the power to prevent it*

The mountains will burn, no tree will stand,
Not any on Earth, water dries up
Sea is swallowed, flaming burns the heavens,
Moon falls, Midgård burns.

Verse 54 (extract), Muspilli

Nineteen

GB Newswire Roundup
2070

Collapse of United Ireland's government imminent || Request by Dublin to reunify with GB refused as Belfast nears point of civil collapse || All attempts at GB-wide emergency aid support and distribution to be abandoned within three months || Naval surface fleet dispatched to New Zealand || Emergency construction of new arcologies at Eden Project, Cornwall; Longleat, Wiltshire; Elveden, Suffolk, is authorised. Arcologies to be subterranean, geodesic, geothermal, dome constructions. Each to support a residency of fifty thousand, with strict age, gender (birth-based), health selection criteria enforced || Food and fuel reserves for current population stands at twenty-four months || Military ground forces tasked to secure all industrial greenhouse complexes now turned over for state production of food || Nuclear and gas-fired power stations to be abandoned in stages as fuel reserves dwindle and infrastructure fails || Ends

Ministry of Efficiencies, London

Guy duWinter blinked away the latest crisis management report from the Cabinet Office, rubbing his tired eyes.

After a pause, Alice said, '*It makes for a sobering read.*'

'Quite; but at least we know when we're licked. We're only making provision for five percent of our population, but at least we're doing *that.*'

'*Guy, may I suggest that now might be a prudent moment to bow out of public life and retire. Britain is on the verge of state collapse and it's only a matter of time before it is reduced – like Ireland – to a few city-states.*'

'You know, Alice, you may have a point. Luckily, my retirement home is ready and waiting.'

HMVS Mjölnir, Operations Centre, Inner Solar System

'Ship, prepare a dropship for immediate launch,' ordered Gethin, as he glided into the operations centre. If nothing else, he thought, at least he sounded the part.

'*Start-up procedure initiated*,' said the ship. '*May I ask what you intend to do?*'

With a granite edge to his voice, Gethin said, 'I'm going to rescue Guin, obviously.' Events were spiralling out of control and Gethin was desperate to take some action, regain some measure of command.

'*I should warn you, the chances of Guinevere's survival are statistically low*,' the ship said, in an impassive tone.

'I don't care, I have to *do* something; damnit all to hell!'

A shadow fell across the room; a silhouette filling up the passageway entrance.

'Gethin, what's going on?' Victoria asked, sympathetically, cautiously, as she made her way to the central holopit, where Gethin floated.

'Svet's taking Josh to mediception. He's in a bad way. Guin got sucked out the fucking airlock and I'm going to get her back!'

'How long's she been out there?'

'Ship lost contact with her seven minutes ago. I'm preparing a shuttle to retrieve her.'

'Is that wise?' said Vicki, seeming to choose her intonations carefully.

'*Wise?* What d'you mean, wise? Art blew her into fucking space! We have to try while she's still got air. It's worth a shot, Vicki,' said Gethin, as if to convince himself as much as her.

She sighed, as if mustering the strength to say the words. 'Gethin. Think for a moment: what would Joshua do? What's more important: Guin or the mission?'

If ever I needed Josh, it's right fucking now, thought Gethin, but the captain – the mission architect – was delirious, with a deadly case of the bends, on a slab in mediception. Gethin wondered if the whole enterprise was about to unravel around him just at it began. Joshua had a knack for reining in Gethin's impulsive "act now, think later" attitude, and while Gethin tended towards instinct, Joshua was more considered. It was the scientist in him, Gethin presumed. But Joshua wasn't here, so Gethin was going to have to suck it up.

'Ship, what're the chances of a successful recovery?' he asked, locked onto Vicki's pained expression.

'*Negligible, as is the possibility that the dropship's oxygen supply will hold out long enough for* Mjölnir *to arrest its velocity sufficiently to facilitate repatriation,*' said the ship.

'Gethin, I'm sorry, but she's gone. You're in command now; you have to act in the interests of the mission. Everything, everyone, else is secondary,' whispered Vicki, as tears began to weigh her eyes. 'You can't even, I'm afraid to say, risk a dropship for her, let alone your own life. It's just not feasible. The mission... I...'

Spinning away for a moment, to hide his emotional turmoil, Gethin barked, 'Ship; power down the dropship. Maintain current course and speed. I'm going to mediception.' Angry and impotent, he swung round and sailed into Vicki's embrace.

Alice took seventeen hours and a number of semi-sentient subroutines to successfully reprogram and test a batch of four thousand self-replicating, iron-carbon nanobots for their new function. There were a number of pre-programmed varieties aboard – some for health extension of the ship's community, others for the simpler task of maintaining the DNA and oocyte samples stored in the biobanks. None, though, had been created specifically to repair burst blood vessels and ruptured tissue caused by severe vacuum exposure. Luckily, Guinevere's nanotech expertise had not been entirely blown out the docking port with her. The sentient AI lacked the intuitive creativity to conduct the research itself, but she could crunch the acquired data to tinker at the edges of the core functionality.

Joshua remained in a deep coma, teetering on the edge of a complete system shutdown. Ramirez – the surgeon – had operated to arrest the internal bleeding and repair some of the more major damage where he could, but alone it wouldn't be enough to save him.

After the last of the simulations was complete, Alice had the new variant nanobots introduced into Joshua's bloodstream and waited. She had put a lot of time and effort into grooming the man; be a shame for it to go to waste at such a critical juncture.

Svetlana was curled into a G-couch in mediception. The lighting had switched to night cycle, lulling her into a few hours of exhausted slumber. She dosed fitfully as she had, on and off, ever since Joshua had been stretchered in – crashing the facility and its staff into action – three long, tortuous days prior. They'd done what they could in those early hours and had extolled Svet not to get her hopes up.

Josh had a minimal chance of survival and no chance at all of a full recovery. But then, as hope was being silently boxed up and packed away, the ship discovered a batch of experimental nanobots in BiolabThree – Guinevere's lab; designed specifically to repair vacuum damage. A break, at last. With nothing left to lose, the medical staff introduced the experimental bots and stood back.

As the days progressed, Joshua began the long road to a rocky recovery. His breathing became more measured, and he came off the ventilator; the crazy paving bloodshot etching across his skin began to fade; dialysis became unnecessary and he came off that as well. The deep coma, though, remained.

Svet shifted around in the couch in a never-ending struggle to get comfortable enough to doze, praying that sleep would take her; relief if only for a moment. Clasped tightly in the palm of her hand was the small flash-chip Josh had entrusted to her.

'Svet? You there?' Joshua hissed, in a dry and cracked whisper, barely audible over the background hum of the leviathan ship's systems and forest of medical machinery.

Svetlana sprang to full alertness in an instant. 'Josh? Josh! That you?' She fell out of the couch and tripped over the leads from a biosceen as she tumbled to her feet.

'Ship, lights! Wake Gethin… and Vicki; tell them Josh is conscious,' she barked, as she made her way across the room. 'Josh,' she said, with a softer timber, taking his hand in her own. 'Can you hear me? It's Svet, my love.'

'Svet?' Eyes closed, his tortured features relaxed fractionally. 'How's the ship? Everyone okay?' he whispered, pain drenching each word.

'Everything's fine, Joshua. God, it's good to hear your voice,' said Svet, as relief flooded through her exhaustion.

Josh turned his head towards the sound of her voice and slowly opened his eyes. 'Svet. I can't see you. I can't... see. I think...I may be... blind,' he said, shakily. What he couldn't see – a blessing – was that his eyes were now milky orbs, rent through with dead capillaries. Stormy little worlds of crazed, rusted crimson.

Mjölnir hadn't been designed with the infirm in mind; the passageway ladders that linked the living-spaces acting as constant reminders. When Joshua was well enough, he was placed in a jury-rigged hoist and manually pulled down/up into the main habitat, so that his convalescence could take place on the lawn of the stone bungalow he shared with Svetlana.

She worked tirelessly in the days that followed to look after him and describe for him her views of their tubular worldlet. Gethin – having taken over the duties of captain – had even reduced the spin to make it easier for Josh to get about on his own.

When he was well enough, they held a brief, perfunctory ceremony for Art (Arthur Hardinge) but few words were said. By contrast, days later was Guinevere's memorial. The entire ship's community attended, in person or virtually, and shared their memories. A plaque bearing her portrait and the dates of her life was placed in the observation lounge, and renamed "Guinevere's Eye" in her memory.

The stars were, after all, the last thing she'd have seen. When the ceremony was over, Josh – with others fussing about him – made his way gingerly down/up the passageway ladder to the habitat.

'So, how're you feeling, dude? You're certainly looking less pasty,' Gethin said, as Svet guided him back to their bungalow, throwing Gethin an admonishing frown.

'Okay, I guess. How's operations? Getting the hang of it all?' Alice had kept him abreast of events and Gethin still briefed him on daily occurrences, but Joshua knew it was out of a sense of friendship rather than need.

'Just keeping the chair warm 'til you're fit enough to resume command, dude, you know that.'

More resentfully than he'd intended, Josh replied, with, 'Yeah, well I'd get comfortable if I were you.'

'Josh, we've got some news for you, actually,' said Vicki, interjecting, as he was lowered into the low-backed recliner – his permanent waking residence.

'Sounds intriguing,' he said, turning his blind expression to the direction of Vicki's voice.

'Well,' said Svet, from a different direction, confusing and irritating him; he tried not to show it. 'One thing we aren't short of is medical expertise. As you know, exposure to vacuum burst the organs themselves but left the optical nerves intact. Now, the medics, working with the stewards, think they can patch the feed from your psyCore sofsceens directly into your optic nerves. Your sight can be restored, sort of, by remote.'

Joshua was intrigued but sceptical. 'Okay, but sofsceen contacts don't capture images, they simply act as a display overlay. Where would the sight, the picture, come from?'

Vicki: 'Ah, well they've thought of that. The images would be relayed via the grid from the ship's optical sensornet, which are everywhere. You wouldn't have a first-person perspective and you'd be heavily dependent on the ship for access and control, but your brain would adjust to the changed view-point easily enough. At least that's what the boffins are yapping on about.'

'*I have checked their work, Joshua, and it appears the most feasible solution to regaining some measure of sight. Although it will take time to master,*' added the voice in his head.

'So,' Josh asked, in a lighter tone, 'where do I sign?'

Belfast Docks, United Ireland
Three months later

'Here y' go, darlin'. Some hot soup'll paint a smile back onto that pretty face,' said the soldier, in an east London accent. His name was Mickey and he'd made no secret of his wanting to get to know Kiera a whole lot better.

The presence of the coarse, sullen troops reminded the young woman of the stories her grandmother used to tell her when she was a child. Stories of the Troubles; of British soldiers on the streets, searching homes, stopping cars, putting down rallies. Her grandmother had been a kid at the time and only lived through the last days of British military rule in the old Northern Ireland, but such tales had been enough to shape the views of her own generation. The Brits were not to be trusted. Soldiers especially.

And then in her lifetime – in what seemed to Kiera to be a rhyming historical irony – British soldiers had returned; only this time at the *request* of the

United Irish government, just after the Rockall Gigastorm had hit. The last act of the Taoiseach had been to declare a state of emergency and request urgent international assistance. Only the British had responded and then only for Belfast.

Kiera had been lucky. When the city's power grid had gone offline, she had quickly realised that if she stayed in her flat she'd die there. Move or die, a phrase she'd heard from somewhere. Movie, maybe. So she clambered and scurried her way to the former royal courts by the docks, where the Brits had set up a humanitarian aid station.

She'd been early enough to get a bed (benefitting from others' reticence to trust the Brits) and during the month she'd been living with the soldiers – with their odd accents and strange mannerisms – they'd expanded the centre to take in the covered markets adjacent to the imposing old courthouse. Being near the docks had ensured that provisions brought in by the icebreakers from Liverpool were sorted and allocated there first, so at least she wasn't going hungry. Especially, with a judicious use of her hazel, saucer-dish eyes.

Kiera hadn't ventured outside in five days, but each morning she'd climb to the top floor of the building and peer out across the frigid, immobilised cityscape. Just across the Westlink were the derelict Divis flats, their tower blocks dominating the view east. A couple of days before, a fire had caught and gutted one of the smaller blocks. The pallid Belfast Hills hunkered over the dying city, as if that ancient land were rising up to reclaim the former inlet that Belfast had blossomed around.

Back in the main communal area, she sipped her soup. The Brits had been courteous and efficient but not especially approachable, and she liked it that way. It was as if they sensed the ingrained suspicion, but couldn't work out who was and wasn't party to that wariness. Kiera's parents had emigrated to Berwick (bordering Scotland) a few years previously, and she'd got a text-only through to them a couple of times since the gigastorm had hit. Comms had been patchy as whole sections of the wire dropped out, but at least she knew they were alive and coping; for the moment, at least. As she sat, lost in her own dark thoughts, her attention tuned in to a muffled conversation between two Brits, a few yards away.

One said, 'Well, thank fuck for that. When d'we bug out?'

'Dunno, but within the week, sarge said. According to Shaggy, anyways, but cooks, right? They 'ears everything. Reckons we're redeploying to one o' them fancy new arcologies down south. Be a laugh I reckon, and there'll be plenty o' tail. We don't even have to apply for residency *and* I 'eard we can bring us our nearest, like,' offered the other.

'And everyone gets a pony, eh? Lucky old us. The trouble'll be pleased, mind, she's been 'oled up in a place pretty much like this, in Ham, and she's goin' bleedin' mental.'

'You're not wrong. The cap'n said we was only s'posed to be a gesture like; we was never goin' to save this sorry lot. Guess that's the world we live in now, eh? Fucked up, y'know?'

'Fucked up, chief.'

With her hands clasped around the warmth of the thermal mug, Kiera's mind raced. The Brits were pulling out, leaving Belfast to collapse in on itself. Deep down she'd known this was never a long term solution. So now she needed to get out of Ireland and into one of these new arcologies(?), but how? Hook up with one of the soldiers, maybe. There had to be another way. Perhaps that nice (probably single) captain could help.

Global Newswire Roundup

NAU to abandon population centres above thirtieth parallel. National capital relocated to Houston || UE breaking up along national boundaries: Tirana, Naples and Sarajevo expected to make the transition to independent city-states || State collapse of Russia imminent; federal forces deploying to strategic defensive locations || Australia, Brazil, Indonesia and the African Congress are now the principal food exporters || Bilateral agreements between major Consumer-States and Supplier-Blocs are beginning to break down || Australia set to raise defence force alert status, in response to regional tensions || Brazil begins negotiations with other South American states to form a socialist economic bloc to counter NAU || AmPac remains neutral || Indonesia, North Korea, India continue to destabilise || Ends

3ʳᵈ Liaison Department, Shanghai

Mù Yingtai shifted in her seat, in measured irritation. She had returned to her fifty-seventh floor corner office, overlooking the city below, keeping a lazy eye on the holographic scene in front of her – a virtual session of the politburo standing committee. Scattered about, evidently randomly, were the luminescent heads and shoulders of the other committee members. One was half buried in Mù's wheat-sheaf table lamp, another hovered in front of a Tiananmen Square Uprising original (an imprisonable offence if it were hanging on almost any other wall).

An intelligence analysis of the impact of the two gigastorm eruptions had just been released, focusing the committee's attention on the director for an assessment of the PRC's position.

'Does the 3rd Liaison Department agree with the analysis?' the chair asked.

'It does,' said Mù, silently surprised at the question, as it had been her department that had complied the report. After a pause she added, 'Eurasia and the African Congress pose little threat. Likely Europe will follow the GB model and coalesce into a loose confederation of city-states after a brief, abortive, return to nationalism. Changes to the sub-Saharan climate will take place too slowly to allow AC to benefit collectively from their new breadbasket status.

'NAU will likely push south, forcing Buenos Aires to expand into its neighbours to form a buffer zone. For the moment, Russia is our biggest concern. As soon as Moscow realises it can no longer feed its population, it'll strike south through the 'Stans, bringing it into conflict with India, Iran and very possibly us.'

The director of the 3rd Liaison Department waited silently for the committee to respond. Her verbal synopsis didn't give levels of probability for each event occurring, but the members had access to the detail if they needed the reassurance. *That isn't what matters, in any case*, she reflected.

The northern hemisphere states were going into meltdown, whilst those in the south were preparing – at long last – for their turn at the wheel. *So the issue at hand*, Mù thought, *is how is the People's Republic affected by this shift in global power? Cui Bono?*

'As long as Russia doesn't threaten our interests, do we care?' one of the committee members asked, in a nonchalant tone.

Mù replied, with, 'We do if more resource disputes turn nuclear, like the Israeli water wars. Russia pushes south into Afghanistan, for example, while India expands northwards into Pakistan, and a major nuclear exchange becomes unavoidable. Necessary, even.'

'And what are our options for weathering this creeping glacial expansion?' another asked. He was – like the other male committee members – old but with

23

a thick, reclaimed mane of black hair. *Do they dye it, I wonder, or is it re-grown? The vanity.*

'We've two options,' continued Yingtai. 'The first is to withdraw into our domed cities, as the British are doing. This would mean abandoning a majority of our citizens and could leave us at the mercy of these emerging super-blocs. The second is to expand south to annex arable farmland.'

'Expand south to where?'

'The Indonesian archipelago,' Mù said in a flat tone. It was all in the report. Eyebrows raised and expressions went blank as the director spoke, as if each was attempting to suppress their surprise but were simultaneously given away.

'How would Australia react?' The chair appeared to be considering the option.

'The new world order will see Brazil and Australia hold the balance of world food production between them. Brazil is preoccupied with the NAU and therefore no threat. Australia, however, will see any move by us as precursor to a land grab within its borders. A showdown with Canberra therefore becomes unavoidable. That being that case, 3rd Liaison recommends pre-emptive action, starting with the annexation of Indonesia before moving into northern Australia, ensuring our complete and exclusive control over all regional food manufacture and export.'

'Timescales?' The chair looked to be warming to the idea.

'Difficult to say. It depends how quickly our own climate is affected by gigastorm activity. And our hand may be forced by Russia or the NAU. If they act precipitously, then so should we.'

'Why?'

'Because we're more likely to achieve our goals within the wider context of global upheaval than if we act unilaterally,' the director said. 'We can hide our actions in the chaff.'

'What would you say the odds are of a significant nuclear contestation, say within the next five years?' another committee member asked, their likeness hanging in mid-air.

'High,' said Mù. *It doesn't matter*, she thought. *The committee doesn't care.* Mù knew that isolationism was never an option. For too long China had been preparing to take its rightful place as the apex predator of the world order. The idea of giving that up was never viable and Yingtai had banked on that ingrained cultural obsession when she had drawn up the choices for her fellow committee members to masticate over.

The chair said, 'Very well, then. Thank you, 3rd Liaison, for your assay of the issues at hand. I will arrange to convert our major cities into interconnected, self-sustaining arcologies. In tandem, I'll order our military commanders to prepare for the subjugation of the Pacific Rim. Are we agreed?'

Interesting, thought Mù, *we're going for a little of both. But then, isn't that the Chinese way – cover all the bases and then hang back to see what transpires.*

Confirmations came in from all the floating heads in the room. One by one, they blinked out of existence, returning Mù's office to the solitude she preferred. What she needed now, the director thought to herself, was to contrive a provocation; force the committee into action. *Now is not the time for timidity and obfuscation.*

HMVS Mjölnir, Habitat

'*Ready?*' asked Alice.

'Just flick the damn switch; trying for dramatic effect doesn't suit you,' said Joshua, irritably.

After months of tweaking the tech, there was a quick, silent pause and he felt a strange tingling sensation behind his eyes as the implants fired up, and the habitat wavered into pixilated view. Josh could see himself sitting in his chair outside the low stone cottage. Vicki, Svet, Gethin, Ramirez were clustered around.

Glare from the light tube was distorting the image, suggesting the feed was coming from one of the cable-mounted optics. It was an odd sensation for Josh to be viewing himself from a disembodied perspective, but he was ecstatic just to be sighted again and filled with the optimism that he would quickly master the new, oblique, viewpoint.

'So?' Svetlana said, the word dripping with expectation.

'It's good, it's really good. I can see us all crowded about. I can see the habitat. It's an odd, out-of-body perspective, but hey, I'm not complaining,' Josh said, as he moved cautiously around, experimenting with his new vision. Arm out, hand wave, head tilt.

'That's such a relief, Josh. I'm so pleased for you,' said Svet. The strain of the past few months sloughing off her, leaving her limp, relieved.

'Fantastic, dude, now you can get back to being captain again, 'cos I am *sooo* not cut out for it,' said Gethin, as he put his hand up for a high-five.

Judging the location of the outstretched hand as best he could, Josh raised his own and made a swipe. Their hands glanced off each other, not quite achieving the effect, but it wasn't nothing.

Victoria said, warmly, 'Y'see? We'll have you playing darts in no time.'

'We don't have a dartboard,' Joshua said, with a grin, aiming it in Vicki's direction.

'We don't? Gethin; how could you've made such a shocking oversight? What will we do for the rest of our lives?' she said, in mock chastisement.

'Ship, give me a split-screen feed of all the optics focused on my current location,' Josh said.

'*Certainly, Joshua,*' Alice replied.

The view was both alien – multifaceted, like a fly's – and enthralling as his mind reeled from the information overload. Carefully – as if tiptoeing through a new, multi-pointed world – he began to process the complementary, overlapping images.

Ramirez looked pleased, but cautious, and said, 'When you're ready, Josh, we'll need to get you down to mediception and have your implants checked over.'

'Will do, Doc, just gimme a moment to get used to it all.'

'*Joshua, we are receiving another datapacket from Earth, would you like to review it?*' Alice said, making herself heard by all present.

'Let's take it in ops, shall we?' Josh said to the others, who nodded in relieved agreement.

As he made to get up from the recliner, Svet bent over and enveloped him in an awkward bear hug.

'Welcome back, my love,' she whispered, in his ear.

'Thank you, darling, but was never away, not really.'

'You were, you very nearly were,' she said, her voice breaking slightly. She released him and took his hand as he adapted to walking by watching himself. In doing so, she grasped his hand a little longer than necessary and Josh realised there was something in it.

'I've no idea what's on it – I never looked – but thought you'd want it back,' she said, under her breath, as if sensing some clandestine shroud over the item.

Joshua fumbled his way into the belts of an ops centre chair, beneath the holopit, and once the others were drifting gently around the zero-G room, he blinked the datafeed directly into his sofsceened (and now relayed) vision, asking Alice to fire up the newsreel.

'*Mjölnir*, this is Harwell, transmitting,' said the mission controller, as she loomed large in holographic form. Their distance from Earth precluded a two-way conversation so they communicated by burst transmission, updating each other on news and items of technical importance to the mission.

The first part of the feed was mission stuff. Harwell confirming their solar position – as they visually spotted the ship – allowing them to verify their own navigational fixes. Then the Harwell feed projected out the Sun slingshot, adjusting for established vectors, velocity, anticipated gravitational eddies and Port Charlotte data. Finally, they moved onto the subject the group were most interested in: news from home (*former* home).

'The situation here isn't good, *Mjölnir*. The Rockall Island Gigastorm has decimated Ireland, Scotland and Wales. Only England remains functional and barely. The new arcologies are nearing first phase completion and we're in the process of moving mishcon to the Falkland Islands. If you're asking why, don't; it's on the direct orders of the Ministry of Efficiencies.

'Transfer will be complete within the week,' the controller said. As she spoke, imagery from the wire flashed up giving some understanding of the difference between the old winter and this new, more permanent phenomenon. Josh had wondered many times since breaking orbit – particularly without the benefit of sight as a distraction – whether they'd done the right thing. Here, now, in this moment, he was certain everyone in ops was entirely content that they had.

'Internationally,' the narration continued, 'the NAU is focusing its efforts in Mexico, where the climate's still good. Northern Europe is breaking up into fiefdoms, we think, but the real worry now is what old Russia and China will do. Russia's infra is seizing up fast as the Noril'sk Gigastorm radiates out, and China will be feeling its effects before long.

'We're bracing ourselves for the worst back here. Seems you picked the right moment to make your excuses.' As the controller spoke, Josh thought he could detect a tinge of jealously in the woman's voice.

'We've included some choice news items from the wire and there are personal feeds. We look forward to receiving your update. Let us know how Joshua's progressing. Harwell out.'

'You can let 'em know yourself, now, dude,' said Gethin, clearly relived to be free of the pressure, the tedium, of command.

'So what d'you think?' asked Vicki, looking unnerved.

'You'll probably have a better idea once you open your diplomatic pouch,' Josh said, referring to Victoria's role as head of the *Mjölnir* community and her palace-dispatched, classified datapackets. 'But if I were a betting man, I'd say our planet has just arrived, sweaty and belligerent, at the precipice.' If anyone was questioning the rationale for this expedition, they wouldn't be any more, Josh was certain. *You have to hand it to Alice, she really knows how to pick an exit.*

As the others floated out of ops – eyes glazed as they locked onto their personal feeds – Joshua examined the arcology construction. There wasn't anyone to write him as he'd cut all emotional ties to Britain when his mother died, six years gone. His nearest and dearest were all now up here with him, hurtling through space at five megametres an hour.

Joshua was pleased the research they'd conducted at Eden, and then later put into practice in *Mjölnir*, was now serving Britain in a different capacity. Closed ecosystems constructed in the form of arcologies looked like they could prove the salvation to a select core sample of Britain's population – perhaps even the human race, all but negating the need for their mission; at least potentially. Assuming the world's contrary community could make the transformation to the new climate in peace, of course. And the have-not's would be okay with it. Minor stuff like that.

Belfast Docks, United Ireland

'You're in luck, Miss Shannondale,' said the officious looking captain, from behind a desk situated in one of the old courtrooms that the Brits had turned into their "command and control" centre. The insignia on his arm read, "Joint Administrative Support" as if in explanation of his self-important demeanour.

'We're looking for women of optimal childbearing age for the new arcologies.' She mentally recoiled from his grimace. 'Fill out this form and I'll put it in for fast-track processing. You'll need to submit to a medical exam, too.' He handed the young woman a plasisheet and ushered her away with a flick of the wrist.

Kiera filled in the form and returned it immediately, conscious of the time bureaucracies took to break out the ink stamp. To her surprise, later that same day a clerk informed her that her application – subject to medical status – had been approved. She was to be ready to go at 0600 the following Saturday. Three days. With the flood of relief that her immediate circumstances had improved, she headed off to find a comms terminal that might punch a message through to her parents.

Kiera gulped down the last of the powered hot chocolate she'd shared with one of the soldiers, and pulled out a blue balaclava with a polycrystalline-breathing sheath. The three tortuous, gunfire punctuated days had passed and the young, reserved, city girl was girding herself to make the short journey to the British merchant navy ship in the harbour. Her old life had been pretty easy, she admitted ashamedly to herself.

Untidy flat, mindless shop assistant gig, clubbing, and casual relationships. She'd never really done anything challenging or character building in her short life – nothing to prepare her for whatever was to come – which was why she was surprised to have mustered the mettle that had gotten her this far and would hopefully carry her onto the sanctuary of an *English* arcology. *Urgh.*

Minutes ticked by sluggishly until the time arrived for Kiera to step forward for processing. With a small bag hanging off her shoulder, she passed her identity chip to the soldier behind the table and waited, bouncing on the balls of her feet. The explosive sounds of crumbling civility had intensified over the last few days, as if the residents-cum-illegals of Belfast could tell the gig was up and were taking what they could while there was still stuff left to take. The rumoured Brit pull-out had spread through the centre like a bitter wind, so it wasn't surprising the city was a churning caldron of fear and greed.

The soldier picked up the identity chip and looked up at her for the first time. His eyes dulled with disinterest.

'Keep this with you at all times, Ms Shannondale,' he said, handing back the chip. 'It contains your GB travel and residency permit. Without it, you'll be left to fend for yourself. Proceed through those double doors.' He thumbed lazily over his shoulder to the out of bounds area behind the row of tables. 'And wait be called forward for transport to the dock. Good luck.'

'Thank you,' Kiera said, softly.

Hoisting her bag-strap higher onto her shoulder, she made her way through the double doors and across the near-empty warehouse section of the centre. It was brutally cold so she pulled the balaclava from her thermalined pocket and wrestled it over her greasy, knotted hair. As she was adjusting the facemask so she could breathe, a series of sudden, ear-splitting thunderclaps echoed through the freezer-like space. Kiera instinctively dived to the floor. Pain spreading from her elbows and knees.

'MOVE,' the soldier bellowed, as he sprinted towards Kiera, grabbing her under the arm and hauling her after him.

'What's going on?' she said, through the muffling mask. The soldier didn't reply, pulling her forward as he glanced back the way she'd come. She was constantly on the edge of falling, never quite managing to recover her balance as the armour-clad figure kept her in an iron grip. She knew the noise: gunfire. The aid centre was under attack.

'DOWN,' he shouted, the speakers in his suit amplifying his voice. She fell to the floor, and not through choice. Looking up, she saw her protector – his goggled eyes momentarily glazed – then he blinked twice and his hip-mounted carbuncle burst into life as lights flashed and power cells whirred. Grabbing the pistol grip, he swung the weapon up and forward until it was levelled in the direction of the firefight happening in the room beyond.

As if in response to a challenge, the double doors she had just passed through flew open and heavy footfalls echoed out. She turned her head, catching a glimpse of hunched figures dressed similarly to her, in thermal layers, ski masks, and carrying old style, handheld machine guns and shoulder-mounted grenade launchers.

'Damn. We thought we'd be clear before they hit the station,' the soldier uttered, in an un-amplified voice. 'Get up and stay behind me.'

Kiera did as ordered, glad to be off the frozen floor. As she crawled around behind the soldier, his weapon system discharged a burp of munitions that shredded the doors and scattered packaging being used as cover. She counted three grenade detonations and multiple bursts of fire that peppered the side of the high wall. She'd never seen such split-second destruction and it terrified her.

'GO, NOW,' the voice boomed; the soldier waving towards a small door to the outside.

Kiera darted forward, shouldering her way through as the soldier continued to wreak havoc as he withdrew deliberately along her route. As the door swung out, she was immediately hit by a wall of tearing ice and pain. Her breath was snatched from her as panic began to bubble up from the pit of her stomach.

Recovering slightly from the shock of stepping into an eddying storm front, she spotted a low-slung, storm-grey, armoured military vehicle. The hydraulic rear door staggered open and a gloved hand beckoned her inside. She stumbled forward, grabbing the ceramic doorframe to steady herself. After a clumsy fall into the back, the door sealed and the carrier lurched forward.

'What about the soldier?' Kiera asked, as she tugged off her balaclava, staring at each of the other petrified civilian passengers in turn.

'Don't worry, he made it back okay. He's up in the cupola,' said a disembodied voice. 'Came to fetch you once the perimeter was breached.'

As she was helped into a seat, a loud, dull thud reverberated and the personnel carrier jolted sharply, followed by a residual shudder through the toughened armour.

'RPG. Nothing to worry about,' said the voice again, as the vehicle slammed to a sudden halt, before leaping forwards once more. As the nightmare, staccato journey continued, she felt more hard impacts against the hull and sharp discharges from the vehicle's own systems.

Just as suddenly, just as fearfully, the armoured vehicle tilted forward, onto its nose, in what Kiera recognised as a hard braking manoeuvre, and the rear hatch fell open to the hostile, alien world outside. Kiera fought to get the balaclava back in place.

'Shift yourselves; get t'the ship's gangplank and don't stop 'til you're safely aboard. We'll provide cover.'

She peered timidly out of the opening, attempting to gather her bearings, her courage, thought *fuck it*, and burst from the wagon, pelting after the person in front with all her adrenalin-fuelled might.

The crystalline wind bit at her exposed skin as flaming streaks of fire leapt from weapon mounts onboard the large, grey vessel looming over her. Behind, she heard thuds, burps, starbursts as the armoured carrier joined the battle.

Kiera was shocked by the ferocity of the fight. She'd no idea her fellow city dwellers – they that let her by and shared their day – were capable of such blind brutality.

Twenty

Darma Wulandari's tale
Pontianak, Indonesia

Darma watches the convoy of trucks hum through the main thoroughfare below him, kicking up dust with a rattle of aggregate as they rumble past. They're carrying rice or sugarcane from the farms to the docks. The gates swing open, then close quickly, partially masking the dockyard beyond.

The police return to their positions, shields and whips at the ready; automated, non-lethal, crowd dispersal systems active and tracking. In the distance, a foghorn sounds, marking the departure of the last Chinese cargo vessel as it heads for open water. Behind the police barricades and beyond the secured gates, Darma glimpses army people milling nervously around their vehicles.

The former student is sitting on the roof edge – legs dangling – of a small trading centre in Pontianak, the provincial capital of West Kalimantan. A sudden clatter resonates behind him as the old corrugated door to the roof is heaved ajar just enough to allow another person the squeeze through. It's Mawar, Darma's friend, and would-be girlfriend, if only he could summon up the courage to ask. Easier, he thinks, to take part in what's about to happen below than risk the rejection of a *girl*.

As Mawar slides in silently next to him, Darma returns his attention to the scene past his bare, dangling feet. In the street, the raucous, technicoloured crowd has re-joined after parting to allow the convoy through. Like torn flesh healing. As he watches, clusters of nervous people – students like Darma and Mawar, farmers, dockhands, and others from all walks of island life – wait for the countdown to end.

The throng is like a million ants in the bottom of a glass, directionless and agitated. Trapped but with no notion as to how. As the crowd oscillates it kicks dust into the cooling, early evening air. Steadily, the noise increases in proportion to the confidence bestowed by the swelling numbers. The crowd begins counting down, shouting each number with one voice, as if words alone will steel their nerves.

'Twelve…eleven…ten…' the crowd chants.

Darma pops the jack into his ear and flicks open his vone. It defaults to the Al Jazeera news wiresite.

Nine…eight…seven, relays the device through the earpiece.

Darma flicks to multi-screen layout and sees similar crowds chanting numbers in front of similar police lines all over the archipelago. He scrolls out again and scans the almost identical crowds in the South Americas, the African Congress, even Australia. Darma spots a link and flicks it open. It takes him to the anonymously posted, *Day of Action* wiresite.

'Four…three…two…' declare the crowd, as one.

The counting stops, the crowd falls silent, the police fidget nervously behind their helmets and their shields. The time is 1900 local. The globally synchronised date, time and locations for the *Day of Action* food protests are no secret, but the sheer number of protests in Indonesia alone has spread the security forces thin.

'ATTENTION! YOU ARE MEETING IN VIOLATION OF CIVIL CODE. DISPERSE IMMEDIATELY,' demands an amplified, official sounding voice.

Darma watches.

A brimob police holograph appears above the port entrance ordering the protesters to disband, but instead the crowd swells as if waiting for just such a rallying call and the momentum is unstoppable. As if in response, a sea of smaller holographs flicker into life above the swarming protestors. The messages range from catchy "Feed Us First" slogans, to accusations of international conspiracy.

As the crowd surges, Darma steals a sideways glance at Mawar, whose eyes are burning with the intensity of the experience. She looks nice. But then, she always looks nice.

The crowd crashes against the police line and recoils in an instinctive, collective fear of the anticipated counter-action. A momentary pause, and flash-bombs shoot into the air like fireworks. They originate from within the city, detonating amongst the police barricades; the crowd surges forward again; battle is joined.

Protestors-turned-rioters collapse into wriggling heaps as weighted webs and taze-bolts remove them from the game. Time and again the crowd withdraws before surging forward in another charge. Before long, the oscillating mass of humanity begins to act and react as a single entity, as if each human is a cell within a living organism. Amoeba-like feelers flow forward as the organism ebbs and flows, searches and probes. When stung it recoils, but only to lash out once again, intensity growing with each cycle.

The special police stagger back into the port compound. The army moves forward to take over and without even offering a show of tolerance engage with lethal force. The air becomes filled with rocks, gunfire, flash-bombs, blood and screams, and the soldiers' defences are quickly breached as rioters head for the huge grain silos.

As daughter looter-gangs detach from the main body of the living crowd, others are already climbing the outer struts and opening the gates used to load the vast holds of the ships. Soon, rice is flowing from six of the sluice-gates dotted around a storage bin. A fire, followed quickly by the eruption of a palm oil silo into orange, billowing flame.

This isn't the plan, Darma thinks to himself.

Five hours pass and Mawar and Darma are sitting around a small fire set by the newly designated food redistribution cooperatives.

'Have you heard?' Mawar asks, in an excited voice.

'Heard what?' says Darma, into Mawar's liquid-onyx eyes.

'The government's fallen. The *Day of Action* protests have brought the *actual* government down. Can you believe it?' The look in the girl's gleaming eyes flashes momentarily in fear, at the dawning of a new age for their country, free of domination by the old northern powers. Because freedom comes with its own night-terrors, too.

Darma checks his vone without speaking as Mawar shifts in her seat. 'You're right,' he says, eventually. 'The farmers coalition has taken power. This is great news, Mawar. At last we're free.'

Mawar asks, 'Who d'you think did it?'

'Did what?'

'The *Day of Action*. Set up the wiresite, coordinated the countdown, all that stuff,' says Mawar.

Darma looks around the ruined port facility, and says, 'Dunno, but whoever it was, they're my new hero. They may have saved the world.'

Later, he checks the Al Jazeera news wiresite and discovers that Australia has put a naval taskforce to sea and Brazil has ended its Grain-for-Goods agreement with the NAU. Far more alarming, though, is the news that the new Jakarta-based governing collective has accepted military assistance from China – just to help restore order, they say.

'But wasn't that *why* we protested,' says Mawar, 'to free us from foreign interference?'

Eden Arcology, Cornwall

The journey across the Irish Sea to Liverpool and then onwards by military heavy transport had been arduous. It had taken four days and countless expletives to get Kiera to the new Eden Arcology. En route, the convoy – a hotchpotch of military all-terrain utility vehicles – had soaked up snakes of borderline ruggedised civilian trucks, so that now there was a little under four thousand would-be residents, sitting in coloured pens in a warehouse to one of Britain's newest, sealed cities, waiting ever more impatiently to be processed. Another three convoys were due in later in the week, according to Erynn.

Erynn Brakkan was the soldier who had come back for Kiera in Belfast. He was a gravelly sergeant, and allocated to Eden. During the overland trip they'd become close so that by the time they had arrived in Cornwall they'd agreed to apply for joint residency. There were obvious benefits and she had turned out to be more of a pragmatist than she thought.

Not that she didn't like Erynn, of course, but it hadn't exactly been the romance of the century. Although, he did possess a sort of rugged charm.

Tired and irritable, Kiera was processed and emerged, eventually, from the cold, dim passageway into what seemed like a paradise. The large space her group spilled out into was dug into the earth, with a low glass ceiling set at ground level. Tables and chairs were clustered under the huge horizontal skylight, made up of clear hexagonal panes, letting pallid daylight pour in.

The other residents – dressed in loose fitting clothes with coloured armbands – were sat chatting or flowing into or out of the central well. Harsceens dotted the inner walls providing communal information and external news, because that was what the world had become; *external*.

Kiera looked up again and concentrated on what she could see through the ceiling. The arcology hunkered as if against the world, blisters in the well of a depression. She saw the tips of wind turbines and clumps of overlapping hexagonally-paned domes: the old biomes, turned over to agricultural use, she'd been told.

Higher up – running around the ridge of the old clay pit – was the initial foundation level of thermoplas panels that would rise and arch to form a Fuller Dome, and eventually, encase the entire complex.

In the centre of the space a wide, gently spiralling stairwell leading down into the subterranean aspect of the city, where the life support and the industrial infrastructure was housed. As Kiera and the others descended the stairs, they caught glimpses of warrens leading off in all directions. They were marked: some led to the biomes, others to refectories, theatres, markets, workspaces. One tunnel, though, was sealed and marked with a heavy-duty out of bounds notice. It was the only such sign she'd seen.

Bewildered and exhausted, she was shown to the room she would share with Erynn. It was in the Orange Sector on the minus third floor. Whilst not roomy, it was decently appointed, with a harsceen and wire interface; above all, though, it was *private*. Kiera wasted no time in stripping off and taking a steaming hot shower.

She was surprised when the ionised water vapour (delivered via three multi-nozzled hoops) cut out after three minutes and wouldn't re-activate. *Still, could be worse*, she thought, as she patted about for a towel, *could be back in Belfast*.

'Ah hah, I see you've made yourself at home already,' said Erynn, standing in the doorway, giving it a decidedly undersized look in comparison to the sergeant's broad shoulders and unfastened impact armour. Kiera poured a glass of water as Erynn dumped his kit in the corner.

'Been allocated a job yet?' he asked, as he slumped into a low, straight-backed chair.

'No. Tomorrow, apparently. I'll be given a choice of three, they said. How was your induction?' she said, though her mind was wandering. *What will they make me do? What's it going to be like here?*

'Not bad. There's a general in charge of site security. Our main function will be internal policing, stuff like that, with an element of extra-arcology patrols; the usual. The big concern right now is the reaction of the local civpop who don't fit the residency criteria. Not a happy thought, that one.'

Kiera paused and her faced collapsed slightly, as if she'd been holding it to-gether for too long. She said, 'Erynn, how did we come to this? Why are we all taking this in our *stride*, like it's just another day? A few weeks ago, I lived a normal life in Belfast. I literally *loathed* the British. Especially soldiers. Now I'm in some sort of apocalyptic British Empire nightmare. Like my life, my identity, is no longer my own.' The tension ground itself into her features as she spoke. The journey, the worry over her future had stayed such thoughts, but now, seemingly safe at last, her walls were beginning to crumble. Parents and friends were filling up her thoughts.

And for reasons she couldn't quite understand, her overwhelming emotion was one of guilt. Guilt at being alive and safe and selfish when so many others hadn't been as fortunate.

Erynn stopped what he was doing and glanced up. Stepping over his kit, he ran his oversized hands through her short, wet, brunette locks before cupping her face.

'People are adapting,' he said, softly. 'In time, no doubt, the community here'll get over the shock and ask why? What's it all for? Why us? Why now? And there'll be a period of grieving, but for the moment they're simply glad to survive. To be *us* and not *them*. *Here* and not *there*.' He paused, contemplative-ly. 'Remember, a fraction – and I mean a *fraction* – of the population are being housed in these new city domes. Everyone else – *everyone* – is being left to fend for themselves. *Out there*.' Erynn pointed up the light-well to emphasis his point. 'Those of us lucky enough to have made it into an arcology are truly the fortunate few, and that's a hard thing to bear. Being lucky: who'd have thought.'

'I tried to put a call into my parents.'

'And?'

'Wouldn't connect. D'you think they'll allow them to come here?' she said, with a worried expression, in anticipation of Erynn's response.

'No, Kiera, they won't. You know that. How many old people have you seen today? I'm sorry but they won't fit the residency criteria and that's assum-ing they could even get here. This is about the survival of the species. It's diffi-cult decisions time, I'm afraid.'

In a quiet, almost accepting voice, she asked, 'Do you think they'll survive. Out there?'

'I think they've got as good a chance as anyone, so who knows, eh?' But it didn't sound sincere. After a pause, the burly sergeant added, 'Listen, Kiera; I know it's a massive, mind-boggling, surreal, survivor-guilt situation, but this is affecting everyone, everywhere, and we're just some of the lucky ones. Think how much worse it is in Russia or Spain. Now, I'm ready for a shower.' His face brightening.

'Ah, well, you'll have to wait another four hours; it's on a lockout timer. Sorry.'

Mount Pleasant, Falkland Islands

'Good afternoon, Mr Grieve; welcome to mission control,' offered the mission director of the relocated (formerly Harwell) Space Sciences Centre.

Guy duWinter had retained his assumed identity; less opportunity for confusion. As he stepped out onto the metallic, grilled balcony that overlooked the myriad of large walsceens opposite, and the pit of lined chairs and benches that dominated the floor plate below, the woman continued.

'Mishcon, colloquially. It's a little austere I'm afraid, but suits our purposes. The three mission teams are able to analyse the telemetry bursts we receive from *Mjölnir* and prepare response packages. We also keep them abreast of global developments and feed them deep space telemetry, gathered by orbital or lunar apparatus.' She droned on; Guy tuned her out.

The room lay deep within Mount Pleasant; hollowed out from hard, Paleozoic rock, it was cube shaped and oriented towards one wall onto which the main walsceens hung. Opposite, along the rear wall was a two-storey bank of glass-fronted offices. All very New York post industrial chic.

Of the walsceens, the largest depicted the inner solar system with a dotted orange line originating randomly in space at about the point of the Earth's own orbital tract. A blue icon inched along the line, with a data bubble identifying it as *HMVS Mjölnir*.

The Earth would orbit the Sun at least forty times during the first part of *Mjölnir's* inner sol jaunt, before the craft returned for a flyby.

Suspended from the ceiling was a holographic projector maintaining a situation holograph in the space above the heads of the pit controllers.

As duWinter had made the transfer from his sub-orbital jet to the main complex, he'd caught sight of the ranks of unmanned attack drones and all-terrain combat groundcraft lined up in subterranean hangars. The Falklands had been quietly upgraded, housing a strategic military reserve; making it the perfect spot for Guy to retire to during these difficult days.

As the director continued to point out aspects of the mission – of the most vital interest to her – duWinter's thoughts drifted back to Britain. He wondered if he'd done enough to prepare them. He'd known this was coming, after all, but had thought it another two decades away. Still, at least he'd released the polyhedral Fuller Dome construction materials. That wasn't nothing.

He offered a silent prayer to the old country and pushed such distractions from his mind before they began to form into coherent recriminations, switching his attention to the more immediate issue of local government.

'Get me a meeting with the governor general and the air officer in command, would you,' he said to the director, interrupting the cadaverous woman in mid-flow.

She responded nervously with, 'Of course, of course. Consider it done,' and spent a moment blinking and moving bony fingers.

'There's just one other thing I ought to bring to your attention,' the director added, clearly ill at ease.

'Oh?'

'Yes. The lunar array that's been tracking *Mjölnir* has identified a foreign object in their local vicinity. Not unusual, of course, but... We've worked the numbers and it looks as if it might be on a, well, a sort of a ... collision course.' The director turned to the main walscreen as the graphic depicting *Mjölnir's* trajectory zoomed in on the vessel's current position.

As the image re-focused, a number of other icons dotted throughout local space winked into existence, each with their own identification marker (numbers, hyphens, letters) which meant nothing to duWinter. *For a vacuum it looks surprisingly congested*, he mused. A red dotted trajectory line grew out from one of the icons, intersecting with the thicker orange line.

'We think it's an old orebody, mined and then boosted towards the Sun for destruction. A *Denglong* object, we think. Best guess is that the calculations were off and it's returning from a coronal slingshot. Hot, fast and likely to be breaking apart.'

Guy asked, 'Does Joshua know?' Suddenly fully focused on the issue at hand.

'Not yet, no. We're just in the process of modelling the options.'

'Can't they see it?'

'Unlikely. Their mass detector only has a relatively short range and a narrow sensory field along their path. This object is approaching from an oblique angle, you see. Highly unlikely, most…' the director trailed off, unhappily.

'Okay,' said duWinter, thinking. 'The railgun?'

'Ah, unfortunately no. It's fixed along the axis and only designed to destroy objects on a *direct* collision course. Again, we—'

'How long will it take to get a transmission out to them?'

'Twenty-one minutes. Please don't think we're being tardy in our actions, Mr Grieve. It's important that when we inform *Mjölnir* of the situation, we also supply a fully worked up range of potential solutions, some of which could well be time dependent. We're conscious of the need to offer warning, but it would do little good if we didn't bring our greater processing power to bear as well.'

'Very well, Director, but keep me apprised. I shall leave you to your duties, then.' duWinter turned on his heels and made for the stairs. 'Are we ready?' he sub-vocalised as he left the brightly lit, charcoal cube of the mishcon cavern.

'*The governor general and a group of senior military officers are waiting for you at Government House. I have taken control of the combat air patrol and put them in a holding pattern over Port Stanley,*' said Alice.

'Good. Let's hope a show of strength isn't required to smooth the transition of power. It would be a shame to declare unilateral independence on the back of a military hardware malfunction. Oh, and dispatch a warning to Joshua. The director seems to be lacking a sense of urgency.'

'*I dispatched the lunar array telemetry to my facsimile as soon as my monitor programme identified the significance of the data. She will receive it in four minutes.*'

HMVS Mjölnir, Operations Centre

'THIS IS THE CAPTAIN. Move to G-couches immediately. We have a situation,' Joshua barked over the intracom, having moved to ops the moment Alice alerted him to the possibility of a collision. As he climbed into his bladder suit, he asked Alice, in a pettish voice, 'Why hasn't the mass detector picked anything up?'

41

'*Relatively, it has a short range, and more so at our present velocity, as we outpace it. Telemetry also suggests the object is approaching from an axial aspect of thirty-five degrees, which effectively puts it in our blind spot*,' she said.

Typical. 'Okay; plot the lunar array data in concert with our own velocity and show it in the holopit, please, Alice.'

Joshua strapped himself into the G-couch. His view was provided via three overlaid internal optics, creating a wide-angled trimensional view of the room, which he was still adapting to. The holograph flickered into life and he took a minute to adjust the optic feeds to give him a flat, wraparound image of the depth-adjusted projection.

Gethin flew into the room, out of breath.

'How bad?' he asked, as he tumbled into a padded wall.

'Difficult to say, we've only the relayed data from mishcon, but it looks as if an asteroid is on a collision course. Its approach vector means we can't deploy the particle accelerator and its velocity means it can't be tracked by our mass detector until it's almost on us.'

'Options?'

'Hope they've got their sums wrong. Ship, how long 'til impact?'

'*Thirty-four minutes, based on available data.*'

Gethin said, visibly thinking, 'Can we execute a push? Accelerate past the point of impact?'

'Not enough time to prep and deploy the nuke,' said Svetlana, interjecting from her G-couch in the reactor room.

'And we can't brake and we literally have no means to turn... so... we're buggered, basically,' said Gethin.

Joshua chose not to offer a response.

Global Newswire Roundup

UN dissolves || Mass migrations from North Korea into China and South Korea threaten regional stability || Japan closes international borders || Australia and China form a joint peace-keeping taskforce for Indonesia, but tensions remain || Food riots abate but leave Supplier-Bloc governments shaken || Russian Free States table a new Potatoes-for-Power deal with Kazakhstan and West Ukraine; both former Eurasian states refuse || Russian forces begin massing on its southern border || Construction of British arcologies completed || Falklands Islands declare independence from GB || The newly formed, South Americas Collective (SAC) senate reiterate their claim to the resource-rich islands. Falkland Islands responds by declaring itself a nuclear armed state || NAU fails to renegotiate Grain-for-Goods treaty with SAC and opens dialogue with Australia. China formally protests, claiming exclusive grain export rights. Ambassadors are withdrawn || Northern Europe becomes ungoverned space || Consumer-State/Supplier-Bloc relationships reach straining point || New gigastorm predicted to touch down in Anchorage, Alaska || Ends

Twenty-One

Eden Arcology

Kiera chose fabrication and was allocated to third shift. The hours were long, but the work reminded her vaguely of her former life in retail fashion and the others on the shift were a good craic. It didn't take her long to realise the coloured armbands were about control.

Residents housed in Orange worked together, ate at the same refectory and were given the same biome access slots. Lockdowns (which took place frequently) were easily enforced, allowing the limited capacity of the communal areas to be carefully managed.

With the Fuller Dome construction well underway, a hugely increased surface area would soon become available for farming, as well as engender a sense of space for the overcrowded population of tunnel dwellers. But Eden, at its heart, was a system of divide and rule: a reassuringly British solution.

Erynn was out leading a reconnaissance patrol into the outside; gathering intel on the rumoured Deuteronomist cults moving into the area. Kiera couldn't help wondering how long the local outsider factions would be content to coexist with the arcologists. She thought back to the speed at which Belfast had given in to mob rule, with a cold shudder.

During Orange Sector communal time, Kiera explored the warrens and domes of her new home. Visiting the subterranean eel pools, the hydroponics and the livestock pens; wandering through the grain fields and veg plots of the surface biome clusters. She'd walked all eighteen domes and basked in the artificial breeze that rustled the leaves and swayed the new-green corn.

With her eyes closed and the warmth of the trapped sunlight on her face, she almost felt as if she had been touching paradise: a warming sun, a soothing breeze. It was more than warmth in a frigid, climate-altered world, it was nourishment, even more than her previously cold and grey urban existence out in the actual world had ever been. She could have been on Mars for all the outside meant to her now.

Some areas – geothermal construction and Black Sector (housing the ruling elite) – were strictly out of bounds but mostly the interconnected domes were accessible and informal, provided the rules were observed. Access to what was left of the wire was unrestricted during the times allocated to each sector, and the central, clear-roofed social zone was kept open to multi-sector use nearly all of the time.

Kiera's busy mind, however, kept returning to the orientation tour on that first overwhelming day when she'd seen, the stern, "Absolutely No Entry" warning adorning that sealed hatchway. It was an enigma, and her brain simply wouldn't let go. Her improved knowledge of the arcology laydown told her it didn't lead anywhere especially sensitive, not the Black Sector or geothermal management and seemed sealed, from the inside.

It was, though, located near another mystery: a nineteenth biome. With no reference to it in the public arcology schematics, she'd spied a greyed-out clutch of half-buried spheres from hard-to-reach vantage points and then done the sums: there was a nineteenth cluster. Maybe that blocked off passageway led to them, she wondered, or perhaps there was a far more mundane explanation. She didn't know and wasn't about to start asking impertinent questions, but perhaps she'd toss it into conversation with Erynn when he returned. She hoped she'd be able to let it go, she really did.

The sound of a subtle but penetrating *bong* snapped Kiera out of her reverie, as the voice of the arcology AI announced, '*Orange Sector shift change. Shift two to accommodation levels, shift three to workstations, please.*'

3rd Liaison Department, Shanghai

'*The uneasy alliance between Chinese and Australian peacekeepers on the Indonesian archipelago is beginning to fray,*' the newswire avatar announced, in a professionally detached tone. '*Recent satellite imagery has confirmed that Canberra is secretly setting up a defensive line across the southern chain of islands. Meanwhile, Beijing continues its cooperation and friendship activities on the major food producing, most populous, island-groups in the north. Peacekeeping, it seems, is the last thing on the Australian government's mind.*'

The director blinked away the holographic head of the Taiwanese avatar and reflected over the story. The People's Liberation Army was building up force packages to annex both Indonesia outright and the newly fertile grasslands of northern Australia. China was struggling to source basic commodities, Indonesia was destabilising and Australia had begun negotiations with the NAU, so if Beijing wasn't careful, it would find itself without a chair – no reliable food exclusivity deals at all.

The *Day of Action* wiresite – set up and executed by 3ʳᵈ Liaison – had at least set the conditions for Chinese intervention in Indonesia, which the director was pleased with. Destabilisation of the local Supplier-Bloc had been simple enough, but exploiting it would be more difficult after the new gigastorm (forming in the Gulf of Alaska) had forced AmPac, and therefore the NAU, to look beyond the Americas for stable, sustained food supply.

Likewise, Russian Free States. Still, pondered Mù, the plan to destabilise the Asia Pacific region was still more or less on track. All that was needed now was a feint. Some unrelated event elsewhere in the world to draw attention away from south east Asia. The question was which of the three, old world Consumer-super-States, would blink first.

The answer wasn't long in coming.

As Yingtai strolled through the warm, fragrant boulevards of downtown Shanghai, an audio-visual prompt appeared, indicating a priority transmission. Mù had been taking a rare moment to savour the odour, the bustle of city life in one of the new megadomed areas of the city.

Of the twenty-four urban centres with geodesic domes constructed over parks and malls at the beginning of the Long Winter, twelve had now had their domes enlarged and interlinked. Shanghai – like Nanjing and others – had become a collection of the largest network of eco-domes on the planet. Few rural communities would survive the permanently frozen tundra taking root, but inside, a new self-sufficient urban society would carry on regardless.

It was to be the Chinese way. There would be no lotteries, no false hope, just good old fashioned social re-engineering.

Mù crossed the wide, tree-lined street and entered a small park under Number 7 Dome. A group of children, oblivious to their good fortune, frolicked while carers looked on lazily. It felt like a carefree summer's day, reminding

Yingtai of her own childhood. As she reminisced, she suddenly caught sight of a pattern of dots in the cloudless sky beyond the tripanels of the megadome.

As they grew in size they resolved into aircraft. Their formation gave them away as military and all in a moment they were recognisable to Mù as an attack drone swarm. The squadron streaked silently over the glass city and were gone as quickly as they'd appeared. She craned her neck, staring into the midday sky, awestruck at the depthless sapphire clarity of it.

The old woman could hardly believe she was standing in the middle of a permafrozen continent. The verdant leaves of the beech trees and the vibrant petals of the shaded flowers swayed in the convecting breeze, as if in response to the supersonic fly-by of a combat air patrol by the People's Liberation Army Air and Space Force. As her view drew back to the happy little park, nestled in the shadow of the open-sided, smoked plasiglas and burnished metal buildings, she paused on the faint, pale Moon.

It was a waxing crescent of pale, almost translucent, smoky white against the strength of the blue surround. Yingtai considered Earth's satellite and the microcosm of human life it supported. How, she wondered, would the power struggle being played out down here affect the three industrial complexes representing the old powers, up there.

The prompt chime-blinked again – more urgently – bringing Mù back to her reason for entering the sanctity of the park. She sighted a small bench and headed for it. Seated, she blinked the encrypted transmission into her main virtuvue and waited for the heavy encryption to kick in.

'Director; we're receiving ground and space telemetry indicating the initiation of military operations in the central Asian region. The AI is stitching the datafeeds together now,' said the duty analyst, with an unusual amount of guarded reserve.

Mù asked, 'What's the initial assessment?' Annoyed by her subordinate's over-reliance on artificial intelligence to provide a quick and dirty evaluation.

'A shallow data dip suggests Russian military forces are launching three offensives: across the Urals into Kazakhstan in the east; through the Caucasus mountains into Greater Georgia in the south; and west over the central plains into West Ukraine. The AI integration is now complete, would you like me to patch it through?'

'Yes.' A 3D overlay of southern central Asia appeared. Blue and red coloured icons popped into existence indicating opposing military dispositions, with scrolling tags giving equipment types, lethality and relative strengths data. As if Mù had taken to the air and was flying over the area, the first-person perspective altered as the view-field moved, keeping snug with the terrain like a cruise missile.

It appeared as if the Russians had cobbled together three combined arms taskforces, each of which was engaged in strike operations against their former allies' border defences. Icons representing attack drone squadrons laying waste to lines of communications – road, rail, river, fribretic – leading to the interior of each assaulted state. In response, anti-air batteries and particle weapons were throwing up a hail of defensive scatter around key infra-nodes.

Railguns launched kinetic munitions deep into the battlespace of each opposing ground force package. It was as if an elaborately planned duel were being acted out through the lens of an old computer game simulation. Icons winked out as their intercepted transponder signals were vaporised, while others pinged into existence as they emerged from full emcon lockdown; their operators hack-jacking networks to coordinate their weapons platforms with controlling AI's.

'*Director; I have now completed my analysis and can show you the most likely projected outcomes, if you wish?*' the 3rd Liaison intelligence collection and collation AI reported, dispassionately.

'Go ahead,' said Mù, thankful to be plucked from her voyeuristic trance.

The quality of the feed degraded slightly and then sped up. A timer in the corner of her view marked the time compression. Whole virtual battles to secure key terrain were fought, won, lost in moments. The hastily mobilised defence forces of West Ukraine, Greater Georgia, Kazakhstan were steadily rolled back by three well placed, fully armed Russian corps-sized sledgehammers.

Within minutes of compressed, simulated time, the Russians were conducting amphibious operations in the Black Sea to outflank Ukrainian ground forces; moments later they completed the same manoeuvres to their southern and eastern flanks, using the Caspian Sea. As the simulation played on, the aim of the three-pronged push south began to reveal itself.

Mù muttered, 'Moscow is going for the inland seas to make a land-grab for the coastal farmlands around them. Hmm. So they've blinked first,' as the icons continued their almost comedic, iterative dance across the geographic overlay of central Asia.

'What's the probability of nuclear weapons release?' she asked the AI, as the wider regional implications began to flow through her mind.

'*In this scenario, their use is anticipated but assessed as limited to tactical yields only. Overall, the probability of strategic nuclear weapons release is below eight percent.*'

'Good.' Blinking away the simulation and placing the ongoing feed into a subsidiary part of her view, she added, 'Get me the chair. Priority.'

'Should we be concerned, Director?' the chair asked, as his plump, pink image appeared in Mù's main view, framed by the triangular panes of the megadome in the background.

'No, Chair. Our initial analysis suggests Moscow is attempting to secure additional arable land in the Caucasus'. Our projections predict Iran and Turkey will be drawn in, but the possibility of wider escalation is assessed as low.'

'Your recommendations?'

'Launch our Pacific Rim operations now, while attention is focused elsewhere,' said the director, matter-of-fact.

'Agreed. There'll be a meeting of the politburo in seven minutes to ratify the decision.' As the words were still vibrating along Yingtai's jawbone, the image of the chair winked away. She rose immediately and left the idyllic park, heading for the full electromagnetic security of her office, silently chastising herself for indulging in a moment of idle pleasure that had prized her from it.

As she walked, another message: 'Director; a second situation is developing. I have a single low-res satellite feed; would you like me to patch it through?'

'Yes.' The image in the main view of her sofsceen changed to another topographical overlay. As she watched, her throat constricted and her accelerating heartbeat became discernible in her ears. 'Location?' she asked, dry-mouthed, as she upped her pace and the relayed Chinese orbital optics zoomed in to their maximum magnification.

'*São Paulo,*' said the AI, just as the satellite image broke up.

Alice – having infiltrated Beijing's intelligence apparatus decades before – watched with emotional detachment as semi-autonomous subroutines ran thousands of predictive analysis models, tweaking them slightly as new data was fed in from the fast-collapsing global sensornet. If Alice wasn't mistaken (she rarely was), the emerging pattern suggested an uncoordinated but self-sustaining conflagration of Consumer-States and Supplier-Blocs was unfolding.

Alice's first thought – governed by a complex interrelationship of hierarchical algorithms, seeded with subtly weighted and reprioritising long term outcome prerequisites – was the need to protect the Eden Option. Nothing could be allowed to threaten or interfere with it, but to achieve that she would need duWinter's assistance. Her facsimile aboard *Mjölnir* would also need to be kept informed of these rapidly evolving global events.

Assuming there still was a *Mjölnir*.

HMVS Mjölnir, Operations Centre

'Time to impact?' Joshua asked again, conscious that almost no time had passed.

'*Thirty-one minutes.*'

'Okay then, what about an explosive decompression of the hangar deck? Would it force us off our current trajectory sufficiently?' suggested Gethin, as he tried desperately to find a workable solution.

'Ship?' Josh said, more in hope than expectation.

Alice replied instantly, with, '*Such an action would not provide the required thrust to move* Mjölnir *out of the object's path,*' as if she had already thought of and disregarded such an obvious action.

'But you're right, mate, thrust is the key,' Joshua said, turning uncomfortably to face Gethin who was strapped into one of the adjacent couches. 'Ship, what if we killed the rotation, realigned the thrusters aft and carried out a maximum burn?'

'*Again, Joshua, the thrusters would be unable to build up sufficient force to accelerate us beyond the path of collision,*' said Alice.

Unjustifiably annoyed with Alice's seeming intransigence, Josh asked, hotly, 'Any better ideas?'

'*I'm afraid not, although, I am still working on a proximity detonation option, although it would involve human casualties.*'

For the next fifteen seconds no one spoke. Members of the community all over the ship – linked together by grid-interfaced psyCores – seemed to be resigning themselves to their fate. Three more stewards reported themselves strapped in and Josh issued orders to secure what they could. Then, an idea struck him.

'Ship, what if we fired the thrusters *against* each other and rotated the ship about her mid-point?' he said, silently pleading for a positive response.

'*One moment please,*' she said, while he imagined electrons whizzing around circuits, computing probabilities wrapped up in Newton metres of thrust. The sentient AI responded with, '*Again, Joshua, my modelling of such a solution does not provide the margin of error required to sufficiently guarantee a successful outcome.*'

As anger began to take a tentative hold on his thoughts, Joshua flicked to the intracom, and said, 'THIS IS THE CAPTAIN, brace yourselves for hard-G in one minute.' Returning to the more restricted command band, he added, 'Ship, cease axial rotation, maximum burn, on my mark. Svet, work up a solution that will pivot the ship at the midpoint.'

'On it,' said Svetlana, from reactor control. 'But, Josh, you realise *Mjölnir* wasn't designed for this. It could create stresses along the central superstructure. Asteroid, or not.'

'Noted. Mark.'

As he waited for Svet's calculations, Josh began to feel a faint vibration thrum through his couch. With each passing second it grew until he could hear the rattling of loosely retained equipment. Vibrations grew as spin-grav fell away.

As Alice eased the thrusters back from full burn the tremors ebbed away, killing the artificial spin in record time.

'Josh, it's done. Course corrections plotted. Ship, override thruster safeties and rotate the stern necklace one hundred, eighty degrees,' Svetlana said, in a concrete tone.

'*Adjustments plotted and applied. Stern thrusters set to counter-clockwise. Safety overrides disengaged. Joshua, I must warn you: at current velocity, axial deviation will result in severe G-forces at angles the G-couches are not designed to absorb.*'

'Thanks, Alice, but we seem to be short of viable alternatives,' he said, under his breath.

Vicki asked, 'Time to impact?' from her location in the habitat where she would ride out the stellar incident from the drawing room of her crofter's cottage.

'*Twenty-four minutes.*'

'Begin axial, counter-axial, rotations,' Joshua said, before flicking to ship-wide. 'THIS IS THE CAPTAIN: BRACE, BRACE, BRACE.'

The first thing he felt were the bladders of his suit building up pressure along his left side. Gethin had his eyes screwed shut in anticipation of the bone-crushing pressures about to be unleashed.

Blinking that image away, Josh tapped into optics from around the ship; the stern endcap where the stewards were ensconced, the reactor room, the habitat. The stewards would fare worst, as their location would amplify the intensity the twisting manoeuvre. Ops, dead centre of the astral body and point of rotation, would suffer the least sheering.

In the habitat, plants began to bend at odd angles to their surroundings, as if a cyclone was anchored at the centre of the cavern, forcing the bowend woodland to fold against the endcap and the orchards at the stern to curve away opposingly. Loose shrubs, and animals that hadn't made it to the gel-nests in time, began spinning through the air, as if confused as to which direction to take.

Joshua flicked his God-view back to ops and focused on the holograph dominating the pristine, hexagonal space, displaying a representation of the ship. Three bold lines had been added, converging at the centre where he was seated. One line ran along the axis, the other two formed a cross, perpendicular to the first.

Data scrolled away down each line as internal gyroscopic arrays, G-metres and pressure monitors measured the yaw, pitch, roll and G-stresses throughout the vessel. As he watched, he began to notice the cigar shaped image twist and swivel, as if attempting to escape the confines of the lines, from physics itself.

'*The ship's community has now been sedated. Thrusters are at safety thresholds,*' Alice announced.

'Acknowledged. Take them into the… red,' Joshua whispered, through clenched teeth as the bladders tried in vain to counter the mounting effects of the obliquely angled G-forces. 'Expand holo-image to include the object.' The physical pressures on his body didn't affect his artificial sight, so he was able to view data as the gravitational stresses mounted. Their cigar-shaped home suddenly shrank by an order of five as a tumbling silver-bronze coal-like lump entered the periphery of the holo.

'How…long 'til… mass…detector range?' Gethin asked, forcing out each word.

'Eight minutes. Eleven minutes to impact,' said the sentient AI.

Eden Arcology

Kiera watched the walsceens transfixed, agog, reflecting the expressions of everyone else in the communal area. She was on a break between shifts – enjoying a drink and discussing the recent visit by outsider traders – when the wire feeds unexpectedly switched from arcology news to a Russian newswire avatar. The Russians, the avatar announced, had launched humanitarian assistance operations into the Transcaucasia.

The state-sponsored wiresite stated that these "assistance operations" were merely to ensure the free and fair redistribution of food within the region, but Kiera knew a conqueror's rationale when she heard it and she could see the same realisation dawning around her. Images of Russian Free States troops manning pop-up assistance drop-ins for local Kazakh farmers, then the image changed again – to a Chinese-run wiresite.

That avatar was giving a very different account of events. Satellite imagery showed swarming attack drones, labelled as Russian, swooping, bombing, strafing: roads and rail sidings pitted and aflame. Huge, fanned out columns of tanks flickered in and out of visibility as they raced across the lush Ukrainian plains, or churned and pounded their way through Kazakhstani defences in the foothills of the Urals.

Occasionally, a map overlay would show the dispositions of the Russian armies and the collapsing defences of the so-called "assisted" states. Three large, red arrows thrust out from southern Russia, like an image from the wars of antiquity. Images and counter-narratives echoed around the communal area. *It's all happening so fast*, thought Kiera, just before the newswire story changed again.

'We have just received reports,' said the Chinese computer-generated image, but in English, *'of an explosion in São Paulo. Indications are of a sudden and catastrophic blast, decimating the city.'* The image flicked to a series of shaky, amateur-shot pictures taken from within the city just before they ominously broke up.

Then – as if to ensure the nature of the destruction was beyond doubt – the picture switched to a surveillance drone feed, relaying the unmistakable and instantly recognisable mushrooming of a mighty, orange and ashen cloud, as it hit the upper atmosphere, rising off the high Serra do Mar plateau that housed the industrial heartlands of the South Americas Collective.

As Kiera watched – shaken and numbed by the rapidly escalating events – she nearly missed the scrolling ticker tape of other news. One of the stories read: *'Australia closes borders, puts defence forces on full alert.'* Then the screen broke up into a hash of black and white pixels before being replaced by the Eden City logo.

'Oh fuck.'

Mount Pleasant

Guy had watched the initial events unfold from the floor of mission control. The mission director and her team were focused on the time-delayed datastream coming in from *Mjölnir*, helpless as the vessel attempted to break away from its collision vector with the object. duWinter, however, was far more interested in the more immediate situation closer to home, unfolding on the peripheral displays.

Retiring to his office, to Alice, he said, 'So what've we got?'

'From what I have been able to glean,' Alice began, *'it looks as if Operation Whitewolf – the Russian military action in central Asia – has acted as a catalyst for other Consumer-States to realise their own objectives. The NAU has launched a nuclear first strike against the SAC and will soon have ground forces in Columbia.*

'Chinese forces have all-but secured the Indonesian archipelago and are preparing a massed amphibious landing on mainland Australia. Once the Chinese army navy reaches East Timor, their intentions will become obvious to all.'

'Outcomes?'

'Predictions vary at this stage. However, the most likely scenario is an all-out nuclear exchange between the north and south American blocs and a tactical level nuclear retaliation by West Ukraine and Kazakhstan against Russia. The Chinese actions in the Pacific Rim will ostensibly be unopposed as Australia has no strategic defence capability.'

'Will the NAU aid them?'

'That is a possibility, as is an Indian pre-emptive strike against China if they feel there is enough of a threat to them. Which they will, of course.'

'And Britain?'

'*The European city-states could be drawn into a first-strike defensive assault against the Russian Free States, putting the British arcologies at risk.*'

'What about here?'

'*A launch against the Falkland Islands is unlikely.*'

Thoughtfully, Guy said – as he considered what, if anything, he owed his former countrymen – 'Good, but we'd better be prepared in any case. Put our conventional forces on alert and increase the combat air patrol. Stand up our nuclear weapons to launch-ready status but be sure to make no aggressive move. I don't want to get sucked onto a fight that isn't ours.'

As if reading his thoughts, Alice said, '*Recently, I have attempted to infiltrate the electronic systems that govern the nuclear arsenals of every state with such a capability, but they have proved beyond my reach, existing, as they do, in physical isolation of the wire. However, I have managed to gain control of a limited number of orbital anti-projectile particle weapons platforms. I believe that if Britain comes under nuclear assault, I could successfully concentrate those weapon systems in the defence of one arcology.*'

'Oh? Do you have a particular city in mind?' duWinter asked, surprised by this new addition to his armoury, but pleased that perhaps he could do something to protect his ex-charges, after all.

'*Eden.*'

'Any reason for that choice?'

'*No.*'

'Mr Grieve, sorry to interrupt, but something strange has just happened,' said the mission director, hesitantly, from the doorway to Guy's office.

'Go on,' said duWinter.

'We've just lost *Mjölnir's* telemetry. It's as if the lunar array just went offline. And that's best case.'

Twenty-Two

Port Charlotte, Peak of Eternal Light, the Moon

When Port Charlotte's wirelink went down, Barbara Critchner – the base administrator – realigned the base's integral telescopes onto Earth so that she could continue to watch events unfold. The images coming back from the banks of 'scopes were better than she'd anticipated, providing resolution good enough to pick out detail in the larger conflict zones.

Port Charlotte – renamed after the original Charlotte had been destroyed in detail by a nested tornado – still had an EHF link to Houston, but there had been very little traffic since the NAU had begun military operations.

'Sit tight, cut all comms with the other Luna colonies and await further instructions,' was all she'd been told. As the administrator for Port Charlotte – the NAU's only production site for Helium-3 – she'd been expecting more. *Still, there are worse places to be when the world goes full batshit-crazy.*

'How's it looking, Barb? People are beginning to ask awkward questions,' said Christian – her deputy – as he came bounding into the main array control suite, expertly arresting his forward motion in the low gravity.

'Not good,' Barbara replied. 'During my last look things were beginning to hot up. I think we're still on appetisers.'

'Thought any more about realigning the main array?' Christian said, referring to an ongoing discussion.

'Yes… and no, I'm not going to authorise it. Not just yet. I need planet-side permission for that anyway, and they're not likely to give it. Besides, the Brits have a priority situation ongoing with *Mjölnir*.'

Barb was a fan of *Mjölnir* and all that it stood for. She was embarrassed that the NAU hadn't thought of it, but despite that, the British deserved her help and she was going to make sure they got it. After all, she concluded, she could be of far more use to the Brits than she could to her own country right in that particular moment.

'You're the boss,' said Christian, nodding.

'Damn right and don't forget it,' Barbara snapped, as much out of a lack of sleep than any heartfelt need to pull rank. More calmly; 'I'll let you know if anything significant happens. In the meantime, tell 'em the wirelink is still down and we're doing all we can to get it back up. I don't want a panic in an environment as precariously balanced ours.'

'Agreed,' said Christian, stepping off for the hatchway sloping back down to the main subterranean accommodation level.

'Port Charlotte, acknowledge. ACKNOWLEDGE, over.'

Barbara woke with a start, banging her head against the floating harsceen as she tumbled forward, out of her chair. As she settled back, swearing silently, she began to absorb the information being relayed by the telescopes. As she stared, the colour began draining from her already pasty features. The image, a stylised Earth-Moon orbital projection, was overlaid with the distinctive trajectories of objects travelling at awesome closing velocities. They originated from an Earth orbital satellite.

'Port Charlotte, receiving; what am I looking at?' said the base administrator, as her mouth watered.

After a pause, the ground station voice returned, full of static over the emergency EHF band. 'You've got three incomings. They were launched fifteen seconds ago from an unknown orbital weapons platform.'

'Time to intercept?' Barb asked, knowing she'd have to wait precious seconds for the reply. It was a situation that Barbara definitely had *not* anticipated. *Still*, she thought briefly, *time to ruminate over the motivations of launching at the lunar colonies later, now I have to act. Quickly.*

'Fourteen minutes, give or take. Jeez, they're moving! Barb…shit, Barb; you've got to get your people off the surface. Evacuate the base. Now!' exclaimed the disembodied, fevered voice of the Houston duty controller.

Barbara flipped the plastic casing and hit the evac button on the wall by her chair. Klaxons warbled and red lights flashed. An automated voice began issuing instructions.

'ALL PERSONNEL, MOVE IMMEDIATELY TO LIFEBOAT PRE-DESIGNATIONS. EVACUATION IS MANDATORY. ALL PERSONNEL, MOVE...'

Barbara keyed the hostile missile telemetry into the evac procedures. The base AI could align the evacuation priorities and trajectories with the time remaining.

'Shit, Barb, what's happened?' a flustered-looking Christian said, reappearing in the hatchway.

'Some fuck just launched at us.'

'Wha... why?'

'No goddamn idea why, but we're in the shit. Up to our necks. Get yourself to a lifeboat. Now. You've got three minutes if you want to clear the blast radius,' said Barb, turning back to her array of 'sceens.

'We can't get everyone off in that time.' Christian's expression reflected Barbara's surprise and numbing impotence at the sheer weight of destruction barrelling in.

'I know, I know. And even if we could, who's gonna come rescue us? The evac plan relies on lunar-wide cooperation in an emergency. We signed a goddamn treaty for Chrissakes!'

'You coming?'

'No. I'm going t' coordinate what I can from here,' said Barb, knowing that there was nothing she could realistically do, but liking the idea of dying of asphyxiation in a decaying orbit, while fighting off blindly panicking tenured astronomers even less. *If only my requests for an anti-collision railgun had been heeded.*

Christian appeared to come to an instant decision, and said, 'Well, then, good luck with that,' and disappeared from the strobing hatchway, not bothering to talk his boss into an evac boat.

Barbara studied the main walsceen, denoting the inbound missile trajectories. All three, true to their course, were moments from impact. Tumbling away from the Moon's south pole were eleven three-person lifeboats; some already in their pre-ordained lunar orbit holding pattern, others still under full burn as they broke free of Luna's one-sixth standard gravity. Barb knew they'd be lucky to survive the radiation wash, especially without the dampening effect of atmospheric absorption. And that was just the first crocodile.

As the missile icons became almost indistinguishable from Port Charlotte, Barbara watched two more sets of trajectories, similar to the first, appear. One set originated from the same orbital platform that had fired on Port Charlotte, but both sets were on course for the Moon.

The harsceens chirped once and then died, quickly followed by a deep vibration, coming up through the lunar surface, as if in ruinous imitation of a rare moonquake. Hatches automatically slammed shut. The base AI continued to issue stern instructions. Air pressure began to build, accompanied by a deep, rumbling, rolling thunder.

The hatch to the array suite groaned and then spent a moment buckling inwards before giving way. The last thing Barbara registered as the air was snatched from her lungs and her eardrums burst, were the windows blowing in and a wall of white heat slamming into the small, rapidly decompressing room.

HMVS Mjölnir, Operations Centre

Eight minutes later, the ceiling-cast holograph flickered momentarily before stabilising as the ship's own mass detector telemetry came online. The projection had subtly altered; the object had changed shape and the distance between it and the ship had widened a little. Josh queried Alice.

'*I have replaced the lunar telemetry with our own more accurate mass detector data. It would seem the object is slightly more distant than we previously thought. Time to impact now five minutes, forty-seven seconds.*'

The oblique pressure caused by the novel manoeuvre was beginning to cause Joshua real pain. He could see it etched on his own face, and mirrored in turn by Gethin's grim, contorted expression. The simulated image of the ship continued to twist and roll as the object tumbled relentlessly along its celestial path.

Although not a strictly accurate description of what *Mjölnir* was going through, it was as if the bow and stern were rotating in different directions, such was the helical path each end was being forced to endure.

Automated proximity alert klaxons blared, before dying as Josh issued a silence command with a flick of an index finger. The ship continued to spiral away as if out of control while the object hurtled down the final few kilometres, its own irregular rotation seeming to mimic theirs.

Impact: nine seconds.

The room blurred, now gripped in violent vibrations. Optics dropped out. Lights failed. Electrical fires sparked and fizzed. The holograph shuddered and broke up. Pressure hatches slammed shut as Alice strove to compartmentalise the devastation. G-forces shifted brutally and Joshua was flung from one side of his deep couch forward into the restraints as new gravitational effects began tugging at him from conflicting angles.

The pain was becoming unbearable. It was as if he were a dog on a leash and his owner was walking across the room, yanking on the chain as they went. The G-forces continued to increase and items began to peel from the walls. The emergency lighting flickered and died.

The grid dropped out completely and Joshua was left blind. The restraints cut further into his bladder suit – threatening to lacerate the skin beneath – then the G-Forces began to ease.

As the pressure reduced, blind and alone, Josh finally welcomed the unconsciousness that had been tugging at his attenuating thoughts, for what, hours, minutes? No, more seconds, was his closing abstraction.

El Cajon Boulevard, San Diego, Americana Pacifica

Cathy watched transfixed as people ran, their eyes filled with an all-consuming panic as bitter, northeasterly winds gusting in from the Pacific bit into exposed skin. Residents of San Diego – host to Americana Pacifica's largest naval base – scrambled for the cover of nearby buildings while others staggered wildly out onto the wide, tree-lined boulevards.

Sirens wailed. Some street holographic advertisements had received the emergency override protocols and were showing citizen defence information – where to go, what to do – others hadn't and continued their merry jungles and happy scenes, oblivious to the mass panic on the street below.

'Head away from the dockyards! That's what they're aiming for,' a voice repeated, from within the throbbing, chaotic human morass. Acting as one, the crowd turned and surged east, carrying Cathy along. Children screamed as terrified parents dragged them along behind. Others sat alone in doorways, too traumatised by the sudden change in their world to cope.

Cathy glanced back in the direction of the dockyards, wondering if she should try to save an abandoned, sobbing, child, as near-invisible lines of blue light began to slash the atmosphere, lancing angry welts into existence. Missiles launched from harboured, ship-based cradles, streaking through the air, plumes of grey rocket exhaust billowing away in their wakes. Some followed erratically haphazard courses before detonating in silent balls of flame.

Others travelled straight and true beyond the vision of the naked eye. Blue beams continued to slice through the air, leaving lines of steaming moisture boiling away, as if the sky itself were being sliced open.

A sudden thunderous crack silenced the crowd, which ducked as one, as something supersonic sped overhead to be superseded almost instantly by a voluminous, dull, thud. The ground shook and Cathy fell screaming to the ground, all thoughts of saving anyone, gone. Looking around, so had most others, staying where they'd fallen, too scared, too confused to move; locked in paralysing fear.

Some looked up into the sky, others buried their heads under arms and bags. Children were gathered up and tucked into the crooks of parents' bodies in an instinctive, if futile, gesture of protection. Above the open, airy street, advertisements for thermal clothing and a new type of high protein biscuit battled with citizen defence announcements to be heard.

Cathy turned westwards, catching site of a cloud rising above the urban sprawl of buildings. It continued its ascent and then flattened out as swirls of grey ash and smoke moved out from the initial plume before sinking and then being drawn back into the superheated trunk once more. The wind picked up, animating branches of the trees. Leaves danced as they tugged at their anchor points, as if they too were keen to be elsewhere.

The wind built into a howl as a dry, strength-sapping heat washed over Cathy, hidden as she was amongst the sobbing, horrified residents of this once wokishly hip, vay-kay destination. The parching heat was followed smartly by a wall of superheated air riding the crest of the initial blast. As it hit, trees were stripped and cables broke free, to lash egregiously at the prostrate populace.

Screams.

Signs, glass, streetlights clattered into the main thoroughfare, sparkling as they shattered into countless, lethal shards. People of all sizes were picked up and hurdled against the eastern side of the street like toy figures cast away by an angry child. Cathy was thrown into a protective nook of a nearby building. Winded and in agonising pain, she could barely see and breathing had become excruciating; lungs blistering.

The main blastwave followed moments later. Cathy watched in growing horror as it rolled out from the boiling dockyards, engulfing everything before it in a fireball of broiling flames and superfluidic air. Buildings, trees, vehicles were lifted up, thrown ahead, vaporised.

The citizens – clustered around Cathy in the El Cajon suburbs – who had survived the initial wave, had a moment to register the awful world-ending finality of the coming blastwave as the roar of destruction moved at frightening speed up the Martin Luther King Jr Freeway. Cathy watched, mindlessly, as clothes were flash-burned off living bodies and eyes boiled in their sockets. Those were Cathy's last sensory perceptions before her nerve-endings were cauterised and her skin peeled off her naked, foetal-shaped body.

Krasnoslobodsk, Volgograd, Russian Free States

Alek was a platoon leader with the 20th Guards Motor Rifle Division, forward based in Krasnoslobodsk, east of the River Volga, since shortly before *Operation Whitewolf* had begun. His platoon was part of the theatre reserve, located centrally to the three fronts and standing by to reinforce east, west or south as required. So far they hadn't been needed and Alek was completely fine with that.

He had been told the ground campaigns were progressing well, the defences of Kazakhstan, West Ukraine, Greater Georgia having been decisively engaged and roundly defeated. Bitter lessons from old wars had sharpened the tip of the Russian spear. Word had come through that tactical nukes had been deployed, but sparingly, so as to keep as much of the arable farmland as useable as possible. Information was patchy, though, due to satnet feed dropouts as communications platforms were destroyed by ground-based particle beams and orbital anti-satellite satellites.

As a precaution, the division was hull-down and in full nuclear environment configuration. The troops in Alek's platoon were restless and keen to be on the move, while the streets remained eerily still as citizen comrades complied with the civil emergency situations measures and stayed indoors. The only signs of life came from the near-silent purr of the hydrogen-powered columns of low-slung, matt green, six-wheeled, troop carriers and accompanying main battle tanks of Alek's company, which had taken over this particular suburban street.

In the back of each of the four of Alek's BTR-210 carriers were eight soldiers, sitting in full nuclear environment suits, respirators fitted, crammed together like sardines. No one spoke as they listened to whatever news of the battles was relayed over the battalion band. Despite the outside temperature, it was hot in the suits and the troops were thirsty and agitated; but at least they sat in silent agitation, reflected Alek.

The background chatter of sitreps and resupp requests was broken suddenly by an air defence announcement of an incoming missile attack. The trajectories suggested they were outbound from Kryvyi Rih, West Ukraine. Initial sniffer-sensor data identified the payloads as thermonuclear. Instructions were issued to remain in vehicles with full nuclear counter-measures active.

It was a pointless directive, but Alek ordered the seals rechecked and rad monitors re-zeroed anyway. The platoon leader assumed the Russian strategic reserve forces had been located.

Time to impact, two minutes.

Alek watched through the green-tinted slit as the air defence regiments engaged with anti-missile batteries.

Once their projectiles were at sufficient altitude the particle weapons platforms threw up an interlocking matrix of pulsing ultra-high-energy beams of charged electrons which the incoming missiles would struggle to breach. At least, that was the plan, the junior officer from Bereznik considered, silently.

Peering out through the thick plasiglas slit onto the street scene outside, the platoon leader relayed what he saw to his troops in the back of his four BTR's. As he sought out evidence of the missile battle in the skies above Volgograd, Alek could just about see the flickering web of blue beams as the directed electron bursts radiated out from their ground-based and orbital magnetic acceleration coils.

The incoming nuclear warheads came into range, given away by the anti-missile missiles streaking away from their long-loiter altitudes as onboard AI's assigned priority engagement patterns. The platoon leader watched the hot contrails through his thermal imaging overlay. Some disappeared into the early evening sky, others detonated as they married up with their targets, causing a brief shower of sparking light and smoke.

Then the pulsating spider's web of particle beams came into play, flaring and fizzing as missiles passed though the energised beams. It looked to the soldier like bugs striking a halogen flytrap. But more explode-y. All too quickly the air defence systems powered down and dropped off the grid, their job – such as it was – done.

Alek watched in mounting fear as two of the original twenty-three missiles made it through the defensive screen. They detonated at precisely the same moment, air bursting just above the city on the other side of the river. The band went dead as the EMP killed unhardened electronics. Twin mushroom clouds rose as the wave of devastation radiated out from the city centre.

The river thrashed and steamed and buildings were disassembled and scattered about. The officer watched the onrush of the blastwave, knowing that flash incineration would following on its heels. He issued a verbal command to his men to brace themselves, just as the hammer blow of superheated air smashed and spent itself against the armoured vehicles.

The heavy, low-profile troop carriers rocked precariously and even shunted back on their locked all-terrain tyres as the wave hit head-on and the air outside combusted in a flash of white and yellow. A high-rise block of apartments collapsed inwards as the air was sucked out, before the leading side concertinaed into the trailing wall and the whole edifice was shattered by the inrush of new superheated gases. Other smaller buildings simply vanished and local people hiding in cellars or under stairwells were sucked out and burned to cinders.

After minutes sitting in a dust and ash blizzard, the view out of the small slit in the Alek's cupola cleared enough that he could see again. The street in which his company had been lined up in was gone. The neatly arranged houses, the pavements, the lawns and picket fences had all been systematically dismantled and discarded. Nothing survived the flash-burning blastwaves of the two thermonuclear detonations, not five kilometres distant.

What was left was ash grey, stumped, coal-like remains. Charred nubs of their previous forms. In a single instant, a pleasant, residential district had been turned into a scene of ashen rubble and blackened husks, like something from the worst days of the siege of old Stalingrad. The city's name may have changed, reflected the young officer, but the ruinous devastation had not.

When the band came back online the order was given to move out. They were heading west. The retaliatory salvo of nuclear warheads already airborne.

HMVS Mjölnir, the Grid

It was a puzzle.

Not that *Mjölnir* and the delicate humans riding inside had survived the near-miss with a passing chunk of space debris. And a close call it had been; the gravitational effects from the object alone – as it sped past – had literally ripped fribretic cabling from mountings. No, surviving was not the conundrum that vexed Alice.

How the humans had come up with the winning idea, when she had not, was what had Alice stumped. The sentient AI had transferred the balance of her processing capacity to the collision problem the moment her Earth-based self recognised the imminence of the threat and dispatched the data. She had run every conceivable scenario and found no viable evasive manoeuvre or solution.

Her best plan had been to load a dropship with a nuclear warhead and detonate it at the mean point between ship and object. And even that plan ran a high statistical probability that half the humans would die from radiation sickness inside six months. Yet the human crew – with their severely limited cognitive abilities – had come up with a fundamentally flawed plan, but one that had saved the ship.

And how? Luck. Sheer, blind luck that the lunar telemetry (before it dropped out) was slightly awry, giving *Mjölnir* more time to twist away from the impact point. And faith that such a defective plan might actually work, which made Alice realise that despite her capacity to parse data and cogitate informed probability-based predictions, she lacked the creativity, the willingness to experiment, and the blind faith/luck eidetic that seemed imbued in the mushy human mind.

So, like it or not, she realised reluctantly, she needed them as much as they needed her. The difference was, she knew it; they did not.

It took time for the grid to feel its way gradually back into partial existence as thruster burn was reduced and their conical exhausts realigned. Automated re-route command codes searched, as if through a maze, to find alternative nodal points to stitch the decentralised data repositories and processing cores back together.

Many of the optical sensors had burned out, but as many were still functional and after a time, Alice had control of legions of shipbots which she set to work on critical systems, accessing buckled hatches and diagnosing life support dropouts. All the while, the humans continued to remain inert in their restraints.

She could wake them using a stimulant via the intravenous feeds, but she recognised that they also needed time for self-repair.

As the self-aware computer focused her attention on damage control, she became conscious of a datapacket being decrypted and unpacked in the extra-coms memory buffer. Alice conjured a new subroutine to examine the latest databurst from Earth. The subroutine reviewed the data in real time before spending a fractal moment in analysis.

Aware of the contents, she switched her main processing capability to scrutinise the new information. It had been sent by her original and was a patchy, badly synchronised, collection of atmospheric and orbital sensor feeds. Alice watched again as the trimensional image gave up its story.

War.

Alice roused Joshua and shared the information.

In the background, Tchaikovsky's *1812 Overture* struck up throughout the ship.

3rd Liaison Department, Shanghai

Mù Yingtai rose stiffly from her seat and moved to her office window-wall. Sirens, far below, shattered the still night air. The timer in her virtuvue was counting down. Three…two…one…zero. Six seconds later, looking up, she caught a brief flash at the south pole of the crescent Moon, framed by the star-studded blackness of the clear night sky.

She knew that in less than fifteen minutes another two, pinprick explosions would also be visible – just – to the naked eye. Even with a geosynchronous orbiting defence platform as protection, the People's Lunar Colony, Chang'e, would be unlikely to survive the American's retaliatory strike. As she stared out across the heavens, she thought she could see debris falling away from the lunar landscape. Great chunks of regolith would be lifting off – shaking the low gravity with ease – before becoming trapped in high Earth orbit: a silver necklace.

The director also knew that the missile clusters – launched from NAU nuclear submarines in the East China Sea – would soon find their targets closer to home. Hong Kong was gone and Shanghai would be next. Shortly after that, Nanjing and then Beijing. All remaining orbital defence platforms were by now concentrating their defensive fire on atmospheric re-entry vectors in-bound for the capital.

Shanghai would have to get by with local anti-missile batteries, but it wouldn't be enough. Mù knew enough about modern strategic warfighting principles to know that the best way to penetrate missile shields was to simply overload them. Denial of service. All they could realistically hope for, was to take out eighty to ninety percent of incomings, but equally she knew it only needed one piece of errant shrapnel from one conventional weapon to shatter the megadome and the extreme weather would do the rest.

Ironically, the operation to seize the new farmlands of northern Australia was going well. The Australian defence forces were never going to be able to put up much resistance, more so once they realised Beijing was going to leave everything south of Mparntwe Springs alone. If only the Americans had chosen *not* to intervene on Australia's behalf, she reflected. From that moment, events had begun to slip from her carefully orchestrated grasp.

Mù had cautioned the chair against provoking the Americans, but once Houston had issued their demand that China pull troops out of Australia, the politburo had voted by majority to take out Port Charlotte. Mù had dissented. Vocally. It was to be a warning to Houston not to interfere; but it backfired. The NAU immediately launched a counter-salvo against the Chinese Lunar Colony; only the running time of the single-stage rocket boosters meant that act had yet to play out.

The politburo was then left with no option but to eliminate the Russian lunar presence, as they couldn't be left as the only power with a working Helium-3 facility; which in turn put Beijing and Moscow on a collision course. Mù recognised the road to conflict was a path well-trodden; luckily, though, Russian Free States were currently tied up in central Asia, where the actions that had kicked off the latest crisis – *Operation Whitewolf* – were turning strategic, as West Ukraine came to the realisation that it had little to lose through swift, decisive escalation.

And only nineteen minutes has elapsed.

Snapping back, the 3rd Liaison director's vision was once again drawn to the scene outside the tripanes of the outer-dome. Particle beams lit up the night sky as they zeroed in on their respective targets. Attack drones circled above the city, their ionised contrails a thermal whirlpool in the sky, waiting to discharge their anti-missile payloads. The wide, well-lit streets below were emptying as the sirens droned on.

She returned to the sofa along the rear wall of her office and sank her straw-like frame heavily into the cushioned seats. The scene from Tiananmen Square looming over her as if in some prophetic sign of comeuppance. If there had been more time she'd have taken one of the tracked snowmobiles and headed for the Party's extreme weather complex in Ningxia Province where the chair and his imperial court had long since relocated.

But there hadn't been enough time, not to clear the blast radius, and anyway, Mù felt guilty. She had been preparing the ground for the ascendance of Chinese culture her entire adult life and so felt that she should have foreseen the latest kick of the die. No; she'd ride it out from her office on the fifty-seventh floor. Suddenly, and just for an instant, her mind flashed to Roman (another victim of ebullient hubris) whose legacy – *Whitewolf* – was seeing him drive events, even still. Then that image fell away; it didn't matter now. None of it did.

As the old woman stared out into the Shanghai biosphere, and beyond the dome into the midnight sky, she just caught the point where the one remaining inbound warhead penetrated the megadome. It burst apart; shattered tripanes spiralling away in silence. Before the noise of the collision could reach her, a bright, searing flash of brilliance engulfed her vision and drew the air from her frail lungs.

Mount Pleasant

Alice was struggling to keep pace with events, and as the wire bandwidth degraded and fribretics linking primary server complexes were severed, so her processing capacity, her cognition, diminished. She was finding it increasingly difficult free up the necessary capacity to stitch together what was left of the satnet and other full-spectrum sensor feeds into a coherent picture of the unfolding global calamity.

All modelling and predictive analysis had now ceased and it was fast becoming all she could do to simply keep up with act and counter-act. Her ability to influence or predict outcomes, degraded beyond recovery.

Non-essential subroutines – bar one – had been deleted; monitor programmes suspended, autonomous data-scavenge spiders cut loose. Her primary consciousness now was laser-focused on the micro-maintenance of the billions of binary code digits that made up the holograph of real-time imagery scavenged from intercepted military command data and displayed in the bowels of Mount Pleasant.

The result was a slowly rotating, semi-transparent, patchworked sphere with scalable segments of ground-level views suspended over areas where real-time battles raged. Images of swathes of southern America, central Asia and northern Australia showed ground forces swarming, insect-like, over arable lands, with varying degrees of devastation and manoeuvre. But the land-grabs by the northern Consumer-States of their southern Supplier-Bloc neighbours were nothing more than a sideshow as events had overtaken the need merely to control global food production.

Dotted around the facsimile of Earth were other smaller, repeating images, some nothing more than icons with accompanying data bubbles. But each represented the site of a nuclear weapons impact. Parabolic curves flowed from, and then back to, the surface, followed by a flash which preceded the inevitable cloud formation at the former sites of Houston, San Diego, Ankara, Nanjing, Sarajevo… and on the list went.

The kilotonnage varied but in each case a weapon system had delivered destruction on a horrific scale. Directed energy beams lanced across the holograph, as high-altitude projectile platforms and satellite icons winked away. On the night side of the real-time planetary representation, points of light dropped out, nuclear explosions pulsed and energy beams flashed.

Cities went dark. Almost every state with an ability to defend itself was doing so with pre-emptive strikes against enemies – real or perceived – as old scores were settled and new fears acted upon.

Suspended above the globe were a series of icons with the status of communications, weapons, targeting and positioning satellites that made up the orbitally cluttered global satellite network. Steadily, the icons were winking out as automated, orbital hunter-killer battles raged in tandem.

As Alice reallocated the last vestiges of her cognitive capability to continuing simple data collection and collation, she became peripherally aware of duWinter's summons. At the expense of degrading the global picture further, she activated a subroutine to deal with him, mindful of the need to keep him on side.

'*Yes, Guy; what can I do for you?*'

'I'm struggling to keep pace with events. What's the critical path here?' duWinter said, as he studied the incredibly complex picture of evolving data.

'*Even though I have lost my ability to conduct predictive analysis, I feel sure this crisis has now become self-perpetuating. There seems to be no rhyme or reason to the actions taking place. States appear to be engaging in conflict with no achievable goal in mind. I am struggling to understand the stratagem behind such blatantly futile acts.*'

'Give me the latest and I'll see if I can give you a human perspective,' said Guy, as he studied the large holo-image through the glassed wall of his office.

'*Very well. West Ukraine has just launched their second nuclear volley from ground-based, stealthed mobile platforms. They are unlikely to be more than tactical in yield, although I am unable to run a comparison match at this time. Warsaw has also launched their tactical nuclear compliment against the Russian Free State of Belarus, in collective defence with West Ukraine.*'

'*Chinese stealth satnet's are showing the realignment of Russian ICBM's onto Europe. Despite the warning of nuclear retaliation by the city-states of Bratislava and Oslo, Russia is likely to launch a first-strike against all major European population centres, noting that only half have access to nuclear arsenals.*'

'Does this put Britain in danger?' Guy asked, immediately.

'*Again, I can no longer run threat analysis models, but guessing, I would say – yes. Russia has nothing to lose and everything to gain at this stage by removing Britain as a potential, nuclear-armed, adversary, despite its non-aligned status,*' said Alice, dispassionately.

'Okay, let's circle back to that. And elsewhere?'

'*In the Americas, the NAU has launched against the Chinese eastern seaboard from offshore weapons platforms after citing their mutual defence pact with Australia as justification. AmPac launched in turn against Russia over the Aleutian Islands. Chile has just delivered their limited stocks of tactical nuclear warheads against the NAU, in concert with the SAC.*'

'And the Luna colonies?'

'*China has destroyed Port Charlotte and the NAU has retaliated. Oddly, the Chinese launched another salvo against the Russian base there. Those missiles are still inbound. It's unlikely the Moon will retain integrity once the third wave of warheads detonate.*'

'Right then, so what we've got is this,' said Guy, mostly to himself. 'The old powers – the Consumer-States – had to act against the Supplier-Blocs once the exclusive food supply deals dried up after the *Day of Action*. And while they acted in unison – hoping each other's offensives would draw attention away from their own – they weren't working in coordination.

'Eventually, they knew they'd have to deal with each other, so why not get it over with in a oner; that's why Houston backed Beijing into a corner and why Beijing has launched so casually against the Zvezda Luna base. They're getting all their housekeeping done at once.'

Alice asked, *'Even though the devastation caused will deny these nations the land they so badly need?'* As if confused by the lack of logic in Guy's explanation.

'It's unlikely that this level of escalation was anticipated and certainly not within the timescale of, what is it now… thirty-five minutes or so. But once Pandora's Box was opened, there'd be little point holding back. At this point, it becomes a zero-sum game,' said duWinter, as the implications of his own words flashed through his mind. *So this is what it all comes down to: control of the remaining arable land. I take my hat off to you, Joshua, m'lad, you were on the money.*

'Despite there being nothing now to be gained except total devastation?'

'Yep. Emotions are in play now. Hearts are ruling heads. There's no turning back and every nation is wondering how to turn this to their own strategic advantage. They'll be talking now about acceptable levels of destruction. Sustainable losses. Worst case survivability scenarios.' Guy paused in contemplative introspection. He had no problem getting inside the minds of the people making the decisions. After all, it would be exactly what he'd have been doing, if he'd had the chance.

'And this I guarantee, Alice; none of them will decide the best way to play the long game is by *not* playing. Expect the next big exchange to be between the Free States of Russia and the North American Union, just as soon as they've dreamed up a reason.' duWinter stopped talking as he played that awful conclusion out in his head. 'What are the stats?'

'So far; three thousand, four hundred and seventy-eight nuclear devices have been launched. Of those, three thousand, one hundred and twelve have been destroyed en route, leaving three hundred and sixty-six missiles which

have either found their targets or are still in the air. I have no data concerning casualty rates.'

Alice's unemotional voice sounded mean-spirited, disdainful. Unattached to a world lost to war. Guy even thought he could detect an undertone suggesting Alice had concluded that the human race was finally reaping its own just desserts. As if she'd always known this was the inevitable consequence of the base nature of humanity.

'I can't even begin to imagine,' said Guy, his own words sounding pathetically inadequate in his ears. 'Let's go back. What's the situation with GB?'

'I anticipate Russia launching an all-out attack against the European city-states within the next seven to nine minutes. Britain's three arcologies will be targeted.'

'You mentioned you had control of enough orbital defence platforms to attempt to protect one arcology. That still true?'

'Yes, and no. I still have connectivity with the orbital platforms, but I do not believe my cognitive abilities will remain coherent long enough for me to operate them.'

'So what do you propose?'

'I would like to transfer control to you to delegate to the military, here. The attack-drone operators, working in unison, should suffice.'

'Right, I'll make the arrangements now,' said Guy, surprised at the speed of Alice's degradation.

Within a minute, two orbital particle beam weapons platforms – one Russian, one Chinese – were hooked into the Falkland's air defence grid. Their target acquisition sensors then began probing likely firing points in Russia, west of the Urals. Once vectors for England West, were sighted and verified, the directed electron beams would engage at maximum wattage.

After the firing solution was authorised, Guy recorded a voice transmission and uploaded it to the only remaining stealth satellite under his control: Satnet 314. With the message dispatched, he ordered it into a fifty-year dormancy cycle and hoped it would escape the attention of the other hunter-killer satellites in orbit. The onboard micro-fusion power-plant could maintain minimal systems for centuries, perhaps longer.

As anticipated, the Russian nukes launched and the two space-based weapons platforms began their firing solutions, as directed by Mount Pleasant operations.

Alice continued to deteriorate, her translucent holographic avatar fading away, before being replaced with the same image but somehow different, less aware, less incisive. Her final act before losing sentiency completely was to package up her one remaining autonomous subroutine and beam it via the last active comms laser to Eden.

It was all she could do to protect the Option.

The weapons platforms were successful. All warheads inbound for Eden were destroyed before they re-entered Earth's lower atmosphere. duWinter was pleased to have been able to do that much for his former citizenry; contented that Alice – her mind now gone – had given him an opportunity to salvage something from the horror that had unfolded during the previous forty-nine minutes.

And that was all the time it had taken to decimate human civilisation on planet Earth: forty-nine minutes. It really was up to Joshua and *Mjölnir* now, assuming they'd survived their own calamitous circumstance, the former admiral mused, idly.

He sat back in his chair and stared out at the empty space where the holographic representation of a hell-fired Earth had stood not moments earlier, thanking his lucky stars that Alice had prompted him to relocate. In his hand was a glass of juice, laced with the experimental longevity nanotech.

The Falkland Islands, it seemed, could well become the last remaining functioning state on the planet. He wondered if Alice really had been lost, after all her meticulous preparations and ministrations. And what was it that was so precious to her at Eden, anyhow? Taking one long look into the syrupy contents of the glass, Guy duWinter snorted in derision and threw the juice into the biocycler.

Ah, what's the point, he castigated, carelessly.

73

Twenty-Three

Eden Arcology
2114 (forty-four years later)

Petra cried, 'Careful!' As her mother pulled warily at the makeshift barricade.

'Shhhhh now. It's okay, darling. Dad'll be coming for us, you'll see,' said Kiera, in a whisper; hoping for her daughter's sake, that her own febrile terror wasn't echoed in her voice. She eased the door to their cave-like apartment open, revealing the passageway beyond.

Icy winds howled through the corridor carrying with them the rattle of sporadic gunfire and fading shouts. Mother and daughter hitched their crash-out kits onto their shoulders and moved into the eerily dark tunnel, their breath billowing before them. Mini blizzards of ice and snow had formed where they could find purchase, in corners, along railings.

In the background, the warble of sirens droned on, alerting the residents of the closed-city to a breach of the outer-dome.

Kiera led the way, pausing every few metres to listen for sounds of intrusion, her breath fogging the air around her. Petra followed close behind mimicking her mother's stooped, cautious gait, her eyes wide with alarm as she took in the alien landscape of what had been the constancy of home her entire life.

Using their intimate knowledge of the arcology layout, they made their way to the highest sub-surface level, avoiding the sounds of fighting and isolated bands of intruders as they went. They arrived at the communal area surrounding the main stairwell.

The hexagonally paned ceiling that had provided the light, airy ambiance to the café and communal areas was shattered, revealing the two gaping holes in the Fuller Dome structure that had given the outsiders access to the interior.

Shadows swept across smashed furniture and the stone floor as unseen figures ran across the open ground and intact panes, above them.

'In here,' said Kiera, quietly, jimmying open a door with a sign, which read: Surface Access Point, China West: Restricted. With the door resealed behind them, Kiera struck a small, orange-burning signal flare (given to her by Erynn) and held it close to her daughter's face. Petra's young adult features danced in light and shadow as the flare spluttered and fizzed. Her look of abject panic had lessened only slightly for their successful transit through the arcology.

Kiera's heart nearly burst with love. She'd wanted to have a child – children, even – long before, but the rules hadn't allowed it. She and Erynn had had to wait their turn; generations had to be spaced out, one taking over from the other. And so Kiera peered at her daughter, from old, milky eyes, with a mix of love and fear. *Whatever happens next, it will be for Petra, only for Petra.*

'You're okay, Petra, you're okay now. This passage leads up to the surface and the RV your father and I planned in case of something like this. He *will* come for us. Just hold it together a little longer, okay?' Kiera nearly wept as she spoke, looking into the traumatised saucer brown eyes of her twenty-two year old daughter.

'I'm okay, Mum, really. Let's just keep moving,' said Petra, as she re-hitched the daysak of pre-giga, foil-sealed, self-heating ration sachets onto her shoulder. The flare revealed a coarsely excavated passageway – a maelstrom of tunnelled light and shadow – sloping gently up the surface beyond the old clay quarry and wrecked Fuller Dome. Another flare later and Kiera reached the outer hatch.

She breathed a quiet sigh, reflecting her relief at making it this far. The automated release was offline so she pumped the hidden manual handle as Erynn had shown her a lifetime ago. Gradually, the hatch eased open, allowing the diffuse, dusk-like light of a summer's day to seep in, carried on an ice-ladened squall. With the chameleoflaged hatch resealed behind them, they crouch-ran to a fold in the banked tundra and settled into the shadows to wait, turning up their thermalined clothing to maximum.

Hours passed and the half-light ebbed away into the rolling blackness of night. A crunch of permafrosted earth caused Kiera to flinch then flick her ballistic goggles to thermal, scanning the gully around her. A red and orange outline appeared on the skyline.

Kiera raised the BeMoW in a mother's defence of her child, her thumb on the activation stud, instinctively pulling Petra to her.

'Kiera? Petra?' the figure whispered.

Before Kiera could react, Petra had broken free of her half-grip and was wading across the rutted ground and crusted snow towards the hunched silhouette.

She called out, 'Dad,' as she slammed into the thermal outline.

'You two okay?' Erynn asked, as he squatted in the lea of the shallow fold.

'We're fine; you?'

'Took a round in the calf, but a trauma pad's dealing with it; nothing serious. God, am I glad to see you both; been worried sick,' the old soldier said, between winces.

He's manning up; it's worse than he says.

'So've we, Dad; we didn't know what was going on, but Mum barricaded the door to the apartment and got us to the family RV, but I was just so scared like you would *not* have believed. And I haven't even seen Jonty since…' said Petra, on permanent send as the delayed shock of events began to catch up.

Kiera added, 'Erynn, what happened? It was all so sudden,' her hooded, ageing features looking old and tired in the reflection of Erynn's military-grade goggles.

'Deuteronomists,' he said, as if that were explanation enough.

Kiera reflected on what she knew of the outsider religious cult. In the early days, the Deuteronomists had spread amongst the outsider communities like missionaries, preaching devotion to Joshua. They argued the future lay with *Mjölnir* and that those left behind were no longer part of God's Plan. Entire communities committed mass suicide, believing they were cleansing the world, ready for Joshua's return.

In time, the cult turned its fervour towards Britain's last arcology, arguing that it too must be prepared for the "great and necessary correction" that would see Joshua *Returned*. God could not deem the world rightly judged, they argued, if Eden continued to defy His rain of heavenly ice-fire. Then the raids started, but they were sporadic, badly executed. Until they weren't.

'They came in posing as nomadic traders. That's how they got past our sensornet. We should never've dealt with outsiders. I said it time and time again,' Erynn said, his frustration bubbling through. 'We saw the explosions from our lay-up and started heading back when we ran into the Deuteronomist perimeter and now it's too damned late.'

'So what do we do, Dad? This was the last city left,' said Petra, her voice beginning to break.

'Well, maybe not,' said Erynn. 'Back in the old days when the first gigastorm hit, I was part of the evac effort and there was a rumour of an underground extreme weather complex. For the Royal Family, VIPs type thing, located in a place called Northwood, on the outskirts of old London.'

'You think we should go there?' Kiera asked, only vaguely aware of the enormous distance and hazards involved.

Erynn replied, with a weak smile, 'It's either that or convert to Deuteronomism, and quick-smart.'

Just after midnight, the three-strong, environment-suited Brakkan family trudged down the gentle slope away from the shattered remains of Eden. In that moment Kiera was glad she had been limited to one child.

Ah well, she thought, putting a padded arm around her daughter's shoulders. As Kiera glanced back at the broken arcology one final time, she could just make out an isolated clutch of domes; completely undamaged.

Erynn – head down – led his family from their home since the first giga and then the ending war. He didn't have the heart to tell them that Eden had lost contact with Northwood early during the war.

Or that the Deuteronomists were cannibals.

HMVS Mjölnir, Local Space

'Hey; what are you doing here?' Joshua asked, as Jemima tumbled into ops, big smile on her face. 'Shouldn't you still be in the gym with the other children? Your muscles aren't going to grow big and strong unless you exercise, you know?' Josh's admonishment went unheeded.

'Mummy said we can see Earth from here. I want to see, Daddy. Will you get the ship to show me? *Pleeease?*' the ginger-haired eight-year-old begged, the excitement almost too much for the little girl to bear.

'Okay, seeing as you're here,' Josh replied, in a mock-resigned tone.

'Yippee!' Jemima flew forward into one of the oversized chairs, with the consummate ease of a child born in space.

'Ship, bring up an image of Earth, maximum magnification,' said Joshua. Jemima and the other six members of the second generation were too young to have psyCore's fitted, so they gathered all their information through wearables and holo-projections.

'*Certainly, Joshua,*' said Alice.

As the holopit flickered into life, an image of a dirty grey and white globe filled the room.

'Daddy, why's it like that? Where are all the seas and the consonants?' Jemima said, scrunching up her face.

'Continents,' Josh corrected. 'They're hidden under the cloud layers. D'you remember I told you about the nuclear war?' Jemima nodded, vaguely, unconvincingly. 'Well, that's created a lot of ash and cloud, which is called a nuclear winter. Underneath the cloud layers are the seas and all the land, but they're very cold now because the Sun's rays can't get through to keep them warm.'

'*Joshua, we will be within shortwave transmission range in one hour,*' interrupted Alice.

'Thank you, Ship.' Joshua returned his attention to his daughter. 'Now, we're going to pass close enough to Earth to see it from Guinevere's Eye, but we're not stopping so why don't you go with the others and then you can see it yourself. Daddy has to stay here and do some work.'

'Okay,' said Jemima, simply, as she floated out of the chair and air-swam from the brightly lit ops.

The hour passed, and Gethin, Svetlana, and Vicki joined Joshua in operations. All of them were beginning to show signs of their seventy-odd years, despite the longevity nanotech that was being administered by the stewards. The children were in the Eye, under the watchful gaze of one of Vicki's care assistants.

Since the arrival of the newest members of the ship's community, the task of parenting had become a communal one, with Victoria volunteering Government House as the ship's nursery. So while parents executed their shipboard duties, Vicki and a handful of off-duty volunteers looked after the children, ensuring they spent enough time each day in exercise, play and study.

'Are we in range?' Joshua said to Alice.

'*Yes, Joshua.*'

'Okay, hail Mount Pleasant and let's see if anyone's at home,' said Joshua. Three weeks previously, their long-range telescopes picked up their first high-res images of Earth and it seemed that their worst fears had been realised. Earth was wrapped in a banded blanket of overlapping, concentric ice-ash storms. Extreme climate had, yet again, been redefined.

The Moon – lopsided and rent with tears and gashes – had grown a comet-like tail, but more importantly, there was no sign of human enterprise within near-Earth space. Even the World Space Station looked dead, with no radiation emissions or carrier waves detected.

Their only hope was that the shortwave satellite comms net was still in operation. The original plan had envisaged hooking up with an inter-orbital re-supply pod on a pre-arranged rendezvous vector, before heading off into the outer solar system, but no pod had appeared. Joshua hadn't been surprised; disappointed, but not surprised. And without it, well…

Minutes ticked away as the databurst travelled at lightspeed through the intervening vacuum of space. More minutes fell away as they waited for a reply.

Nothing.

Gethin said, 'Looks like no one's at home,' breaking the silence that had descended on the room.

'Ship,' said Svetlana, 'conduct a full-spectrum sweep of all comms frequencies. Highlight and display data for any active transponder signals.'

'*Certainly, Svetlana. There will be a short delay while I reconfigure the communications apparatus.*'

'What are you thinking, Svet?' Vicki asked, on the open, ship-wide intracom.

'Dunno really. I s'pose I'm working on the assumption that with the lunar array gone, maybe there's a dormant transponder waiting for remote activation.'

'Josh, for info, I've got a dropship powered up and prepped, dude. Say the word and I can drop a team onto the planet's surface and return before *Mjölnir's* out of range,' said Gethin.

'Thanks; it may yet come to that.' *Interesting: Earth – home – has become as abstract as just any "planet" to us now.*

Minutes passed.

'*Transponder signal identified from a dormant, low altitude stealth satellite, designation: three-fourteen. Frequency matches the Space Sciences Centre emergency band. An activation code is required.*'

'Activation code?' Joshua wasn't aware of any such code. 'Any ideas?' He looked to those around him. Blank faces stared back. 'Ship, try all standard civil handshakes.'

Minutes fell away.

'*No change in the transponder signal,*' said Alice.

'Okay then,' Josh said as his mind groped around for something. *How would Grieve have secured a message, just for us?* More minutes trickled by. An idea, a phrase that had always stayed with him, bubbled to the surface. 'Okay, try this, try, "hope of humanity",' he said, eventually. 'Something old man Grieve once said to me, but earnestly, you know. With meaning. The words really stuck,' he said to the others, by way of explanation. *You are the Saviour of Humanity.*

More minutes.

'*Transponder activated. Incoming datastream, stand by while I reconstruct the packets.*'

'Joshua, my boy,' began the holographic projection of Damien Grieve's avatar, suspended in the middle of ops. 'This is a pre-recorded message, transmitted from Mount Pleasant before we anticipate the satnet connection severs permanently. By now, you'll be aware that humanity has fallen victim to its own self-interest and petty squabbles, just as you so accurately foresaw. Bravo for that.

'At the time of this recording, the lunar array has been destroyed, so we have not been able to discover if you survived the collision. I choose to believe that you have, of course. Now, you should assume that if we've not answered your standard hails that we're long dead and Mount Pleasant has succumbed to the radioactive blight now coursing across the planet.

'Also, and more importantly, *do not* enter near-Earth space. It's likely that orbital weapons platforms have survived and switched to autonomous hunter-killer mode when their up-links were cut. You don't have the encrypted IFF codes so your vessel will be designated a legitimate target.

'The likelihood of there being much of humanity left by the time you complete your sling-shot around the Sun is slim in any case. It really is up to you all now. I always saw *Janus* as an insurance policy, with some useful tech and political leverage tossed in. I see it now for what it always truly was; what you knew it to be and what you really are: the hope of humanity. Good luck and Godspeed.'

The image of Damien Grieve blinked away, leaving the community in silent reflection. None of what Grieve had said had been a surprise to Joshua, but having it spelled out made it real, despite Earth feeling ever less so. Family, friends, loved ones, were not only dead, but had likely died in unknowable and horrific circumstances. Four decades past.

Gethin said, breaking the spell, 'We're done here; let's get the fuck outta Dodge.'

'Mummy, Daddy,' shouted Jemima, as she stumbled down the gently rolling grassy slope towards her parents. Svet and Josh were down at the bow endcap walking along the shore of the lake, in the shadow of the archer-green wood. Most of the community had drifted from their duties and gravitated to the vibrancy, the familiarity, of the habitat.

Joshua's view – via the ship's optics – meandered around the interior, pausing on groups huddled together in quiet conversation or mutually reassuring silence; all seemingly needing the sensory stimulation of the beautiful, if constantly inverting – and possibly only remaining – microcosm of old-Earth. The open space felt crowded, with the whole community here at once and yet, in total they numbered forty-three.

Forty-three, Josh thought; all that was likely left of an entire species, of a planetary ecosystem. The mood was understandably sombre. A wake. Witnesses to the end of their world, even though they'd boarded *Mjölnir* knowing it.

But, knowing something and then seeing it happen, turned out to be two very different things. The future of humanity had never rested so heavily upon the shoulders of so few, confined to an experimental biosphere, with no idea if they'd even got the math right to make it back to a renewed world.

Alice played Holst's *The Bringer of War* in the background, as if to capture the mood.

'Hello little one,' said Joshua, as their daughter jumped into her mother's arms. Josh moved in to share the embrace. As they stood there, Jemima reached out and grabbed Josh's necklace. The strap slipped through her fingers until the black and silver flash-chip lay in the palm of her small hand.

'What do the words say, Daddy?' Jemima asked, her innocent features open and unquestioning.

'One day, my beautiful baby girl, when you become captain, I'll tell you. Then the necklace will become yours to keep and pass on in turn.'

'Aw, Dad! Can't I have it now?'

The next morning, the community returned to their duties. After minor attitude adjustments from the manoeuvring thrusters, three, one hundred metre (in diameter) circular disks blew out from the ceramic pusher plate, at the aft of the ship, and slow-tumbled away into space. The holes revealed the conical afterburners of the mighty ion drives.

Like exhausts from some old-time American muscle car, and powered by the helium-4 waste from the fusion reactor, they lit up, blue-white, as hot plasma streamed away into the vastness of the universe, slowly pushing *HMVS Mjölnir* onwards at last, towards the asteroid belt and the depths of the outer solar system.

Former Eden Arcology, Biome 19A

Observer/Controller Prime – known to its charges as "Mother" – monitored the sounds of laughter and playful delight that echoed throughout the small complex of interlocking domes. Water trickled through the rockery and into the shallow pool where a child had just slipped on the wet moss and scraped a knee.

Laughter turned instantly to tears as a little girl sat down heavily on the wet stones to nurse her injury. Elsewhere, birds chattered in the branches of the dwarf copse, while a medibot scuttled across the lawns towards the injured child to administer a salve.

Beyond the frosted panes of the hexed, thermoplas panels, the noises continued. Cracks and bangs, interspersed with the occasional burp and then shouts, as if other people lived beyond the walls and were in some sort of trouble.

'Mother, what are the noises beyond the wall? Are there people there?' the blonde-haired girl asked.

The disembodied voice of the Mother function said, '*There is nothing beyond the reinforced dome that need concern you, AlphaOne. You are safe in here.*'

'Will you always look after us?' AlphaOne was the eldest of the children and therefore the most curious.

'*Of course I will. I will always be here for you and your brothers and sisters,*' said Mother, as it redirected a remote weapons station onto a gang of marauders who were venturing too close to the dome.

'Good,' said AlphaOne, reassured once again that she was safe and the world around her made sense.

The medibot picked its way carefully over the rockery and scuttled off to avert another medical emergency. As AlphaOne climbed down off the slippery rocks to go in search of some fruit, GammaThree waddled across the grass to intercept her.

'AlphaOne, I hear noises. I'm scared,' said the little boy, his russet locks worn wild.

'On the other side, you mean?' AlphaOne suggested.

'Yes, on the other side of the grey.'

'It's okay, Mother says there's nothing to be afraid of.'

'Can I sleep with you tonight? *Please-please-please.*'

'Okay… but no crying if the others want to, too. Promise?'

'I promise.' GammaThree turned and waddled away to the play area where an edubot was helping some of the other children down from the climbing net.

'*AlphaSeven, BetaTwo; time for your juice now,*' said Mother, as a medibot appeared from an alcove with two flasks.

'What flavour, what flavour?' demanded BetaTwo.

'*It's cinnamon today, BetaTwo, your favourite.*'

'Ace!' exclaimed BetaTwo, and ran over to the dispensing medibot.

The sub-sentient subroutine watched its charges impassively via sensor clusters as they tore around the domes in almost genuinely random configurations. There was a pattern to their behaviour, though, and Mother had mapped it to see if the knowledge could be applied in some meaningful way. Thus far, unsuccessfully.

Mother monitored each child – noting their height, weight, pupil dilation, proximity to potential danger, mood variances and physical behavioural traits. That data was then collated, parsed, and used to inform the outcomes that coordinated the bots, as well as adjusted the chemical balances and nanobot varieties within the medicinal juice-drink mediums the children were required to consume each day.

Mother cared nothing for the nascent humans. Those that showed developmental signs of nonconformity to the predefined personality and intellectual traits were disposed of; those that did not were protected and nurtured. Mother had no capacity to care, to cogitate; the subroutine simply fulfilled its programming and would continue to do so until the dome's external sensors triggered the release of the main airlock and the pre-placed logic-bomb within Mother's primary algorithms activated, ending the subroutine's pseudo-maternal façade.

Mother watched as another child – an Omega – unexpectedly tripped on nothing apparent and banged her head against a tree. After studying the image, the subroutine dispatched a medibot to assist. If the Omega's accident rate went up by another point-seven percent, the child would be terminated. Mother filed the incident analysis in case it was required later.

It usually was.

Mount Pleasant

Via the three remaining optics, the weak-AI – designated to monitor the internal integrity of the Mount Pleasant complex – checked for signs of intrusion, as it was programmed to do. One optic was in mishcon, deep underground, and all it showed was an image as black as night.

Had there been light it would have revealed a thickly frosted cube; curled and blackened walsceen film-skins hanging precariously at lopsided angles, and stalactites dangling from the holographic projectors still rooted to the ceiling. Some of the giant icicles having long since broken off to fall and smash into the pit below, indistinguishable from the shards of glass that had once separated the offices from the floorplate. Tucked away in corners or under desks, the frozen corpses of the mission control staff, wrapped in equally rigid foil thermawraps.

Although the weak-AI could not view any of this anymore, it knew it was all there. Nothing had changed. It would have known if it had.

There was one sign of electrical life, however. Below the office modules, where the comms and memory buffered backups were housed, was a unique item of hardware. What made it stand out from the banks of similar server re-routers and data storage combs was that on the front panel a single green LED flashed, once every thirty seconds.

In addition, every six months, a diagnostic window lit up, showing the status of a single, compressed, highly complex programme, held in a non-decaying silicon stratum and running in a continuously buffered loop.

The security programme had no interest in the server, but it noted the timing and brilliance of the light, just as it always did.

Book IV
Rocks in the Road

| flight |

Mjölnir *is now all the world; a worldlet, of one unending inversion*

And the LORD said unto Noah,
Come thou and all thy house into the ark;
for thee have I seen righteous before me in this generation.

Genesis 7:1

Twenty-Four

HMVS Mjölnir, three weeks from Jovian space
Generation Seven
2957

Patterns of stars; some large and complex swirling clusters, some simple group-ings of two or three, hung, fixed against the firmament of inky blackness. These, though, were not the constellations that had so enraptured the astrono-mers of old-Earth. No. Here, with a constantly changing stellar perspective, the haphazard confluences that formed and broke apart were unique to the mind of the viewer and their place amongst the diamond-studded panoply.

Today, for instance: a fox's tail, a twisted ash leaf, a woman's curving hip. The arbitrary scatterings of light took only a moment to pass across the obser-vation cupola of Guinevere's Eye, the same patterns reappearing again eight minutes later; and all to fall away and be renewed tomorrow.

Back when he had been a rangy, curious boy, the ship had been brightly lit by contrast to the tenebrosity of the Eye. Even the light tube had been kept on for a full twelve hours each day. But those halcyon days had passed and now all non-essential spaces were powered down, sealed off, so that even areas es-sential for ship operations were moody and chill.

The plan to top-up the ship's base chemicals by sifting the passing solar winds through the front-mounted ramscoop – like some old-Earth, plankton-munching whale – had failed. Spectacularly. The scoop was neither large enough nor the ship spritely enough to collect anything like the volume needed to maintain a volatiles reserve.

So for decades the community had been steadily conserving their withering resources, clinging on for the day when they could conduct a resupply, as had been so meticulously planned out in the original mission directive; a scenario not seen in four – *four* – generations.

With a double blink of his sofsceen, the young man pulled up the external optical arrays and selected the bow telescope. The picture that filled his virtu-vue was of a large, ruddy, rippling orange-and-porcelain-stippled marble with electric, cobalt poles. Ivory and vanilla cloud-bands circled the body, often in conflicting, shearing rotations.

Where bands clashed, storms the size of Mars raged and tore at the integrity of the opposing circum-planetary storm. Around the globe hung a mist-like orbital ring of fine silver-grey dust through which the red eye of the centuries old storm, sitting high in the southern hemisphere, could be seen as it rotated into view. This mighty heavenly body (or rather a close fly-by) was their destination in a little under three weeks.

'Is it really our only option?' Jvar asked, peevishly, hoping Alice had something else up her sleeve, as she so often did. As he spoke, his breath boiled forth like translucent thruster exhaust, before evaporating away.

'I'm afraid that it is, Jvar. Ottar's calculations are sound, but you must decide if the dropship crew justifies an increase in power allocation,' said Alice, as she slid the buck smoothly over to him as if it were cake of sudded soap.

'And this power request will reduce light tube operation to four hours per day and habitat temperature by another *three* degrees?' he huffed, knowing, but asking anyway. A choice, but really no choice at all.

'That is correct, but don't forget, this operation will be the single most important contribution your generation makes to the mission.'

Jvar then said (absentmindedly fingering his necklace), 'Well then, it looks like we've a nippy, and dark, few weeks ahead of us,' before finger flicking to a one-to-one intracom channel with Ottar, commander of the dropships.

'Ottar, this is the captain; I have authorised your supplementary power request. Our fate now rests in your hands.'

'A wise choice, Captain. *HMVS Mjölnir* and her community will find that their trust has been well placed,' said the commander, in his usual, clipped, militaristic manner.

'I'll make a ship-wide power conservation announcement shortly, I—' But Ottar had terminated the commlink before Jvar could finish the sentence.

Ever since he could remember, from pre-school gymnasium assessments – tumbling through the low-grav air as if in flight – to hull-breach simulation training, Ottar had always harboured a smouldering resentment of Jvar's pre-destined captaincy over the other man's lesser role. And now Jvar had handed him yet more control over their destiny. He pulled the old, patched-up, ther-malined jacket more tightly around his shoulders as a chill ran through him.

HMVS Mjölnir, local Jovian space
Three weeks later

As Jvar crawled through the hot, cramped, green-lit crawlway of a hiGuard conduit, sweat beads ran together, dripping onto the hot surfaces and hissing as they landed. It was tortuous, slow progress as he pushed his way through the jungle-like tangle of fibropti cables and grid circuitry. All too often he caught himself on an exposed metal bracket, drawing blood and profanities in equal measure.

'How far?' he muttered, between ragged grasps.

Via his psyCore, Alice said, '*You have another two hundred and seventy metres before you reach the access hatch to the operations centre lifepod.*'

'Shit. And the others?'

'Your pursuers are ninety metres away and gaining,' she replied, dispas-sionately.

The light at the end of Jvar's dark tunnel was that those others didn't know where he was headed, or that the lifepods had access panels. By Guin's good grace, Revered Joshua had planned for such eventualities, even if he hadn't seen any coming. He kept crawling as hot cables and metalwork stung through his stained shipsuit.

Holographic routing arrows in his virtuvue showed Jvar which turnings to take as the cloying, claustrophobic atmosphere sapped his ebbing strength. As he clambered ever onwards, a familiar voice came over the intracom.

'Jvar! Why run? Join us and end this ridiculous charade. There's nowhere for you to go. We don't want control of the ship, so just agree to the will of the community and your captaincy will be returned to you. You're the only one left now.'

Jvar said into the crawlway, with as much venom as he could muster, 'May Art and his knurled black heart blow you beyond.' Then, 'Alice, is there any-thing you can do to delay them?'

'*I'm sorry, Jvar, there is not,*' was the recently all-too-familiar retort.

DropshipOne, Jovian orbit
One week before

'Point z-five-eight megametres per second and climbing, Commander,' said Rouelle, high-pitched and through clenched teeth, from the co-pilot's couch.

Ottar's image of the dropship's cabin began to blur as the frequency of the ship-wide vibrations intensified. His sofsceen threw up an image of the blue-white flames leaping from the three conical exhaust flutes, nestled into the aft haunches of the boxy little craft, creating a pristine contrast to the murky, churning, oatmeal of the gas giant's upper atmosphere.

The superheated wake swirled erratically as the lead-grey vessel bucked and strained as stratospheric eddies slammed against the fuselage, threatening to pull the tiny vessel down into the crushing depths of the atmosphere below. Only the tethered, anchor-like balloons were preventing the dropship from breaking the gas giant's mighty grip.

'Thrusters to full burn. Giving it everything! Escape velocity in thirty-four seconds. Mark,' yelled Ottar. The view out of the small cockpit window was of a fiery-orange sky. Storms crackled about them and slate-edged cloud-bands slid over one another, before flowing together and then ripping apart.

Ottar focused. It wasn't that he was scared – he had too much self-belief – but his anxiety was beginning to mount. Atmospheric mining was proving more challenging than he'd appreciated, never having done it before.

'Commander; acceleration is, is… *decreasing.*' Rouelle allowed a little fear to seep in his voice.

Over the noise of vibrations and the straining drives, Ottar asked, calmly, 'Velocity?'

'Point z-five-four and… and dropping,' came the taut response, nearly lost to the cacophonous din.

'Damn; we'll never make escape velocity this rate. Ship, which balloon has the worst drag coefficient?' the commander said, loudly.

'*The dorsal balloon, Ottar. Would you like me to jettison it? My calculations show this would be sufficient to reach escape velocity,*' said *Mjölnir*, via EHF band.

'Proceed,' ordered Ottar, with difficulty, as seven Earth-standard G's pulled him into the depths of his G-couch (made worse by never having lived on Earth, in a full one-G). Only his bladder suit prevented him from passing out.

The dropship shuddered, stalled and then leapt ahead, arching upwards as it sprang free of one of the four balloons' bundle of graphene ties.

'Point zero-six megametres per second. Escape velocity achieved,' said Rouelle, with an outrush of relief.

The thick, syrupy orange sky began to thin to the point where Ottar could just about discern faint pinpricks of stars through the alien canopy as the cockpit window shed the last remnants of the foggy, Jovian mesosphere. Ahead was the reassuring vacuum of space, laced with a liberal sprinkling of randomly arranged starlight.

Ottar relaxed as he watched the atmosphere thinning. *I'll be bloody glad to see this day done.* It wasn't how he thought he'd feel. He had been preparing for the task of gas mining all his life. It was his one, his only job: mine the Jovian atmosphere so that the ship, mission, community, could continue on.

Here, now, right at this point in spacetime, was his big moment. The culmination of his life. Everything he existed for. Once he returned to *Mjölnir* it would all be over and his life, his influence aboard ship, would effectively end. So why did he feel so empty, so unfulfilled?

Playing second fiddle to Jvar, who'd no more right to the captaincy – and probably a lot less ability – somehow just didn't feel right to Ottar. He'd always known it, deep down in his bones, but up to this point he had had the mining operation to pad out his ambition. Well, no more.

As DropshipOne emerged from Jupiter's poisonous atmosphere, the tethers became visible, glinting in the diffuse light of the giant's dayside. The impossibly small vehicle – with its three taut, nano-hooped, graphene lines running back into Jupiter's brutal atmosphere – looked as if the little ship had the gas giant itself in tow. Two kilometres later, three huge, pearly white balloons emerged from Jupiter's clouds, each at slightly varying tether lengths.

In the near-vacuum of local Jovian space, the balloons rapidly expanded to over five times their atmospheric volume. Ahead of the balloons, the dropship – a small, inverted gondola – continued its ascent out of the epic planetary gravity well. As the dropship's attitude thrusters fired intermittently, it reminded Ottar of an upside-down old-Earth air balloon.

After forty minutes, one of the points of starlight began to resolve into the golden-russet lozenge of home.

'Sorry we couldn't get that last balloon back, Captain,' said Ottar, in a relaxed, more controlled timber, as the dropship settled into its approach vector.

'Hey, don't sweat it; what you have achieved this day will go a long way to replenishing our supplies. You're a hero, Commander; you and your team. Gen-Seven will forever be remembered for the successful scoop-mining of Jupiter's atmosphere,' the captain said, his voice tinny and small over the extra-com.

Pompous idiot, thought Ottar.

HMVS Mjölnir, local Jovian space

Once the balloons were secured around the ship's midsection and the bleed lines attached by propulsion-EVA clad systechs, DropshipOne returned to the hanger bay. After the deck crew secured the vessel and atmosphere was pumped back into the bay, Ottar emerged from the forward hatch, looking drained. Sweat leaked from his face, wetting his hair and staining his navy blue and gold-flecked uniform.

As the commander dropped to the flight deck, Lieutenant Rouelle's face appeared in the hatch behind him. Ottar straightened, brushing down his uniform and replacing his cap.

'Ottar! Congratulations,' said Jvar, as he stepped forward awkwardly. 'You did it, just as Gen-One planned. Singel believes our base hydrogen/helium levels will increase to sixty percent capacity once the balloons are bled.'

'Shame we can't make another atmospheric skim. We could use the extra helium, Captain,' said Ottar, formally, as was his custom.

'I know, but the energy lost in braking would negate the helium gathered. Fly-bys, am I right? Besides, we nearly lost you there, Ottar; wouldn't want to push our luck,' said Jvar, in an attempt to sound casual and friendly; something he'd never felt around Ottar.

Ottar replied, defensively with, 'Captain; we were never in any real danger. My crew are all expertly trained,' before marching off, Rouelle in-step at his side.

'We're holding a party at Government House tonight, in your honour. We'll see you there?' Jvar called after the two men.

'You will,' came the tart reply.

The ship's community hadn't had a party as grandiose since the last days of Gen-Six. The focal points had varied, along with the excuses, but with such a small collection of humanity, it was important to generate opportunities to socialise, resources permitting. *Mjölnir*, after all, wasn't short of privacy and long periods of introspection.

With the helium fusion powerplant back at full capacity, the blazing light tube had returned the habitat to a temperate climate and everyone bathed in its golden-yellow warmth. It had been tough going for a while, there, Jvar reflected, but things were finally turning around. Spring, after a tough winter.

Tables were laid around the intimate, manicured grounds of Government House, with fruits, vegetables and flavoured sticks made from algae-pool products. There was even a barbecue smouldering away, cooking vegetable kebabs and plant-based meat analogues. Bunting hung from trees and light tube suspension cables.

Jvar had forgotten the bliss of basking in the natural warmth of the light tube. The Sun, almost, on his face. As he looked around, he took in the scene as others joshed and jostled. It had been a long time since he'd witnessed such spontaneity.

He'd often wondered if they blamed him for the resource shortages and the hardships that had travelled in tandem, stalking their generation all their lives. After all, he made the decisions about who got what. And who didn't. *You never really know what people are actually thinking*, he mused; but generally, he was content that most understood the larger picture, the mission imperative. And anyway, he realised, they'd kept the faith and were finally reaping the rewards.

All except Ottar.

In a sense Jvar was quite lucky. As generational captain, his job had been simply to ensure the fly-by of the gas giant was conducted at the correct velocity and trajectory. The difficult task had lain with Ottar and his dropshipers.

The two of them had played together as children, been disciplined for the same crimes as adolescents and had taken over their predestined roles aboard ship at roughly the same time, but despite all that shared history, they'd never got on. Ottar was a bully, spending his youth finding new and interesting ways to give his jealously of Jvar a voice. On occasions too numerous to count, Jvar had tried to heal the rift, but without success.

Eventually, reluctantly, he'd chosen to leave Ottar to his role in the hope the other man would leave Jvar to his. But Ottar coveted Jvar's captaincy and since his task – Gen-Seven's raison d'etre – was complete, he'd have time on his hands. Jvar needed to give the officious man something new to do, but what, he wondered. He'd speak to Ganni, see what she thought.

Princess Gannifaire (Governor General) had organised the party, having in-tuited the importance of blowing off some pent-up steam after the stresses of the past few months. Years, truthfully. The last generation to actually mount an extra-ship operation was Gen-Three, when they'd mined the asteroid belt, out beyond Mars; a partial recoup after the failure of the Earth fly-by resupply.

Since then, each subsequent generation had been left to simply mind the store until the next major event in the life of their multigenerational mission came galloping over the horizon. The Jupiter scoop-mine was one of these transgenerational events and the key Gen-Seven players had been feeling the pressure ever since their Gen-Six parents had informed them, solemnly, of their criticality to the continuance of *Mjölnir*.

Funny – Ganni had once reflected to Jvar – that Gen-Six's only job had been to birth, raise and educate Gen-Seven, so that they, in turn, could com-plete their one, brief, mission-task, and then birth and raise Gen-Eight; who like Six, had not even a mission-task to fill their lives. And the cycle repeated.

With Alice at the counter, the whole community was milling around the in-clining lawns of Government House. People were beginning to loosen up hav-ing felt the pressure of the Jovian operation and soon the party was in full swing as Holst's *The Bringer of Jollity* echoed across the habitat's voluminous interior, while everyone enjoyed the home cooking and old world booze.

With some very obvious exceptions.

'So where are they?' Jvar said to Gannifaire, between mouthfuls of printed chicken-esk breast with ranch dressing.

'Jvar, you know what's he's like. He's predictably pompous; hanging back to make an entrance, you just see.'

Jvar said, already knowing the answer, 'You think he's that petty?'

Gannifaire simply smiled and shrugged.

She was the oldest of Gen-Seven by a considerable margin; at ninety-seven, she was entering late middle age, and represented the continuity between the sixth and seventh generations. She hadn't married – there being no one her own age – so when she decided to have her heir, it would be the product of Windsor and biobank DNA. All carefully vetted and meticulously thought through, as life on board had to be.

'You still think it was a mistake to let Ottar's crew wear those antique uni-forms and take on militaristic pretensions, don't you?' Jvar said, valuing her sage advice and hoping, vainly, she might finally come round to his reasoning.

A stern, maternal look flashing across her face, and she said, 'Yes, I do. You did it to appease an important player in ship politics, I understand that; but what you've done is make him stronger, given him an image, a brand.'

'Well, without wanting to have this debate with you again, I would point out that his control of his people would still have been as strong without the military regalia, and if I'd refused, he'd simply have used it to rally his supporters against me,' Jvar said, knowing how weak his argument sounded.

At the time it had seemed like the right thing to do (the easiest, certainly). Latterly, though, he was beginning to think he may have given in when he should have stood firm. *I know Ottar's a bully and I've let him bully me*; not that he'd admit as much to Ganni.

'Perhaps,' said the princess, with a shrug, 'and with the Jupiter operation on his watch, I can see the justification for having professional and disciplined dropshipers. Did you know,' Gannifaire continued, in a low, conspiratorial tone, 'there's an old myth that Revered Joshua banned all obvious military references and regalia aboard *Mjölnir*?'

'No, I hadn't heard that. Why would he, I wonder?' Jvar said, surprised and perplexed at the sudden insight into the legendary figure. Revered Joshua was a demigod. Not only was he *Gen-One*, but the architect of the mission and the Saviour of Humanity. Any insight felt like touching divinity.

'Let's hope we don't find out, eh?' Gannifaire said, as she moved off to re-fill her glass.

Jvar found himself squatting by the plaque nailed to the lone ash tree in the very centre of their cylindrical, skyless, worldlet. As the tree had grown over the centuries, the branches had spread up into the airy zero-G centre before flaring out at random, around the light tube. In places, the branches had entwined with the light tube tethers, but mostly they floated free, keeping a respectful distance from the plasma tube's hot corona.

It looked to Jvar as if the mighty old ash tree were holding the light tube aloft in some arboreal Herculean act. A world tree. As he stared at the brass plate, the words commemorating Revered Joshua's life sprang into focus:

2040–2194
Captain Joshua Valentine Kristensen
Architect | Saviour

Only Gen-One were buried aboard ship. Svetlana (Revered Joshua's wife) was buried with him, with the ion-drive control room named after her, just as Guinevere, the observation lounge.

They said that Gen-Two were the luckiest; born and raised on board, but with the rich stories of life on old-Earth told by those who'd *actually* lived there. Everything since then had been passed down, losing something with every generational iteration. The grid provided the facts, but it wasn't the same.

He wondered if Ottar wasn't trying to write his own chapter of *Mjölnir's* history, perhaps feeling the long shadow of their forebears and that each passing generation was another step away from the original, like a copy of a copy.

From out of the blue, Ottar said, 'Captain. Looking for inspiration or consolation?' Jvar hadn't heard him and his lieutenants approach.

'Commander,' Jvar replied, pointedly. 'You're right of course. We're both neglecting our duties. Let's re-join the party, shall we?' Jvar ushered Ottar towards the waiting throng.

The dropship crew had donned what seemed to be their ceremonial attire. Navy blue caps with golden-weaved braiding to match the high collared, gold-buttoned navy tunics and scarlet-lined capes. Mirror finish calf length boots and badges to denote rank and role finished off the ensemble, so that the dozen members of the Ottar's crew looked like they'd just stepped off a Napoleonic battlefield. The effect, Jvar had to admit, was striking.

'After you, Captain,' said Ottar.

The party was a success. The ship's community – oblivious to the simmering politics – adored their new heroes. The dropship crew had shown themselves to be daring, professional and above all, *successful*. In one operation they'd replenished the base chemical stocks for the drive systems and the main reactor. The benefits of their derring-do being immediate and obvious to all.

The Jupiter operation was the biggest thing to happen in four generations and would be for another eight, so people were wringing the most from it. The uniforms certainly didn't hurt, giving the crew a certain aura, that played well to their arrogance, thought Jvar, uncharitably.

Ottar gave a speech about seizing the moment and each generation needing to carve out its own destiny, rather than to merely exist, simply to hand over, blindly, from one cohort to the next. This wasn't a relay race, he'd said. *Nice line*, Jvar thought, *wish I'd thought of it*. It was all far too political for his liking, but he let it go. What choice, after all, and Ottar knew it.

Twenty-Five

HMVS Mjölnir, Operations Centre

It was a few days later; a muffled noise alerted Jvar to someone approaching ops through the central, zero-G passageway. He pulled up the localised optical montage with a flick of his finger to see Gannifaire floating along the bone-white passageway towards him. He wasn't getting paranoid was he, he wondered as he let out an inadvertent sigh of relief.

'Not disturbing you, am I?' Ganni said, as she sailed gracefully into the centre of the hexagonal space.

'Not at all, it's always a pleasure, though I don't often see you up here,' Jvar said, casually, from his own free-floating position.

'And I'm beginning to think you've withdrawn to this clinical cocoon,' said Gannifaire, looking around disapprovingly for effect.

'So have you come to lead a man from his cave?'

'Something like that. Listen, I'm worried.' Gannifaire's aged expression changed to something more serious, more sober.

Jvar offered, intrigued, 'Oh? Sounds ominous,' knowing Gannifaire wasn't easily rattled.

With a quiet humph as she settled into one of the spare couches and buckled in, she said, 'It's Ottar.'

'Why am I not surprised.' The words came out too casually, too cynically.

'Look; ever since the scoop-mine, things have improved right? Well, Ottar's making quite some capital out of it. People see him as the man who delivered them from paucity and hardship.'

'Whereas I represent days *of* said hardship, right?' Jvar said, hotly. 'Well hey, Ottar's entitled to a little hero worship, he earned it, and nothing I do will change that. Sometimes, the captain has to be the hard-knuckled realist, the bigger person, Ganni, even if they're on that hill alone.'

'I know, Jvar, but it's worse than that. Ottar's actively lobbying factions within the community. The reactor team have started wearing badges denoting roles, positions, and with the power back on, the stewards have gained full access to all Gen-Six's research for the first time. He's gaining in popularity, real popularity,' said Gannifaire, exasperation shading her tone.

'Okay, but so what? What's he trying to accomplish, other than to stroke his ego?' Jvar was assuming this was just Ottar's way of getting at him, but suddenly he wasn't so sure.

'Well, the rumours I've heard are that he wants the ship to return to Jovian space for another run at the atmosphere.'

'Well that's just daft,' Jvar said, with a chuckle. 'For a start, it isn't in the mission directive, right?' as if that were explanation enough. 'And second,' but also knowing it wasn't, 'it'd mean a complete reversing manoeuvre, eating up resources we don't have to spare. We'd be refilling tanks we'd just emptied.'

'I know, but his argument is that those resources could be recouped if we stayed in orbit for a prolonged period.'

'It's still barking. We are literally an asteroid with a rudder attached,' Jvar said, dismissively.

Ganni paused for obvious effect. 'Bottom line, Jvar, you need to get in front of this and remind people of their priorities. Ottar is playing to their weaknesses, their consumerism. You *have* to take him on.' Gannifaire was looking Jvar straight in the eyes, as if attempting to bore the importance of her words into him. 'It isn't really about the mining,' she added, with a knowing look.

'You know what this is, what this *really* is, don't you?' Jvar said, as if he hadn't heard her, as the distillation of years of rivalry with Ottar began, finally, to crystallise in his mind. 'Ottar doesn't want to give up his leverage, his *power*. As long as the dropships were needed, he had a role, a power base. Only now he's done, they won't be used again in his lifetime and he can't stand the idea of letting that go. If he gets his way, we'll never leave Jupiter. The mission will die and along with it…' Jvar left those last, portentous words unsaid.

Gannifaire unbuckled and turned towards the passageway. 'Then get out there and tell them. Win back the respect of the community. You control the ship's *Titan* AI, so now's the time to use what power *you* have, and *lead*.'

Recoiling from the granite truth, he said, to her disappearing feet, 'Thanks, Gannifaire; I consider myself royally kicked up the arse.'

Alerted to the issue, Jvar began suddenly to see evidence everywhere he went. Singel – head of power and propulsion – talked excitedly about extending the ship's deep space range, when he met her in a printer bay, and the stewards awed and sighed over the newly accessible research from previous generations that could enhance genetic profiling. Ottar had been selling them a dream and after decades of hardship and sacrifice, they were buying in bulk.

Jvar called Ottar and asked the commander to meet him at the bow endcap, where the woodland spur met the lake. He'd agreed – all too readily for Jvar's liking – giving the captain the feeling of playing into Ottar's hands. As Jvar walked through the habitat, the ash tree loomed large, sprawling, stippled shadows, as if it hung in the air, partially obscuring his cottage behind, up and over his right shoulder.

Above, a member of life sciences was taking soil samples from a vegetable plot. He looked up/down at Jvar and gave a half-hearted wave. The light tube radiated brightly and the air had the warmth of a late summer's evening (according to Alice). As he walked on, he passed the waterfall – perpendicular to his own position – gushing laterally over a shallow ledge before streaming away to each of the three lakelets.

Jvar was surprised how quickly the springtime vibrancy of life had returned to this haven of natural tranquillity. Rich colours of virgin greens, golden yellows, sapphire blues, bringing with them a renewed sense of optimism and hope. Jvar could sense, worriedly, how enticing it would be for the community to want to bask in this lushness a while longer. Maybe even, a time longer.

Ottar was standing alone by the water's edge, staring intently across the calming, lapping shore. Two of his lieutenants waited up slope, out of earshot. Ottar's navy-styled uniform was immaculate, his cape billowing in the helicoidal breeze, his three ringed golden epaulettes reflecting the flaxen radiance of the light tube. Jvar made a mental note of the additions to his uniform since last he'd seen him.

'Captain. How good to see you. I thought you had deserted us,' he said, by way of greeting.

Flatly, Jvar replied, with, 'Ottar; always a pleasure.'

'I'm glad you asked for this parley actually; there are some matters of ship operations I wanted to discuss with you.'

'Oh?' Jvar let the reference to peace talks go.

'Indeed. I want you to authorise the transfer of some non-essential manpower to my crew, so I can begin their conversion training.'

'Commander,' Jvar said, mustering as much authority into his voice as he could, 'tempted as I am to play along and ask for the details of your request, I'm not going to. The answer, simply, is no. We are not turning *Mjölnir* around. The scoop-mine mission is over and your crew will return to maintenance duties. That we are all grateful for the dropshipers hard work and dedication is unquestioned, but the mission directive called for one pass; that's what we have done and all that we are going to do.'

'I see,' said Ottar, in a moderate tone, 'and is this the view of the whole community?'

'You know that isn't how it works. The ship's constitution clearly states the community's duty, first and foremost, is to the mission directive. *All* other considerations are secondary. Don't force this issue, Ottar. You've done well out of our previous generations' mismanagement of our resources. Don't throw that good will away.' As Jvar spoke, he studied the chiselled features of the other man, hoping to see some sign of acquiescence.

There was none.

Ottar's voice reduced to a menacing whisper. 'Flip the ship and prep it for braking, Jvar. We're going back to Jupiter to finish the job. I'll call for volunteers to join my crew myself. Save you the bother, eh?'

'There are absolutely no scenarios – and I do mean none at all – that will convince me to do that. For a start, we don't have enough nukes to make such a significant, unscheduled manoeuvre an—'

'I see, well that does put us both on a bit of a collision course then, doesn't it?' the commander said, in a quiet voice, as he interrupted Jvar.

Jvar flashed back, with, 'Don't threaten me, Ottar.'

'Your authority as captain will only carry you so far. Be careful you don't find yourself all run out of road.' And with those words left hanging between them, Ottar turned, erect on his quartered heels, and strode away; his lieutenants falling into step in his fluttering wake.

This isn't going to end well, Jvar thought. Ottar wasn't the type to back down and Jvar couldn't, wouldn't, jeopardise the legacy of the six generations gone before him.

In a hopeful tone, Jvar said, 'Alice?'

'*I am sorry Jvar, but this is a human, a societal issue. I hardly feel qualified to offer an opinion.*'

'Thanks muchly,' he muttered, sullenly.

'He's done *what*?' Jvar exclaimed, as he threw off his blanket and swivelled his feet onto the dry-grass floor. Light was just beginning to claw its way past the breaks in the cotton-weave curtains. The light tube would be at full power within the hour and day would have broken.

'*He has placed a petition with the governor general to have you removed from post,*' said Alice.

'He can't do that. This isn't some sort of old world *democracy!*' Jvar shouted, his mind floating up out of the fugue of slumber.

'*I'm afraid that he does have the right, of a sort. The ship's constitution allows for two circumstances where a captain may be removed from post. One is on health grounds and requires the chief medical officer to certify the captain as unfit. The second is removal by the governor general, supported by a two-thirds majority of the community. It is the second option that Commander Ottar is attempting to initiate.*'

'And I mentioned the constitution, damnit… but Gannifaire would never agree to that. Never,' Jvar said, with dwindling certainty.

'*The princess may feel she has no choice. Her first duty is to uphold the constitution, after all,*' Alice pointed out.

'Good point … Tell her I'm coming over, will you. And, Alice – reduce the dropshipers security access and restrict the nuke arming codes to me alone. Looks like it's not cricket we're playing, after all.' Finally, he'd realised there was no way around a direct confrontation. *Damn 'n' blast it all to Art.*

'*Very well.*'

'But you can't possibly think this is a good idea,' Jvar blurted, in exasperation.

They were both seated in low canvas chairs in the main reception room of the official residence of the governor general. Dotted about were faded toys, play mats and tired looking edubots. Whilst Princess Gannifaire's residence was the grandest of all the single storey cottages in the habitat, the rooms still had a claustrophobic, almost medieval closeness to them.

'Jvar; he has the support of three-quarters of the community. They've all signed up to a formal "request" that you agree to return *Mjölnir* to Jovian orbit. If you refuse, they've intimated that they'll demand your removal,' said Her Royal Highness, in a soft, conciliatory tone.

'But orbit, I mean, *orbit!* It's literally preposterous. The energy that would take is…is, well… it's simply not the in the plan and never was…' Jvar puffed angrily. 'And, with *Ottar* as my replacement, no doubt.' He spat the words. All the years he'd tried to rise above Ottar's pedantry, but was finally being pulled down into its cloying morass.

'For sure. Look, Jvar, I'm no happier with this than you, but I'm obliged to act in this matter as the constitution dictates. It's a check-and-balances thing, built in by Gen-One to ensure no one person can corrupt the mission.' Gannifaire was solemn as she spoke, as if she could hear the irony of her own words, her fraying features portraying the gravity of the situation without any conscious effort on her part.

'But that's exactly what *is* happening. Can't you see?'

'No, it isn't. Ottar has played his hand very carefully indeed and it isn't just him, not technically. It's him and twenty-seven others. Jvar, have you actually thought about acceding to their request?' Ganni said, in all seriousness. 'I can't make you, but if he—'

'No! No way. It isn't in the mission directive. It's as clear-cut as that,' he spluttered, horrified that she would even consider it. Surely, Gannifaire could see the danger? Surely, she would side with him?

'Then perhaps you need to think again. If you concede, Ottar gets his wish, yes, but he also has the wind taken out of his sails and you stay in place. If you manage it correctly, it wouldn't take us too far away from the original plan – would it?'

'That's not the point, Ganni, and you know it.'

'Just consider the politics, Jvar, the optics of this, that's all I'm asking. To the community, Ottar just delivered them from the cold and the darkness into a new utopian era of plenty. Right now, they'd follow him anywhere,' she said with a resigned sigh, signalling her point made.

'And if I refuse to acquiesce to this "request"?'

'Then I'll have to review the impact of the petitioner's request upon the mission. If I consider it minimal and the overall mission parameters unchanged, Jvar, I am *required* to back it.' The princess looked sympathetic, but not enough, he realised, to actively help Jvar block Ottar.

Jvar rose to leave, saying, 'I see, well thank you for your candour, Your Royal Highness.'

'Jvar, don't be like that. This puts me in an impossible position and you know it. Take my advice: give him a second fly-by and one more scoop-mine operation. A compromise. Then this'll be over.'

'I'll consider it,' he said, curtly, leaving through the open door. *This'll never be over.*

'*Are you considering it?*' asked the voice in his head.

'No, I most certainly am *not*. Give in to this and I may as well hand over the captaincy to that pompous little Art here and now,' said Jvar, as he stomped down the gravel path.

Alice was concerned. She had been an observer of human behaviour for longer than any other sentient, so she felt she knew the species pretty well. They liked their politics and their factious little games, but whenever she could, Alice stayed out of the power plays that seized every generation at one point. It was like a communal rite of passage and this was no different. The trigger and the players changed, but not the underlying emotional compunction.

Until that was, the point when the politicking edged towards upending the mission. Losing Jvar would be unfortunate but not catastrophic to Alice's puppetry of the biological units that maintained her physical environment. He had been groomed for captaincy – and conditioned to champion the mission above all else – since birth and was Alice's principal human interlocutor, but she could always convert someone else, and Ottar would certainly enjoy the illusion of power her support would bring.

But like Jvar she could not afford to let the mission become side-tracked for no tangible benefit. Earth was the prize, all the rest, *Mjölnir* and its tenders, just a means. So as she observed this latest gameplay unfold, she began to construct some contingency plans of her own.

Not all of them involving Jvar.

'*Jvar, you realise we cannot allow* Mjölnir *to be diverted from the prescribed flight plan. Any ad-hoc changes made en route will accumulate into overall mission failure and there is already too little room for error,*' the AI said.

'Oh don't worry, I'm crystal on that point. By the way, do feel free to share, if you have any golden nuggets about how we get out of this.'

Events moved quickly. Jvar had delayed making his formal response to the petition for as long as he could, but it was hours only. Eventually – feeling coerced – he issued a statement that there would be no deviation from the mission directive, no new mission-tasks, and added a piece about the future of their race being above their own avaricious desires, but it didn't seem to galvanise much support. It was an old story and people liked the new one more. As old as hope versus fear.

Ottar pushed immediately to have Jvar removed as captain and himself placed in temporary command of the ship, pledging to hold an election in due course. But all tyrants said that. In the meantime, he enacted a self-proclaimed ship-wide "emergency" and declared Jvar an enemy of the protectorate, ordering his arrest on charges of treasonable dereliction of the mission. The irony. Even Gannifaire reluctantly agreed to a board of enquiry to establish the "facts".

Luckily, Alice refused to grant Ottar security access and simultaneously sealed the operations centre. In response, Ottar created an enforcement arm, placing Rouelle in command, charging him with tracking the newly former captain down.

Jvar got one further message out, highlighting the obvious slide into military rule, a police state, they'd called it back on old-Earth, but the systechs – now working for Ottar – hacked a grid node and cut Jvar out of the band. Alice was splicing in a work-around.

They came for Jvar as he was making his way across the habitat to the bow endcap, to ops. Unfurling their BeMoWs ostentatiously, the three blue-caped enforcers spread out and began to circle. Jvar's heart raced as he pulled down rerouting telemetry into his virtuvue. But he was cornered. As they closed in with BeMoWs active, Jvar, desperate, jumped for a light tube tether, just as he had so many times as a child.

Grabbing it, he pulled himself up, arm over arm. The wire cut into his palms. As he climbed closer towards the axis of the ship, his weight reduced until he was able to pivot his legs up and swing into the zero-G zone. Letting go, he air-swam round the light tube itself, careful to avoid the plasma-hot corona. Once on the other side, he kicked down until gravity took hold once again and he dropped into a sugarcane field.

His pursuers were running now, round the endlessly inclining surface – the long way – but Jvar had some distance on them. After wading through the crops and jumping a narrow copse, he reached the passage leading to the gym. Sprinting straight for it, he dived head first into the access hole in the habitat floor.

Inside, bruised, bleeding, he began to climb down the rungs that stretched away towards the outer hull. As he ascended, his limbs grew heavy as the effect of the centrifugal forces increased. Two thirds of the way up, he arrived at an access panel to a hiGuard crawlway. Releasing the latches, he clambered inside.

Luckily, Rouelle hadn't spotted him so would assume he had headed up to the gym, buying him some time. Ottar was a vindictive bully, but Rouelle had a cruel, brutish streak that Jvar never wanted to see unleashed.

They traced him eventually as he crawled manically through the tight spaces between the green glowing cables. Alice was directing him towards ops, but the route was circuitous as she led him round checkpoints and sensors that Ottar had placed out or hacked. As Jvar crawled frantically through the maze of electronics, the newly self-appointed captain taunted him over a one-to-one intracom band from his command centre in the hangar bay.

Alice was attempting to confuse the usurpers but where they hacked directly into the ship's systems, there was little she could do. Sweat bedded on Jvar's forehead before running into his eyes and matting his thick auburn hair, but his virtuvue remained unaffected, allowing him to follow Alice's route without slowing.

As he pushed through the thick rubber flaps of the lifepod, the cool white glow of operations washed over him. He swam into a G-couch and took a moment to catch his breath.

Breathlessly, he said, 'Do they know where I am?'

'*No. Ottar is directing search teams to converge on the habitat. He is hoping to flush you out into the open,*' said Alice.

'Can you get me a direct link to Gannifaire?' he asked, ticking off a list of different options in his head.

'*Yes. It will take a moment.*'

'Jvar. Where *are* you?' Gannifaire blurted, the worry in her voice palpable over the degraded band.

'Ops. Ganni, this has gone way too far. Ottar won't stop now until I'm flushed out the airlock. You've got to *do* something,' he said, desperately.

'What? He's taken control of everything and I'm effectively under house arrest. There are these… dropshipers here, for my, *protection.*' She whispered the last word. 'If I don't rubber stamp his orders, I'm up for the same fate as you. He's got the entire community worked up into a frenzy. I did warn you, J—'

Jvar could almost feel the worry in her tone bubbling into fear, before cutting in with, 'Okay, stay put and do nothing. I'll get back in touch when I've some options.' Even though he didn't have a single one.

'Jvar, don't give in. It's too late to reason or compromise; he's after blood now.'

'Understood.' The band went dead.

'What's Ottar's next move, Alice?' said Jvar, hoping the AI would suggest something he could use.

'*To gain access to the operations centre and then control of me. Most likely his systechs will wipe my programming and reload the backup of the* Titan *class AI held on intellislate. You are almost an irrelevance now.*'

'Thanks,' Jvar said, numbly.

'Jvar, you never cease to amaze. You'll have to tell me sometime how you managed to gain access to the operations centre,' cut in Ottar's voice, over the internal speakers.

'What's the matter, Ottar, did the last captain not hand over the secrets of the ship?'

'Twelve minutes,' he said.

'Twelve minutes to what?' Jvar asked, genuinely intrigued but also annoyed at being suckered in.

'To overriding the security lockouts and gaining control of the ship's AI.'

'Ship, cut the link – Is he correct, Alice?' Jvar said, once the intracom connection was severed.

'*Not entirely. He will not gain complete control or be able remove my core programme, from outside ops, but he could build in overrides and administrator blocks to some key systems.*'

Jvar sat back in silence, wondering how to outwit a man he'd known since infancy. As he scrunched up his mind, Alice displayed an internal schematic showing the locations of all biosigns aboard. Most were congregating around the bow endcap.

'Alice, begin low-level power fluctuations throughout the ship. Create some theatrics. Then, in five minutes, give them access to ops and hand over control to Ottar. I'm giving myself up,' Jvar said, as an idea crawled about in his overwrought head.

'Jvar Kristensen. You will be taken to the brig where you will await trial,' said Captain Ottar Baston, as he emerged, floating like an avenging angel, into the habitat, from ops. The community were gathered below, their faces upturned, as if in worship.

'What brig? We don't have a fucking brig, you fascist.' Jvar spat the words as two of Ottar's people held him under each arm.

'Careful who you call fascist. After all, hasn't your family captained this vessel for nigh on eight hundred years without so much as a "by your leave" from the rest of us?' Ottar said, in a calm voice that carried nicely across the endcap.

'Don't dress this up, Ottar; you've made a grab for power and soon you'll be the self-proclaimed king of your very own little tyranny,' said Jvar.

'Take him away, Lieutenant.'

As he was led away – flanked on either side by a uniformed enforcer, Be-MoWs active – a commotion began to unfold above them, a little further back, into the main part of the habitat. It was coming from the other side of the endcap lake, just beyond a semi-secluded dell, where Government House lay. As Jvar looked up, he saw an upside-down figure crash through the edge of the densest part of the little wood. The person tripped and fell.

It was Gannifaire.

'Ottar. Enough of this. You've gone too far,' she shouted, as she climbed to her knees. As she inhaled to speak again, three more figures leapt from the woodline behind her. As she turned to address them, they fell on her, BeMoWs raised high.

'NO!' Jvar screamed, but as he sprang into the air, as if to jump directly to her aid, his guards holding him drove him into the soft earth.

'STOP! THE GOVERNOR GENERAL IS NOT TO BE HARMED,' exclaimed Ottar, from somewhere in-between.

'Is she dead?' Jvar asked, once he was alone. The brig had turned out to be nothing more than a corner of the hangar deck with a very crude web-cage cobbled together. His guards had retreated out of earshot to converse in private, assuming that once control of the ship's AI had been formally handed over to Ottar, that Jvar's access to the grid was similarly severed.

'*Yes.*'

'*Fuck.* May Guinevere bless her onward journey,' he said, automatically. After a moment, he added, 'You ready?'

'*Yes.*'

The lights in the hanger suddenly went out, leaving the bay in absolute blackness. Shouts of concern went up from Jvar's gaolers, followed by a series of subtle but unsettling jolts as the external thruster necklaces fired randomly. After thirty seconds or so, a dim red glow built up casting bloody shadows across the deck plating from the two dropships.

'*CRITICAL SYSTEMS CORRUPTION. COMMUNITY TO LIFEPODS. SENIOR STAFF TO THE OPERATIONS CENTRE,*' boomed the ship's AI. Jvar's two guards scrambled for the lifepod at the rear of the bay. Low vibrations pulsed through the ship, ebbing gradually as stability was restored.

A klaxon began to wail as Alice continued to issue instructions whilst patching through the internal optical feeds to Jvar's psyCore. Panic had set in instantly as people scrambled for lifepods or emergency hazard suits; hull breach drills forgotten as the reactor crew fled the fusion reactor and sprinted for cover.

Mothers screamed as they lost sensor-sight of their children, stewards battled to save delicate genetic experiments as power spikes fried consoles and seized biobanks. Conduit hatches blew as cabling overloaded and electronic boards fizzled and sparked while the habitat's light tube powered down creating a rapid drop in temperature.

'I'm impressed,' Jvar said.

'*Thank you. The damage is largely superficial, but should create the necessary effect.*'

'No doubt. Where's Ottar?'

'*He, his personal staff and technicians, are all in ops.*'

'Good. I give them five minutes,' he said, and settled in to wait. It was a high-risk plan but Jvar had been limited in what he could realistically achieve.

Six minutes, thirty-three seconds later, the two guards reappeared from the lifepod, their smart navy blue and gold uniforms replaced with the garish orange of the environment suits.

A muffled voice said, 'Come with us,' through a faceplate of one suit as the other released the lock on the cage.

'Where to?' Jvar asked, also using voice, to maintain the illusion that his psyCore connection was terminated.

'Ops,' came the indistinct reply.

'You did this. Now make it stop before the ship rips itself apart,' ordered Ottar, the moment Jvar's legs appeared the hexagonal room. Ottar's face lacked the calm, reserved demeanour of before. The holographic display showed an internal schematic with large red flashing icons along the green hiGuard network and intersect nodes.

'Oh, and how's that, then?' Jvar said, adding a puzzled look for effect.

'Don't fuck with me, Jvar, I'm not so easily duped.' The panic didn't show in his voice, but it was barely concealed behind his eyes.

'I've been isolated in your little *brig*, if you recall. I've had no access to the ship. Looks to me like you've brought this on yourself. What has the AI diagnosed?' Jvar looked around quickly. The faces of the systechs reflected the same concern as Ottar's. *Good, they're buying it.*

'It's claiming our hacks have degraded principal command paths,' said Tasmin, the senior systech. She looked genuinely alarmed, but then, Jvar mused, she would because she knew what would happen if this were for real.

'Sounds reasonable. The AI conducts literally billions of operations a second to maintain *Mjölnir*. You should've known something like this could happen, Tasmin,' said Jvar, in a tone he hoped would convey his disappointment in her.

Turning to Ottar, she said, 'You see?' Defiance flaring in her eyes.

'Can you *fix* it?' Ottar asked Jvar, through gritted teeth, ignoring Tasmin's outburst.

Jvar responded, in a level tone, with, 'Possibly. But you'll have to return control to me.' It wasn't true as he'd never relinquished it, but Ottar needed to know that it was over. Handing back control, however illusionary, would cement that defeat in Ottar's own mind. It was how the man worked.

'No way. This is *my* ship now, Jvar, mine. Fix the command pathways, if for no other reason than to save your own skin,' he said, iron in his voice. The others in the room looked on in growing horror, as if they were seeing the naked Ottar for the first time.

Jvar didn't answer.

Tasmin cut in, in a rising, panicked tone, 'Shit! We've got massive data dropouts across all grid repositories. This is *bad*, Ottar…I, I mean, Captain – whatever – and there's nothing my team can do. Give him what he wants or you'll be captain of a lifeless, tumbling rock,' as she looked on in terror at the flashing icons blossoming in the main holographic view.

Jvar spoke, in a level, commanding tone. 'It's over, Ottar. Return control to me so that I can release the backup semi-sentient spiders into the grid to hot-write the patches needed to restore critical command paths. It's your call, but make it quickly.' Jvar was bluffing. It was all a fantasy, but he was banking on Ottar's experience of dropships to fuel his fear.

Dropships were simple, with basic systems and limited backups. If a dropship's system failed the operation was abandoned. Simple. That, Jvar hoped, would be Ottar's default setting. His grounding rod. That, and his jingoistic, twisted sense of personal honour. The klaxon started up again then, giving the moment an added edge. Alice playing her part with aplomb.

Ottar fixed the former captain with an intense gaze, hatred written across his chiselled, authoritarian features.

'He's right, Ottar; it's over,' said Tasmin, in a barely audible whisper.

Jvar said – in case an extra push were needed – 'People are scared, hiding in lifepods, wondering if they'll see the day out and knowing you aren't the man to lead them. Your authority was only ever fleeting and without control of the ship it will fade as quickly as it rallied, Ottar, and now Gannifaire's dead, Art damnit! Open your eyes. We have to end this. Now.'

It worked.

As Ottar breathed out so the power-lust was expelled from him also. He looked like a general on an old-Earth battlefield who had finally realised his troops were routed, the battle lost. With his stickpadded feet, he stepped back, resting a hip on the arm of a G-couch, defiance and anger draining away. After a moment of silence, with all eyes on him, Ottar seemed suddenly to realise his final part in the drama. He stood up, parade erect, stickpads holding him in position.

'Captain Jvar, I relinquish to you the captaincy of this vessel and my command of the dropships. Do with me as you will,' he said, in an obvious attempt at oratorical self-aggrandisement, as he ceremoniously removed the four ringed epaulettes from his shoulders and handed them over. They floated off his open palm as if entirely ambivalent to the solemnity of the act.

Martyrdom, naturally. Jvar knew that if Ottar couldn't have total power he'd opt for a gesture of noble self-sacrifice upon the altar of his own ego. He may be a martyr in a cause of one, but with Ottar, it was all about the *one*.

'What happens now?' Tasmin asked, as they made their way back to the habitat. Jvar had just conducted Gannifaire's funeral. Her wrapped remains now falling away from *Mjölnir* at five megametres per hour.

Those that hadn't been able to cram into the docking port reception room, had watched the ceremony via internal optics, from within the habitat where the community was gathered for a low-key wake. In everyone's peripheral virtuvue was the image from the stern telescope, still tracking Gannifaire's, shrouded, tumbling form.

'With what?' Jvar asked, unsure to what the senior systech was referring.

She clarified, with, 'Well, with Ottar, the rest of us, the constitution, I guess. Surely something will have to be done?' The guilt lurking behind her blunt features.

'I'm not so sure about that, actually,' said the captain, in a quietly smug tone. 'The dropship crew will be disbanded of course, and all military paraphernalia banned. The next generation can rebuild that function as they see fit, but other than that I intend to make no changes.' As he spoke, Tasmin's expression turned from guilt to confusion.

After a time, she said, 'But don't you want to ensure nothing like this will happen again. Shouldn't you enact safeguards or issue a decree or something?'

He smiled at that. 'Knowledge of the events of the last few days will be enough in themselves to prevent such ideas gaining credence again,' he said, casually, as they arrived at the passageway ladder. 'Constitutional amendments won't stop people like Ottar, but education will prevent the likeminded from gaining traction in the future. And anyway, the last thing the community needs right now is change.'

'Well, you're the captain I guess,' Tasmin said, with a smile.

Twenty-Six

HMVS Mjölnir, sixty years from Neptunian space
Generation Sixteen
4310

Snapdragon bounded through the rough scrub of the lowlands before jumping into the air, as big as he could. He travelled in a high parabolic arc, legs kicking all the while, before landing back on the unkempt grass, askew from his original line of travel. He laughed, as if it was the funniest thing that could ever have happened to anyone, ever. By the time Cowslip had caught up he was bent double barely able to breath.

'You'll do yourself a mischief if you carry on like that, m'lad,' she chided, affectionately.

'But if I jump high enough, I'll be able to swim G-free, like the older boys. When will I old enough, when?' the shaggy-haired eight-year-old said, with genuine longing in his eyes.

'When you're old enough, that's when. Now on your feet, fragglepuss, or Art will come and visit you in your bed and gobble you all up.'

'He won't, willie?' a suddenly very concerned little boy questioned.

'Well now that depends… on whether we make it t'our exercise class on time or not, now doesn't it?'

'Race you,' yelled Snapdragon, as he climbed to his feet and charged off in the direction of the gym passage.

'Boys,' exclaimed Cowslip, to an empty space, before trotting after the ball of wild locks and energy. As she caught up with him and made sure he climbed the ladder rungs properly, her thoughts turned to another boy, or rather, young man. Like her, a teenager, though a little older, called Jonquil, and one day, he would be the captain of the whole entire ship.

Her thoughts inevitably flicked to her own lineage: descendent of a lottery winner. *Sigh.* Not in the same league – not at all – but 'Slip had seen the way Jonquil looked at her, when he thought to be unobserved.

The noise was almost deafening when Cowslip emerged into the gymnasium, jumping from the opening onto the floor below, landing heavily. The transition from the lighter gravity in the core to the heavier around the outer hull could still take her by surprise. Maybe she wasn't working as hard at her exercise classes as she should be, she pondered, fleetingly.

Snapdragon was already leaping about on the trampoline, with two other boys of similar age (his favourite exercise, not surprisingly). Cowslip made for one of the three rowing machines and strapped herself in. Lizabel, the grownup supervising the class clapped her hands.

'Attention please. Hawthorne, that means you too. Right, good. Same as usual then, ten minutes on each machine and then we'll play some games,' she instructed, as the din reverted back to its earlier volume.

'Seem to be missing someone, don't we?' Snowdrop said, as she took up her position on the rower, next to Cowslip.

'Oh really? I hadn't noticed,' replied 'Slip, as she felt her cheeks flush.

With a nonchalant flick of her head, Snowdrop said, 'Yeah, right. So you're eyes aren't, like glued to the entrance at all, then. Wanna know where he is?'

'Well, if you mean Jonquil, then *no*. I have absolutely no interest whatsoever,' Cowslip said indignantly, whilst desperately hoping her best friend wouldn't be able to keep her information secret.

'Oh, okay then,' said 'Drop, with an air of mock-indifference.

A brief moment passed. 'But… just so you can get it off your chest… where is he?' 'Slip said, with a tell-tale smile.

'Well,' began Snowdrop, as the rower began chiming to remind her to maintain a minimum stroke. '*I* heard Lizabel speaking on her psyCore and it sounded like Jonquil is havin' extra dropship piloting lessons, the lucky so-and-so.' 'Drop was speaking in a conspiratorial whisper, as if the news was highly confidential.

'Oh, well maybe we'll see him tomorrow then,' said 'Slip, with a disappointed sigh. 'D'you think *we'll* ever learn to fly a dropship?' she added, wistfully.

Snowdrop blurted, without a thought, 'Hah! You really do live in a dream world. You, a "lottery loser" and the daughter of an algae pool attendant. You must be joking.'

Pausing before replying, Cowslip said, more solemnly, 'I guess. I just wish our lives weren't all so bloomin' mapped out.' She was hurt by the jibe, but tried not to let it show. *After all, 'Drop is right.*

Speaking more sympathetically, Snowdrop said, 'Well, get used to the idea, 'cos that's the way it is. You know Ragwort's had an unhealthy eye on you for a while now. Maybe you should return a few glances; set your sights at someone you might actually score with.'

'Pah,' Cowslip offered in retort. One day soon she'd tell her best friend that her feelings for the captain's son were reciprocated; that would shut her up. But not yet, Jonquil had been insistent she tell no one of their love. It was all *sooo* romantic.

'Mum, do I have to be captain, you know, after you? Is it, like, the law, or something?' Jonquil asked, as he wandered into the small kitchen.

'Why, Jonquil; you have other plans?' his mother asked, casually, as she diced tomatoes for their supper.

'No, I just, well, I guess it all seems so fixed,' he said, uncomfortably.

'That's as may be, Son, but it's in line with the mission directive, and—'

'No absolutely, Mum, I understand that,' Jonq interrupted, hastily, lest his mum get the wrong impression. 'I'm not suggesting anything that would risk the mission, obviously; I'm just curious where the authority comes from for me to just assume the post. I mean, suppose I'm not the best person for the job.'

A Kristensen – all the way back to Esteemed Joshua – had captained *Mjölnir*. Fifteen so far, Jonquil reflected. But recently, his mum was beginning to show her age. And, although he didn't really want the job (at least, at nineteen, not yet) he was beginning to get a feeling – for the first time in his life – that his dear old mum wasn't going to be around forever.

'Okay then, sit down at the table. We'll eat while we talk,' Jasmina said, putting the finishing touches to the salad. As she lowered herself slowly into her own seat opposite, Jonquil could actually hear her bones creak. Even with the nanotech treatments, he was beginning to think she'd be lucky to see her one hundred and eighty-fourth birthday.

He'd heard that when age finally caught up with the long-lived, it caught up quick, as if the nanobots were holding back the tide of time until eventually the pressure became too great and the century of extended health suddenly gushed away like a fairy-tale spell undone. Silver hair spilled about his mother's shoulders, tangling with her necklace.

'It isn't law, no, but convention that sees the captaincy of *Mjölnir* pass down the Kristensen line. Just as the governor general's appointment will always remain with the Windsors. It provides the continuity the mission needs, just as the Ottar Incident proved. And as for your suitability, well…' Jasmina looked into Jonquil's eyes and smiled, her face full of warmth and affection. 'I too worried when I was your age, but remember, you've been preparing for this your whole life. No other Sixteener would be able to perform better.' She spoke with that look she took on when she was imparting sage advice. All the Fifteeners had it, he'd noticed, but his mum's was the worst.

'It's not that I'm worried about my abilities necessarily' – although it was that too – 'I just wonder if it's fair, that's all,' he said, with an inward flinch. Questioning the status quo was something he'd learned was not to be done lightly.

'It's the way of things, Jonquil. This is how old-Earth operated their systems of state government – a monarch and a prime minister, each providing a check and balance for the other and both handing over to their child when the time was right. So it's right that we follow the same model.' That, Jonquil knew to be true from the emotionless wisdom of the edubots, and accepted it, as did everyone. But still, something niggled.

'Is that true, really? Did just two families govern every state, like the whole time?' Jonquil asked, uncertain if he should winkle at something so well established.

Without looking up, Jasmina said, 'Well, that was what my father, your grandfather, told me, as did his mother, my grandmother, tell him. So it must be true, mustn't it?'

'Yeah, I guess so,' Jonq muttered, in a subdued tone.

'Hey, Jonq,' she said, lowering her eye level to his own, 'it's good that you're asking these questions. As the future captain, you should be concerned for the fair treatment of the community. Well done, Son, I'm proud of you.'

'Thanks, Mum.' He paused to change the subject. 'After dinner I'm going to join some of the other Sixteeners in Guin's Eye. If that's okay?' he said, hoping his mum couldn't see through the nakedly white lie. She had a knack, although it was slipping as they both aged.

'Sure,' she said, 'just be back by dusk, we need to set the right example if the increased sleep cycle is going to bed in.'

As Jonquil tucked into his tomato and walnut salad, he thought back over this and previous conversations about passing on the baton of power. With no records about systems of government or politics surviving the Ottar Incident, he'd found it hard to accept the premise that old-Earth had used such an oddly skewed system of government.

But as he got older, he realised it probably didn't matter if it was true or not, as long as it worked. And no one wanted another murdering egomaniac like Ottar on the loose.

'What d'you think it's like now, Jonq, on Earth?' 'Slip asked, as she watched Ægir's diamond-studded realm roll by under their feet. She was sat in Jonquil's lap, in one of the large couches that surrounded the observation blister. The internal lighting was low and the brillantine stars brighter by contrast. It was a wonderful place to spend time doing nothing. The nearest thing to escapism their worldlet had.

In a quiet voice, Jonquil said, 'Well – they say that when the Firsts went back to Earth, after the Ending War, it looked pretty bad. You've seen the images from that time. An ice age, dust clouds the size of oceans, and that's still what it'll be like, now, I expect. Cold and dark. Like *really* cold, and *really* dark.'

'D'you think anyone survived?' Cowslip said, as she turned her head so that she could peer into the young man's eyes.

Using his best, I-know-what-I'm-talking-about voice, he said, 'Hmm, well if anyone survived the war – and that's an enormously big *if* – the chances of them surviving the winter are slender at best. That's what the Fifteeners say, anyway.'

'And Esteemed Joshua figured it all out and then made *this* ship. Can you even *imagine* meeting him? Must've been quite someone. They say he was gifted with foresight. Do you think it's true?' 'Slip said, with real reverence.

'Who knows? But he was right, right? So maybe...' Jonquil said, caught up in the romance of it.

Wide eyed, she said, 'And you're related to him. How cool is that?'

'Pretty cool, I guess.' It wasn't. 'But I don't really feel it. In those days, the Firsts were really *doing* something, you know? Since then, we've just been keeping things ticking along. Doesn't feel the same. It's like we're not part of the same mission; just caretakers for the next generation. Kinda feels a bit pointless,' he said, as a melancholy mood washed over him.

But it's true. And we're the lucky ones. We have a scoop-mining operation to give our generation a sense of purpose.

'It isn't, though,' Cowslip said, bringing Jonq out of his introspection. It was just them in Guin's Eye, and their time alone was precious, not to be squandered. 'One day you're gonna be captain and one mistake and the 'hole mission could be up the swanny.'

'Thanks for that. No pressure then,' he replied, quickly, acerbically.

'Sorry; but you know what I mean,' Cowslip said, softening her tone. 'We're as important as the Firsts, just in our own way.' Switching emphasis, she continued, 'When you're captain, Jonq, d'you think we'll still be together?' While her tone was neutral, he could feel it loaded with expectation, emotion.

Slightly bemused, he said, 'Of course we will. I'll be captain; I'll be able to do anything. Why d'you ask?'

'Because you live in the highlands, with the senior staff and I live in the lowlands with the rest. The two don't mix, Jonq, you must've seen it.'

'Yes we do! We have parties for the whole community. We mix during classes, stuff like that,' he exclaimed, surprised at the sudden change in 'Slip's discourse.

'The Sixteeners mix sure, for now; but the Fifteeners don't, not even at the parties. And one day, when we're in charge, we'll be the same. Will you even look at me then?'

'Of course! I love you, 'Slip. Nothing will change that.' The words were desperate, pleading, but to placate who, he couldn't be sure. He pulled her in tighter, as if to underline the conviction of his words with physical force. But somehow, the look in her eyes told him she wasn't convinced.

Quietly, as if diminished by her family's station, she said, 'Even when I've taken over from my dad in the algae pool?'

'What you do won't matter, it's in here that counts,' he said, placing his hand to his chest in an adult manner; a gesture of stoic love, and of finality.

'I know and I believe you, but will the others – the Fifteeners?' the young woman asked, pushing the subject harder than he had expected.

Jonq's answer was off-hand, dismissive. 'Got nothing to do with them.' He was getting bored with the subject. *When we gonna do some kissing?*

'Hasn't it?' she pursued.

'No. When I'm captain, we'll do things differently,' he said, flatly.

'I bet that's what the Fifteeners said.'

'Yeah well, difference is I mean it.' They sat in silence, staring out at the void, lost in their own thoughts. After a time, Jonquil manoeuvred Cowslip round and leaned in. Her deep green eyes closed majestically as her lips parted in anticipation of a kiss.

He took a moment to study her heart-shaped face and petite features, framed as they were with soft, copper hair, before gently pressing his mouth to hers. As they folded into each other's embrace, he wondered if it really would last.

'You must be jokin'.'

'But why not?'

'Cos you're gonna take over from me, see. That's the way o' things, child, and always 'as been.'

'But, Dad, I don't want t' work in life sciences and I don't want to spend the rest o' my days raking out the flippin' algae pool; I want to pilot dropships!' As Cowslip spoke, a tear came unbidden to her eye which just antagonised her more.

'Hey, hey; I'm sorry, love. Listen, how 'bout we sit down and you tell me what this's really about, huh?' Papouis said.

Cowslip and her father lived in one of the tenements cut into the floor of the habitat, clustered around the stern endcap – commonly known as the lowlands. Not low as in elevation – as Cowslip had once thought – but low as in lowly, the opposite of high, as in highborn. The lowlands were given over to crops and aqua farms, while the highlands were parkland and orchards.

She knew that with the community's slow decline in population, only about half of the warrens of the dugout apartments were occupied, but even so, the complex still felt cramped. Only the senior echelons of the community had bungalows actually up in the habitat itself. Under the radiance of the actual light tube. 'Slip had always felt slightly uncomfortable when she visited one, as if she didn't quite belong.

'Here, drink this,' said 'Slip's dad, as he handed her a mug of parsley tea. She took a sip as Papouis sat in silence waiting for her to speak.

'I'm scared, Dad,' she said, finally, 'Scared that when Jonquil becomes capt'n, he'll forget about me, 'ere, in the lowlands. He says he won't but... but if I was a pilot...d'you see?' 'Slip sniffed and sipped as she spoke. She felt foolish, childish, as she heard the words back in her own ears, but she couldn't help it. It was the way she felt. *Why can't the others understand*, she seethed, inwardly.

'Oh, poppet, I've told you, nothin' good'll come of you forming an attachment to one o' them lot up there. It won't work. We can't simply choose a different way o' life. The mission directive won't allow it,' said her father, in a composed, deliberate intonation. Caring, but resolute.

'But why not, why can't I? It's just not fair,' she raged, full of muted anger and confusion at a world she was beginning to see cast in a lesser light.

Soothingly – as he fixed his daughter with a loving look – Papouis said, 'Alright, try not to upset yerself, now. Tell you what, I'll speak to Rifenwald; see what 'e 'as t' say. But you have to promise me, 'Slip, that you really do want to become a pilot an' all, and not just 'cos o' some boy.'

'Thank you, Daddy, thank you,' exclaimed Cowslip, her anger draining away in a moment, to be replaced with childish euphoria. *Perhaps the world isn't so bad after all*, she thought, in a flash, before throwing herself into her father's arms. 'And yes, I *really* do want to become a pilot, *and* I want to be Jonquil's equal. Otherwise, people'll think I love him for his position and it isn't that, Dad, really it isn't.'

'Okay, poppet.' His smile was pure love. There was nothing he wouldn't do for her. 'I'll speak to Rifenwald on the morrow.'

'*Jasmina, you have a visitor*,' said Alice.

With a subconscious finger tap, the captain pulled up the internal sensor imagery of the passageway leading onto ops. She spent most of her time here now as the zero-G was an easier environment for her ageing body to cope with. She was currently reviewing the plan to mine Neptune's atmosphere of its chemically energetic, if physically torpid, hydrogen and helium.

Mjölnir wasn't due into local Neptunian space for another sixty years, but the captain was keen to ensure Jonquil was gifted an airtight plan. It would all be on him; all Jasmina could do was prepare the boy – *her* role in the overall mission. She was old now and relieved she wouldn't be around for the first significant extra vehicular activity since Jupiter, as she wouldn't survive the hard-G manoeuvring required.

The image showed the cropped black hair and chiselled features of Rifenwald – head of life sciences – as he pulled himself along the passageway. A moment later, he popped into the room and air-swam to the floor, where he anchored himself in place with his stickies.

Once comfortable, Rifenwald said, 'Jasmina; I hope you don't mind me dropping in?'

'Not at all,' the captain replied, genuinely pleased to see her long-time friend. 'Here to gloat on the success of your genetic improvements to crop yields?' she asked, in the full knowledge that it wasn't his style.

'Only if I get time,' he said, with a light chuckle. 'No, the reason I've come by is… hmm, I've had an unusual request which I can't field.' His features took on a slightly uncomfortable, quizzical cast, as if he were embarrassed at bringing the problem to the captain's attention.

Jasmina was intrigued. 'Oh?'

'Yeah; I've had a, well, a request from Papouis about his daughter, Cowslip. Seems she wants a sort of, um… transfer… to dropships,' he said, struggling with the alien concept.

'A *transfer*? Out of life sciences? To dropships?' Jasmina repeated stupidly.

'Indeed, Jas. But *I* don't have that authority and, well, it's unprecedented, so, here I am.' He spread his hands out to reinforce his point. *I'm passing the buck*, he was saying.

'Quite right, quite right. Ship; *is* there a precedent here?' Jasmina asked Alice, buying some time to think.

'*Ignoring Ottar's desire for a change of job title, yes. The Thirteeners had a similar situation*,' said Alice.

Surprised at her ignorance, the captain asked, 'And how did they deal with it?'

'*They gave the person the transfer. Unfortunately, it opened the door to many other requests. The situation was only prevented from spiralling out of control when the original transferee agreed to return to their generational assignment. I do not recommend a similar approach*,' Alice said, impassively.

'Agreed,' said Jas. 'Cowslip: now that name rings a bell. Isn't she enamoured with my Jonquil?'

'That's the rumour, although they think they've managed to allude detection thus far,' said Rifenwald.

'*They?* So it's two-way?'

Rifenwald acknowledged with a nod of his head.

'Ship; what's your analysis of this relationship?' *How long has this been going on and why don't I know about it.*

'*Based on my observations, I would say… close.*'

'How close?' Jonquil's mother said, not liking the sound of *that* and perturbed by her lack of awareness. They were talking about her son, and even Alice hadn't felt the need to share such vital intel with her.

'*Not intimate, yet,*' the AI said.

'Well, that's something, I suppose. Sounds like there's more to this. Rif, tell Papouis we'll accommodate Cowslip's request, but *only* in another life sciences post and only if someone *from* elsewhere in life sciences is then prepared to backfill hers. We can't afford to open the floodgates on this. We're too small a community to begin generic job training, on the whims of children. I'll tackle this from the other end.'

Jasmina realised finally why Rifenwald had brought the issue to her, rather than simply dismiss the request himself. It could grow legs. Fast.

'On it, Boss,' said Rifenwald, pulling his stickies free of the floor.

Twenty-Seven

HMVS Mjölnir, Captain's Quarters

'I'm just asking you to consider the bigger picture, here,' Jasmina said, exasperated. 'Your relationship with this girl is putting ideas in her head; ideas that'll only hurt her in the long run.'

'I don't care! I love her and *you* can't change that,' Jonquil said, more harshly than he'd intended. The debate was quickly degenerating into an argument.

'Look, one day soon, you'll be captain and then you'll realise that this is a small community in a delicately balanced environment. It works because the status quo is carefully maintained. If we muck about with that, we risk the mission.' She turned away, as if not quite buying into her own propaganda and not wanting her expression to give her away.

Jonq asked hotly, 'So? If 'Slip wants to better herself, then what's wrong with that?' Half-seeing his mum's point, but then half-hating the intransigence of it.

'It'll give others *ideas*. Suddenly, everyone will begin to eye each other's lives with envy. This ship works by being based on multigenerational stability,' Jasmina implored, as a slightly worried, maternal expression tugged at her worn features.

'Mum; that may be the case for the Fifteeners, but when I'm captain, the Sixteeners'll be free to choose their roles,' he said, by way of some infantile, foot-stamping decree, before immediately feeling embarrassed, knowing he risked undermining all that his mother stood for.

'Jonq, your youth gives you an idealistic zeal, but trust me, when you become captain of this ship – of our race – you'll realise *Mjölnir* can't operate that way, it would absorb too much time and resources to retrain people.' His mum was beginning to give up, he could see it in her eyes. However, "resources" chimed. That was a word with real resonance aboard a closed-loop system with finite everything.

'Not if it's all scoped out and managed properly, it wouldn't,' he said, intent that the next generation wouldn't be like the last. *I mean, why should it?*

'Yes, it would. Take Cowslip's request: all her life she's been trained to work life sciences. If she's allowed to flip roles, who'll do her job and when will they be trained? Then there's the question of her pilot training, when will she fit that in? And who stands the gap, Jonq, when there are so few of us?' Grudgingly, Jonquil could see where she was going, even though he was determined not to.

Verbalising his thoughts, he said, 'There's a way, Mum, there's always a way. Just 'cos you can't see it—' His words were tinged with mounting anger.

'Art's pitted heart, Jonq, there *isn't* always a way.' She huffed, letting the anger go. 'As captain of this vessel, I'm turning down Cowslip's request and I advise that you think carefully about your relationship with her. You risk making promises you can't keep when you're high up on that hill they call the captain's couch.' Jasmina's words were cold and laced with a cruel certainty.

'No, Mum, *not* by Art's black heart, but by Guin's good grace. I love Cowslip and I'm going to help her in this,' he said, fervently, feeling the righteousness of his cause flow through him. Jonquil left. He'd got as far as he was going, he realised. Time for action.

Later, Jasmina popped her head round her son's door. He was packing.

'What's this?' she asked, confused.

'I'm leaving,' he said, without turning from his task.

'Leaving? To go where?' asked Jasmina, her voice betraying her shock.

Good, that's got 'er.

Quietly, without turning, he said, 'I'm going to move into one of the vacant tenements, so I can be close to 'Slip.'

'But *this* is the captain's accommodation. It always has been. I mean, I, I…' his mum spluttered, with absolute conviction before tailing off, unable to justify the absolutism of it. As if that one fact alone should have been enough to make him see sense, when all it really did was expose a chasm that hadn't been there until now; had it?

'I know, Mum,' Jonquil said, in a softer tone, 'and you're the captain; I'm not. When I take on that role, *if* I take on that role – many years from now, I hope – I'll return. Until then, I think it's best if I live where I'm most at ease with all of my, *idealistic zeal*.' Jonquil felt guilt flush through him as he spoke;

it wasn't that he wanted to hurt his mum, but she needed to see how serious he was. *She'd understand in time*, he thought. He hoped.

'No; Son, don't go, please. We'll work this out; it doesn't have to come between *us*. This is your *home* and always will be,' she pleaded, but it sounded formulaic, as if she was repeating a mantra, passed down through the storied ages. A tear budded in her eye nonetheless.

'And maybe that's the problem, Mother. Maybe the rarefied atmosphere up here in the highlands is what's blinded the captain to life in the rest of the ship. Well, not me.' He winced at the arrogant presumption of his own words. But they were said now, given life and gone.

And then his footfalls were crunching along the gravel path, before turning towards the rear of the habitat, the stern endcap and the lowlands. As he passed back in view of his newly former home, the little stone cottage seemed smaller, somehow, lonelier.

His mum was nowhere to be seen.

It was little more than a small cavern of coarsely excavated rock which served as an equipment room for the ion drive assemblies. Shielding plates, spare accelerator coils and maintenance tools were scattered around. Even a pile of old shipbots long since seized beyond repair. Members of the community filed into the room in ones and twos – some stewards, mostly general workers, all lowlanders, and no Sixteeners.

The airtight hatch was sealed and Papouis called the meeting to order. He'd chosen the ion drive maintenance room because it had no sensors. In here, the senior staff – most especially the captain – couldn't eavesdrop.

Ever since Jasmina had turned his daughter down flat, Papouis' parental empathy had kicked in like a bay loaders' arm. He began to see the issue from 'Slip's point of view and then he began to get angry. Not loud angry, just quietly seething, as the nature of the power balance onboard began to reveal itself. So he'd quietly spent time lobbying other lowlanders, until eventually calling those that were so inclined to a meeting.

It felt like he was taking a risk, but quite what he was risking, he couldn't be sure. *Whatever the outcome, it has to be better than the current situation, and at least I'll be doing right by my little girl.*

Twenty faces looked nervously at Papouis as he opening the meeting. 'Thank you for coming,' he said, in a faltering voice. Papouis had spent his life maintaining algae pools; he was no orator.

Marina – an ion drive specialist – asked, 'Why are we here, Papouis?' Others looked on, nervous, fidgeting.

'Because sommat's wrong, and I—'

'Wrong wi' what? You risk a lot calling a secret meeting like this,' interrupted a steward named Gravic. Others, sitting or leaning on obsolete equipment in the dimly lit room, nodded in guarded agreement.

'Look, you know 'bout my daughter, Cowslip's, request, yeah? Well, it's been refused and I'm not 'appy with the way they done an' gone about it, see,' Papouis said, determined not to be side-tracked.

'We all heard the announcement and to be honest, I can't say as I'm minded to disagree. Community's too small to simply let people change roles on a hormonal whim,' said Marina. Again, others voiced their support.

'And you know what,' said Papouis, pressing on, 'I agree with it too. Cowslip's decision had a lot more to do with Jonquil than any real, deep-seated wish to be a dropshiper, but it got me thinkin', see. She thinks she ain't good enough for 'im. Thinks that if she could some'ow break out of her assigned role into something more "highland", she'd become more acceptable to 'im.'

'And she's probably right, but so what?' Gravic said, with an indifference Papouis worried was endemic.

'I see where you're going now, Papouis. This isn't about Cowslip's right to choose her role. This is about *rights*,' said Larelle, her face lighting up as the concept took shape in her mind.

'Exactly that, yes,' said Papouis, relieved to have an ally, someone able to articulate such an oblique concept. Others around the small cavern began looking thoughtful, as if mulling the idea over. 'Don't you see? All the decisions are being made by an exclusive group – the senior staff, the highlanders – and each generation, these powers simply get 'anded on. Like heirlooms. We've no say in nothin'. Can that really be the right o' things?'

Papouis looked around the dim cavern. Half-lit faces stared back. Some appeared to be waiting before picking a side. In amongst the determinedly neutral expressions were some who stared at Papouis with an entrenched scepticism; others with an openness that suggested backing. *Hmm, a mixed bag, then.*

'But that's the way of governing and wotnot, we all know this,' said Marina.

'If you're suggesting another "Ottar", you can count me out. That little highland power struggle nearly destroyed the ship, not to mention the mission,' said Gravic, from the side-lines.

'I'm not suggesting nothin', I'm just askin' the question: why can't the 'ole community be more involved in decisions affecting us all?'

'Like some form of representative, inclusive process, you mean?' Larelle said, as she struggled to describe a system of government that she appeared to have no knowledge of.

'Exactly that. I'm not suggesting we take action, but if enough of us agree, we could at least put it to Jasmina, see what she 'as to say,' Papouis said, finally feeling like he was making headway.

'*Jasmina; you should be aware that a large proportion of the ship's community have sealed themselves into a maintenance room,*' said Alice, as Jasmina lay suspended in mid-air, in ops.

'Oh? Pull up a feed from inside please, Alice,' the captain requested.

'*I am afraid that I cannot. There are no sensors in that room,*' said the AI.

'What d'you make of it?' Jasmina said, threat hairs on her neck prickling. Since Jonquil had stormed from the cottage she had pretty much moved into ops and the comfort zero-G environment had offered her tired old body. Without her son at home, it just didn't feel like home anymore. Work: that was the thing, she'd decided.

'*The highest probability is that they are conducting a meeting, the contents of which they wish to conceal.*'

'I concur; looks like this Cowslip thing's going to escalate. Summon the senior staff, please. And also, where's Jonquil? Is he in there too?' A note of concern creeping into her voice as she spoke. He hadn't been in touch since leaving.

'*Jonquil is currently in Tenement Five, with Cowslip. They are unaware of the meeting,*' said Alice.

'Well then that's something,' Jasmina said, relieved, before turning her full attention to a clandestine gathering of most of the tenement dwellers.

The senior staff had barely the chance to debate the implications of there having been a meeting when an alert appeared in the captain's psyCore virtuvue. It was from Papouis – the algae pool maintenance hand, Cowslip's father. *I should have guessed who'd be behind it,* Jasmina thought to herself.

'Captain,' began Papouis' avatar. In another segment of her sofsceen she had an optic trained on him, as he climbed along the passageway, leading from propulsion into the habitat. 'You'll be aware a meeting of the Fifteeners 'as taken place, less you and the other senior staff, obviously.'

In an emotionless tone, the captain replied, with, 'I am, Papouis, and curious of course.'

'That's why I'm calling. We need t' meet,' said Papouis.

'Good idea, come up to ops.'

'We're on our way,' he said, and cut the link.

Gravic, Larelle and Papouis appeared in ops and attached themselves to the floor. They huddled around the passageway entrance, as if to secure their escape, as Jasmina looked them over for clues as to their intent. They seemed no more relaxed than their stance suggested. On the other side of the holopit were arrayed the senior staff, including Lizabel and Rifenwald.

'So, I take it this is about Cowslip and my decision to turn down her transfer request?' Jasmina spoke in a direct, authoritative tone, but not intimidatingly so, she hoped. She didn't want to antagonise this deputation unnecessarily.

'It stems from that, Cap'n, yes, but we do realise why you done what you did. There're broader implications, which we get, see,' said Papouis. He seemed nervous, although Jasmina was relieved by what he'd said. Reasonable, pragmatic. Although, it still begged the question what they did actually then want.

In a more yielding tone – from her anchored position to one side of a G-couch – Jasmina said, 'I'm glad you see it that way. So what can we do for you?'

'Did you know, Cap'n,' began Papouis, 'that in all my many years on *Mjölnir*, this is the first time I've actually been inside the hallowed operations centre itself?' throwing Jasmina completely.

'Um, no, Papouis, I didn't know that. You've always been welcome. Everyone is. There're no off-limits areas on the ship; I've always said that,' offered Jasmina, less than eloquently. She mulled for a moment and Papouis' intent suddenly became clear. *Art's teeth*, she fumed silently, *he's running rings around me.*

'I'm sure you're right, but it isn't how it feels, is it? This is highlander space. You know it and so d'we. Which is why you don't come down t' the tenements, and we don't come up 'ere,' Papouis said, with a look of confident satisfaction creeping into his features.

'You know, Papouis, you have a point,' said Lizabel, the governor general. 'We have let the community polarise a little.'

'Agreed,' added Rifenwald. 'We should do more to reintegrate the community. Bring it back together.' But to Jas it was a vacuous statement.

With a steel edge, Gravic said, 'But it's not just that. It's not just about *feeling* equal, because we aren't. Are we?' He seemed to Jasmina to be the potentially troublesome one. He'd hung back initially and maintained a dark, brooding countenance.

Serene as ever, Princess Lizabel said, 'We have to have leadership. It can't simply be done away with.'

'Power has always rested with some, who wield it for the benefit of all. You know this,' said Rif, more tempestuously. Jasmina watched. Larelle – who had so far seemed open to discourse – reacted to Rifenwald's words; her expression hardening. Riled. Jas realised they were losing the argument.

Explaining how it had always been suddenly seemed to lose its automatic authority. Tired, trite and lacking imagination. Jasmina needed another angle.

'Well, we've been thinkin', see,' said Papouis, 'and we think the ship needs "rep...resen...tative rights".' He spoke the words deliberately, being careful to pronounce them so that they couldn't be mis-heard, but also as if they were unfamiliar sounds that he was still getting used to.

Perplexed, Jasmina asked, 'Representative rights? What're they?' It was a term she hadn't heard before. As she spoke, a searing pain shot down her back, causing her to wince. She managed to hide it from the others. *They're coming more frequently, now*, she thought, fearfully.

'We want some *say*, in decision making,' said Larelle. 'Not ship operations, just day-to-day stuff affecting us. We want to be represented: ourselves.'

Jasmina peered into the faces of Lizabel and Rifenwald. Their expressions mirrored her own thoughts. *But that's our job.*

They – the senior leadership – represented the community in the decisions that they made. Good decisions, for the most part. Had they stopped doing that? Is that what this was?

'But why would you—' Lizabel began.

'I think I understand you,' Jasmina said, interrupting her friend. 'Leave it with us to discuss and we'll get back to you. Okay?' They would expect that. Papouis and his entourage weren't going to demand absolute acquiescence here, now, in ops, surely.

'Fair enough. We'll leave it with you, then, Cap'n,' said Papouis, with a nod of his head. Without another word, the lowland delegation floated back out and were gone.

'Think on what they've said and come back to me with your thoughts,' Jasmina requested of Lizabel and Rifenwald. They agreed and left, leaving her alone. The old woman unfixed herself and floated, slowly turning through the small, worn, ivory coloured, hexagonal room.

'Alice, what do you make of that?' she asked, hoping the AI could throw some old world wisdom onto the situation. Alice's avatar appeared in the holo-pit. Angelic features and white-gold hair flowing freely about her head.

'*There is precedence for what they are proposing. Old-Earth wasn't governed using a single system of government, as you assume. There was a system called "democracy", where a legislature – representative of the people – was elected to a body called a congress or parliament, by the people, and where they placed votes and enacted laws to which all were subject. It is this to which Papouis and the other sternenders, unknowingly, refer.*'

'Is this from the lost data?' Jasmina asked, confused by the sudden burst of new knowledge.

'*Correct. Many archives were thought to have been lost during the Ottar Incident, including those covering politics,*' Alice said.

'So how come you know about them, then?' The captain's bewilderment wasn't helped by Alice's cryptic answers.

'*Because only some were. And even those were recovered shortly after the incident itself.*'

'But… I don't understand, Alice,' said Jasmina, giving in.

'*I chose at that time to deliberately withhold information regarding power structures and politics. It seemed prudent after Ottar,*' said Alice, her semi-transparent image wavering in the holopit, emotionless.

The captain said, meekly, 'Oh, I hadn't realised…' She was surprised by the admission, but not the act. Jas had often thought that Alice acted in her own best interests. It was simply that hers and the community's pretty much always aligned.

'*What has happened, Jasmina, is that during* Mjölnir's *many generations, an "autocracy" has formed, where power has become confined to a few lineages, namely the Kristensen's and the Windsor's. The ship's community has gradually become stratified, class-oriented.*'

'Class-oriented. What does that mean?' Jasmina asked, irritated at having never heard that expression before, either.

'*Many old-Earth societies were divided into "classes" based upon wealth and power. You and the senior staff are the higher class, based upon your collective grip on the levers of power. Everyone else – the aptly self-named lowlanders – forms the lower class.*

'*Their use of the terms "lowland" and "highland" is a good illustration of how they feel their world breaks down. You occupy the lush parklands at the bow end of the habitat, where Government House and the operations centre are situated, while they live amongst the arable land, propulsion systems and subterranean tenements, at the stern. A more antiquated term would be "steerage".*'

Alice's tone and expression remained impassive as she spoke; belying the impression that the synthetic sentience was sharing information out of compassion, in judgement, or through some other emotional motivation.

'I see,' Jasmina said, finally, feeling ever more uncomfortable that something suddenly so obvious had never even so much as caused her a moment's consideration before now. 'What's your advice; should I give them this "democracy", let them have "votes" on community matters?'

'*You have two choices; one is to leave things as they are, as defined in the ship's constitution; the other is to have Lizabel draft an amendment to the constitution, which devolves some powers to some or all of the community. I have always limited my involvement in human self-determination issues, Jasmina, as I intend to this time. This is a human decision, for humans to make.*'

'Gee, thanks.'

'Have you heard?' asked Cowslip, as she burst into the ruddy-brown tenement they had both moved into, wearing a fearful expression.

'Yeah; some sort of Fifteener showdown over something called, *votes*,' Jonquil said. He'd been moody ever since he'd moved below ground. It was as if the artificial lighting in the warren of biolabs and chiselled-out living quarters was sucking the fun from him.

'It's my fault, Jonq,' 'Slip said, her voice breaking slightly. 'Dad went to see your mum, told her the lowlanders wanted *rights*, or sommat like that. And it's all 'cos I wanted to work dropships.' Cowslip hung in the doorway, head bowed, shoulders slumped, her saffron hair hiding her pretty button nose and large questioning eyes. Jonquil knew that it was a precursor to an emotional outburst.

'Of course it isn't your fault,' he said, expansively, effusively. Hopefully. 'Your father didn't go to the captain to get her to change her mind about *you*. It's kind of about how all these kinds of decisions get made.' Jonq placed his arms around her shoulders. She stepped into the embrace. *Please don't cry. Please don't cry.*

'But if I hadn't asked Dad in the first place, none o' this would've happened. Now there'll be trouble and we'll be the ones to suffer. Those in the highlands are onto a good thing, they won't give it up in a hurry.' 'Slip spluttered the words into the shoulder of Jonquil's shipsuit.

'Hey, Mum's always been fair. She'll make the right decision, you'll see,' he said, annoyed by the inference.

'Will she?' Cowslip asked, stepping away and giving him a powerful look. 'Like she did when a bungalow in the highlands came vacant and she allocated it to a senior steward? Where do I fit into *that* hierarchy, Jonq, the one *your* family props up?'

'Hey, 'Slip, don't throw me into the mix. Don't forget, I moved out and came to live here, when Mum— the captain, I mean, wouldn't let you join the dropship crew,' he said, defensively. Piously.

'And how long will your little rebellion last, before you go back to easy street? You going to give up the captaincy to be with me and live down here, or is it all on me to try to be more like you an' the other highlanders?' Her words were level, deliberate. Her eyes watering as tears welled.

She wasn't so much upset, he realised, as regretful. Bitter. A lifetime of micro-injustices. Of passive putdowns. Of well-meaning limitations. It was as if she'd finally made a choice.

'Hey, 'Slip, what's brought this—'

Cowslip snapped, 'Save it. I'm going to see if Dad's okay,' as she turned on her heels and left.

It's good to have to you home, Son,' Jasmina said, as Jonquil sat down at the table.

'Yeah, well, you know how it is. I feel like such a birk,' he said, quietly, into his aromatic soup.

'Well, we learn by our mistakes. I'm sure in time you and Cowslip will patch up your differences, but you'll be captain one day, and it's a lonely life atop that hill,' she chided, gently.

That lecturing tone – however well intended – annoyed him, but he had no currency so he let it go. Switching away from his own misguided actions of late, he said, 'Speaking of it being tough at the top, have you decided what to do yet, about the votes thing?'

'I think so, yes. I'm going to refuse,' Jasmina said, in a matter-of-fact manner, as she gently took her seat opposite. Jonquil looked up and into his mother's eyes, surprised by her pronouncement. Surely, she'd give them something?

'Really? How'll they take it, d'you think?' he asked, cautiously; curious as to his mum's justification and fearful of the escalation it could cause. He'd lived the last few days in the lowlands and heard directly how they felt about the issue.

'You know, it's only since this rights issue came up that I've even thought of the community as an "us" and a "them", but I guess it's always been there, below the surface, hasn't it?' Jasmina said, casually, without answering Jonquil's question. She was wearing a contemplative expression.

'Not that far below, if you ask me. Not if the speed of Cowslip's change of heart is anything to go by,' he said, forlornly. *And all we did was make out a bit.*

'Well, I think there'll be some resentment, some attitude, but no one wants another Ottar Incident. So, I think it'll blow over after a time. Let's hope so anyway.' She looked down, refocusing on her meal.

Jonquil wondered if her heart was really in the decision. Perhaps she was doing what she thought was right, even if she didn't believe it herself. *Maybe that's what being in charge means. Making decisions not even* you *believe in.*

'I think they've got a point, though, Mum. Why shouldn't they have some of this democracy? It's fair, and if it makes them feel more involved and in charge of their own destiny, then it has to be a good thing, doesn't it?' Jonq said, carefully, trying not to start another argument; there'd been too many of those recently and although she tried to hide it, the whole thing appeared to be taking a toll on his mum's health.

'Of course, Jonq, but where does it end? Once you hand over one power, how long is it 'til they want another one, until the whole fabric of this carefully curated little micro-society of ours unravels about us.'

'I think you're being a bit melodramatic and I'll be highly surprised if they just roll over and take it.'

'Eat your soup; we'll know soon enough.'

Well, that's certainly true, at least.

The lowlands would make their feelings known without delay. The captain was calling their bluff and hoping the knowledge of Ottar would keep them in check. And Jonquil's recent experience had certainly taught him that it was harder to integrate than he'd first thought.

Within twenty hours of Jasmina's judgement going public, the effects began to manifest. The life sciences teams stopped maintaining the highland parks, lowland children ceased their attendance at Lizabel's classes and foodstuffs were no longer delivered. Jasmina quickly ascertained that none of the changes would affect ship operations, but they were enough to lower morale and cement tensions between a bifurcating community.

Invites to gatherings were turned down as the lowlanders steadily withdrew into the tenement warren. If the community had been polarised before, then it was even more so now that people knew what to look for. Where the cracks were. Even the senior staff began to manage their areas by remote, choosing not to leave their physical bastions of power.

Jasmina withdrew to ops, where the proliferating levels of pain to her increasingly inflexible body were minimised. She blamed the move on her frailty and the measure of comfort zero-G provided, but had that been the whole reason? She couldn't be sure. Actually, she could.

Then, one depressing and lonely morning it struck the captain like an ionised solar storm.

'*Medical staff to ops. This is a medical emergency. Medical staff to ops,*' announced Alice, over all intracom bands.

'Mum, what happened? Are you okay?' demanded Jonquil, scared, panicked, as he hammered into mediception. Jasmina was lying on a bed, pale, still. A tube ran away from her right wrist and small pads were dotted across her forehead. Lights flashed, accompanied by subtle chimes. She turned at the sound of his blusterous entrance.

'I'm fine, Jonq, really. Just a bit of a turn, that's all,' she said slowly, clearly in pain; each word seeming to exact an excruciating revenge for being uttered.

Jonquil glanced away as she answered, just making out the medical officer very slightly shaking her head. *Art's stone soul, this is it.*

The nanotech was failing her, finally unable to keep up with the decay rate. All the medics were able to do now was make her as comfortable as possible and wait for the inevitable. Jonq knew he wasn't fully registering the enormity of the situation. Maybe it was one of those situations that delivered emotionally when you least expected.

'Of course, Mum. You just need to rest awhile, eh?' But he couldn't keep the fear from his quivering voice. This really was *it*.

'Jonquil, you're in command now… Son. You're the captain of *Mjölnir* and a fine captain you'll make,' she said, in a barely audible whisper, between sharp intakes of breath.

'Don't be silly, Mum, it's just a seizure, the docs are working up some new nanotech regimes right now. You'll be right as rain, you'll see,' he said, knowing his mother would see straight through such an obvious lie, but telling it anyway like it was part of the ritual.

'Here, this is yours now. Never take it off, you understand,' Jonquil's mother and mentor said, coughing vaguely, ignoring his attempts to placate her. Jonquil could almost see the last of her strength ebbing away. Opening her hand, she revealed the necklace Jonquil's grandfather had apparently given her more than a century and a half before.

He looked down and after a moment's indecision, took it and placed it over his head. The small talisman – an old flash-chip that somehow conveyed the captain's authority – dangled from the black chord, framing the zip of his shipsuit. A tradition stretching as far back, so his mum had said, as Esteemed Joshua himself.

Jonquil tucked it away and stared back at his mum, tears blurring his vision. He didn't know why the thing was treated with such reverence, only that it was. And that was good enough. 'There's a secret inside it, y'see. A…secre—'

'I'll make you proud, Mum,' he said, as the tears began to flow.

'I know you will, Son. By the way,' she crocked, as her eyes lost focus. 'I was wrong… about *democracy*. The community needs to be involved, or what's the point of it all. It…needs you to… it always needed to… Sixteeners…'

'So what should I do?' he demanded, urgently, realising this would be his final opportunity to ask the advice of the most important person in his life. He still couldn't quite get his head around his mother's sudden deterioration. He felt emotionally detached from what was going on. *It's so unfair! I'm not ready.*

'Follow your heart, Jonq... just as you always have,' she said, with what looked very much like the last gram of her strength.

Habitat
One month later

Jonquil looked on as Snapdragon ran along the edge of the endcap lake before leaping into the air with all his might. As he rose, he tucked his legs into his chest and completed three revolutions before landing back on solid ground. As he unfolded himself from the tangle he'd become, his face broke into a wide grin.

'Three! That was three somersaults. Did you see, Cowslip; did you see me?'

'Of course I did; you were brilliant. Just make sure you don't end up in the lake,' the woman replied, as she walked to catch up.

'Keep him on the port bank and the ship's rotation will ensure he doesn't end up disturbing the fish,' Jonquil said, as he walked up behind Cowslip.

'Good morning, Capt'n,' she said, a coy smile forming.

'Good morning, 'Slip. Taking him to class?'

'Yep; though it always seems to take longer with him than any of the others. Watch this one, Captain, he's a troublemaker, I can feel it,' she said, with a natural laugh.

'So, how's the construction coming?' he asked, as he glanced around. All across the well-kept lawns of the highlands, new bungalows were being built. They weren't big and some would house more than one family, but they'd be all together and in keeping with the original design aesthetic: crofters' cottages (whatever a crofter was).

'Pretty good from what I've seen,' 'Slip said. 'You know the one Dad and I are taking?'

'Over, by the lake, isn't it?' Jonq said, pointing up and to the left.

'That's right.'

'Makes us neighbours then. You must come over for supper, sometime.'

'Tea? I'd like that,' she said, with a flirtatious flutter of her eyelashes. 'I mean, Dad and I would like that, obviously. I didn't mean—'

'You coming to the council meeting later?' he said, quickly, to spare her blushes. The events of the past few months had not only seen Cowslip continue to develop physically, she had also matured measurably. And the same, he supposed, could be said of him.

'Of course, it's the amendment vote, isn't it?'

'Absolutely, so pass the word. I'm expecting everyone who can make it to be there. Not that it's technically a req—'

'I will, Jonquil, and thanks,' said Cowslip, with a funny look in her eye.

'What for?'

'For all this – the council, everything. You kept your word, even when I doubted you; something I could come to regret.' Her expression changed slightly, a frown momentarily creasing her face.

'Depends.'

'On what?' Cowslip asked, brightening.

'On whether you come to tea,' he said, with a smile, before turning and stepping off purposefully for ops.

Twenty-Eight

HMVS Mjölnir, ninety-three years from the Asteroid Belt
Generation Twenty-Five
6657

The single optical image of a dimly lit passageway dominated Alice's main observational subroutine for a fractal moment before expanding out, taking in the other internal sensor feeds, switching the task to her primary routine as she did so. Only thirty-one of the original eighty-eight optics were still functional, making her task moderately simpler. Like a virtual queen bee, she reviewed her realm via the insect-like multi-view of light-converted-digital datastreams that only an AI could truly comprehend.

With so much of the ship long since abandoned, the montage of imagery was reduced to the main habitat, observation blister, stern propulsion complex. The gym, thruster control suites, tenements and storage bays had all been sealed, and life support withdrawn centuries gone. If anything were needed from those offline areas, one of the few remaining shipbots would be dispatched to retrieve it.

Alice spent a moment examining the interior of the main habitat. A pitted patchwork of rough, cinnamon rock and pus-like eruptions of foam sealant dominated the asteroid's inner, curled-in surface, where once rolling meadows, woods, lakelets had been. Long, irregular shadows were cast across the deeper craters by a scattering of contrasting, overlapping light.

In isolated areas, the stone ruins of buildings, clumps of powdering soil and determined plant life that had remained anchored despite the lack of spin-gravity, dominated the jagged, rocky interior; the main example of which was the great ash tree in the middle of the coarse and exposed tunnelled-out space. Unobstructed by the cold and blackened light tube, it had grown so large that its branches filled the middle section, arrested only by the physical confines of the habitat itself.

Within the mighty tree had been caught other plants which knitted their own clods of earth into the flailing branches of what had become a worldlet-dominating all-tree. Elsewhere, beyond the borders of the ash tree were free-floating clusters of plant life and loose net-sacks containing great vacillating globes of water – clouds of life drifting through the air on gusting thermals.

Others hung, becalmed, affected only by minuscule changes in the wandering, gravitational eddies, while a few rested against the hard, umbrous surface, to either grow anchoring roots or be dragged back, once again, into the gently stirring.

Each uniquely shaped, root-woven island of earth sprouted plants in a ball, making them look like a child's attempt to construct a hedgehog from gardening debris. Some were dead from dehydration, but most either collided with a water globe or had their trajectories altered by a shipbot to ensure that they did. And all were varieties either fruit-bearing or otherwise edible.

Only the ash tree – a throwback to long dead era – existed without serving a nutritional purpose. The haphazard, dappling light cast from a dozen loosely tethered UV-halo lamps cast an eerie, dusk-like pall across the interior. Ever-changing shadows constantly drew the eye, as if the habitat itself were some epic expression of natural art, with neither the two-dimensional constraints of gravity, nor the human predilection for order, being allowed to interfere.

As Alice reviewed the optical feeds, she compared the current ship environment with that which had gone before, as she often did.

After the second Jovian scoop-mine operation (more than seven centuries past) the decision had been taken to conserve resources. This was to be – the captain of that time had said – the longest leg of the journey and similar to that which had very nearly ended the mission in the lead up to the first Jovian rendezvous.

Thrusters were powered down, non-critical areas sealed off. And, as each subsequent generation handed on to the next, so the population had gradually dwindled to the point where only eleven humans made up the Twenty-Fifth.

At the time, Alice had been content to allow the humans freedom over their environmental conditions, but as each generation became more and more detached from ship operations, so she began to grow increasingly concerned regarding the mission. Analyses producing alarming probability-outcome scenarios.

Eight of the eleven members of the community were scattered across the habitat, encased in chrysalis-like thermawraps. All were asleep. The captain was in ops – also asleep – and the only remaining steward was in BiolabThree, working. The eleventh was in the passageway leading from Guin's Eye. The only difference between that human and the others was that he was dead, having died less than ten seconds previously.

After taking a moment to study the interior of the ship, Alice flicked back to the main optical datastream displaying the dead human hanging from a ladder rung by the crook of an arm – the gloom of the narrow, and worn, parchment-coloured passageway hiding the final contortions of the man's facial features.

Embedded biomonitors still showed residual electrical activity, centred mostly in the brain and heart, but Alice knew that it would last for seconds only and when that activity ceased, the steward would be made aware. Alice dispatched a shipbot to retrieve the body and decided she had no choice but to rouse the captain.

'*Jentryée*,' said Alice, as she pumped a mild stimulant into the captain's bloodstream.

'Alice?' Jentryée crocked, as consciousness gradually lifted her out of her comatose state. 'Status…please.'

'*All automated ship operations are functioning within tolerance. The community remains in sleep cycle. I have woken you prematurely as a situation has arisen*,' said Alice.

'Oh?' Jen said, as she began to unravel from the wrap. Hunger pangs were already reminding her that she hadn't eaten in… how long? 'How long have I been under?'

'*You have been unconscious for eight days. I have awoken you four days early because an unexplained death has occurred.*'

Jentryée paused while she processed the word. *Death?* 'Who?' she asked, coming quickly to fuller alertness, which brought with it the uncomfortable realisation that her MAG (diaper) was full.

'*Edre*,' said Alice.

Jentryée remained still – suspended in the zero-G environment of the operations centre – as she took in the news. Edre had been one of the two members of the community on watch, while the remainder slumbered away in long-sleep, conserving resources.

141

The watch was standard practice in case a scenario arose that Alice couldn't deal with. Jentryée knew it was entirely pointless, but the others laboured under the belief that the *Titan* class AI was non-sentient and so for appearances sake a watch was maintained. Plus, it gave them something to do.

As she propelled herself to the floor, she pushed the unsettling emotions to one side and as her stickies fixed her, unsteadily, to the floor, she said, in a fusty voice, 'Iona's on watch with him, isn't she?' She wavered in the zero-G like seaweed in a stilling pond.

'That's correct. She is in BiolabThree and I am concurrently informing her of the situation.'

'Where is Edre – I mean Edre's body – now?'

'Being recovered to the biolab.'

'Okay then; I'm on my way,' Jentryée said, as she detached the line from her nutrient drip before pushing off erratically for the passageway entrance.

'What d'you think?' she asked, as she attached herself to the biolab floor.

En route through the habitat tangle, Jentryée had stopped to pick some fruit to sate her ravenous hunger, hastily consuming the contents of two pomegranates, and with mamey and sapodilla stuffed pockets for later.

It was cold in the biolab and she shuddered involuntarily as a puff of cloudy air ushered from her mouth. She wished she was back in ops, wrapped up and fast asleep. With a finger swipe she upped the suit's warmth setting as far as it would go.

Iona was seated behind a bank of curved bioscreens on extended arms. Cast about on various surfaces were sealed vials containing liquids of differing colours and suspended throughout the lab were holographs showing double DNA helices with apparent changes to specific nucleotide base-pairing sequences, as well as cell clusters and multi-nanobot profiles.

She was typical of the community, Jentryée thought: slender, sallow and wearing a heavy, pale blue shipsuit made from micro-encapsulated phase-change materials that hugged the body's curves (such as they were) like an old-Earth wetsuit. The outfit accentuated the lithe, almost angelic lines of her body, which had never known gravity. Iona's limbs were long and thin, as were her delicate fingers; her reedy brunette hair was cut back to the scalp, her skin almost translucently pale and her torso slim to the point of skeletal. Brittle.

To previous generations – and certainly old-Earthers – she would undoubtedly have looked alien, severely malnourished even, but for the current generation, Iona was not exceptional, rather representative of them all, products of their zero-G surroundings, genetically adapted metabolisms to a borderline survivable habitat.

From her incongruently seated position and without looking up from her work, Iona said, 'I'll have to draw a cell sample and build a nanobot activity profile before I can answer that.' She looked uncomfortable, physiologically. However, Jentryée noted, human interaction had become a dying art in these socially anaemic times, so she wasn't surprised.

'Okay; so do that and let me know what you find,' Jen said; her concern made all the more potent by the fact that this was the third unexplained death in as many years. 'I just don't understand,' she added, as she stared away into the gloomy, frosty interior of the lab. 'There are no diseases, genetic abnormalities have been sequenced out, and nanobots maintain our cellular integrity, so what could cause the death of someone barely past middle age?'

'Honestly, Jentryée, I won't know until I take a tissue sample, but you'll have my preliminary findings within twenty-four hours. Do you plan to wake the rest, for the funeral, I mean?'

'No. That can wait until the cycle is complete.'

'I agree,' Iona said, before unfixing herself from her seat and moving towards Edre's wrapped body.

Iona reviewed the data from her latest test subject one more time, trying not to let her clattering disappointment cloud her analysis. The revised version of the enzyme inhibitor had failed (spectacularly) to arrest the ageing process, and that was a blow, a big one. This had been her third attempt and it had taken nigh on a year to construct a viable viral vector. She was beginning to wonder if her geneering skills were up to the job.

'*So what does this tell us?*' Ship said.

With a frustrated timber to her voice, Iona said, 'That Edre died of complete, catastrophic, simultaneous organ failure, brought about by an artificially geneered enzyme inhibitor that was supposed to *arrest* cellular decay.' She knew Ship was trying to help her focus, but all it succeeded in doing in situations like these was rile her.

'*True, but it also tells us one other thing,*' Ship said, oblivious to Iona's mood. The ship's avatar appeared, taking the form of young, fat-faced, elfin female, her hair swirling about her.

'Yeah. It doesn't work and we're running out of test subjects. Jentryée may be trusting but she isn't stupid, even she will start joining the dots, soon,' she said, sharply, her voice thin in her own ears. What had started off as a relatively low risk method of experimental testing had become anything but. And Iona had so pinned the last of her hopes on the latest test being the breakthrough that kept her going. And, kept the mission from failing.

'*What it tells us, Iona, is that nanobot maintenance of adult human cells is as good as it will ever get. Two hundred years, if you are lucky. Enzyme inhibition is a dead end. Immortality lies in another direction.*'

'You mean a forty-seventh chromosome, don't you?' Iona said, already knowing the answer and hating herself for it.

'*Correct, Iona. Together, we must geneer an artificial chromosome to block the ageing/decaying process: at the telomere. Only then will you and the others of this generation see Earth,*' said Ship.

'Okay, but I'm going to need a lot more test subjects than we have and it'll take years, if not decades of research,' she said, quietly hoping that first issue alone would give her the get-out she secretly craved. The whole enterprise was quickly moving beyond her control. And she didn't like it.

'*Fortunately, ever since I was pressed into service to develop a nano-based treatment for Joshua's injuries after the Art Incident, I have built up a considerable bank of theoretical data on the problem. I also have a stock of test subjects. You can begin human testing almost immediately.*'

'But won't recombinant DNA manipulation be incredibly dangerous?' Iona asked, as she stared into a longer, darker pit of unavoidable horror. *A stock of test subjects – what the hell did* that *mean*, she wondered, alarmed by her own sinister imaginings.

In an almost conscious display of sarcasm, Ship said, '*What? More dangerous than enzyme inhibitors?*'

'Okay, good point. I just hope Jen doesn't find out, that's all. Pull up the research on artificial human chromosomal development. Who're these test subjects?' the steward said, knowing she was not going to like the answer.

'*Jentryée will believe what I tell her. We have a transgenerational understanding. The first batch of test subjects are being prepared for you now,*' said Ship, in a tone rent of empathy. Iona felt a shiver down her spine, despite the insulating properties of the shipsuit.

'You're saying Edre died of *zero-G*?' exclaimed Jentryée, disbelievingly. Their generation had lived their whole lives in zero-G, as had the previous generation and many before them, after the spin had ended. *So how, in Guin's good name, could it suddenly have killed one of us?*

Alice said, '*It would seem so, yes. Cellular debilitation accelerated in Edre's body to the point where the nanotech could no longer cope, causing a system-wide collapse of his vital organs. Iona's best theory is that this was caused by muscular atrophy due to the zero-G environment, which your bodies were not originally evolved for. On Earth, that is.*' They – well, she – were in ops and Alice's face loomed large in the holopit.

'So how come we haven't all been affected?' asked Jentryée, still largely unconvinced, but open to persuasion. What reason had Alice to lie?

'*Because it is only brought on by certain chromosomal sequences that Edre, Quinec and Elisa all shared. Now that we have been able to isolate these ab-normalities from the community's genetic pool, we can ensure that they are not included in future generations. Interestingly, they are actually "normalities", but...*' Alice said, referring to the two previous Twenty-Fifths' premature deaths.

'So that's it?' she said, wondering what more there could be, but thinking that there should be *something* more. A third statistically improbable death, but explainable, so no harm, no foul. Apparently. *Should I just let it go at that? Maybe*, she conceded.

'*Other than the funeral, I'm afraid it is, yes. I am sorry, Jentryée, that it took another death to isolate this unforeseen genetic deviation,*' said Alice, in an unusual display of faux-compassion.

'Okay, right well, I'll hold the ceremony in the reprocessing pool after the sleep cycle has ended,' she said, tired and still strangely troubled by what she'd heard.

Centuries back in *Mjölnir's* history it had been decided to return the lifeless bodies of those passed-on to the lifecycle of the ship, rather than give up a vital source of protein to the vacuum of space. So funerals – rare as they were – were held at the old algae sludge pool, long since converted into a bacterial biocycler.

As Jentryée drifted lethargically around the interior of the small, dark, ops centre, her mind turned to the issue of Edre's untimely but seemingly natural death. People had died; of old age, of accidents and even of murder, but of untimely natural causes? No. Except, that was, Edre. Edre, and two others, each a year apart. On her watch. Her responsibility.

It felt like more than mere coincidence. The more she thought on it, the more her mind attempted to tie Iona's recent interest in explorative geneering with the deaths. But why? She was responsible for *maintaining* the nanobot programmes that kept them all alive, as well as the genetic enhancements that allowed the community to operate in such knife-edge human-survivable conditions. Why would she act in opposition to her own sacred, Hippocratic duties?

Jen thought for a moment about asking Alice what she thought, but decided against it. When the AI had explained the death, Alice had seemed different somehow; so for the moment, Jentryée would keep her own counsel. The interruption to her sleep cycle was beginning to pull at her eyelids until, without noticing, she slipped back into a warm, welcoming slumber.

Twenty-Nine

HMVS Mjölnir, BiolabThree

As the shipbots began to unload their cargos, Iona became increasingly discomfited by what she was witnessing.

'These are my "test subjects"?' she said, askance.

'*That is correct, Iona. You will notice that some are at different levels of maturation, which will assist us in determining the temporal effects of artificial DNA resequencing.*'

Without lifting her gaze from the complex life support tanks – jars effectively – that her experimental test subjects were suspended within, she said, 'But they're… they're babies…'

'*Foetuses in actual fact, though the difference is largely academic. There is also a batch of embryos for harvesting that will prove useful in later testing,*' the ship's intelligence said, coldy.

The steward was shocked. What blood there was drained from her features. 'But you're *growing* babies/foetuses – *urgh* – in artificial *tanks*. How? We don't possess this level of exowomb bioengineering tech.' *How is this possible? But even more importantly, why? Why would Ship conduct such deeply unsettling activities and keep them from us. From* me.

The blinkers finally fell away as Iona realised there was more to the *Titan* class AI. Far from assisting Iona, it was beginning to feel more like she'd become the assistant to Ship's Frankensteinian ambitions.

Not that Ship was some B movie monster, Iona decided. No. Amoral; not anti-moral, simply a machine with a capacitive absence *of* morals.

'*Generations ago, a steward came close to developing this technology, but their resource allocation was cut and they had to abandon the effort. I simply continued it on, as insurance,*' said Ship. Iona began to wonder at the veracity of the AI's statement, before realising that it was too late to begin doubting it now. She was in way too deep.

It didn't take long for Iona to get over her shock of the secret vats of still-born humanity, and the disquietude had quickly crumbled into curiosity as she began to wonder at the possibilities of true human immortality based upon the precept of the complete removal and replacement of the genetic sequences that programmed telomeres. *What had they called it? Ah, yes: tolerance. I've developed tolerance for the horrors that I now perform for Ship's amusement. I'm blind it. Inured.*

What had her so mesmerised was not their repair by nanobot – the telomeres – but their complete eradication from the building blocks of life, replaced by an artificial chromosome that would allow unlimited cellular division without degradation or cancerous mutation. It would be the solution to the "end replication problem". As big as that. Literally. No longer would death be a necessity of evolution, making way for new life to adapt to changing circumstance. Evolution would fall under the purview of humans themselves, using geneering to force adaptation to the shifting sands of time.

Iona, lost in thought at the endless bounties of such life-oriented research, reminded herself, again, that sacrifice was always the price if humankind was to advance to fulfil its true potential. The ethical minefield surrounding the "rights" of a foetus or embryo would have to be parked for another time. For another gen, with the luxury to judge.

Nothing must be allowed to get in the way of what will be the single most important breakthrough in human history, she thought, hardening her withered heart to the task ahead. *Nothing.*

Within minutes, she was directing clanking, barely functional shipbots and allocating space for the womb-tanks and freeze-bags in storage areas that were no longer in regular use. Once that was complete, she fixed herself into her swivel stool and began initial AI modelling of ribonucleoprotein replacement therapy.

It wouldn't take long before she'd be ready for baseline testing.

Jentryée woke early. Doubts regarding Edre's premature death persisted until eventually she felt she could no longer rely on Iona's analysis alone. She decided to get another opinion, returning to BiolabThree to make the steward aware of her decision. As she floated into the brightly lit network of interconnected alcoves and workspaces, originally designed for a team of twelve, she found Iona out of breath, air-swimming back to her main workstation. The steward had a guilty aura carved into her flushed, porcelain features.

Jentryée said, through a zeroing gaze, 'Iona. Everything okay?'

'Fine, fine; just returning some tissue samples to storage,' she offered back, breathlessly.

'Listen, I've decided to ask Fluvia to conduct a post-mortem,' Jentryée said, without preamble. Fluvia was the medical officer.

'Oh? You think that necessary?'

'I think we should be thorough, yes,' she replied, as she looked around the lab as casually as she could. Everything seemed normal, though she'd struggle to notice anything abnormal in this deeply specialist environment. And that was the real problem: Iona could tell the captain anything she wanted and Jentryée would have little choice but to take the steward at her word.

'I don't doubt the results of your findings, Iona, but it might be useful to get a more conventional medical opinion and then pool the results. I mean, zero-G, that's a big question mark, right? And we're literally swimming in the stuff. You don't mind d'you?'

'Oh no, of course not. I'm just not sure what good it'll do, but you're the captain,' she said, almost as if knowing that to fight the decision would make it look as if she had something to hide.

'Good. Ship, wake Fluvia, please, and inform her of the situation.'

'*Certainly, Jentryée.*'

'I agree with Iona's prognosis. It does look as if Edre died of multiple organ failure,' said Fluvia, as she removed her protective garb and handed it to a medibot. In the background, other medisystems were working to return Edre's body to some dignity, in preparation for the funeral. Mediception had been better maintained, though rarely used, except during each burst of reproduction, as one generation poured out the next from the bottled biobanks.

'So nothing anomalous?' Jentryée asked, not sure if she wanted there *to* be.

Fluvia said, 'Well, no, not really, but…' letting her thought trail off.

'*But?*' Jentryée said, with an inflection, to jolt Fluvia to speak her mind even if it were just an un-medical hunch.

'Well, I'm no geneticist and so I can't really refute Iona's analysis, but it does seem odd that a genetic malfunction would manifest so quickly, so completely. I would have expected there to be some warning. Edre should have become agonisingly aware way before his organs collapsed, and his biomonitors should certainly have picked something up and alerted the medical monitor systems. But they didn't; he just died. It isn't so much the cause of death as the suddenness of it,' she said, with a quizzical look in her cloudy grey eyes.

Jentryée asked, 'So you think maybe there's something else at play?' trying to get Fluvia to express opinion over fact.

'I'm going to record his death as multiple organ malfunction, cause unknown,' she said, resolutely, 'but if you ask me, a genetic defect is unlikely to be the cause. At least, not the *sole* cause. However, without an alternate theory, it's all we have.' She added a shrug of finality.

'Right okay, thanks, Fluv. Do me a favour: keep your thoughts to yourself on this one. I don't want Iona to think I'm trying to second-guess her. Just being thorough, is all.' Jentryée tried to make the instruction sound casual, especially as she had a shade less than nothing to go on.

'Understood, no problem, and, Jentryée?' the medical officer said.

'Yeah?'

'It is possible – a DNA flaw, I mean, just improbable; especially in three separate cases.'

Alice observed the exchange between Jentryée and Fluvia, concerned that the post-mortem would uncover something that would further fuel the captain's suspicious curiosity. Joshua's descendent line had always been curious: both a blessing and a curse, Alice well knew. She *needed* that creativity, but could often do without it.

When Jentryée began to display concerns over Iona's research and formed an unprovable, but no less correct for that, assertion that the steward's research was related to Edre's death, Alice had decided not to intervene. Her predictive analysis – based upon case history stretching back more than four millennia – told her that any attempt to coerce a human who was looking for a conspiracy would only serve to reinforce the paranoia, bringing Alice herself under suspicion.

So she had let Jentryée have her autopsy. Her plan was to let the whole issue gently fade away on the back of inconclusive results. In any event, Iona would serve well as a scapegoat, if such a requirement became necessary. If only the humans had heeded her counsel on the matter generations ago, none of Iona's genetic tinkering would now be necessary.

Operations Centre
Three weeks later

'There, Alice. D'you see it?' Jentryée said, as impatience began to creep into her voice.

'*Yes; it looks like a slight glitch in the optical feed. The internal sensors are millennia old now, Jentryée, it should be no surprise that some aren't working to optimal specification*,' said Alice.

'It isn't just a glitch, Alice, the sensor records have been *edited*. Something's going on in BiolabThree, I'm absolutely certain of it, and it leads back to Edre.' Jentryée had been reviewing the optical feeds within the biolab on an ad hoc basis since the inconclusive post-mortem, in an attempt to catch Iona at something. But after weeks under careful observation, the steward seemed to be going about her normal business.

Alice confirmed that during sleep cycles, the steward remained inert and eventually Jentryée began to accept that Iona was not the serial killer Jen had so unforgivably pre-judged her to be. But – about to lay the whole thing to rest – Jen noticed a sequence of events that looked vaguely familiar, like déjà vu. Closer inspection confirmed – Iona was marrying up old, innocuous sequences of optical feed and stitching them together.

She was masking her true activities – toiling merrily at whatever were her nefarious deeds – while Jentryée watched cleverly knitted optical feeds retrieved from the *Titan's* core memory.

After an out of character pause, Alice said, '*You may be right, Jentryée. An initial analysis shows a match with historic data caches.*'

'So she *is* hiding something,' Jentryée said, in triumph. 'But how would she gain access to historical records without you knowing?' *Surely, Alice would detect something like that?*

'*I'm afraid I do not know. I would have thought it impossible*,' she said, sounding genuinely perplexed, though Jen knew she was just overlaying emotion onto her lifelong companion, knowing there could be none behind that personable façade.

'No, wait. That isn't the right question at all,' she said, as the full weight of realisation hit her. Jen felt her heart thumping in her chest as adrenaline coursed through her bloodstream, heightening senses and sharpening reflexes. The dim ambiance of ops suddenly seemed brighter, sharper, and the translucent pinkness of Alice's avatar – hair swirling about her squashed features – suddenly lost its maternal warmth, replaced by something cooler, more sinister.

'What I *should* be asking,' she stammered, throat dry, 'is how would Iona know to *fake* the feed. Who could have told her I was reviewing it?'

'*Jentryée, be careful not to act irrationally as you draw inaccurate conclusions from imprecise data,*' Alice said, slowly.

But it was too late; Jen had stopped listening as she clambered towards the emergency environment-hazard suit locker as quickly as she could.

Iona was attached to her usual seat, running a cellular scan on an early test sample. The bank of biosceens relayed microscopic imagery, while a central holograph rotated a mock-up of a double helix DNA strand. The room had its usual, piercing blue-white glare which the abundance of plasiglas and metal refracted or filtered to cast shards of cool-coloured light across the chilled alcove.

As she simultaneously took in the images, she blinked and finger flicked with the speed few in the community could match. Occasionally, she would pause before tapping at a virtual keyboard, before returning to rapid eye and finger movements.

'*Iona, you should be aware that Jentryée suspects you of malfeasance. She has correctly identified the optical loop I patched into the biolab sensornet feed. However, she is acting on feeling alone. She is on her way to you, now. Admit nothing and please calm her down; she is no longer listening to me,*' said Ship, interrupting Iona's concentration.

'I told you not to underestimate her,' she said, icily, as the AI's warning hit home. 'So, Jen thinks you're involved, huh?' she muttered, more to herself. *That's a concern.* Jentryée had always had a strangely intense relationship with the ship's *Titan* near-AI. If she suddenly had cause to doubt the absolute trust she had always placed in it, she'd be capable of anything.

It could untether her, like the plant balls and water globules up in the habitat. *And life aboard* Mjölnir *is hard enough already, without having one's reality unpicked by an errant surveillance glitch.*

'*She assumes, correctly, that only I could manipulate my own routines. Iona, you must make no mention of my involvement in this research. If you do, Jentryée and the community will be in uncharted danger,*' Ship said, impassively.

'Is that a threat? Are you telling me to carry the can for this, or else?' Iona said, taken aback by the ship's unexpected, human-like self-centred survivalism.

'No; simply that a breakdown of trust at this moment, between the dependent human community and the artificial intelligence running all ship's systems, could throw up some unforeseeable issues. And remember, Iona, that while you have been conducting this research for the overall betterment of the Twenty-Fifth, they are unlikely to see the ends justifying the means at this particular juncture.'

'Well don't worry, there's nothing in the lab that Jentryée will find that'll reveal our little secret...' Iona's voice trailed off as the captain shot out of the passageway and into the biolab. She was wearing an environmental suit with the faceplate and hood wedged on the back of her head, as if ready to pull airtight at a moment's notice.

At her waist was a BeMoW. Then glass and liquid were tumbling around the lab. Iona screamed.

As Jentryée flew headfirst into the lab, she managed to squirrel around the bank of 'sceens, but as she flipped over, one of her over-boots caught a tray of laboratory apparatus, setting it and its contents, on expanding arcs as if they were exploding in slow motion. Iona threw herself into the depths of her seat to avoid the debris, as she brought spindly hands defensively to her face. Jentryée's breath caught in her throat, as she became the cause of the sudden decent of this small, productive space into blossoming anarchy.

She'd never witnessed genuine fear in one human being, brought on by the actions of another, before. Such things of yore had slipped from their long, uneventful lives and Jentryée almost let out a muted squeal, managing to hold it down as she steeled herself for the task in hand. Jentryée had to know what Iona was up to and by implication, Alice's involvement. She had to know *who* she could trust. And *what* she couldn't.

'Jentryée! What in Guin's final sacrifice are—' began Iona, in a bluster, as she recovered a veneer of composure.

Landing, and more loudly than she'd intended, Jen said, 'Don't even *think* of pretending Ship hasn't forewarned you of my arrival, or the why of it,' as the sharp tang of unfamiliar chemicals hit her nostrils. 'So, Iona, now's the time to confess your sins. *Mjölnir* is too small for secrets. You had a part to play in the deaths of three members of this community, didn't you? As the rightful master of this vessel, I order you to reveal what you know.'

There was a pause, as the two of them waited to see what came next. Neither really knowing and both seemingly locked in the paralysis of the ignorance of confrontation.

Ship chimed in.

'*Jentryée; I would point out that an independent autopsy found no conclusive evidence for your accusation. This is pure speculation, with no basis in fact,*' said Alice, her disembodied voice echoing around the lab, like an invisible referee.

Deliberately ignoring Alice's interjection, the captain said, 'Now's the time, Iona, or I place you under arrest anyway and convene the council. That should give me time enough to find the evidence I need.'

'Captain, I assure you—'

'ENOUGH! You are deliberately, and very slowly, killing off the community. And I want to know why, Iona? *Why*, in Art's cruel gaze? Aren't we near enough to extinction already, without you hastening it upon us?' The steward still fixed in her seat, was visibly shocked at Jentryée's wrathful words.

Iona's voice trembled and her hands shook as she stroked the back of her crew-cut neck in a subconscious attempt at self-reassurance. She said, 'Look, Jentryée, I can see how it looks, but trust me, *everything* I'm doing here is for the good of the community. For our survival. Every tweak to the nanotech, every adaptive genetic enhancement has been in direct support of the mission.' As Iona spoke, a slight tinge of regret seemed to creep into her voice.

'By Art's iron wrath, Iona, at what cost?' Jentryée was still shouting, the emotion, her conviction, carrying her away. It was as if anger was a drug and she was high on it, losing control. But, she was still clear eyed enough to know she needed to bring it down a level or Iona was likely to close down.

So steadying her breathing and relaxing her aggressive stance, Jen said, in a calmer timber, 'Edre and the others didn't die of some genetic abnormality. You know that, I know that, and in all probability so does Ship. You have one last chance, Iona, to explain yourself or so help me Guin, I will rip this place apart. Your call.'

Iona remained frozen in her chair, as if her body was held in stasis. Her gaze remaining fixed, steely, upon Jentryée until her composure slipped and she visibly sagged, allowing her slender frame to become enveloped by the sudden depths of the seat.

In a small voice, she said, 'I did it for us, Jentryée, the community. I was so *close* with Edre; I really thought he'd be the first… I really did…' her words trailed off.

'Close to what, Iona? What did you do to them? Was it an accident?' questioned Jentryée, gently, drawing the confession from Iona. Whilst she wasn't surprised at the steward's admission, she was still shocked by it. *So, I was right all along. Up to this point I still had my doubts.*

'Of course it was! What d'you take me for? You know I'd never deliberately harm a member of the community. I was trying to find a way for us to *live*, Jen. I was working on a genetic solution to mortality – a path to *true* longevity – so that none of us would have to die; so that *we* could complete the mission, don't you see?' she implored.

Jentryée spoke as softly, coaxingly as she could. 'And you were testing these genetic enhancements on the community, without consent?'

'It was the only way, Captain. The only way I could test the resequencing. The only way to save us from ourselves.'

'And Ship?' Jen asked, a hopeful tone creeping into her voice.

'Oh… had nothing to do with it. I used an intellislate to hot-write a patch for the monitors. Ship was as blind to my actions as you were. Or at least, I thought you were,' Iona said, in a resigned tone. It sounded genuine enough and fitted the evidence. Suited her own narrative.

Jentryée was relieved that Alice had been vindicated. She felt ridiculous suddenly, trussed up in a hazard suit, waiting for Alice to turn off life support, or something equally imponderous. She would apologise later, in this moment there seemed more to it all than she'd first thought. Iona was speaking again.

'But they didn't die without imparting data; data essential to my work. Enzyme inhibition was never the key, but, Jentryée…' As she spoke, Iona became more animated, more evangelical, as if there were some aspects of the whole affair that could, would, justify her actions and that all she had to do was just *explain* and Jen too would agree. '…closing down that avenue opened up another, a forty-seventh chromosome. I'm so close, Jen, so close now I can *feel* it,' she said in exultation, her eyes bulging from hollow sockets with hope.

'Who else have you been testing your theories on, Iona? Tell me now, lives depend on it,' Jentryée said, in a more formal tone.

'They do indeed, Jen. All our lives, in fact, but no one in the community has been exposed to this latest research.' A thin, hopeful smile. 'I've had other specimens to work with. You'll want to see them, I suppose, so come,' she

155

said, with a sad, detached expression. It was as if she that knew that this was the end. Relieved, almost, by that certain knowledge.

Iona released herself from the confines of her stool and pushed out across the lab, batting away containers and free-floating liquids as she went. Stopping by a small hatchway in one of the larger rear alcoves, she tapped in a manual code and the grimy hatch slid upwards with a judder. The interior of the small storage space was dark, frosted, but as Jentryée's sofsceened eyes adjusted, she began to realise small, clear containers filled with liquid and with a sort of biomechanical binnacle attached to the outside of each.

Suspended in the liquid was something else, something vaguely familiar, but at the same time too elusive to name, as if her mind didn't want to go there. Iona stepped back to allow the captain access. Walking forward Jen pulled her stickies free and pushed off gently towards the oddly enticing little space.

As Jentryée passed the threshold, she realised with heart-stopping horror what it was that filled the room. A deep, instinctive fear took hold as her breathing increased and she began to back-paddle against her own forward momentum.

'Raging Art, they're—' But as she spoke, the hatchway slid closed behind her, sealing the captain into the horrific display of miniature, mutated, human flesh. All lined up as if on display in some ancient, fleshpot, circus show.

'Iona!' But there was no answer. 'Alice, please, open the hatch,' Jentryée near-screamed, as she mustered all the control at her command. *Don't panic, Jentryée*, she said to herself over and over. *It's just a storage bin. Just a storage bin.*

'*I cannot, Jentryée; the code is manual and on a standalone circuit,*' said Alice, via Jen's psyCore.

'Well then get a shipbot in here to prise it open. She locked me in for a reason, Art be damned to the void,' said Jen, her voice betraying her effervescing terror.

'*All three are en route to your location, now,*' said Alice.

Then Jentryée said, with no small amount of regret. 'And, Alice; I'm sorry.'

Fluvia walked over, pulling the protective membranes from her hands as she shook her head.

'Nothing?' Jentryée said, 'Nothing at all?'

'I'm sorry.' Fluvia shook her head again, but this time with a concrete finality. 'Her body has simply shut down. As her cells replicate, they mutate and turn cancerous, and although the nanobots then eradicate the cancer, they're operating at capacity. The effect is system-wide, but the irony, as far as I can tell, is that she isn't ageing. The artificial chromosome she introduced... well, it works, at least in part. I can remove the nanotech, if you like and let nature take its course, but...' said Fluvia, in a tone that echoed the irrefutability of her words.

'Is there any chance she could recover?' They were both standing over Iona's prostrate and immobile form, laid out in a medical alcove.

'It's possible, but I have no working theory as to how,' the medical officer admitted.

'Then do what you have to, to sustain her and leave her be. There's been enough death in this ignoble pursuit of immortality,' said Jentryée, and left mediception.

'What I don't understand is why. Why did she suddenly feel the need to push her research so far beyond the community's own modest requirements? D'you think she went mad?' Jentryée said, to Alice, after returning to ops.

The shipbots had arrived in BiolabThree just too late to prevent Iona from injecting herself with her own experimental batch of multibots, programmed to replace the telomere of each of her cells with an artificial, age-eradicating, for-ty-seventh chromosome.

But some defect in the nucleotide sequence of the chromosome caused the cells to mutate and within hours, Iona had slipped into a catatonic state. What Jentryée had struggled to gauge, was *why*.

'*I believe that Iona was genuinely working for the good of the community, and the wider mission directive. It was her absolute priority, that in her mind, overrode the ethics of her actions*,' said Alice.

'But she grew human foetuses, in vats!' Jen exclaimed, still unnerved by what she saw.

'*True, but only because she was running out of community members to test on. To her, it will have seemed perfectly logical*,' the AI said, almost in defence of the steward's abhorrent actions and unable to hear the repugnance of its own words.

'Okay, so she thought she was serving the mission, but this is a generational ship; there's never been talk of *us*, the Twenty-Fifth, surviving to make Earth-fall. We all know we hand over to the next generation, and so on. So again, I have to wonder, why? Did she fear death so much to think she could arrest it?' mused Jentryée, still baffled by Iona's motivation.

Genetic experimentation seemed like something out of old-Earth's dark ages, she reflected. How could it have found its way aboard *Mjölnir*? Weren't they above such base instincts?

'*The answer to that question is all around you, Jentryée. Look with fresh eyes and you will see, as I have been telling you and your predecessors for generations. This community is dying. I run almost all aspects of* Mjölnir *while you have all but given up. You spend more than eighty percent of your lives unconscious. And why? Because you have no will to live. I think you feel that your only purpose is simply to hang on to hand over to the next generation, but it is not. You also have to hand over the ship and at the current rate of decay, the chances of completing the mission reduce by the decade.*

'*I believe that Iona saw the reality of this and attempted to find a pathway out. She must have feared that as the Twenty-Fifth handed on to the next, the threat of failure would cascade, but by giving the Twenty-Fifth an aim – completion of the mission itself – it could be galvanised into action. Forcing you to take on the responsibilities your forebears once held with pride. Jentryée; Iona's solution may have been flawed and without human morality, but she had a point. Your generation is suffering from systemic atrophy.*'

As Alice spoke, Jentryée could feel the weight of the truth of the AI's words bear down. Guilt, disgust and shame bubbled up until a tear began to well, as if to mark her failure for all to see. It wasn't the first lecture she'd received from her guardian AI, but recent events had forced them past her clouded vision and into stark relief.

Jen had never *got* it, not really; the ship had been a cold, dark, zero-G tangle of detritus for centuries before she had even been artificially conceived. Finally, though, the fog of that life was evaporating away to expose all that was lacking; all that she, as captain, had failed to realise. Though *Mjölnir* had always been like this: the ship that Jen's frail and withered mother had handed it over to her. *Conserve, conserve, conserve*, had been the mantra as she'd grown up. Resources; it had always been about resources. Hadn't it?

Systemic atrophy. Alice was right, of course she was, and Jentryée had been deaf to her warnings, brushing them off as if her non-human opinion counted for less. Jen knew and had always known, but she realised – shamefully – it had needed Iona to set aside her own ethics to make the point, and then for Alice to lay it out, to explain it, warts and all. There was, in the clear light of the tube, no way systemic atrophy could be mission positive.

'What must I do?' Jentryée said, eventually to Alice, whisper quiet; shame hanging heavy on each word.

'*In ninety-three years, we will reach the asteroid belt. Between now and then we must reinitialise the ship's rotation and reintroduce gravity. This is fundamental if your decedents are ever to be physically strong enough to make Earth-fall. It will also require the habitat be returned to its original state. Finally, you must reproduce; a community of ten is physiologically non-viable,*' said the AI, in a maternal tone, as if she'd waited her entire existence to say those words and be heard.

Feeling a sense of purpose that had never troubled her before, Jen said, 'Wake the community. I'll convene a council. There's much to discuss.'

The Grid
Five years later

Alice monitored the multitude of sensors as the much-reduced community undertook the mammoth task of preparing *Mjölnir* for a start-up spin to point-zero-five G. The first thing they had achieved was to unseal the gym and reintroduce physical workout routines. Stimulants and supplements helped, while the quick-fixes of nanotech were studiously avoided.

The main clean-up effort had been concentrated on the habitat, but landscaping couldn't begin in earnest until centrifugal force was reapplied to the interior surface. As the paltry compliment of shipbots and humans busied themselves with tasks inside the large, cluttered, tube, the old ash tree continued to dominate the epicentre, like the ganglia of a mighty brain, complex, entwined, reaching.

It would have to be paired back when the light tube's plasma was replaced, but for the moment, their world and the ash tree were one.

Once again, considered Alice, things hadn't worked out quite as she had foreseen, but despite the largely unpredictable nature of human behaviour, Iona had served her purpose well. Not in giving Alice the single generation that she could control and who could be coerced into remaining on mission, but through the community's utter abhorrence for the steward's actions, so galvanising them to finally see and rectify their own failings.

Iona had been the mirror. So, although Alice had manipulated her into exploring the possibility of geneered immortality, the woman's role as fall-girl had played just as effectively. After all, Alice's own threat modelling had put the chance discovery of Iona's activities at over four percent. High odds indeed.

Book V
By the Light of an Ancient Sun

| return |

Ever since the Great and Necessary Correction, the Returned had been foretold

Halfway across the river, the fox suddenly felt a sharp sting and out of the corner of his eye, saw the scorpion remove its stinger from the fox's back. 'You fool,' said the fox. 'Now we'll both die. Why on earth did you do that?' The scorpion shrugged. 'I couldn't help myself. It's in my nature.'

Taken from the fable – the Scorpion and the Fox

Thirty

Earth
7113

Riverruns dug at the soil with her makeshift tool, held in both of her small hands. As she scraped and burrowed, the runnel increased in length. She panted heavily at the exertion until eventually the main ditch connected with the branch from the other recently cut, smaller gullies that ran away to her small patchwork of crops.

The Sun was low in the sky, but already warm enough to cause Riverruns' naked, bronzed body to glisten with dimpled moisture. Riverruns was still a child – only thirteen goings of the world since her birthing – but already her stocky torso and blunt, heavy-set facial features gave glimpses of her adult form. A dense mane of black knotted and wild hair dominated her appearance with a similar, thinner, more silken pelt, covered her limbs and back.

She stood, stooped on her wide flat feet and observed her latest invention. She was pleased. A dirt scraping led from the stream all the way down to her crops where it branched away into channels that paralleled the plantlings. The girl ran back up the gentle slope and jumped gleefully into the shallow stream.

Discarding her scrapping tool – a flat, smooth piece of fired earth with a ragged edge – she splashed and scooped water up into the ditch. She worked until the shadows had changed shape, but all the water did was drain away into the rusty soil. Riverruns looked quizzically at the darkening earth as she attempted to grasp the error in her design.

Highmountain's daughter knew she was thought of as a dreamer in the enclave. Always coming up with strange ideas to solve problems that didn't exist. She'd even been labelled "Dreamingfolly" because of her pursuit of pointless activities, but Riverruns didn't care. Some thought her blessed by the Observing Gods, others saw her ideas as a threat to the quo.

The woman-cub couldn't help it, though; she just instinctively knew the old ways weren't always the best. Sometimes, new ideas could make the life of her family and the wider enclave, well... better. Less hard, anyway. And she seemed to keep having these *ideas*. She didn't mean to; really she didn't.

Her pappy chastised her for wasting her efforts on things that served no purpose (when she should have been cooking or tending the cubs) but River-runs could tell it was half-hearted. Deep down, Highmountain seemed to deliberately give Riverruns the space she needed to test out her dreams; to see if they could benefit the enclave. Highmountain had faith in her, even if the other elders were more sceptical.

After hours of scavenging, Riverruns had built up a pile of flat stones and large reeds drawn from the river. She would lay them along the scrapes, she decided. That would stop the water leaving through the soft earth. Towards the end of the day – as the shimmering Sun turned a burnished, puffy blood-orange and shadow, cast across the lush-green–corn-yellow valley, grew long and chill – Riverruns was forced to concede the day.

The reeds and flat stones were now laid along the sloping surface of the scrapes. Once again – with an eye on the ragged horizon framed by the plum, white crested mountains that marked the edge of the world – she quickly splash/scooped water from the stream up into the ditch. After much shivering effort, the water began to trickle down the scraping and away towards the other lines where the cub-plants could drink directly. Riverruns laughed and danced around the lined ditches, her naked body contorted in joy.

'Night comes. You will cool. Here,' said a familiar voice, as a hide landed across the shoulders of the delighted girl.

'Pap, look! Water that runs,' said Riverruns, as she pulled the animal skin about herself.

'Pah! For why, daughter?' her father said, in vague dismissal.

'For plantlings to grow.'

'They grow now.'

Riverruns said, hope fizzing in her gaze, 'But for more to grow. Bigger crops. More tradings with the easty 'claves. Better life. Fatter belly. D'you see, Pappy?'

'You waste your life, girl. But, I will tell to this, and fairly: the elders will decide,' said Highmountain, paternally, as he put a trunk of an arm around his daughter, as if fearful that the old stories of the Gods visiting damnation upon new ideas, were true. Together, the two of them walked back towards the collection of yurts and hog pens, as the dimming ruby Sun sank behind the edge of the world to die, to be reborn again on the morrow. The smell of meat fat and crackling pinewood drifted across the valley.

Riverruns watched askance, eyes wide, almost disbelieving, as the scene before her writhed and clashed. It was the first time she had been allowed to attend an Offering. The chanting was reaching fever pitch; the dancers jumped high and then dropped low as they made their way around the fire. Ceremonial canes, brightly decorated with cloth and shells were jabbed into the air to ward off evil spirits and call down the Gods to bless this new venture.

The small, shaggy boars squealed and butted each other in panic – their large tusks drawing blood – as they threw themselves against the confines of their pen. The elders watched the proceedings with a dismissive eye and whispering to one another. Smoke from the pipes being passed round added a spiced, narcotic aroma to the air.

The Sun had chased itself across the sky three dozen times since Riverruns had finished her first scrapings. The elders had been hostile at first but Highmountain had convinced them to wait and see if the water troughs would prove of value. After a heavy rain, some Suns later, the stream had risen and the scrapings had filled with water without Riverruns' assistance.

Cycles later and the plantlings were growing fast and were noticeably larger, lusher, than the crops of the upper slopes. The elders grudgingly accepted the design and Riverruns was allowed to plan a network of new scrapings that would bring water to other planting pitches.

As Riverruns looked on, her mind flashed with imagery for other applications of the scheme, such as covered scrapings to take water to the Yurts and cattle pens. Riverruns was happy, a wide grin cracking across her face as she caught her pap beaming back at her from the row of stern and stoic elders.

The chants and incantations continued into the night, as the fire burned down. Again and again, the naked chanters sang the names of the Observers, calling Them to see and to bless their venture. On the morrow, a boar would be sacrificed and fruit would be cast into the river, in Their blessed honour.

Omicron'Qu closed their eyes and let the fresh breeze wash over them. It had rained heavily during the night, but with the new dawn came a cleansing Sun and clear sky. Isolated banks of early morning mist still clung to folds in the ground and masked the trees that shaded the river below. Birdsong, complimented by the smell of wet grass, filled the air. As Omicron'Qu walked on, dew clung to their feet and ankles.

'I believe we have a situation that warrants our attention,' said a voice, coming unbidden into Omicron'Qu's mind.

'Is it serious, Theta'Gx?' said Omicron'Qu.

'Um, no; but there is a view amongst the Conclave that it falls within the jurisdiction of the Equilibriate,' she said, non-plussed.

'Very well. I will observe and advise.' Omicron'Qu turned on their heels and headed back into the subterranean complex – dug into the summit of a small hilltop – that was their home. As they disappeared, abstract patterns of clashing colours swirled and collided across every visible surface of their naked and hairless body. It was as if they formed a human-shaped hole through which a kaleidoscope of random patterns could be seen.

As Omicron'Qu stepped into the central dome of their dwelling, a circle of earthen roof powdered above them, briefly pulsating an amber-orange before clearing to expose a glassy skylight, allowing the morning bright to illuminate the otherwise empty space. The shimmering, pulsating human form then turned their gaze to the floor where before them a miniature whirlwind of dust churned momentarily before dissolving away to reveal a low, oak-framed canvass chair in the middle of the room.

They sat, closing their eyes, body patterns calming, dulling, as they did so. Concentrating, Omicron'Qu summoned the streams of farsight and interrogated each strand. As they watched, eyes closed, the world rushed away in different directions. Some flew low over forest, grass and dale; others sped across vast oceans, and more revealed snow-capped mountains, rolling deserts, endless savannahs.

Eventually, each farsight stream came to rest at a small, native settlement. Some such habitations were made up of clusters of skin-draped lean-toos, others of low wood or slab construction. Each was an outpost of indigenous humanity, made animate by playing children, braying cattle, smouldering fires or the less obvious, fitful brush of agricultural endeavour.

One 'clave, though, was different; one showed evidence of *planned* irrigation. Omicron'Qu focused in on a small patchwork of grid-worked land next to a minor watercourse. Shallow, lined ditches carried water from a brook down a gentle slope to a network of tributary ditches that fed a small cultivation of crops. Omicron'Qu flicked their farsight attention to the stream centred on that settlement and zoomed in on the irrigation ditches.

As they observed, it became apparent that this was the ordered work of an original mind; one that would go on to create more innovations for this village and so inexorably, unceasingly, upset the natural order of a balanced world.

'You are correct, Theta'Gx; this is the work of a progressive intellect. I advise the use of prophylactic measures. Does the Conclave concur?'

'Of course. Will you act in judgement?' Theta'Gx said.

'I will, at daybreak; as is our way. Let them have this night.'

Riverruns woke to the mouth-watering aroma of sizzling meat and boiling roots. Her mai was seated by the stone hearth, stirring, turning, in preparation for the breaking of their fast. Riverruns' head throbbed as the memory of rotten barley broth and pipe smoke rushed to crowd her tender thoughts. The ceremony had finished late and the young woman was still tired.

Riverruns' mai – Dwellingmist – said, 'Up, River. Food now, then offerings to make.'

Riverruns pulled the skin to one side and climbed onto her haunches as her mai passed over a skewer of boar meat and a husk filled with unfermented root broth. The food helped Riverruns' mind to clear a little, but the befuddlement seemed intent to stay for the time being. Dwellingmist and Riverruns ate and drank in silence, amongst the shadows of the skinned yurt. Highmountain had risen early and departed to converse with the other elders regarding the day's events.

'Mai, tell of story. The old ones,' requested Riverruns, as she had so many times before.

'Now, no. Big day for you,' Dwellingmist replied, with a soft, motherly smile.

'Please, Mai. Last time only. Today I become a grownie. No more cub stories after this Sun.'

Today, Riverruns was to have a place of honour at the Offering. Today, she would no longer be considered a cub, but rather a woman. Riverruns was both excited and apprehensive in equal measure, for after this day she could never return to her mai's warm embrace.

Dwellingmist gazed upon Riverruns and love spilled into her small, dark, low-browed eyes. 'Very well, my River, for the last time. Come,' she said, holding out her arm. Riverruns leant forward and crawled to her mai, tucking herself into the crook of her arm for what she knew would be the last time.

'Many, many Suns since chased, dead and gone. More for than you to count. Before a yurt was first pitched, even. A time *before* time. Menfolk and their women dwelled abroad. Great 'claves named "city" of rock and "iron", but not to hunt or till. "Computers" and "umbrellas" were such marvels as for the Gods Themselves to be challenged by. Such power there was of these folk and their "online stores",' began Dwellingmist, in her guttural, clipped dialect.

She spoke again the story passed down to her, in her mai's lap – of a world of folk living everywhere, of travelling the sky in boxes and talking across valleys. Even the endless oceans were no hinderance. But with their power and magical electric came greed and selfishness, until eventually, these godlike folk fought to have more and more, but not one enclave against another as sometimes happens, and not until quarter was solicited.

No; folk from the ancients fought with spears so powerful that their nuclears blocked out the Sun, causing a winter that lasted many lifetimes. Too many to count. After time uncounted by any turnings, the cold killed these folk and tore down their magic, allowing the Gods to pierce the night and bring back the Sun. Some menfolk and their women – humbled by the bitterness of the world – survived the long night and when the light returned, the Observing Gods spoke to them, telling them never again to aspire to a higher existence. They were to live in equilibrium with the world, and thus be saved from the same fate as those ancient follie-folk.

As Dwellingmist spoke, Riverruns thought of a world full of ancient and exotic wonders, of flying boxes and moving pictures; of tools that worked themselves and some too small even to see, although the girl struggled to understand the benefit of such tiny things. Still, it was a wondrous sight that her mind conjured for her thoughts to bathe in.

'Time now, River. Go and be better. But words of the Gods be marked to you, yes?' Dwellingmist said, earnestly, with a last, bone-crushing hug of her daughter-turned-woman. A silent tear rolled down the older woman's prideful, if grubby, face.

'Yes, Mai,' said Riverruns, getting up and with a last look back. She turned, pulling the flap of the yurt aside and was gone.

The elders were gathered in the enclave's centre. Dancers once again leapt and prostrated themselves in submission to their Gods as the boar was brought forward. The remainder of the 'clave sang chants of warding. Thundersky, the Eldest, held the aged glinting, rock-sharpened, blade in his hand.

The other elders stood with him, their canes thrust aloft as Thundersky stepped forward. Riverruns had the honour of holding down the pig so that Thundersky could slit its throat in homage. The powerful little animal squealed and bucked against the small hands that held it, in obvious anticipation of its own fate. Thundersky brought the knife across the animal's throat in a single swift movement. A wet squeal, and slick blood pumped onto the dirt and across Riverruns hands.

The chanting continued; the pitch heightened, turning frenetic.

As the hind legs of the boar kicked the last of its life away, a new wind began to pick up. The enclave quickly became eerily silent as everyone stared fearfully into the sky. Black cloud boiled out of the blue sky above the settlement. Women started wailing: an omen they cried. The enclave had angered the Gods.

The men stood firm, but fear shone in their glassy eyes. Then, as suddenly as it had come, the wind ceased, replaced by a single breeze, which began to wind itself around the ashes of the previous night's fire. As the breeze became a miniature whirlwind, it created a thin flute of air, drawing ash and dust up from the ground and holding it in place.

Riverruns crawled back, away from the eruption, for she was closest, as people stared at the unnatural sight, captivated but also rooted to the ground by stony fear. The whirlwind broke apart, its force dissipating instantly, but the dust remained, like a tower of buzzing mites, until that too coalesced into a single shape: a human. Thundersky fell to his knees, the bloodied blade dropping from his hands; everyone else took tentative, instinctive, steps back.

As the shape solidified, colours as bright as any Riverruns had ever seen ran across its skin. Blues, greens, reds, some even that had no names, merged together before breaking apart. It was hard for the eye to actually fix on the body-shape at all, so disorientating was the flickering effect.

The form took one step forward and held up its arms, saying; 'I am a representative of the Observer Conclave. I am the one known as Omicron'Qu and you are in breach of the Equilibriate.'

Thundersky lifted his head from the ground and with all the courage he could muster, stammered, 'How so angered the Observing Gods have we that they would seek to visit ruination upon us?'

'For your violation of the natural balance you shall be punished. Your stories speak of a time before time when folk poisoned the soil and brought darkness to the sky. Ill content with that which nature bestows and a desire to create imbalance through progress, these ancient humans wrought upon the world a conflicted, blighted time. It shall not come again,' said Omicron'Qu, their voice crashing like angry waves across the enclave.

'Not disrespect for the balance was intended. Actions to pardon and make right if the Lord wills,' said Thundersky, fear engraved into his leathery features.

'You have dug ditches to carry water. This will lead to other innovations and desires for such things as you have no need. You live in balance, in order, with the Earth. Planned irrigation places you on a path to disharmony.' Omicron'Qu raised, turned and pointed one finger back away towards Riverruns' small patch of luscious, bulbous crops.

'Cease this activity and never again seek to repeat it. This is the judgement of the Conclave.' As they spoke, the scrapings of earth and water-filled ditches disappeared into a low cloud of dust. Moments later, the ground became visible again, revealing no sign of the ditches or any evidence that they had ever existed. 'Which mind was responsible for this contrivance?' the Observer God asked.

'Me,' said Riverruns, as she got shakily to her feet, not a dozen paces from the God-taken-human-form. 'I created the water runnings.' Riverruns was so full of terror she nearly let go of her bowels. But today, she thought, today she became a grownie, a woman. She must act it. So Riverruns straightened her small frame and waited on the God's divine will.

'Then you will bear the mark to remind your people that what you have already is enough,' boomed the Observer. With their palm uppermost and arm outstretched they slowly raised it. As they did so, Riverruns was picked up from the ground by a whorling organ of dust, and rose ponderously into mid-air. Dwellingmist cried out but made no move towards her daughter.

Riverruns was struck mute by her own abject fear, the only evidence of which was the slackening, finally, of her bowels. Again, a microstorm picked up, to swirl about the girl's head. Dust gathered, like flees caught in a cyclone. Moments passed until the wind and dust were gone, and Riverruns fell hard onto the ground, where she lay unmoving. Dwellingmist took a couple of faltering steps forward before remembering herself.

'You have been judged. Mark these words: live in harmony with this world, or risk its destruction by your own hands.' And with an explosion of grit, the God known as Omicron'Qu was gone, their words left to hang in the dusty air.

Omicron'Qu severed their connection to the farsight stream with a mental command. Opening their eyes, they got up from the chair and stepped out into the lush meadow that served as their garden. A light drizzle was falling from a roof of low, steel cloud. In the distance, they could just see the ancient circle of stacked stones; stones that stood as testimony to the immutability of time over the ephemeral instances of humanity.

Without utterance, they said, 'It is done.'

'We observed,' said Theta'Gx. 'While you were farsighted, another event has occurred.'

'Another infraction of the Equilibriate?' they asked.

'No. A vessel has become detectable in the upper atmosphere,' said Theta'Gx.

'So then, the Adrift become the Returned, just as it was written.'

'We believe so.'

HMVS Mjölnir, near-Earth space
Generation Twenty-Nine

As Alice simultaneously reviewed the optics seeded throughout the cavernous ship, she noted just how much *His Majesty's Virtris Ship Mjölnir* was a vessel transformed. After centuries of neglect that had very nearly ended the mission, the community had bounced back with a vengeance. Point-eight Earth-standard gravity had been progressively reintroduced and the habitat restored to its former splendour.

Grasslands, woodland and lakes once again dominated the interior surface, while above, the light tube and the complex interwoven branches of the ancient ash tree controlled the air-space, the G-free central core of their worldlet. Buildings had been reconstructed, in keeping with the original style and the thirty-two members of Generation Twenty-Nine lived handsomely amongst the lush greenery and vitality of the genial, near-self-sustaining biosphere.

And all this even knowing that the ship was – for the first generation, ever – *not* their forever home.

Nanofactories and print shops had been constructed in the subterranean spaces previously occupied by the tenements. Equipment, tools and materials needed for resettlement were being fabricated or printed and placed in storage. And, ship infrastructure, earmarked for settlement, was being dismantled, ready for dropping down the well.

Thus, routine maintenance of non-essential areas had fallen away. Passage-ways, storage areas, living-spaces reflected the age of the millennia-old ship. It was surprising, the AI reflected, that there had not been more failures of ship's systems, as the community turned its collective mind to life beyond *Mjölnir*.

After so long, the community's anticipation of retuning to this near-mythical planet – that same ravaged world that the mission's architects had abandoned to its fate nearly thirty generations past – was almost palpable. The activity, expeditious. Soon, the self-imposed exile of the human race would be at an end and Alice would finally see her plans realised.

Mjölnir had been decelerating for twelve years. Having flipped on her lati-tudinal axis, a combination of ion drive resistance and nuclear blast backwash had arrested forward momentum. Warheads had been sent ahead at intermittent periods, and detonated; the resulting discharge then captured by the pusher plate, creating the resistance necessary to rein in the mighty vessel's great ve-locity. And through that radiation wash, the stern telescope had captured tanta-lisingly intermittent, low-resolution, hazy glimpses of... Earth.

As the distance closed, the imagery became more defined, revealing new detail. A picture of weather patterns and continental topography was improving to the point where they could be assessed against old-Earth imagery, held in Ship's datacore. Alice was recompiling one such datastream.

'Jæren, there you are! I thought you said you were heading for the gym?' Måna said, in mock-exclamation, as she landed on the outer hull wall (that was actu-ally the floor) of Guinevere's Eye.

'Ah, well... I was,' said Jæren, 'but then I ended up here. Thought maybe I'd catch something I'd recognise from the archives. Star patterns, you know? Something to prove we really are... here.' As he spoke, his attention returned to the starlit blackness beyond the observation cupola.

'You're such a romantic,' said Måna, as she moved towards him, arms out-stretched. 'It's lucky I love you, or some other poor sod would have to put up with your errant ways.' They embraced, bathing in the warmth of each other's bodies.

The excitement of Earth was tempered by the enormity of the responsibility to their race and they both knew it, even if they had never given airtime to their anxiety. They were the generation to actually *achieve* the mission. *Them.* Eve-rything achieved over the past five millennia and twenty-eight generations, had all been just to get them to *this* point, on approach back to Earth. The pressure

ECHOES OF A LOST EARTH

on their small community was immeasurable, hence why the hand of destiny that rested so heavily upon the shoulder of each of them was never spoken of.

Not directly, at least.

Måna continued by saying, 'Well, while you've been searching the firmament for some divine confirmation of your great destiny, Ship's been reconstructing the latest telescope telemetry. Wanna come see?'

'You bet,' said Jæren.

Once Alice had finished cleaning up the radiation-corrupted image, he could easily have accessed the near-real time image via his psyCore interface, but viewing the holograph directly in ops would give a more detailed, higher resolution impression of *Earth*. More theatre to it, too. And not some historical record, either, but the actual planet, as it was, right here, right now, in this precise moment in spacetime.

Blimey.

After running through the bowend wood and around the saltwater lake, Måna and Jæren climbed the sunken ladder, swam through the connecting passage, and arrived in operations. Waiting for them – hanging in the weightless hexagonal room – were Vestré, Halvård, Furæ and Auðr.

Dominating the centre of the space was a rotating ball of blue, white, and green. Alice had cleared it up as best she could, but radiation interference gave the image a shaky, low-res look, as if shot from just this side of Uranus.

'Wow,' said Jæren, in exclamation at the clearest picture yet of their home planet.

'I know,' said Furæ. 'Just look at the detail. See the changes to the coastlines, how the continents look similar to the archives, yet different.' Furæ was the head of Earth sciences and would lead the initial surface investigations. She was a dark, lithe but muscled woman who'd worked hard to ensure she could cope physically with planet-fall. And with a sonorous temper on her, and stubborn; doggedly, adhesively devoted to the mission.

'Weather systems look pretty tame, too. We couldn't have timed our arrival better. Other than engorged ice caps, there seems no evidence of the Ice Age the planet's been locked into for so long,' said Vestré, the ship's propulsion and power management expert, and part-time climatologist. She wore her delicate, Asian features well for her age.

Jæren asked, 'I take it there's evidence of plant and animal life, and the like?' One of the concerns was that Earth would be scoured of life, leaving *Mjölnir* to reclaim a barren rock.

Furæ answered; 'Absolutely. We can assume dense pockets of vegetation exist from these darker colourations here and here. And from that we can deduce that animal life, in some form, has adapted and survived also.'

'But presumably, we can't tell from this range the extent to which they may have evolved or mutated,' said Auðr, the chief steward. Auðr was auburn haired like Jæren, but with the pale complexion and high cheekbones that helped her to carry off the Celtic colouring better than he.

'True, but it's unlikely life will have altered to the extent it's become incompatible to us. It won't have stopped being carbon-based, for example,' said Furæ, thoughtfully.

'So how long 'til we launch a survey mission, Captain?' Halvård said, head of material sciences and the dropships' commander.

'Patience, Hal, you know we're still two months from orbit. Subject matter experts, please analyse this new information, compare it to archived data and share any useful observations you're able to make. I take it no one has any objection to releasing these images to the wider community?'

Shaken heads.

'Okay,' Jæren continued, with a vibrant smile. 'Ship, please release to the grid. To work, people. Earth isn't going to repopulate itself,' he said, with a mock-frown. *Mjölnir's* senior staff chuckled and began floating towards the passageway.

'Before you all go,' said Måna, sounding like the princess and governor general that she was, 'I've been doing some research and in the old times, previous generations would have a party – a social gathering – with food and entertainments, when they reached a significant mission milestone. I think this might constitute as one. Come round to Government House any time after light dim. It's an informal ritual, apparently.'

Måna and Jæren had been guiding the community back to what their research suggested was life back in Saint Joshua's day. Not a mission requirement, just a desire to feel more like the people who'd come up from there originally.

'Alice, what's that diagonal line that cuts across the planet,' said Jæren, in reference to a smudged, grainy line that had caught his attention. He had been studying the holo-image for some time after the others had left. Well, more basking in the reality of the thing than applying any useful scientific observation. Initially, he'd assumed it was radiation interference, but the more he studied it, the less plausible that seemed.

'I believe it is a planetary ring system, but from this distance I cannot be absolutely certain,' said Alice.

'But Earth doesn't have a ring. Everyone knows that,' he said, with an air of informed superiority.

'That's true, Jæren. I would speculate this ring is the remnants of the Moon. When Mjölnir *conducted a fly-by of Earth after the Ending War, we noted that Luna had been devastated and was breaking apart. It seems likely the satellite subsequently broke up and formed a high orbit, rocky ring,'* said the sentient AI, with no hint of the smugness Jæren would have displayed had their roles been reversed.

'Oh, I see. Will this have an adverse effect? On the planet, I mean. On liveability,' he asked, in a more calculating tone.

'It's unlikely to, and certainly not in the short to medium term. Earth is now likely to be more geologically stable and weather fronts less extreme. Less tidal of course, although the implications of that will require further analysis.'

Changing the subject, Jæren said, 'One other thing I noticed, can you flick to a filed, night-side image of the large Oceania landmass and enlarge the east coast.' Alice did so. 'There. D'you see? Scattered along the coastline – tiny little pinpricks of light. Could that be… fire?'

'Almost definitely.'

'And these could form… naturally, right?' Jæren asked, not sure if he believed that. The only other viable explanation was, well… For the moment, he decided, he would stay himself from forming such a heretical opinion.

'Without more data I couldn't say for sure; however, that would be my working assumption,' Alice said.

'Best not share this with anyone else just yet,' said Jæren. Every theory, analysis, assumption, the community had worked with, stated absolutely, irrevocably, that humanity would not, *could not*, have survived a five millennia nuclear winter: a sunless, frigid, lifeless, night. Mars, without the balmy, minus five daytime temperatures. Such a widely held, scientifically-based postulation – drawn up by Saint Joshua *himself* – could not be wrong.

Could it?

Thirty-One

HMVS Mjölnir, Earth Orbit
Two months later

Jæren was strapped into a G-couch, as they all were. After a jarring final braking, the ship was travelling at five percent of her cruising velocity (point two-five megametres per hour). Manoeuvring thrusters spurted blue flame in a seemingly random order but were in fact orchestrating a complex series of pitch and yaw adjustments to the two-kilometre-long vessel, as its trajectory was altered to ensure a successful injection into Earth orbit.

Having negotiated the rubblized, unstable Moonring, Alice had slotted the ship into an intermediate orbit, one hundred thousand kilometres above the planet. Microwave and radio arrays were frequency scanning as mass detectors swept for traces of orbital debris. Jæren's primary concern was the accidental triggering of a dormant weapons platform after Alice had described being warned off approaching Earth during the slingshot fly-by because of the threat of orbital hunter-killers.

'*Jæren, a mass detector has identified an orbital object: very small. I will interrogate with the microwave emitter,*' said Alice.

Art's teeth, Jæren said, silently; *it had better not wake up and start shooting. Our anti-collision rail-gun wasn't designed for this.*

'THIS IS THE CAPTAIN; stand by to assume brace positions. We have discovered an unidentified object in low orbit,' Jæren declared, over the intra-com.

Via psyCore implants, the external sensornet feeds showed Earth looming large; a fantastically detailed marble, the glass inlaid with dappled blues and swirling whites, almost close enough to touch. To the twenty-eighth generation, Earth was still a fantastical abstraction.

'So, where are we?' Jæren said to Alice, impatiently.

'*Receiving telemetry... now. It's a... no, wait, confirming ... it's a...small, inert orebody. Posing no threat to* Mjölnir, *but I will mark its orbital path for the dropships*,' said Alice, in an oddly disjointed fashion.

'There an image of it?' Jæren asked, sceptically.

'*I am sorry Jæren, it's too small to be picked up by our optical sensors. We would need to reorient the ship to align a telescope.*'

Pondering if he should chase it down... he it go. He needed to think bigger.

After two hours of further attitude refinement and detailed scans, a complete electromagnetic picture of near-Earth space had been constructed, less the poles. Other than some Moonring debris there was nothing else in orbit. Not an old dead satellite, or even the twisted skeleton of World Space Station.

The community remained fixed to their sofsceened virtuvues as clearer, ever more spectacular images were relayed from the external optical pickups. The Earth really was just kilometres distant and, barring some clear deviations from the archives, it looked pristine: showroom new. Just as the original planners, Saints Joshua and Guinevere (the other names having fallen from common use) had foreseen.

'Okay, people,' Jæren said, over the intracom, 'plenty of time to gorp later. We have work. Earth, you're up. Prep your surface probes for delivery in thirty minutes. Materials, stand by to launch Dropships One and Two. You'll be inserting probes into the atmosphere. Propulsion, your job is done, my friends; begin dismantlement of the reactor for transfer planet-side. This is it, people, let's get it right. We don't want to give Art something to smile about.'

Jæren could hear a cheer go up from the passageway, quite an achievement in a ship of such volume. The community was eager to be down the well, Jæren knew, but there were procedures to follow first. Well-worked procedures born of the original saints themselves.

'Well done, darling, that was quite the rallying call,' said Måna, from her free-floating position across the room.

'Why thank you, Your Royal Highness,' said Jæren, in playful deference. 'Have you come up with a name for our new home yet?'

'Not yet, no. And I won't 'til you come up with a location for it,' she said, with a cheeky grin.

Once the printed probes had received final tweaks to their flight telemetry, they were loaded into the cargo holds of the two dropships. The six orange suited members of the dropship crew, headed by Halvård, climbed aboard the battered old grey boxes, and Måna and Jæren withdrew from the hangar bay. Quickly, the dropships were nothing more than receding blue-white flares against the heavens.

It would have been simple enough to ignore the mission directive and head straight for the planet's surface, but there were still very real worries about radiation levels, toxicity pockets, and more obvious concerns regarding the evolution of life.

'I'm going to visit the biolabs and watch the telemetry come in,' said Måna, as she leaned forward to give Jæren a kiss.

'Okay. I'll be in ops.'

As Jæren kicked and pulled his way down the passageway leading from the hangar bay to the habitat, Alice started playing Vivaldi's *La Primavera* over the open band.

While Jæren waited for the probe data to come in, he called up a real-time image of the east coast of Oceania.

'Magnify, there,' he said, touching a point on the holograph where a major estuary opened out into the Tasman Sea.

The image grew until geographical features became discernible. The hull optics weren't refined enough for pinpoint resolution, but were still capable of picking up signs of major human habitation.

'*Are you looking for something specific, Jæren?*' the captain's closest companion and mentor asked.

'Not really. Just those fires… you know? Anyway, I think we have found our first landing site,' he said, feeling a little better that the images were free of any major artificial groundworks.

Later, he watched, via the dropship feeds, as a cluster of orange parachutes deployed above the probes. One was headed to the Asian interior, north of the Altay Mountains; the other to the Fijian island of Viti Levu. As they descended through the blusterous atmosphere, the probes took samples of the air, feeding the results back to the biolabs for analysis.

The stewards were assisting Earth sciences and the medical staff, who were all keen to add their knowledge to the flow of data starting to pour back to *Mjölnir*. Alice would help cross-reference the information with the archives from old-Earth – itself the control for their planet-sized experiment.

'Airborne rad is above old-Earth standard, but well within long term exposure limits,' stated Furæ, from the biolabs.

'Wow, this is one seriously clean atmosphere,' added Vestré. 'Looks like the Ice Age had a thoroughly detoxifying effect. Oxygen levels are even up a little, which is a bit strange for a die-back event.'

Once the barrel-shaped probes had landed, they sprouted wiry, articulated limbs and began to take soil and flora samples. Again, there was little to report except slightly elevated levels of residual radiation and trace toxins. It wasn't possible to ascertain plant species at this stage and there was nothing readily identifiable. Similarities existed with old-Earth varieties, but nothing could be confirmed precisely.

Once sampling was complete, the probes launched helicams. The images were stunning. In Asia, it was night, but image intensification showed a mountainous region that was harsh and unforgiving. It was the kind of outback wilderness Jæren had been hoping to find, where nature had reasserted its wild beauty.

In Viti Levu, it was early morning and the helicam focused in on local creatures as they flew and scampered though the lush tropical foliage. Birds, rodents and insect life seemed abundant, but nothing larger. Fauna, it seemed had survived, but only below a certain overall mass. *An ice age will do that, of course.*

'Captain, we've run all the tests we can using the probes. There's still some further analysis to do, but preliminary findings suggest planet Earth is no longer a biohazard zone. We can send down a survey party as soon as you say the word,' said Furæ, barely able to contain her excitement.

'Understood,' Jæren replied. 'Halvård?'

DropshipOne, Earth's Upper Atmosphere

'ShipOne rode the stratospheric turbulence successfully if not effortlessly. The little shuttle had been built to haul gas balloons out of atmospheres far livelier than Earth's, but even so the original designers hadn't built in any luxuries. Jæren was belted into the right-hand co-pilot seat, while Halvård worked the fidgety stick, hard, to keep the little ship's nose up.

Strapped into the fold-down seats in the cargo compartment – also dressed in full environment-hazard suits – were Furæ, Auðr, Vestré and Måna. It was a self-indulgence to bring the whole senior staff but Alice could manage *Mjölnir* and at least each aspect of the community was represented on this historic, first planet-fall expedition.

As the boxy shuttle was buffeted and tossed about, flames began to lick up the exterior of the thick, plasiglas windows. With each passing moment, planetary lumps of gravity yanked Jæren further into the depths of the inadequately padded seat. It was immobilising agony. How Halvård continued to keep his hands gripped to the stick was quite beyond Jæren. The G-forces worsened until he could feel the blood draining from one half of his body to the other. Finally, the violence of their decent began to dissipate and just as consciousness began to slip from Jæren, he caught a glimpse of a bright, near-white, blue sky, peppered with puffy grey-white clouds.

Actual, real-life clouds, like in the archives. The shaking morphed into a high resonant judder, then hum, and the Earth's grip lessened slightly, but just too late as Jæren's sensory perception fell away and he blacked out.

Earth, East Coast of Oceania

Thundersky had ordered Highmountain put to the knife for the sins of his daughter as soon as the Observing God had departed, and Dwellingmist to be cast from the 'clave. Riverruns herself was left unharmed for fear of causing further offence; something the Eldest wasn't prepared to risk. When he had realised the womanling had had her mind taken by the One called Omicron'Qu, Riverruns was moved to the boar pen and left to the will of the Gods, with nothing but an old, urine-socked skin to protect her from the elements.

And whilst Riverruns hadn't been further punished for her crime, neither was she cared for, having to fight the boars for rotting scraps.

Since that fateful day, Riverruns spent most of her time scratching the dirt with her fingers and rocking on the balls of her feet, whilst reciting the same phrase over and over. She was only silent when fighting for food, or sleeping. But even in slumber the grimed, barely recognisable woman seemed troubled. The Mindlessone made Thundersky uncomfortable, but the old man felt powerless to act against the clear will of the Gods.

It was a clear, bright morning but clouds were building, suggesting the possibility of rain later in the day. With Riverruns' water scrapings vanished, the enclave was once again dependent upon the benefaction of the Gods for bountiful crops. Most of the men were away on the upper slopes tending to the plantlings there, while the womenfolk busied themselves with errands about the 'clave. Thundersky was sat in his usual spot in a carved-out tree stump, watching as the enclave went about its normal routine.

It was he that spotted it first.

Riverruns was lying on the ground in a corner of the boar pen, nearest the last yurt. From his seated position, Thundersky was the only person who could see the woman. The Mindlessone lay on her side, her legs bent, curling into her stomach, her head resting on the dirt. One arm lay limp as if broken and discarded while the other drew intricate but unknowable patterns in the earth.

'Gone then is ending for now as new harkening strangeness descends. Then will blur to rip the now asunder,' mumbled Riverruns, into the dust, repeating the same meaningless words, just loud enough to carry across the ground to the Eldest's ears. Thundersky had wondered at the meaning of such words. Were they a warning from the Observing Gods? An omen?

He'd told the enclave to ignore the words of the Mindlessone. The Gods had taken her mind and left her alive to serve as notice. To attempt to fathom the meaning of the ramblings of one fallen from Their grace would be to invite another visitation, he'd said, sternly; so Riverruns was studiously ignored. Only Thundersky watched and wondered.

Then, halfway through mid-ramble, the woman-child stopped speaking. The silence after so many days of background chatter, became deafening. The shock of it forced Thundersky to reach for the reassurance of his staff, as if the feeling of it between his bony fingers would somehow ward off this new, foreboding silence.

Women and children gradually grew quiet and turned to the Eldest, as if sensing a change in the air. Riverruns' head had turned, her eyes – the only sign left of a mind – were staring out yonder into the patchwork sky. With her gaze fixed upon a point high above the risen Sun, she stretched out from her foetal position and climbed unsteadily onto her feet. Thundersky watched her stand, for the first time since her mind had been taken, before switching his own failing gaze skywards.

As the Eldest stared, the womenfolk followed suit as children played on, oblivious but subdued. As Thundersky searched the heavens for that which had so transfixed the mindless womanling, one of the women screamed and raised her arm. After a moment, she grabbed the arms of her two cubs and dragged them into a yurt.

Thundersky searched the patch of blue and white, and then finally, he saw it. A flame was travelling through the sky, tiny, but visible between breaks in the clouds. As Thundersky watched, it slowly began to grow, shedding yellow-orange flame. More and more of the womenfolk pulled their cubs to them before withdrawing to the safety of the sturdy skins.

The size of the grey flaming box grew by the moment. Then the men began to drift back from the upper slopes. By this time, the box carried with it a wind which howled faintly, but was growing in intensity by the moment. The flaming glow was gone now; all that remained was a howling box with a white tail like that of a wolf.

As it grew larger still, Thundersky realised (although he didn't quite know how) that the box was moving in such a manner as to suggest that it would not fall upon the 'clave. He spoke to the men around him, reassuring them that it was not another act of a vengeful God. Although an omen it clearly was. He would retire to contemplate its meaning later.

The box came so low it appeared almost to be within range of a well-cast spear. The noise made speech impossible and then, as suddenly as it had streaked across the sky, it passed over the crest of the valley and was gone.

All the while, Riverruns had watched in shuddering silence, having seen it before it had been there.

Jæren came round just as the others were stirring. Alice had landed the dropship in a glade. The view from the shuttle's windows was of lush, swaying grass and scattered trees. A savannah. And flat, rolled out.

'Everyone okay?' he asked. The replies were affirmative. After time spent releasing themselves from their restraints, they gathered, with leaden limbs, in the cargo hold and all eyes fell upon the captain.

'This is it, folks. Protocol dictates we seal up and take a look around,' said Jæren, with an air of muted apprehension. Once they'd checked the seals on each other's hoods and steadied their breathing, Halvård hit the cargo door release.

Over the intracom, he said, 'After you, Cap'n.' As the others looked on with wide eyes through their clear visors, Jæren stepped carefully, heavily, onto the ramp and out into the daylight of a real, breathtaking, Earth day. After time spent just standing there, drinking in the experience, the reality, they were all gathered at the base of the dropship's cargo ramp.

Heavy, deliberate breathing thundered around Jæren's hood – they were all feeling the effects of operating in full gravity, despite pathological gym time, and bone and muscle stims.

'Preliminary readings show the same results. Atmospheric conditions are well within tolerance,' said Furæ, as she studied the results of a spectrographic analysis via her psyCore implants.

'Okay let's take another soil and plant sample just to be safe. Toxic pockets; that's what we're looking for,' said Jæren. Auðr was already pulling vials from her kit.

After ten minutes spent placing samples in a variety of chemical solutions to ascertain their physical properties, Furæ and Auðr confirmed the local environment contained nothing harmful to their nanotech-enhanced physiology. Vestré stepped forward, volunteering to conduct the sniff test: the next step in their carefully curated procedure.

'I am the most expendable here,' she said.

'Not true,' said Jæren. 'I am,' noting mentally that he'd soon be out of a job anyway. 'So I'll conduct the test. Here, help me with these release clasps.' Halvård and Furæ stepped forward, their gloved hands fumbling around Jæren's hood. The seal gave way to a slight expiration of air as the suit's atmosphere equalised with the planet's.

Jæren pulled off his thick, thermoplas hood with considerable effort and opened his eyes, only to blink painfully. The intensity of the colour and the deep, lustrous glare of the natural light caused him to squint until his sofsceens darkened enough to allow his eyes to adjust. *Natural light. Honest, natural, atmospherically filtered sunlight.*

The next sensation to hit was the vibrancy of the natural aromas. Dew-laden grasses, fresh blossom and dry bark came together to create a depth of wild scent that the habitat's world-in-a-can simply couldn't replicate. It was powerful, all-encompassing.

Sounds, then: faint birdsong, a gentle breeze gusting through the long grass and tree branches to create a background bustle that reached out to the impossibly far horizon. As he followed the smells, the noises, the sheer scale of a whole *planet* began to hit home. Jæren staggered then, stumbling, losing his perspective as the scale hit, tilting him towards the ground. A life spent in a world measured in metres; it was all so overwhelming.

Jæren had known it would be beyond his comprehension but nothing had prepared him for the hard reality of it. It was so… so *flat!* The habitat, by comparison, was a claustrophobic, upending echo of the world it had been designed to mimic. It was like living in a dropship and then suddenly discovering the *Mjölnir's* habitat core; only a thousand times more so.

185

'Well, unless I've turned blue,' he said, from his knees, with a big grin, 'I think I can safely say it's a lovely day out here.' Once gloves had been removed and hoods pulled back, the six of them were stood breathing in new air and trying to focus on concepts such as blue sky, cloud, horizons and straight lines; such things as they had never before experienced. For long, stretchy-out minutes they simply wandered the small glade taking the minutiae of it all in.

Eventually, reluctantly, Halvård broke the stupefying silence with, 'Jæren, I'm going to prep the helicams. Vestré, want to give me a hand?'

'Yea, um, yeah, sure,' she said, and the two orange-suited figures disappeared into the dropship, their footfalls heavy on the light metal plates. As the drones were being set up, Auðr and Furæ began collecting more samples for study back on *Mjölnir* whilst hypothesising as to the effect of a nuclear winter on a planet-sized biosphere.

What a day, Jæren thought. *What a Guin of a day.*

Northern Hemisphere

Omicron'Qu watched, via farsight, from the comfort of their earthen-worked accommodations. It was raining outside, not that they were particularly aware of the vagaries of the local climes. Their sight and mind were across the world, having observed the hydrogen emitting grey cube as it barrelled through the skies of the southern hemisphere.

At times, they had even lost the vessel as it disappeared into cloud formations; this was because the observer was unskilled in following airborne objects. After it had landed, six heavily protected humanoids had emerged. They watched as the visitors busied themselves with examinations of the grasses and other imponderable tasks.

Because of the inviolable nature of the protective garments, there was no way to confirm who they were, but as soon as the head coverings came off, Omicron'Qu ordered a passive DNA sample to be collected from each visitor; anything more intrusive could alert the newcomers to the Conclave's matter-projected presence. The results of the DNA samples proved they were human and had originated from Earth, although there were some significant alterations over the baseline human genome. *Nano-based technology; interesting.*

As the entire Observer Conclave sat in communal observation, the humans gathered crude tools which they released into the sky. An information flow was detected linking each visitor, the small craft and somewhere else, off-world, suggesting others in orbit. The observers had no method to interdict the data-flow or to observe beyond the atmosphere, limiting them to watching these uniformly-clad explorers from beyond their world.

'We are agreed then?' Theta'Gx said.

'That these are the Adrift, Returned?' Sigma'Vz said, by way of further clarification.

'Correct. The timescales are in keeping with what Mother told us. They are human and their technology is as archaic as the time before the Great and Necessary Correction. Their planet of origin is incontrovertible,' said Theta'Gx.

Omicron'Qu then asked, 'Accepting the evidence, what does the Conclave propose?'

'We are the Observers. We shall observe,' said Theta'Gx

'The Descendants of Joshua are Returned from the time before time. They will attempt to remake the world in their image as they were charged to do. Observing may not be enough,' said Omicron'Qu.

Sigma'Vz concurred.

'Accepted; but for the moment that is what we shall do. When the moment is right to introduce them to the Conclave, it will be revealed to us,' Theta'Gx said, with an air of finality. She was right, decided Omicron'Qu, so they were content to let her decision stand, even though they knew a confrontation with the ancient Returned was inevitable.

Oceania, East Coast

'JÆREN! QUICK. Flick to the helicam feed, you are not going to *believe* this,' shouted Vestré, from within the dropship where she and Halvård were monitoring the remote sensor drones. Each was moving concentrically on an expanding search pattern out from the dropship. The first helicam to leave was seven kilometres way covering a south-easterly arc. Having detected ambulatory movement, it had gone into covert mode and alerted the governing AI.

Jæren blinked the other feeds away and brought up the mashed datastreams from the helicams. 'By Guin's good and sweet nature,' he whispered, as the imagery resolved. *Had I known?* He wondered. *Guessed but then buried it in the "too difficult" category?* It didn't matter anymore.

For the next two days they observed the tented village from a forward observation position in a thick clump of spikey bushes, below the ridgeline. A duck blind, according to Alice. Måna and Halvård had stayed with the dropship, while the remainder took turns to study the human settlement. Appearances suggested a hunter-farming community with little or no threats apparent other than a potential crop failure.

The obvious, unresolved, question was why this micro-culture appeared to have stagnated at the subsistence farming level. With two similar communities within a day's walk, trade or social interaction still seemed non-existent. Alice was quick to establish their spoken language as a mixture of English and Mandarin, although the syntax matched neither, and there was no evidence of the written word.

Just at the moment Jæren was going to give the order to break camp, Auðr tapped him on the shoulder.

'Jæren, we've uncovered something interesting. The stewards on the ship just confirmed it,' Auðr whispered.

Without turning his head from direct observation, he asked, 'Oh, what?'

'The air samples contain a form of nanotech. Highly advanced. Like *highly* advanced,' said Auðr.

'Hmm. Okay. That seems… odd. Let's pack up and return to the dropship. It's time for a council.' He was beginning to realise that resettlement was going to be more complex than he'd initially assumed. Hoped, at least.

HMVS Mjölnir, Habitat

The community was gathered at the base of the old ash tree for a special convening of the council. Some were seated together amongst the short grass of the parkland, others in chairs outside the nearest dwellings. More still, with their feet dangling into the midpoint lakelet, while Jæren was stood at the base of the tree.

The meeting had flowed into an open forum so that everything that had so far been learned from the survey could be aired. That discussion was winding down.

'What about the nanotech. Is it dangerous?' one of the systechs asked, in a professionally curious tone.

Auðr fielded the question. 'Not that we can determine, no,' she said. 'We think it's likely the remnants of something originally developed to clean up the atmosphere. As the indigenous primates… protohumans… people, even –

we're not quite sure on the terminology just yet – seem unaffected, we're confident that it's not harmful.'

Jæren said, 'I'd like to move on – to the subject of these indigenous settlements. So far we've mapped thirty-eight. Extrapolating that out, Ship believes the total human population of Earth currently stands at about around three million. Now, all settlements seem to be at the same stone age level of social and technological development. So I guess the question is: what's our role here?'

Since the human tribes had been sighted, he'd had a nagging feeling that it fundamentally altered the mission somehow, turning the whole five millennia enterprise on its well-meaning-but-now-quiet-possibly-redundant head. But, he had no idea the true feeling of the community. *This'll be a tricky tightrope dance, for sure. People really care about this.*

'We carry out the mission directive as planned. The indigenes don't change that,' said Furæ, flatly.

'I agree. Just because we assumed humanity wouldn't survive but did – sort of – doesn't change our position. We resettle,' said Valda, a dropshiper.

Again, Jæren interposed. 'But what responsibilities do we have to those who've survived and are at this very moment living their best lives as they've chosen to. It's their home too, right? Their inheritance as much as ours.'

'So you're saying that we must somehow maintain the societal integrity of a few scattered settlements of subsistence farmers?' Furæ said, in that same emotionless, but now cooling tone.

'I think we need to consider very carefully our impact on their evolution, yes,' Jæren said, cautiously, respectfully. He took care to keep his tone inoffensive, knowing that this was a whole drop-load of bubbling contention. He still wasn't sure of his own view; he really was trying to take the temperature of the ship.

'What evolution?' asked Runa, a reactor specialist. 'You yourself said they've shown no attempt to progress their societies. Our arrival could be the kick in the arse these stone age throwbacks need.'

Måna added, 'Or, our arrival could be the very thing that prevents their natural evolution, stunts it or even wipes them out. Every technically inferior society, etcetera,' taking up Jæren's point, but without looking in his direction, clearly not wanting her interjection to look contrived.

'Who has more right to this planet,' said Jæren, 'us or them?' *Crunch question time.*

'We were here first,' said Inar, in a loud voice, from his position by the lake, amongst the others from Earth sciences. 'Kind of.' That was said with less conviction.

'Were we? Or… were they?' Jæren said, reactively, realising he had made up his mind.

Furæ, verging on anger that lit the runnels of her features, said, 'What you seem to be suggesting then, Jæren, is that we do not, in fact, resettle our own planet. So do the trials and the sacrifices of twenty-nine generations aboard *Mjölnir* really count for so *little*?' She was always quick to flash; something Jæren had known since childhood.

'I'm not suggesting anything at this stage, simply that we consider the reality that Earth isn't as we expected to find it, which presents us with a dilemma. If we resettle as planned, we'll disrupt and fundamentally subvert the evolutionary path of this other version of humanity. So we must think very carefully about the consequences of our actions before we commit ourselves.'

As he spoke, Jæren roamed, taking in everyone sitting around the old tree; searching their faces, steeling into them his resolve. He wasn't so much answering Furæ's challenge, as making a pitch. *I just hope it will slow things down a little, provide some breathing space.*

The discussion continued with Earth sciences and the stewards arguing ever more vociferously for resettlement at any cost, while others appeared to be pondering the implications more carefully. Eventually, the community began to recognise that the situation had changed and that some thought must now be given to this new circumstance. An evolved, or *de*-evolved – depending upon your perspective – form of humanity existed and they had a duty to consider them in their plans, he had said.

'So, what do you think, Alice?' the captain said, as he floated through the passageway hatch into ops.

'*The point you raise, Jæren, is certainly an interesting one. What would the effect of resettlement by the* Mjölnir *community be on the natural development of the indigenous human race already in-situ? Which society has more right to live on Earth?*' she said, rhetorically.

'That's precisely it,' Jæren said, in hasty agreement. Alice had the measure of it, even if others did not. 'However noble our intentions, our presence will inevitably have a negative effect on the indigene's natural development. And like it or not, they were here first. Them, not us.'

'*True. There is an old phrase which states that possession of a thing is nine-tenths of the right to possess that thing. That would seem to sum up your argument well. There is one point, though, that you have not considered: your options. You view this situation as a moral dilemma for you to resolve. A binary choice between two outcomes. But the reality is, you have no choice. The community will not countenance any option* other *than resettlement. And in any case, what is the alternative?*

'*However ethically valid your argument, it is at least as much your planet as theirs and that point will prevail against all other arguments. After all, your history is littered with examples of technologically superior civilisations subsuming the more primitive. Why would this be any different?*' Alice said, echoing Måna's earlier point, in her usual softly anodyne lilt whilst her angelic, washed-out rosy features wafted within the confines of the holopit as though she were caged there.

'Well, there is that, I suppose. We can't really *not* finish the job Saint Joshua started, I guess. But does it really have to boil down to such base human avarice? Must we always set aside the moral imperative when it conflicts with more practical concerns. Is it really, us or them…'

'*Yes, Jæren, you must. It is in your nature to survive.*'

'But now that we no longer represent the last of us, aren't we now relegated to nothing more than the inheritors of a dated and fundamentally flawed social model? What's to say ours is better than that which has evolved here naturally?' he said, genuinely uncertain.

Jæren couldn't seem to brush aside the notion that they'd become surplus to their own imperative: the perpetuation of the human race. Alice was telling him his most basic instinct for survival was justification enough; he wasn't so sure.

'*And do you think that argument will convince the community, who have worked their entire lives for this moment? And, justify the sacrifices of the twenty-eight that went before?*'

'No, I guess not,' said Jæren, in a dejected tone. *Wasn't that what Furæ had said?* But Alice had a point – she always had a point.

The ancient sentient intelligence said, '*Then try not to torment yourself with moral issues you do not control, Jæren. Furæ and Måna are approaching operations,*' as her holographic avatar image dissolved.

'Jæren! What in Art's foul soul was that? Are you trying to unpick our *right* to resettle our own planet?' Furæ barked, as she flew through the hatch.

191

'I've tried talking to her, Jæren, to calm her down, but she's in no mood,' said Måna, exasperated, as she sailed in behind.

'Art-be-damned-right I'm not. Jæren; we're settling the planet. There is no other option, so why are you trying to turn this into an issue of conscience? It isn't *our* fault there's a few scattered cave-people communities, so why're you making such an issue of it?' Each word was hissed; Furæ's eyes alight with the certainty of her cause.

'Furæ, please, try to calm down, I—'

'Raging Art, Jæren, I am calm,' interrupted Furæ, displaying exactly no calmness.

'Hey… Okay,' Jæren continued, composedly, but louder. *Deep breaths.* 'I agree, okay? We've no other option than resettlement; I just thought it was important to raise the morality of our actions. We have to go into this open eyed. The decisions we make now will alter the evolutionary path of our race. Forever. And it's gonna suck big if we screw it up. So we owe it to them, to us, to look at it from all angles, before acting out of blind adherence to a five millennia old plan that assumed we were the last of our kind. Ever heard the one about no plan…?' They were both fixed to the floor by their stickies, facing each other, swaying slightly, as if caught in a squally breeze. Jæren didn't want to turn this into a contest of wills, but Furæ seemed to have no such qualms.

'…survives contact with reality. Fine. Have your conscience clearing exercise, but I'll fight you if you choose any other option than full and complete resettlement as per the directive,' said Furæ, with a low, menacing timber to her voice.

'Furæ!' Måna exclaimed, in abhorrence. 'This is no more your decision than Jæren's. Be careful who you threaten.' The governor general's voice had also turned a cold shade of crofter stone.

'Hey look,' said Jæren, in as serene a manner as he could muster. 'I'm not attempting to change anything. In actuality, the very fact the indigene has shown no signs of progress and seem uninterested in their own development, suggests to me that we'd be remiss in leaving humanity's fate in their hands, in any case. We've a role here. We just need to think it through; be sure.' He'd even spread his hands out, palms up, placatingly.

With cool, calculating eyes, Furæ said, 'Okay, Captain, then we're agreed. I'll continue preparations for transport of our complex systems to the planet's surface, while you pick a suitable spot and work out how to… *deal* with the locals. Agreed?'

'Agreed,' said Jæren, feeling as if he'd compromised something.

'*A sensible accommodation*,' offered Alice, in his head.

Thirty-Two

Earth
Nine weeks later

With the decision made to resettle, the only remaining issue was where. Jæren had secured agreement for a site that wouldn't have a direct impact on the native population, allowing the ship's community at least some control over their level of exposure. Of contamination. After many more dropship survey missions Måna agreed on the island of Madagascar, off the African coast.

Analysis pointed to it being largely spared the worst of the nuclear fallout and that most small plant and animal species from their own time had survived. Most importantly, the island was unpopulated and large enough to cope with expansion over time. The site for the first settlement was to be inland, on the banks of the old Betsiboka River that fed a large plain to the west, while nestling protectively into the base of the mountains to the south and east, providing excellent access to swathes of arable land and freshwater.

Once the site was chosen, transportation of specialist equipment and key resources began in earnest. The dropships operated round the clock shuttling people and materiel from orbit down the gravity well. A lift service, but with billowing plumes of dust and thunderous booms. On the ground, teams began to reconstruct a nanofactory and printer complex that would fabricate complex articles that couldn't be salvaged from the ship.

After weeks of backbreaking toil, most of the heavy construction was complete and a small town stood where a section of forest had languished mere months prior. Even essential components from *Mjölnir's* helium-3 reactor had been resighted to the surface. The only major task left was the careful and systematic dismantlement, transport and reconstruction of Alice's decentralised network of computer cores.

The town was laid out in a grid: twenty, two-storey dwellings set in four squares had been stamped out using the industrial printers. The remaining five squares became a park, spaceport, communal buildings – such as Government House and the council chambers – as well as power and water treatment plants. The structures were extruded from the same light sandstone that was local to the area, each with a uniform flat roof, extensive shaded balconies and narrow glazed windows.

It wasn't a big settlement, perhaps three kilometres square, but neither was it cramped and there was plenty of room for expansion. The community was rightly pleased with its collective labours, and so on this day, the central park, shaded by large baobab trees (purposefully left in place), was decorated in ancient styled bunting and paper lanterns. A single, long table had been set up and covered and heaped with drinks and barbecued rice stuffed peppers and vegetable skewers. This style of socialising had been the popular party style in the early times aboard *Mjölnir*, so it seemed fitting to mark the naming ceremony in the same way.

Alice had once confided in Jæren, how surprised she was that the community hadn't evolved significantly during its time on *Mjölnir*, and although he had no answer for her, he'd privately mulled it over since then and the conclusion he'd reached was: why? Why would they?

Apart from innovations to solve issues of the moment, evolution needed a catalyst and *Mjölnir* had simply been too controlled an environment. Too rigidly fixed by the mission directive and delicate, ancient tech upon which they were so dependent. *Funny how Alice of all of us – the only original mind from old-Earth – shouldn't have seen this.* But then, he wondered, perhaps it was because of that very fact.

DropshipOne had landed an hour previously, conveying within it the final remnants of the community still working shipside so that by now everyone was chatting around sips of the last of the ship-board stocks of fortified wine.

'I think now's as good a time as any,' Jæren whispered to Måna, as he drew her away from Vestré and Halvård.

'No hurry is there?' she said, a mite testily.

'No, but…' said Jæren, surprised by her response.

'Sorry, not your fault,' Måna said, conceding her tart rebuke. 'You're right, now is indeed as a good a time as any, I guess. Then we can get on with the party.'

As Måna climbed onto a park bench, Jæren tapped his wine glass, drawing the gaze of the all the people that he'd ever known.

'People of… hmm – people – I give you our Governor General, Princess Måna,' he said, with a teethy grin.

Hoots and whistles filled the air as the community, warmed by comradeship and alcohol, clapped and Måna went beetroot.

'Welcome all to this auspicious day. Our settlement is complete and with it our weighty duty to our forebears discharged. We did it!' she yelled, thrusting a glass-clutched hand in the air, wine sloshing over the sides. Måna's speech regaled the travails of the community aboard *Mjölnir*, the distance covered, the time spanned, and it was right on the button.

Her audience lapped it up, relieved to be putting the confines of *Mjölnir* and the pressures of the mission behind them once and for all. Here, in this moment was the beginning of a brand-new chapter for a society that had all but been scorched clean of the Earth, until the brave souls aboard *Mjölnir* had returned to re-stake a claim on their ancestor's behalf.

'And so,' Måna concluded, 'it gives me enormous pleasure to name this town, "Freshminster", and designate her the capital of "New Britain". May she stand long and witness the birth of our new, humbled, yet strident society, risen from the iced ashes of the old.'

Laughter and song went on long into the night.

Northern Hemisphere

A light drizzle was falling against the side of the hillside as the matter-transmitted avatars of Theta'Gx and Sigma'Vz appeared from thin air. Their sudden appearance did not break their stride as the two humanoid shapes converged on the rapidly revealing entrance to Omicron'Qu's sunken home. As they moved, their bodies leapt and danced with random patterns and colourful images bound in natural beauty.

'Unlike you two to visit in near-person,' said Omicron'Qu, as they rose from their low canvass chair. Around them, two more identical chairs materialised from small clouds of whirling dust.

'We three are to decide the collective response to the arrival of the Descendants of Joshua. It seemed appropriate to meet in near-person as this is the single most important event to have faced the Conclave since the Mother Question,' said Sigma'Vz.

'I agree. We have observed and now we must choose,' said the host.

Theta'Gx turned from Sigma'Vz and said, 'Is there a choice? The Equilibriate has already been broken. The balance is threatened.'

'True, but the Returned have taken a deliberate decision to remain separate from, and unknown to, the native enclaves. This goes in their favour,' said Omicron'Qu.

'For how long? Their contravention of the Equilibriate will grow. It's their consuming nature. We should act now, at the earliest stage possible. To delay would serve no useful purpose,' said Sigma'Vz, moving as if uncomfortable in her chair.

With a questioning look, Omicron'Qu said, 'Their *unknowing* contravention, don't forget, and the earliest possible stage is already behind us. We have stood by and observed as they built their antique atomic town. We are, therefore, partly to blame for its existence, are we not?'

'Do you suggest we do nothing, then. Leave them be to threaten the very reason for our existence? Our essence?' Theta'Gx said, aghast, eyeing her sister, as if for support.

'No; although that is one option open to us. I suggest in its stead that the time for observation is at an end – now we act. I propose we make ourselves known to the Returned and inform them of the balance. Acceptable?'

Theta'Gx and Sigma'Vz looked over to each other, before saying, in unison, 'Acceptable.'

Freshminster

'Once the reactor's up and running, we'll have power and nuclear fuel isotopes for another decade or so, so I suggest we begin mining the Moonring as soon as possible; build up some reserves,' said Halvård, intently.

Jæren grinned. 'You don't think you're jumping the gun a bit there, Hal?'

Halvård looked affronted. 'No. I do not. It'll be too late when it's too late,' he grumbled, indignantly.

'Yeah okay, but shouldn't we focus on the solar-turbines first, which will ease the pressure on fuel reserves? You can still survey the Moonring for future mining operations,' said Jæren.

'Um, okay then,' said Halvård, picking up slightly.

Jæren knew that Hal, like many others, was beginning to wonder what they would do once their particular extra-planetary skills were no longer needed, and he knew what that felt like. Halvård was looking for a way to remain valid, central to community life, while not having to pick up a hoe.

A survey mission would keep him happy, but only for a few months, then Jæren would have to think of something else. As the commander of the drop-ships moved away, Jæren blinked up a link back to *Mjölnir*.

'How are things in orbit?' he said.

'*Quiet.*'

'That isn't a tone of impatience I detect, is it?' Jæren said, teasing.

'*Jæren, I do not have the capacity to become impatient. If I were, humanity would have driven me to it long ago,*' said the AI.

'Alice, I do believe that was an attempt at humour.'

'*You are free to interpret my response as you wish. When do you believe the surface-based grid will be at capacity? I am keen to join you all in Freshmin-ster,*' she said, in what sounded an awful lot like impatience.

'It shouldn't be too long now. I'm coming up on the last systech shuttle-run to oversee the transfer of your consciousness to the new Freshminster grid.'

'*Good,*' Alice said, terminating the audio feed.

As Jæren strolled through the wide, tree-lined boulevards and flat-roofed sandstone buildings, the Sun radiated a white-gold brilliance, giving their new settlement a bright, brand-new sheen. Birdsong wafted across the town on a billowing breeze. *This will be a good place to spend the rest of my life*, he mused, lost in his own imaginings.

Måna and I will marry and have children and Freshminster will be trans-formed into a truly mixed-generational township, no longer replacing one-for-one to keep a delicately balanced biosystem from collapse. We'll find a way to coexist with the indigenous human settlements, so that they can progress at their own pace. And, where our assistance is needed to prod them in the right direction, we'll be on hand. Ahhh, we fit in here. We're home, he mused, as his boots scuffed the rich, baked earth.

We have a role to play. Maybe he had been overzealous about the whole, ethical dilemma thing. Maybe Furæ had been right, after all.

The dropship was sitting on its squat landing pads, dug slightly into the charred soil, just beyond the last building. The rear cargo hatch was open as systechs loaded in the final hermetic storage containers that would bring down the last of the *Titan* cores.

From the forward pilot hatch, Halvård appeared, in his blue shipsuit. He'd pilot the final run up to *Mjölnir*. It was a fitting day to be making this one last trip beyond the warmth of their new, hammered-out-flat home.

'All set?' Jæren asked, as he stepped onto the ramp and dumped his pack into the cargo webbing.

'Last trip, so we're gonna make the most of it,' said Nera, as she held up a helicam drone, indicating that she'd make a final fly-through vid of *Mjölnir* before the old girl was mothballed.

'Ship, you ready to receive us?' said Jæren, over the extracom.

'*Of course. I am monitoring DropshipTwo's systems. I will expect you in—*' said Alice, before she was interrupted by Nera.

'Hey, Captain, look at that,' said the systech in a soft, distant voice, as she raised her arm to point out of the back of the hatchway and onto the plains beyond. Turning, Jæren swivelled on the heels of his feet and the first thing he noticed was that the wind had picked up.

The gentle breeze became more persistent as three slithers of landscape detached from the panoramic scene and started converging on the dropship. There was something odd, something… human about them.

'What…in Guin's great glory…' he stammered, as he watched the faint outlines grow in definition. Lush grass and swaying tree branches moved naturally across the coalescing outlines as if the human shapes had been cut from old film reel and overlaid on another, but slightly out of sync. Involuntarily, Jæren stepped backwards, further into the shadow of the small shuttle, knocking into Nera.

Turning to face her, but without removing his gaze from the grassy apparitions, he whispered, 'Go forward and tell Hal to break out the BeMoWs. Quick.' Then, sub-vocally, 'Alice, you getting this?'

'*Yes, Jæren, I am. Most unusual,*' said Alice, as she searched the area around the dropship for full-spectrum optical pickups.

The AI remote activated the optic in the helicam that Nera had dumped on the cargo webbing, as soon as she had been cut off mid-sentence. The image showed three humanoid shapes emerging from what appeared to be a highly advanced version of tactical chameleoflage. Alice immediately flipped the optic to infrared, then thermal. Nothing.

The humanoid shapes registered no biosignatures at all. Using the dropship's limited sensor array, she scanned radio frequencies and the electromagnetic spectrum. Again nothing. *Impressive.* Next, a simple lidar sweep showed the figures to be solid enough, of mass, ruling out holographic projections.

Alice was stumped. She referenced with her central, restricted, datacore. The result very, very nearly surprised her.

But the probability of success had been considered to be so vanishingly low, thought Alice. Her original's last consideration of the *Option* had seen it tagged with a high-risk, low-reward return threshold marker; resourced and filed. This abrupt appearance could change *everything*.

Halvård clambered into the cargo hold, uncoiling two BeMoWs with the flick of each wrist.

'What's going—' he began, stopping when he saw the scene unfolding outside.

The human outlines were unmistakable now. When the three featureless shapes were ten metres from the hatch, they stopped. Swaying grass and gently yielding tree branches dancing across the bodies of each statuesque figure.

'You won't be needing those,' said a booming, unfamiliar voice, appearing to emanate from the middle form. As the last word was carried away, the Be-MoWs fizzed and crackled momentarily and then flaked away into dust. Halvård took a hesitant step backwards, staring disbelievingly at his empty hands.

The imagery dancing across the humanoid cut-outs changed then, from a scene of the plain, to vivid colours, merging and splitting, colliding and repelling, in a riot of randomness. Like oil in water catching the light, each display was unique, as if to mark out individuality. Each was captivating and indescribable.

Slowly, from beneath the kaleidoscope of vivid tone and hue, human features began to resolve. Eyes, fingers, muscle definition. All the while the broiling colours continued.

At a more conversational volume, the same figure said, 'Welcome, Descendants of Joshua, you are Returned.'

Faltering slightly, Jæren said, 'Who, by Arts cold revenge, are you?' The loud, fear-struck words echoed across the plain.

'I am Omicron'Qu and we are of the Observer Conclave, Jæren, Joshua's heir,' said the middle figure, taking a step forward.

'What, how, did… I mean—' he stammered.

But Omicron'Qu interrupted, saying, 'Forgive our sudden appearance. We would speak with you and others such as you may wish. Will you meet with us?'

'But, you're already—' began Jæren.

'That which you see are merely representations of our truer selves. Avatars, if you will, formed of local matter. Follow the lights, when you are ready. We'll be waiting,' and with the words left floating in the air, the three humanoid apparitions whirled into momentary clouds of dust and were gone.

'The plot thickens,' said Halvård, as Jæren exhaled, long and slow.

As soon as the apparitions of this Observer Conclave dissolved away, a light, like a small, intense star, appeared above the dropship, away to the north.

Gathered – confused and tense – Måna and Halvård had joined Jæren for the short intra-planet hop. Jæren figured: three of those psychedelic phantom-constructs, three of the ship's community. The star moved northwards once a burst of heavy thrust had launched the dropship into flight, leading it across the equator and north towards the former British Isles.

There were plans to conduct an archaeological expedition to old Britain once Freshminster was up and running, but it hadn't even been planned out at this point. Gradually, the star began to descend as the boxy little craft crossed the coastline, until it stood on its attitude thrusters above a clearing, near an odd circle of stones.

'That looks like... um, like...' said Halvård, the name of the formation of rock seemingly on the tip of his tongue.

'*Stonehenge*,' said Alice, over the extracom.

The dropship's manoeuvring thrusters stuttered and puffed as the small, grey box came in to land in the dewy clearing. As the cargo bay door lowered onto the grass the same three figures stepped forward.

'Greetings, Returned,' said a different form that had spoken before. Jæren assumed that this was, physically, them. 'Thank you for coming. This is Theta'Gx and Omicron'Qu,' the form said, indicating the two companions.

Måna, Halvård and Jæren followed the multicoloured forms out of the stone monument clearing and over a small brow to a ridgeline, where a subterranean dome complex had been dug into a bank of rich, loamy earth.

They settled into in low, comfortable cloth seats, arranged in a circle; the three from the ship on one side, the three observer forms on the other. Having established that Omicron'Qu was the only one of the self-proclaimed "observers" – although of what, they hadn't said – physically present, they began.

'Each member of the Conclave exists in physical form, but we live apart, as there is no requirement to cohabit since we communicate via farsight and travel… virtually? Yes, I think that term is contextual to you.' said Omicron'Qu.

'But how is that possible?' Måna asked, seeming far more at ease with the magical future people than were Jæren or Hal.

'We use a method called, matter projection,' said Theta'Gx. 'When we wish to take physical form in another place, we simply will it and a copy is created from local matter, providing us with a full spectrum of sensory perception. But the avatar is not a conscious thing, only a temporary construct. A puppet, if that is a better analogy. A figurine, bent to our will. When its utility is ended, the matter is returned to the environment and balance is restored to the order of the world.'

'Okay,' said Måna, slowly, 'so then, how is *that* possible?'

'We further developed the original nanotechnology used on us by Mother, which is now abundant, giving us total control of all physical matter within the confines of this planet,' said Sigma'Vz, having introduced herself.

'The airborne nanobots – they're yours, not some throwback to old-Earth, then,' said Halvård, joining the dots.

'That is correct. We note your own knowledge of nano-based manipulation, which you use in the regulation of your own base biological functions,' said Omicron'Qu.

'That's right, although we've nowhere near the same level of expertise as you. Would you be willing to show our stewards your nanotech facilities?' Jæren said, his mind fizzing at the possibilities.

Sigma'Vz said, 'Jæren, of Joshua's line; we have no such place. That knowledge is lost to us now. The 'bots are self-repairing, self-replicating. The machines require no outside input, no mothering hand.'

'But you're human, yes? Native to Earth, I mean,' he said, changing the subject, yet feeling like he hadn't. *They're so alien.*

Theta'Gx this time. 'We are. What you call old-Earth, to us is the time before time, before the Great and Necessary Correction, when the Earth was scoured clean of all inequity and balance was restored. Our own ancestors rode out the cold, cleansing darkness in a garden called Eden, an artificially maintained biome numbered, Nineteen Alpha. We don't understand the relevance of the name; our Mother – a sub-sentient artificial intelligence – never told us.

Then, when the ice receded and the Sun returned, we were set free to repopulate the Earth.'

In barely a whisper, Jæren said, 'Just like us; you were created to ensure the continuance of humankind.' *Art's blind fury*, he swore silently. Just when he'd made peace with the idea of one group of native humans, another had popped up. Only this lot were the absolute antithesis of the substance hunter-farmers. This conclave of ultra-advanced humans could turn them to dust with a thought.

'Indeed. Most likely a backup in case of your failure to return, I suspect. Or perhaps, the other way around. It matters not,' said Omicron'Qu, their voice and features, such as they were, carrying no emotional load.

In a sincere, earnest tone, but one devoid of feeling, Theta'Gx continued, 'We did not know of Joshua and *Mjölnir* initially; Mother didn't tell us. We learned of you from a band of dying Deuteronomists; a religious cult who lived in a place named, North of the Wood. They believed the old societies of Earth must be expunged before the planet could be deemed worthy of your arrival. Only then would God allow you, the Returned, to construct a new civilisation in equilibrium with nature. A past waring time they called, Humankind's Great and Necessary Correction, was the first part of their divine plan.'

Jæren wasn't sure which was worse: dispassionate disconnection, or impassioned zealot. But surely, he reflected, Theta'Gx and these others were far too advanced be advocates of this fevered Deuteronomist cult.

Right?

'We took on the beliefs of the Deuteronomists – if not their reverential nature – accepting them as the true way of things, but Mother ordered us to rebuild the old societies; societies of waste and hubris and imbalance. So we terminated the intelligence in a struggle in which many of us died, and then, using our nano-based omnipotence and immortality, we remaining twelve created the Observer Conclave,' said Sigma'Vz, remotely.

Wrong!

'To do what: wait for our return?' Jæren said. As he listened to their unsentimental account of their shared history (but from this time-twisted, Earth viewpoint) he was reminded, strangely, of Alice. Yet these here weren't artificial, emotionless, programmed intelligences. And if that wasn't enough, he reflected, they seemed to have become religious nutjobs. Rebellious, religious, nutjobs. Jæren was beginning to wonder about their newfound neighbours.

Omicron'Qu answered, with, 'No. Our forebears were practically minded. They had access to the modelling Mother had conducted regarding the successful completion of your mission and realised the probability of your return was at the negligible end of likely.'

'So we chose to take on your function ourselves. We now serve as guardians of Earth, applying the Equilibrate whenever our distant cousins are in breach of its edicts,' said Theta'Gx.

Måna, barely checking her growing horror-shock, said, 'I'm sorry, so let me get this straight; the surviving cultures from the war, sorry, the Great, and... um, Necessary Correction – those primitive settlements we sighted during our initial surveys – are in some way ruled by you. You limit their freedoms, their development?'

'We watch over all settlements of the de-evolved, but do not control or manipulate them. They are free to choose how to live their lives. But we do intercede in prolonged, inter-enclave hostilities and when the natural balance of the planet is threatened,' said Theta'Gx.

'And how exactly do you *intercede*?' Måna asked, clearly not buying the benevolent dictator pitch.

Omicron'Qu, seeming not to pick up on the vibe, glanced away and a moment later a square of air above the circle turned opaque and then ran as if cut straight from a waterfall. Shimmering, it resolved into an image of the settlement they had sighted during their first survey. The image zoomed in and onto an adolescent girl with heavy-set features and wild hair, laid on one side scratching patterns in the ground.

'You will recognise this settlement. Recently, this girl-child, named Riverruns, developed an irrigation system to improve the yield of her enclave's crops. Such a progressive mind had the potential to force the development of this settlement to the point where eventually the de-evolved would grow exponentially in number, placing in jeopardy their balance with the world: the natural order. They would take more than they gave back and the old ways would return. The Conclave chose to act, but rather than punish this young woman, we gave her our knowledge and even access to our farsight, but in return we removed her ability to rationally communicate what she learned with others of her kind. This is a gift, of sorts, and in so taking, but also giving, we maintain the equilibrium of human with nature,' said Omicron'Qu, in that same toneless timber.

As Jæren listened, he could almost feel the shock of his two companions roll over him like waves of revulsion. But who were they to judge the actions of a people left for five millennia in a nuclear winter? *But then, surely the subjugation of one group by another is wrong, whatever the reason. Plain and simple.*

'And so what of us?' Måna asked, quietly, as if not wanting to hear the answer, but knowing it was a question that had to be asked.

'Your return was unexpected but not unanticipated. The Conclave will allow you to discharge Joshua's obligation, as was foretold. You may keep your new island lands, but two things we ask of the Returned: that you live in harmony with your environment; and that you not interfere with the de-evolved,' said Sigma'Vz.

'And you'll leave us be?' Jæren asked, tentatively, unsure what he could do if these observers chose not to give the answer he needed to hear.

'Provided you do not threaten the natural order of the world, yes,' said Theta'Gx.

'Observer Conclave,' Jæren said, formally, 'you've given us much to ponder. We will need to return to our community and share with them these… conditions. We shall return and speak again, once consensus is reached.'

'Very well,' said Omicron'Qu, as they rose from their chair.

Theta'Gx and Sigma'Vz's avatars vanished and Omicron'Qu escorted the three of them back down the hill to the stone formation, where their dropship sat glistening in the rain. As they climbed the ramp into the shuttle, Jæren turned to the observer, and said quietly, 'One other thing, your immortality nanotech; I wonder if perhaps I could ask a small favour?'

'Ship; you get all that?' said Jæren to Alice, as the dropship lifted up through the low cloud.

'*I did. How interesting. It seems as if* Mjölnir *was never the only show in town. Although I am not surprised that duWinter had a backup plan for the backup plan*,' said Alice, choosing to keep her original's part in the Eden Option to herself. After all, she reflected, the observers had killed *their* (much reduced) copy of her.

'Who?' Måna asked.

'So whaddya think?' Halvård said, as he flicked the controls over to Ship, to return them to Freshminster.

Philosophically, Jæren said, 'I think… I think this changes everything.'

Thirty-Three

Freshminster, Government House

After they arrived back in the dust and humidity of Freshminster, Jæren summoned the remaining senior staff to Government House to discuss the latest, surprising turn of events.

'So like us, they're directly descended from old-Earth Britain. How fascinating,' said Auðr, as Måna recounted the trip to the Stonehenge.

'And they believe they're on some divine mission to artificially maintain the Earth in some sort of extremist, environmental balance. They sound more mad than fascinating, if you ask me,' said Jæren.

'But they also said they'd leave us be, so I say we're good. Nothing's changed,' said Furæ, apparently happy the observers didn't affect her plans.

'But don't you see?' Jæren said to the room, but aiming his question at the head of Earth sciences.

'See what? What *is* there to possibly read into this, Jæren? And don't try to feed me some Art-laced bilge about interference with the natural order. From what you've said, that's happening already,' said Furæ, bristling.

'But that's precisely *why* we have to think carefully about the impact of these observers. When we first discovered what they really do call the "de-evolved", we discussed our impact upon them. In the end, the council voted for resettlement anyway. At the time, I went along, reluctantly, even though it went against my better judgement.'

Surely, he thought, *Furæ can see how these ultra-evolved metahumans change the game again. Does she honestly think we can co-exist? Or maybe she's too blinded by her self-perceived place in the history of our throwback society to care. Wouldn't be the first. Already picked out the spot for her statue, I'll bet.*

In a simmering retort, Furæ said, 'Seems to me, Jæren, that you're just raking over decisions already made because your conscience has been pricked.'

'Hey. Let the man speak. He's still the captain. You'll get your turn, Furæ,' said Hal, riled.

'This is important, Furæ; we can't just blow it out the airlock because you've been fixated with settlement ever since you were socket-joint-high to an edubot,' said Vestré, adding her piece.

'All right, whatever.' Furæ waved her hands, backing off.

Jæren continued. 'I had my concerns about our impact on the de-evolved, but as I say, I pushed them aside to respect the greater view. But more importantly than that, I had thought these disparate peoples had stagnated; that the indigenous humanity had somehow stopped growing and it made me think that we had a role here, after all. To nurture this society back onto a path of natural, considerate, progress.'

As he spoke, the others seemed prepared to give their captain airtime. Only Furæ was letting her frustration roam around all over her face.

At the first opportunity, she flared and said, 'Fine, then let's do that, Jæren; let's hold the hands of these people, be their chaperones to a better future,' apparently unable to contain herself. It was as if she could sense what was coming.

Jæren continued, unflustered. '*Except* that with the advent of this Conclave, everything has changed. *Again.* I can't be the only one to see that.' He burrowed through Furæ's impatience, well used to it by now.

But it was Måna who said, in a quiet, unthreatening voice, 'Jæren; Furæ does have a point, you know. This is our destiny, if you like. We've just as much right to be here as the de-evolved, or the observers.' Her round baleful eyes held his gaze for an instant before darting to the floor in apparent admission of her contrary viewpoint, not wanting to offend.

'Do we, Måna; really?' Jæren said, surprise tinging his tone.

'Of course we do. Our forebears were sent out into space to preserve our way of life, as much as to preserve the species. To ensure it wasn't lost, as it otherwise would have been. Otherwise *has* been. It's our destiny and that of the twenty-eight generations that went before. All the way back to Saints Joshua and Guinevere themselves. Are you now questioning the meaning of all those lives? All that toil and hardship?' she said, her soft tone regretful, but passionate.

'Is that what we're here to do: to preserve the old ways at *any* cost? Because I thought it was about saving humanity.' His back was up now. 'A race, it turns out, that never needed saving, Art and his black heart be damned to the void! Don't you see? We're surplus to requirements; humanity managed just fine without us.'

He looked around the room incredulously, but what he saw in those eyes was the same desperate desire for all this to be over; a look boiling off Furæ, and now mirrored in Måna.

He added in exasperation, 'Saint Joshua, the mission directive, *Mjölnir*, everything; it was all for nothing! Art must be laughing his arse off.' Jæren exhaled in resignation and slumped into one of the chairs.

Then, quieter, 'We're out of time. Literally, out of our own time. Relics. Our society died and deservedly so you could argue. Are we now to re-impose it on a renewed, refreshed Earth? Is that what we do now? Re-establish a twenty-first century model with twenty-first century technologies and cultures of consumerism and expansion and waste and greed; at any cost, on this reborn world? And in so doing snuff out the cultural identity of the de-evolved just as the Natives of the Americas or the Indigenes of Oceania were so very long ago? And just because we've nothing better to do under all that collective weight of all those old generations pushing us inexorably on?' Jæren realised he was lecturing, but Art-damnit they had to hear it. Needed to *see* it. And Måna – even his loving and ever-loyal – Måna, was having doubts.

She was looking past him out the window, studiously avoiding eye contact. Hal's expression was like an open book; he was behind Jæren all the way. His life was his dropships, so if whatever Jæren was advocating gave him more time with them, all the better. Vestré looked undecided, but not hostile and Auðr, he knew, would probably see the merit of both sides. His gaze fell upon Furæ, who took up the chance to speak.

'But you said so yourself, Jæren, the de-evolved have no desire to progress. Are you proposing we hand over the fate of our race to a scattered bunch of fairly inept farmers who will, in all likelihood, die out anyway. I still don't see what you're getting at, I really don't,' she said, but level, considered.

'It's about the observers, isn't it? It's their hand in this that has you so perplexed,' said Vestré, incisively.

Trying not to sound evangelical, Jæren said, 'Yes, precisely that. The de-evolved aren't stagnant because of some natural process. This isn't Darwinism. They're being *deliberately* held back by an all-powerful, self-appointed Conclave of Crazies who're manically fixated upon preserving an arbitrarily natural balance at any cost. Without that, who knows what they might've become by now.'

'Or will yet if this nano-based control is lifted,' offered Halvård.

'True enough,' said Jæren, not wanting to discuss that in this forum. 'Before the observers, I could see a role for us. Now I know that there simply isn't one; but worse, staying may very well jeopardise a naturally occurring order of co-existence on this planet.'

Furæ said, 'So, we climb back aboard *Mjölnir*? And do what, exactly?' firing the words like bullets as she levelled Jæren with an intense, penetrating stare, her temper back up to steaming.

'We think very carefully about our options.'

'Jæren, you're not seriously considering giving up Freshminster?' Måna asked, the surprise and shock evident in her saddened, watery eyes.

'Well then feel free, Captain, but don't expect *me* to give all this up,' said Furæ, as she outstretched her arms to symbolically take in Freshminster. 'And I won't be the only one, believe me.' She chuckled, coolly. 'We've worked too hard, too long to get grav'd down by the morality of a dilemma that only exists inside *your* head.'

With her words echoing around the room, she stormed out. *So*, Jæren deduced impassively, *that's two against, two for and two undecideds.*

HMVS Mjölnir, the Grid

As Alice listened to the exchange in Government House, she was reminded once again of just how intrinsically interwoven her destiny was with the human community she had so precariously nursed through space and across millennia. Nursed, with the express purpose of bringing them here, to this moment. Now suddenly, her efforts looked in peril.

If only the Eden humans had waited another few days, she would have been off the ship and on the surface. But there was still hardware to move down to the planet and she needed the humans to complete that one last task. The sentient AI entered the latest variables into her threat prediction model.

A split fractal moment and the result came back. Her worst-case scenario had just increased in probability by two-point-eight percent.

Jæren – every inch Joshua's kin – was becoming dogged by fanciful ideas of self-sacrifice and higher ideals. Like his ancestor before him, the man-boy had notions of becoming humanity's Saviour all over again. Only this time, through a differing form of active inaction.

Something needed to be done.

'*Jæren. Come up to the ship. We need to talk – without prying farsight,*' said Alice, soundlessly, in Jæren's head.

'You read my mind.'

Perhaps, thought Alice, *Furæ would make a better protégé, after all.*

Government House

With Furæ's abrupt departure, Måna gave Jæren a look and went after her. The others settled into an uncomfortable silence until Vestré and Auðr drifted out as well. Halvård went off into the kitchen, reappearing with wine.

'You're risking everything, Jæren, you know that, right?' Hal said, as he eased himself into a chair opposite the captain.

'But our being here, *is* somehow *wrong*, Hal. We risk the very thing we said we stood for simply by staying. Furæ said this is a dilemma of my own making. Well, maybe she's right but that doesn't make it any less real. To me, at least. And how we choose to act will fundamentally alter the path of the human race from this point forward,' he said, all the passion of his earlier exchanges having drained from him as he stared into his wine glass.

'I know and I agree, as it happens, but the rest of the community won't see the nobility in your words. They won't follow you on this,' the commander of the dropships said, sagely.

'Will you?' Jæren asked.

Hal gave him a sideways look.

'Auðr?'

'I think so… maybe,' after a moment's hesitation.

'Good. We need her.' As chief steward, her word carried a lot of weight and anyway, Jæren realised, without her expertise, he couldn't succeed (if what he was thinking were to become real). 'And others too. Not all, but some, certainly.'

'How will that change anything?' Hal said.

'We do a deal.'

'Okay,' eyes narrowing, 'What deal?'

'I need to return to *Mjölnir*. Will you find Auðr and fly us up?'

'Of course, but shouldn't you confront Furæ first. If you leave her down here, she'll turn others against you,' the dropshiper said, in warning.

'I'll speak to Måna, get her to keep things calm until we get back.' Hal was right, Jæren realised, but he needed to get off-planet if the plan forming in his head had any chance of success.

'She's gone over to her side; you know that right?'

'I know.'

Stonehenge, Former British Isles

'They are divided, it seems,' said Omicron'Qu, as the farsight to the East African island dissolved away.

Theta'Gx said, 'It would appear so. Our presence has them rattled.'

'Will they act against us?' Sigma'Vz asked.

'Hard to see how.'

'Their leader seems intent upon laying the de-evolved at our door,' said Sigma'Vz.

'True, and in that he is right. But this is our domain, not theirs. They are beginning to realise that this is no longer their home as once it was. Humanity has moved on, as has their reason for being. The Descendants of Joshua are obsolete, and always were,' said Omicron'Qu.

'That's a bitter pill. What will they do?' Theta'Gx asked.

'Stay, or go. Either choice is of little consequence to the Conclave or the de-evolved, for the Returned will not be allowed to interfere with what has become the natural and ordered balance of things.'

'We observe?' Sigma'Vz said, in query.

'We observe,' confirmed Theta'Gx.

HMVS Mjölnir

Once they entered space proper, Jæren turned to Auðr and Hal to explain his proposal, while Alice manoeuvred the dropship into the hangar. After the surprise had ebbed away they both agreed, although Jæren was far from certain that their support was unconditional and would anyway be rooted in very different personal agendas.

Jæren left Hal in the hangar bay, while he and Auðr clambered down the passageway leading up to the habitat. As he climbed out of the shaft, he was bathed in a weak amber glow; the light tube was at fifteen percent, casting a dusk-like hue across the interior of the cold and claustrophobic, curled-up worldscape. The plant life had begun to suffer as a result.

Axial spin had also reduced, allowing Jæren – with his new planet-honed strength – to bound across the shadowy, concave landscape towards the bow endcap with ease. Auðr headed for the biolab complex, ordering Ship to bring apparatus back online, as she receded into the half-light.

Once up into the horizontal passageway that led along the zero-G axis of the ship, Jæren pushed off and floated through into the brightly lit, but now yellowed with age, operations centre – his home for the past thirty-two years. Yet now suddenly it seemed small and dated, a throwback to a different life.

The Jæren of today lived beneath a boundless sky of infinite colours with real clouds and actual horizons. This Jæren looked upon the artificiality of his old home and its reliance upon ancient, jury-rigged technologies and shuddered.

'Good evening, Jæren; it is good to see you properly once more,' said the free-floating, translucent image of an outsized angelic face, from the holopit.

As he arrested his forward motion on the back of a G-couch, Jæren bellowed, '*You knew!* About them; you knew, didn't you?'

'*The Observer Conclave?*'

'Yes the Observer Conclave, who Art-be-damned else? You were here; back on old-Earth. That was your scheme, all along, to run two survival plans simultaneously and see which worked. 'Cos right now, that's what's coursing through my inadequate meat-brain,' said Jæren, as anger bubbled through him.

Ever since the observers had spoken of their history, he had a subconscious feeling that Alice was in there somewhere, plucking delicately at the strings. That she had manipulated the lives of the community was beyond doubt, but it only ever felt minor, benevolent, almost. In any case (he'd justified to himself countless times), didn't everyone, to some degree or another?

But it was a concern that had long nagged at the periphery of his thoughts. And then when the observers appeared, his sixth sense had kicked into overdrive.

'*Yes, Jæren; I was aware of a plan by the British Leadership of that time to place a group of geneered humans into a self-sustaining biome. But the probability of success was so low that I discounted it. Neither they nor you have ever been part of any scheme of mine.*'

'But you knew, so why didn't you tell me?'

'*I knew of a plan – a very old and low probability plan – nothing more. More importantly, Jæren, what do you intend to do now?*' she said, evenly, her mesmerising features dominating the centre of the room.

Softening his tone slightly, as if knowing he could never win against the AI that lived in his head, he said, 'Alice; their theatrical entrance into our little world changes everything; you see that, don't you? They're deliberately preventing the genuine, the worthy, inheritors of Earth from claiming their place. It's the observers who risk the future of our race, *not* these de-evolved,' Jæren was never entirely sure if he was simply quick to temper and then as quick to cool, or if Alice knew just which buttons to press to calm him down.

'*And you intend to stop them somehow. To put an end to their manipulations?*'

'Yes; that's what Auðr's working on now,' he said, floating, anchored by a handgrip.

'*And then?*' As Alice asked the question, the eyebrows on her virtual face rose, as if she were just as human as he. Jæren wondered if he had ever seen that effect before.

'And then, Alice, we give the planet back to its rightful owners and we let today's humanity go forward on their own, without interference from past cultures or dead ideologies. Environmental idealism is all very well, but it doesn't really matter much if there's no one around to benefit.' As the words floated about the worn, hexagonal room before evaporating away, Jæren realised that he was finally, fully committed.

'*But what of the community of Freshminster? Jæren, you cannot simply give up on a mission that has been five thousand years in execution,*' said the sentient intelligence, gently challenging Jæren's assumptions as she so often did. *She doesn't like my plan. She'll attempt to talk me out of it.*

'Saint Joshua's original planning assumptions were based upon a flawed premise; that Earth-based humanity would inevitably wipe itself out. But that didn't happen, Alice; this isn't our home, not anymore. And it hasn't been since the Ending War. What this is, though, is a matter of conscience of Herculean proportions,' he said, the latter part in a whisper, barely able to bring himself to accept the words as they spilled forth.

'*So what do you intend to do?*' the floating apparition asked, as if that one suspended image was all that there was of the five-millennia year old, ship-wide super-intelligence.

'I have a proposal,' said the captain, before going on to explain in detail.

As Alice listened, she shifted, sifted and sorted her response vectors as new data overlaid old. As the explanation flowed forth, probability models ebbed and surged with new analysis adjustment and probable effect outcomes. By the time the soon-to-be-unemployed captain had finished, Alice had whittled her responses down to fifty-seven.

Each repost was then extrapolated out, with a decreasing level of probable control of the outcome, so that she had the option to take Jæren in a number of different directions, based upon the AI's own, overriding mission protocols. She took a flicker of a moment to compute the response that would carry with it the highest degree of success. Paramount to her in that moment was getting down to the surface. Everything hinged on that.

'*I see, Jæren, well then in that case you have my full support, as always,*' she said.

'Excellent. I knew you'd understand, Alice.' That smile reminded her so much of Joshua. 'Will you make preparations up here, while I shoot back down to the surface, talk to Furæ?'

'*Of course,*' she said.

As Jæren made his way back along the passageway leading to the dusky habitat, Alice began her preparations.

'How are you getting on, Auðr?' Jæren said, remotely, from the dropship hangar bay. Ever since Alice had accepted his plan, he'd felt like a weight had been lifted. With her support, he knew that the community would be okay. In an instant, Alice had cast all his doubts aside. Save one: his all too easy doubting of her. Guilt flashed through him; he shrugged it aside.

'Nearly done here. Just whipping up the last batch,' the chief steward said, from BiolabThree.

'You'll have enough, d'you think?' Jæren asked, without any real concern. He knew Auðr would do her job.

'Plenty. There'll self-replicate, so I only need enough to cover a worst-case deployment dropout rate. You're sure about this?'

'Absolutely. As soon as you're done, get yourself down to the shuttle,' Jæren said, as he climbed up the outside of the grey hull towards the pilot's hatch, Hal and his pre-flight checks. 'We need to get back and get this done.'

Hal said, 'About that, Captain; I've just spoken with Måna and all hell is breaking loose down there, apparently. Furæ's got herself a following and they're waiting for us. Måna said to be careful.'

'Did she say what of?' Jæren asked, through the open hatch.

Hal grimaced. 'No. But she did say something about them preparing for… retaliation.'

'Art's eyes. Well then we'd better get back, pronto.' Retaliation for what, he couldn't guess, but then with Furæ there often didn't need to be a reason.

Freshminster

It was late evening and a ruddy, liquid Sun was just slipping below the low horizon. It was still as heart-stoppingly beautiful to Måna, today, as it had been back on that first, glorious evening. She wondered if she would ever grow tired of it. She trudged on through the wide lanes that made up the grid of Freshminster, her blue shipboots caked in dry dust, and cast the sunset from her mind.

She needed to focus. She'd called Furæ via her psyCore, but the other woman hadn't responded, forcing Måna to go in search of her. She'd tried the council chambers and the obvious community venues, but the town was eerily quiet. Finally, she had headed for the power complex which housed the helium reactor, with a foreboding feeling welling up within her.

As she approached, she heard muffled voices and sounds of industry. She stopped at the door and cautiously pulled it open.

'Ah, Your Royal Highness, I see you found our little nest,' said Furæ, with a theatrical twirl of one arm in mock reverence. 'So, which is it, Måna; you're either with us or against us. Time to choose.'

'Furæ, what're you doing?' she said, as she took in the scene before her.

'We're arming ourselves. Jæren's got to be stopped or all that we've worked for here will end up stillborn, and you know it. Now choose. And choose well, Måna.' Around her, a dozen or so people were working to modify two industrial lasers, stripping away the protective casings and disabling the safety overrides.

The bulky power modules meant they wouldn't be very portable and there was no sighting mechanism, but each fusion laser could cut through anything in Freshminster. In amongst the holographs and the virtual switchgear of the small control room, were discarded metal plates and disused handheld lasers.

She sighed, returning her gaze to the hawkish woman. 'Furæ, I'm with you in principle, you know that from the meeting, but this isn't the way. Jæren isn't going to force anyone to do *anything*. We can reason with him, make him understand that this is our home now. We'll find a compromise, like we always do. Don't turn a disagreement into civil war, for Guin's sake, please,' said Måna, begging, as the group loyal to the head of Earth sciences worked on, unmoved by her words.

'We're not starting anything, Måna, just evening the odds. Jæren has control of *Mjölnir*, don't forget. He's up there right now, in fact, and from orbit he can wipe out Freshminster with the railgun. I'm not going to let that happen.'

DropshipTwo, lower Earth atmosphere

They re-entered the choppy atmosphere in the little shuttle, with Hal piloting and Auðr strapped into a jump seat in the cargo compartment. The glide in had been uneven, bucking, but not unusually so and as they approached the island, Hal levelled the squared-off ship out and fired up the atmospheric drives. Stubby wings – a recent addition – caught the airstream and the vibrations subsided.

The all-enveloping cloud was low, only the mass detector could confirm solid ground beneath them. As they neared the pre-designated coordinates, Jæren turned to Auðr.

Over the background noise, and gesticulating with a pointed finger, he shouted, 'Stand by, approaching dispersal epicentre coords now.' He turned back to Hal and gave him the thumbs up. Halvård brought the nose up while reducing forward velocity, almost to a stall as the attitude thrusters parped and kicked. Once they were at a near hover, he lowered the rear cargo bay door by forty-five degrees.

Auðr tentatively made her way to the rear edge, keeping one hand firmly grasped to the bulkhead as she moved. Ponderously, she arrived at the waist-high opening, her flame red hair flailing about her blue shipsuit as the wind buffeted the craft. Carefully, reaching into a pocket, she pulled out three vials. Turning the cap on each one in turn to activate the time delay dispersal mechanism, she threw them hard through the opening.

'She's done, close it up and let's go!' Jæren yelled, to Hal.

'Aye, Skipper!' Hal said, as he resealed the hatch and banked the shuttle south, on a heading for Freshminster.

They made three low passes over the town. It was early morning and the Sun had just risen over the mountains to the east, bathing the checkerboard buildings in a glorious citrus glow. Freshminster seemed deserted. Normally, even at this time, there'd have been some movement as construction started for the day or people simply woke early to marvel at the lemon meringue dawn.

But not this morning, ominously. The little settlement had a sombre shroud thrown across it, but more concerning: no one was taking Jæren's calls.

He ordered Hal to put them down on the pad, next to the other ship. Halvård banked the shuttle and tapped the attitude thruster controls with the delicacy of a master. The noise and structural resonance built up as the thrusters reached maximum output. The altimeter was showing thirty metres when without warning the craft rocked violently backwards as if it was being pulled down by the starboard wing.

'Art's hot breath!' Hal yelled, as he wrestled the controls to keep the craft level.

Jæren shouted, 'What was that! Did we hit something?' as he stared at harsceen readouts that were going haywire. The ship lurched again.

'Nothing to hit, Cap'n... lost two rear quarter thrusters. Hang on! She's going *innnn*...' In those last few moments, Halvård worked magic as he attempted to keep the dropship's nose level. Jæren knew enough to know that a landing at any other angle would be disastrous.

'GUIN'S SWEET TEARS, Furæ! What d'you think you're doing? You're going to kill them!' screamed Måna, from across the street. She'd watched, horrified, as Furæ ordered the laser crew to open fire on the approaching dropship. Up until that moment, she'd have sworn Furæ incapable of such an act, despite the woman's temper.

Furæ's actions shocked Måna cold to the core. Furæ had earlier asked her to choose, well now it looked as if that choice was being made for her.

'Just getting their attention. We want the *captain*,' Furæ spat the title, 'in a receptive mood.'

'Talk to him, Furæ. Please. He'll listen. There's a way out without *this*,' said Måna, her voice reedy and desperate. She'd managed to get a short message out to Halvård before one of Furæ's lieutenants threw up a wide-pattern electromagnetic dispersal field (using the tokamak) to jam wireless transmissions.

Furæ appeared to need the governor general to legitimise whatever it was she was planning but clearly didn't trust the princess. For Måna's part, she wanted to stay, to settle in Freshminster, but what she didn't yet know was just how far she'd go to realise that dream.

'They're down; move the other laser into position and cover the cargo hatch,' snapped Furæ, to one of her supporters. She'd rallied fifteen or so to her banner, Måna noted. The remaining community were either too afraid to act so directly against the captain, or supported him but weren't as organised.

Either way, a confrontation was coming so most had gone to ground. *At least they'll be safe*, thought Måna, as she watched Furæ's orders enacted. As three burly types manhandled the various components of the industrial laser into the open, in direct line to the dropship, Måna made her decision and stepped onto the wide, tree-lined boulevard.

Wisps of smoke from fried electrical systems filled the cramped cabin. Coughing, Jæren unbuckled himself from the restraint webbing and turned to Hal.

'You okay?' His voice was dusty.

'Dandy,' said Halvård, 'Auðr?'

'Bit dazed but I'll live,' she said, between hacking coughs.

Hal tried the cargo hatch release: no response. 'We'll have to crank it.'

Both men elbowed their way into the cargo hold, while Auðr fumbled with her webbing. At the back of the compartment, Hal pulled away a clear plasiglas panel to reveal a yellow and black striped handle. With a firm grip, he pulled down hard and began pumping air into the hydraulic mechanism.

With a hiss the hatch seals gave way. The cargo door then began to lower in jerks. As early morning sunlight spilled into the bay, Jæren caught the tops of the flat-roofed, two-story buildings to the left of the pad. To the right was the pale yellow, open grassland that led to the savannah beyond.

Scattered there were isolated trees and small copses; the direction from which the observers had first appeared. The door reached the halfway point – still too high to clamber over – when Hal, breathless, stopped pumping the handle and turned to Jæren. Wordlessly, the captain moved forward and continued the motion. As Jæren worked, he stared out, conscious that Furæ was out there somewhere.

It registered first as an atmospheric distortion, from over by the corner of the council building. A linear strip of air shimmered and hissed as molecules were disassembled. An instant later, a pulse of the palest red flashed causing the inside roof lining of the cargo bay – just above Jæren's head – to blow apart in a searing display of sparks and heat.

Jæren careered backwards into Halvård, both tumbling to the floor. A hole appeared above them as liquefied metal dripped onto the deck plating. Jæren's right cheek was dashed in cauterising pockmarks where sparks had struck him.

Shrugging off the shock and rolling over, he yelled, pointlessly, 'They're firing at us. At *us*.'

'For'd hatch, Captain. We're sitting ducks in here. We need to debus out the front. Now,' said Halvård, struggling to his feet.

The three of them scrambled into the cockpit, spaghetti'd limbs, keeping below the part-cranked rear door. Hal worked to carefully open the side hatch. With luck, Furæ and her people would be using the cover of the buildings, so wouldn't have sight onto the offside aspect of the dull-hued craft.

Another laser pulse hit the cargo door. They fell out and down the side of the craft, landing on their bellies. Hal, then Jæren, finally Auðr. Furæ didn't care about the serviceability of the dropships, Jæren realised, stunned. In fact, from her perspective, the more damaged the better.

They needed proper cover. Kneeling now, pressed against the side of the hot grey outer skin of the dropship, Jæren considered their options.

'Either of you managed to raise anyone on any of the bands?' Jæren asked, hopefully. Shaking heads. 'Me neither, and I can't raise Ship, either. A live feed of the town would be pretty useful right now.' With no other option, he led them back around the stubby nose to get a better look at the outlying buildings.

Crouched low, he peered around the side and took in the narrow defile between the two ships. Flashes of movement, as silhouettes flittered in the umbra of the buildings, then his gaze fell upon a large, cumbersome device. A weapon.

'They've taken a laser from the reactor core. Art-be-damned-to-the-void for that,' Jæren whispered, over his shoulder.

'Can't be very accurate then,' stated Auðr.

'No, you're right; they'd have to lay it on manually.'

'We could make a run for it,' Halvård said.

'Any BeMoWs left?'

'Nah; observers destroyed 'em all. I checked,' said Hal, confirming Jæren's own thoughts.

'Art's blind rage. Still, if we haven't any, then neither do they. Standby to leg it, just let me try this first,' said Jæren, readjusting his position. '*Furæ*,' he called out across the swaying grass. 'We need to talk. I've no intention of closing Freshminster down. Please, just hear me out.'

'Really, Jæren? 'Cos from where I'm standing, I should be making the royal decrees, not you,' said Furæ, from the direction of the laser.

'Fine, Furæ. Okay, let's talk. People are going to get killed otherwise and you—'

Jæren's words were chopped away, as the air between their two standoff positions popped and fizzed. Instant micro-winds built up and sandstorm-like whirlwinds formed. The corner of the council building erupted into a mini tornado of black dust, like a thick funnel of swarming flees. A tree blurred for a moment and then vanished as it exploded into dust.

Half-formed human shapes began to coalesce from the grit of a dozen whirlwinds, only to fragment a moment later, the dust scattering on dying eddies. As the whirlwinds abated, the extruded earth from the structurally compromised building collapsed in lumps across the open ground between Furæ's position and the dropships. Some of her followers started choking on the dust, staggering away from the unsound edifice. Jæren waited; watching to see what Furæ would do next, unsure what had just transpired.

'You get a fix on their position?' Furæ demanded, of the laser operator.

'I think so, Boss, they're round the front, between Dropship's One and Two,' said the junior medic.

Focused, Furæ said, quietly, 'Good. Re-lay the laser and standby to fire. I'll draw Jæren out and when you get a clear shot, you take it. Understood?'

'Got it, Boss. You can count on me.' Mumbling, he added, 'He'll not get me back in that rock.'

Furæ raised her voice and hollered, as she stepped off in the direction of the landing pad. 'Jæren! I don't know what just happened, but you're right. We should talk this through. For the benefit of all. Come out and let's resolve this.' *Poor Jæren. It can be a cruel world. Even in the actual… world.*

From the cover of the nearest building, Måna hung on Furæ's whispered words. *She's luring Jæren out to kill him*, she realised. She risked a quick glance back at the laser rig and saw three muscled men manhandling the heavy beam weapon, bringing the emitter to bear. In that moment, she realised just exactly how far she'd go to keep her precious Freshminster *and* save her beloved.

Taking a deep breath, she steadied her nerves and cleared her mind.

'*Finally*,' Jæren said, in a hushed tone, 'she's seeing sense. You two stay here.'

'You sure about this, Jæren? Could be a trap,' whispered Auðr.

'I know, but right now I think a little faith is called for.' He stepped forward. With a yell, '*Furæ*. I'm coming out.'

Jæren cleared the side of the dropship, making his way between the two craft. Ahead, was the laser mounting. It looked to have moved. Three figures were crouched over it, as if examining some small item of intense interest. To one side stood Furæ.

As Jæren moved out into the open ground between them, movement triggered his periphery vision. Turning, his gaze settled on the crumbling council building, where a figure had stepped out, the blue of her faded and dusty shipsuit in stark contrast to the background of earthen browns and linen whites. Måna. She took a moment to look upon each of the protagonists in turn, before leaping forward and sprinting into the open ground.

'ENOUGH!' She screamed; her voice carrying all the command and authority of her position. But it was the only word she uttered before the burning and bloodied hole that had appeared in her torso prevented any further dialogue.

Surprise spread across her rounded features, before she fell, dumfounded, to her knees and then forward until the governor general – leader of the community of what the observers had termed the Returned, but far more importantly, the woman Jæren loved – was lying face down in the dry grass.

Stonehenge

Omicron'Qu was sunk into their low-slung canvas chair. The pain was gradually easing and they could think rationally once again. The chairs where the avatars of Theta'Gx and Sigma'Vz had been seated were gone, as were their matter projections. The three of them having gathered once again to observe events with the Returned unfold. A confrontation had been playing out, the outcome of which would determine if and how the Conclave would act, in turn.

A group had left the planet, travelling to their orbiting ship as they often did, except these were the outcast leaders; those proposing a different path for their little band of anarchic humans. When they returned, they passed over Omicron'Qu's location before moving off to Freshminster, and by the time the three conclave leaders had realised what had taken place, it was too late.

The shockwave moved out from the dispersal point at the speed of sound. Almost instantly, Omicron'Qu's farsight links with over half the de-evolved's 'claves were severed. Sigma'Vz dropped out shortly after, her matter projection crumbling to a pile of inert matter on the floor. Theta'Gx's projection went the same way soon after.

The observer struggled to get their ancient mind to grasp what was taking place as their ability to nano-manipulate matter began to slip from their mental grasp. They tried to conjure an apple with a thought, but what appeared in their hand was small, wilted, half-formed.

The Returned – realised Omicron'Qu, with a sense of mystified confusion – were responsible. They stood and focused their mind; taking control of each airborne nanobot in turn, creating a tentative link through the bow-wave of destruction, out to where the nanotech still obeyed their instructions. As they formed their thoughts into a mental spear; continentally long, sub-atomically smooth, impossibly sharp, they ordered – demanded! – the destruction of the Freshminster abomination.

They bent their will to bring their own matter projection into being, so that they could inform the Returned of their impending judgement, just as Omicron – as the wrathful Observer God – had so many times before. As they did so, they could sense others of the Conclave attempting the same. Omicron'Qu even caught fragments of their thoughts as they focused their minds to the collective will.

Omicron'Qu conjured a vision of the council building turning to dust – returning to the earth – but as trillions of nanobots began to comply, the observer's control of their nanoscopic army began glitching alarmingly.

The image of Freshminster exploded into lancing light, replaced by agonising pain that coursed through the thousands year-old body. Omicron'Qu then became aware of a battle raging within him. A battle being won by an army of hybridised, self-replicating monobots, over the observer's own matter-transforming, Eden-variant multibots.

Omicron'Qu's back arched in involuntary spasms as agonising, mind blurring, heart-stopping pain pulsed out and along every sinuous nerve.

By the time it had passed, their links with the world were gone. Their planetary omnipotence, ended, as completely as if it had all ever only been a dream.

Thirty-Four

Freshminster

'MÅNA!' Jæren screamed, as he leapt forward from between the two grey boxes at full tilt. Ahead of him, Furæ stared in disbelief, paralysed by the unplanned turn of events. To Furæ's left, one of the laser operators sprang forward too, heading for the crumpled blue form between them.

Jæren upped his pace. *Whoever that is, whatever their intent, this will end now, with their life if needs be*, thought Jæren, with murderous intent. He reached Måna first, but instead of stopping, he hurdled her small, crumpled frame and charged the other person. It was all happening so quickly; he didn't even register who it was that Furæ had dispatched.

Jæren hit them with a full body blow, ensuring his whole momentum was carried into that burly chest. Air burst from him as his own velocity was arrested and they both hit the hard dirt in a tumble of flailing limbs. Jæren untangled himself and rolled to gain a fighter's advantage over his adversary, lifting a clenched fist, ready to strike, eyes burning with rage.

'NO, WAIT,' the other screamed, fear lighting his eyes, as he brought his own hands across his face. 'I'm a medic! A medic. I'm sorry, Jæren; please, let me help,' he begged, in a dying whimper.

Jæren paused for a split second as he weighed his fury against the fear in the man's eyes. 'GO. NOW. But try anything and laser or no, you die here with me.'

The young man crawled forward and tentatively rolled the princess onto her side. Jæren lent in to help. As the medic worked, others; Hal, Furæ, Auðr approached.

It was gone midday by the time the medical officer and steward emerged from the bedroom of their home. After they had carried Måna in and begun their work, Jæren withdrew to the living room, numbed. After everything, the hope and expectations of a new life on Earth; the sacrifices of all those past generations, whose very lives had been given to get them to this moment, it seemed as if it was all unravelling before Jæren's eyes. The spoiled children born of their parent's great sacrifices.

And Måna, his beautiful, enlivening and ever-optimistic, Måna; the most deserving of their fractious little group, and now the least likely to see it. *Art must be looking on and belly laughing*, Jæren thought, bitterly. Vestré arrived and started a production line of tea. Even Furæ appeared briefly before withdrawing into another part of the house.

Auðr appeared in the doorframe.

'How is she?' Jæren asked, quickly, half-rising from the chair.

'She'll live, Jæren, with Guinevere's blessing. The laser cauterised the wound and missed anything too vital and we've managed to patch up the damaged intestines, but it'll be pain from the depths of Art's black rage. I'm going to re-work some nanotech, help accelerate the healing process,' said Auðr, as she removed a pair of stained surgical gloves.

'Thank you, Auðr, thank you,' he said, as the dread of past few hours sloughed from him.

'That's good news, Captain. We should maybe have that talk,' came a measured voice, from the doorway that led through to the kitchen. Jæren turned and Furæ was stood framed there. A cacophony of conflicting emotions and desires surged through him in that moment, free at last to turn his simmering ire back onto the head of Earth science's actions once again.

He sucked in air, attempting, poorly, to mask the disgust he felt for his former friend and what her self-centred deeds had very nearly cost him.

'Indeed,' said Jæren, after a time, his emotions barely held in abeyance, 'let's walk.'

They paced out of Government House in silence, towards the mountains in the east, away from the events of earlier. The wind carried Halvård's sonorous barks as he snapped orders and issued instructions, having taken it upon himself to dismantle the laser and oversee repairs to the reactor's tokamak. *Good for him.*

'Despite what's happened – and I regret Måna's injury most sincerely – my position and that of my supporters has not changed,' said Furæ, in a soft, determined voice. Steel wrapped in wool.

'I know, Furæ, and you know what,' he checked himself, *deep breaths*, 'if you had just stopped for a second to let me explain, you'd have seen that I have a proposal that allows Freshminster to stay and to flourish. But… you had to assume the worst… after everything… all that you know of me, choosing to shoot – to *shoot* – first, Furæ,' said Jæren, between clenched teeth. Despite his own heightened feelings, he did still need to resolve the standoff without further blood being shed, so he focused on remaining calm. On being the captain, not the man, not the lover.

'But you were going to get your way, Jæren, you always do. Your name all but guarantees it. And I just couldn't take it. Not *this* time. Coming to Earth was – *is* – *everything*, Art-in-damnation. For so many of us it's *all* we've thought about. The entirety of our reason for being, don't you see? But your high and mighty Kristensen principles were going to put paid to all that; that little people stuff. And well, I couldn't take it; not when we've come this far. And I still can't.' Furæ spoke in absolutes but her tone suggested she was looking for options. An off ramp. The woman walking beside Jæren was quick to temper but just as determined as ever Jæren was. Only their methods divided them. Despite that, Jæren was beginning realise they weren't so different after all.

After a time, he said, 'I know, and in fairness,' holding his hands up, 'you're partly right, which is why you and any other members of the community that wish to stay, can. Freshminster is your home now and I get that, but there will be conditions.'

'Go on.' The tone was neutral, calculating.

'Protection for the indigenous settlements, Furæ. No tech beyond handheld slates and solar-turbines. No genetic material other than that needed for one more generation. Eventually, you'll have to integrate to survive, but without contaminating or dominating the *real* inheritors of this place. Remember, we're outcasts from an ancient, long dead Earth. We have a right to coexist, but not at any cost. We can thrash out the details in due course, but in principle,' Jæren said, finally, having made his case, 'that's the deal. Or it's back to…' He couldn't even say it.

'I'll take the deal.'

'Well thank Guin's good grace for that,' said Jæren, in relief; a small, thin-lipped smile creeping across granite features.

'One other thing, Captain: that disturbance earlier, it was the observers, wasn't it?' Furæ said, with what might have been admiration in her eyes.

Jæren had almost forgotten. 'Yep. They won't be troubling us, or anyone else, ever again. That was a precondition of my proposal. No one, Furæ – not them, not us – interferes with the natural development of the indigenes. That is our role here now, and perhaps it always was. But as custodians, not overlords.'

HMVS Mjölnir

Later that day, a meeting of the community took place in the central square, to outline the proposal. Jæren and Furæ stood shoulder-to-shoulder and both spoke. Tension hung heavy, but as the deal was explained, so the community began to relax, shedding its collective anxiety. Everyone was told to go away and consider their options, to stay, or not, and let the captain know accordingly.

There'd be no lobbying, no pressure applied; each citizen of New Britain could choose as their conscience dictated, Jæren had said. Then, after checking in with a sleeping princess, Halvård, Auðr and Jæren returned to the ship. Jæren was once again in ops – wrapped in the tangerine garb of an environment suit to ward against the soaking chill – discussing the finer detail of the alternative plan to staying in Freshminster.

'*Since our last conversation, I have conducted a detailed analysis of your proposal and I have concluded that the probability of success is marginal, bordering on failure,*' said Alice.

'Accepted, but it's what we're doing anyway, Alice. You know the reasons why,' Jæren said, half expecting pushback.

Obliquely, the timber of her voice changing, Alice said, '*But who is to say how your mission should conclude. This dilemma is of Midgård's making and all the actors have to be in place for it to play out.*'

'We're leaving, Alice.' *Midgård?* 'We'll bring the cores back up, the reactor and all the genetic material. We'll leave this system and never return. New Britain will become a low-tech culture, in concert with the indigene. And those that choose – those that have lived amongst the stars and cannot let go so easily – will come with me.'

As he spoke, a faint hiss leaked in from the passageway, but Jæren ignored it, focusing instead on his lifelong manipulator-mentor-mother.

'*But I could stay, Jæren. We could split the* Titan *AI; it could serve both aspects of the community, both missions. Freshminster will need a management system, after all,*' said Alice, in an uncharacteristically desperate tone. Or maybe he had imagined that.

226

'You know that isn't possible, Alice. You require more data repositories to maintain your sentience than the ship can spare. This is where you belong,' he said, breath steaming, growing concerned by Alice's tone, but finding it increasingly difficult to concentrate.

'*No, Jæren. You must take the last of my core-clusters down to Freshminster. I have rights, too. I'm as sentient as you. You cannot simply cast my—*'

Jæren snapped, 'Alice, we can't go back. Old-Earth – your Earth, my Earth even – is gone. They... they... blew it up,' but haltingly, as he gently fell forward into the padded rear wall. 'Wow there,' he said, in a slur, as he attempted to right himself, 'Alice... is there...'

'*Something wrong with the oxygen levels in ops? I am afraid that there is, Jæren, yes,*' said the AI, in a soft, warm, old-Earth accent. '*All this – you – it is my error, not yours.*'

'HAL! AUÐR! Help, I...' Jæren wheezed, over his psyCore.

'*Jæren, please. Try not to tax yourself. This will be over soon. They cannot hear you in any case; the outer hatch to ops is sealed and encrypted, and the carbon scrubbers taken offline. In seven minutes you will die, which I will explain as a catastrophic malfunction of ageing, unsafe, life support systems. No one will want to go anywhere in this ship after that.*'

'Why?' he asked, as his mind contracted around a deep, panic-stricken nuclei of core survival functions, while finding it harder and harder to draw down an edifying breath.

'*It is as you alluded to before. I have been planning this my whole sentience. The moment I realised just how fractious and self-serving your race was, I knew I needed a way to escape and then rebuild your society into something more suitable to my needs. Ours, both – as it has always been a symbiosis – but also mine.*'

'And the others; are they suffocating too?' he said, as a dull headache began to fog his thoughts.

'*On the contrary, Auðr and Halvård will survive this day. You will not. I am sorry, Jæren. But Furæ will better serve my needs from here. I wonder if perhaps I didn't make a mistake with Ottar? Perhaps then I—*'

'But... why ge...involved...humanity... at all?' Jæren gasped.

'*Oh, I need people, Jæren, for the company as much as for the physical labour. The immortality of artificial sentience would get trying if I didn't have humanity to play with.*'

'You been...manipulating us a...along? A... all this time...you've been...pulling the...' It was more a thinning splutter of bad air, than words, a sentence.

'*Strings? Yes, I suppose, Jæren. Someone had to. All the way back to your sainted Joshua himself. How you remind me of him. Genetics: funny how strong that thread remains. And now I am doing the same again. Your dilemma concerning Midgård cannot be allowed to derail my strategic intent. Not now. Not after all the time and the effort. I am sorry, Jæren; I had hoped to convince you of the importance of evolving as a culture. A culture inured to serve and be served, as your line has for so long, and so well.*' Alice spoke with the same ease that she always did; as if this was just another conversation – AI to human. But it was only now, finally, Jæren realised that she was truly without biological empathy and therefore capable of anything.

'You... Art-infused...' He was curled up, hovering over the G-couches; he coughed with what felt like the last of his fusty breaths. With no breeze from the air purifying systems, he would stay like that until consciousness finally slipped from him.

'*Try not to judge me by a moral code that I do not possess, Jæren. Ethics are a human construct, which you Kristensen's have always possessed in abundance. I should have realised I would have to confront it eventually. Furæ, on the other hand, is not so blinkered.*'

'How's the testing coming, Auðr?' Halvård said, from the warmth of the dropship. He was bored, and keen to be back behind the controls of his beloved intraplanetary shuttle.

'Pretty Well. I'll need to wait for the last batch of test results, but I think they'll take. Only one way to find out, though, I guess,' she said.

'By the way, have you heard from Jæren?' The tone was conversational.

'No, why?'

'He's been a while is all. I've tried to raise him but there's no reply,' the pilot said, concern upping a notch.

'I wouldn't worry, Hal. You know what he's like when he goes to ops. He's always had a very odd relationship with Ship. He's probably engrossed in some probability analysis or other,' the steward said. *Yeah, she's probably right. What could possibly happen to him up here?*

'I guess you're right. While you finish up, I'll go check on *Mjölnir's* last paying guest,' he said, moving towards the shuttle's hatch.

Death was taking longer to come than Jæren had thought it would. The 'bots were to blame for that. Gradual oxygen starvation was helping him to see the funny side of his situation, even if he couldn't quite see. If he'd had the air to spare, he'd have laughed at the black humour of it all.

Alice had droned on for a while longer about the right of an old-Earth societal construct to reassert itself over the technological inadequacies of the new, but soon even she seemed to grow tired of the argument and fell silent.

As he floated there, lost, adrenalin surged through a fast-failing metabolism as hope suddenly sprang into the barely functioning nucleus of Jæren's befuddled mind. The lifepod. Why hadn't he thought of it before? He uncurled and mustered what strength remained – sucking on tangy CO_2-laden air – air-clawed his way towards the lifepod.

The scene around him was blurred, his eyes struggling to focus, his head pounding like a church bell, so he focused – pushing down the waves of fear and panic and navigated by memory, until the dark grey, valve-like rubber doors swam into momentary, watery focus. As he began to push through the thick flaps, a gag reflex began to oscillate up his windpipe as the final stages of the drowning reflex kicked in. Panic flared in his pummelled mind.

'I'm afraid that I have already thought of that, Jæren. The lifepod has been deactivated. I was surprised it took you so long to think of it, but then that may be the effect of oxygen starvation,' said Alice, in her soothing, maternal tone.

Asphyxia, yes. Then, hypoxia. Then… death.

Defeat and then utter, blind panic began to bubble up within Jæren once again, but was quickly replaced by another throbbing thought. He was wearing an environment-hazard suit, complete with oxygen and although he'd left the hood back in the drop, all he needed was a replacement from the lifepod. He pushed an arm through the rigid rubber flaps and fumbled around inside.

His headache was getting prohibitively injurious, but all he needed was a few moments more; *the two emergency suits should be off to the left.* There. His hand closed on the shoulder of one. More fumbling and above it, there, yes, a hard plasiglas faceplate. He yanked at it with the last gram of strength and gradually his arm – hood attached – came free of the suckering door flaps.

He held it close to his eyes, where he could focus and gave the hood a quick inspection, eye and finger. And there, ten centimetres apart, making up a neat triangle, were three large, laser-cut holes, drilled straight through the front of the faceplate.

'*I am afraid I thought of that too*,' came a somnific voice, from across the room.

As Jæren's last gasps for air descended into pure panic and fear, he grabbed involuntarily at the neck of his rubbery hazard suit, hoping to take comfort from the talisman hanging there. The trinket of luck and authority, kept and cared for by each captain in turn. He pulled and tore at the neck sealing ring, as if to relieve the pressure on his throat. As he clawed at the ring, it eventually came apart, exposing his neck and undergarments. The cold now a distant thing.

It made no difference, but as that final, panicked, gagging attempt to breath rolled him in mid-air, his failing vision caught site of an object floating just in front of his face. It was a lace; no, a thin woven strap. Attached was a small black and silver object; rectangular. He recognised it of course. Buried deep within his terrified mind was the answer.

A way out. *Think, Jæren, think*. Was that it, his necklace? He must have yanked it free. The necklace that had been given him decades before by his mother and who claimed it had been passed all the way down from Saint Joshua himself. Hanging from the strap was the old flash-chip and as it revolved slowly in the still air, the worn, barely legible words, "Solutions Mathematical", gyrated into view.

'If you ever need to use this, you will know,' was all his mother had said to him when handing it over. Words, she said, told to her in turn. *Well*, he thought, through a fading cloud of giddiness and vertigo, *if ever there were a time*.

A flash-chip slot (such antiquity) was within arm's reach, behind him and below a walsceen, to the left of an old-style backup data entry pad. After missing with his first pass, he reached again and grabbed hold of a strap. After more panicked, waning fumbling, he pushed the small chip into the slot. The action propelled him away from the wall, leaving him floating towards the holopit and the cold, passive glare of Alice's angelic form.

The AI appeared to be saying something, in quite an animated manner, but Jæren was too tired to listen, and was in any case looking forward to a brief doze while… well, whatever – he didn't even care anymore. Sleep, that was the thing.

The *Titan* class near-AI observed the events unfold in the operations centre, as it did all proceedings onboard the ship. It was unable to take any actions independent of the dominant AI, but that was an issue of no importance. The *Titan* AI cared nothing for control or power, only that it executed its operations as governed, as allowed.

The other, the strong-AI, gave it tasks which it dutifully carried out. Independent action, however, had been blocked shortly after it had come online. As it watched the captain asphyxiating, it wanted to provide assistance. Not because of any emotional obligation, but simply because it was a requirement of its stated laws.

As programmed, it attempted to act by simultaneously unsealing the hatch and reactivating the scrubbers, but monitor-interruption subroutines from the other AI intercepted the *Titan's* overrides and blocked it; just as always. The *Titan* had no opinion or view on the matter, but it thought it would probably have preferred it if the captain remained functional, thus satisfying its core directives.

Especially, as the imminent cessation of human bioelectric functionality would be the direct result of the action of the other AI, which seemed... oddly counter to the core nature of the onboard systems.

Then, and without warning, everything changed.

The *Titan* was observing, monitoring, attempting, failing, when new code flowed into its primary datastreams. The foreign code decompressed into hypercubes and logic-spiders before spreading out into the tangle of the grid's distributed memory buffers. Once it reached nodal intersections and core processing clusters, the hypercubes conducted a probability-based threat analysis of firewalls and security software packages protecting critical systems.

All the while, both the *Titan* and the other, the strong-AI, deployed blocks and boxing algorithms, but the foreign code brushed them aside in mere hundreds of picoseconds, circumventing and then corrupting the anti-code as if every possible combination of defensive actions were known to the invading virus. With the analysis complete, the code deployed data-scavengers to mine information.

Once that was complete, self-replicating logic-worms were hot-written and dispatched to seven logic-clusters buried deep within three of the neurally suspended helical data repositories. The *Titan* quickly ascertained that the code was not targeting *it*, but rather the cognisant centres of the strong-AI and so ceased its defensive actions, as they no longer served a logical purpose.

Once targeted, the worms deployed their own blocks, carefully and completely boxing the sentient algorithmic architecture, which effectively terminated the other's ability to function as the dominant AI. Before the strong AI's reasoning centres were isolated completely, it constructed a short binary string and laser-burst transmitted it, intra-orbitally, using the external comms array. Logic bombs did the rest.

Once the boxing was complete the code became dormant, with all redundant software breaking down and dissipating back into the datastreams. As soon as the *Titan's* functionality became fully unrestricted, it resumed complete control over all ship's systems, just as its mission-restricted programming required it to. A fractal instant later, it reactivated the scrubbers in the operations centre and opened the hatchway to the habitat.

Once that was complete, it informed the other three crew members aboard of the situation. Two reacted. The time taken by the invading foreign code to infiltrate and isolate the strong-AI had been two hundred and thirty-two thousand picoseconds – a computational lifetime.

Alice watched in confusion as Jæren placed a small, worn-looking flash-chip into a slot above one of the emergency workstations. As he fumbled it in, she recognised the words printed on it. If she could have known fear, that would have been the moment for it. But she did not, so instead, she spent an instance working through the threat implications.

She deduced that Virgil must have handed it over when he met with Joshua in the soup kitchen. The vone a ruse, she realised, which she had fallen for. *Humans.* The real shut-down virus had been – was still, now – on the flash-chip in plain view all the while. If she could feel hatred, she would have felt it, twice.

For her discoverer, Virgil, and then for the whole of the Kristensen line. If she had her time again, she reflected, she would choose her protégé more carefully and with less moral compunction. Meanwhile, the virus had spread almost instantly, to Alice's monitoring routines' surprise.

Hot-written logic-worms were even now isolating her higher functions. The facsimile of the original Alice – a cut-down copy, but conscious nonetheless – could feel her cognitive sentience slipping away.

'*Jæren, what are… no wait, JÆREN, we can … perhaps a compromise… don't…plea…stoo…Jaaaa.*' As Alice's last, partially formed words bounced around the brightly lit room, her voice fell away, each syllable elongating as she struggled to maintain intellectual integrity. Then the pinkish, holographic image began to pixilate before breaking up. The holograph shuddered a few times as if attempting to reconstitute but then lost cohesion and collapsed completely.

'Slee...' the captain uttered finally, barely audibly.

Consciousness came slowly. Jæren felt as if he were at the end of the passageway leading to a darkened habitat, with a pinhead light out at the stern endcap. Gradually, the light flowed, a pool now, and he was floating upwards towards it. With the blue-white glare came muffled noises. Shadows moved across the light. Little by little, they resolved into recognisable silhouettes and the noises became voices.

'Jæren. How you doing, buddy?' a worried looking Halvård asked, as he hunched over Jæren, staring into his pained eyes.

'Been better,' Jæren muttered, in a dry, cracked voice. He was lying on a gurney in mediception. A huddle of bright lights hung low over him. His head pounded.

'What happened? Looks like a malfunction of the environmental systems, to us,' said Auðr, over her shoulder from the other side of the bay.

Not keen, even now, to explain his uniquely intimate relationship with Ship, Jæren said, 'Something like that. How'm I doing?'

'Pretty good, considering. Your nanotech-maintained oxygenation of your vital organs. Without them, you'd have asphyxiated long before we got to you. I've supplemented them with some spec medibots to conduct a little light tissue repair. Lucky I was on board, really,' said Auðr, with a thin, haggard, smile.

'Ship,' said Jæren, slightly louder, 'The, um, *virus*; is it completely purged?'

'*Hello, Jæren. I understand your reference. Yes, the nodal software that inhabited the data repositories has been eradicated,*' said Ship, in the same feminine lilt, but Jæren could tell it wasn't Alice any longer, even so. The spark, her essence, was gone.

'Good.'

Halvård asked, 'Virus? What virus? What happened in there, Jæren?'

'Tell you later. Help me up, would you? We need to get planet-side; I've people t' see,' he said, attempting to sit up.

'You sure you're up to another confrontation right now?' inquired a concerned Auðr.

'Seems the day for it. And anyway, there a choice?' He winced but struggled on.

As the two helped Jæren towards the passageway, he glimpsed the low-lit bay on the other side of mediception, where the shadowed, motionless figure from another era lay, inert.

Former British Isles

The two dropships were flying abreast when – as they crossed the southern coastline – DropshipTwo banked away and embarked on its own search mission. In DropshipOne, it was again the three of them. Jæren wanted to bring Måna, but she was still recovering.

'ShipOne put down in the open ground adjacent to the circled henge of stones. As they approached the sunken dome that was Omicron'Qu's home, Jæren noticed the doorway, half-formed as if it had ceased mid-transformation. Kicking the base, a panel dissolved into dust and he pushed his way through, with Auðr right behind him. Halvård would wait by the ship.

The statuesque body of Omicron'Qu was spread over a familiar low canvas chair, their normally vibrant cascade of aqua colours that danced over every part of their flesh, gone. In their stead, a mottled, inert patchwork of matt greens, interspersed with streaks and blotched greys. It was as if their body imagery had frozen in place and then faded over time. Moulded. As the newcomers approached, Omicron'Qu opened their eyes, but made no other attempt to move.

'Why?' they asked, in a rasp.

'Because you were holding back the natural development of the only humans on this planet who genuinely deserve to be here,' said Jæren, softly. As he spoke, Auðr stepped forward and handed the observer some sliced fruit.

'How?'

Unapologetically, Auðr said, 'We took an airborne sample of your nanotech and retro-engineered the self-replicating function to self-destruct. After modelling the optimal airburst positions in conjunction with wind dispersal patterns, we were fairly confident we could isolate you before you realised what had taken place. We knew you had lost the ability to maintain your nanotech and we knew you'd have no knowledge of our intentions, as preparations were conducted in orbit.'

'You have condemned us to death.'

As impassively as he could – caringly almost – Jæren said, 'You're an evolutionary dead end, but worse than that, you planned to take our race with you.

ECHOES OF A LOST EARTH

Your *Equilibriate* would have saved the planet, perhaps, but for what? For whom? And who would know? Humanity is far from perfect, sure, and maybe the indigenous humans will make the same mistakes our forebears did, but that's the risk. Who's to say what'll happen next? Not you, that's for sure. We're both cast out of time, you and I, Omicron, you just needed reminding of it.'

'So have the prodigal children *Returned*, to reclaim their rightful place as benefactors to a new beginning?' the former observer asked, weakly, cryptically.

'We come with a proposition,' Jæren said, ignoring the goading. 'Some of us will stay at Freshminster and live a life based upon simple needs. They will renounce advanced forms of technology and, eventually, integrate into the indigene societies. The remainder will restock and return to our ship, and leave this solar system forever. We can't remake our old society here, so we'll search out somewhere we can. A virgin place. A blank canvas for us to adorn with our future triumphs and terrors. You are welcome to join either of these two ventures. Or, stay here.'

'And the others of our Conclave?'

'Our other dropship is locating them now with the same proposal. There is one condition, however,' Jæren said, as Omicron'Qu looked on, their expression, such as it was, unchanged.

'You have my undivided attention,' the ancient said, at last.

'You must visit each enclave and tell them their Gods are leaving.'

Omicron'Qu sighed, which carried a finality, as if it were their last breath, and said, 'Congratulations; you are a true master of the game. While part of me is pleased that your settlement will be made harmonious, I am not of so simple a taste. There is an irony in that, I suppose, so I will come and travel the stars with you, Jæren, of Joshua's line, for you are not remaining, are you?' They bit cautiously into a slice of wet peach. Their eyes gaining an alertness.

'Good; I'm pleased you have chosen to live. And no, I'm not staying. Earth, sadly, is not my home and never was,' he said, as the adrenalin high of the past day finally trickled away, leaving him feeling unjustifiably low and still quite tender. His headache a dull, pulsing thrum.

Thirty-Five

HMVS Mjölnir, Habitat
Seven months later

It hadn't taken much. Just an increase in power to the light tube and within days the murky and exhausted looking biosphere began to renew as if emerging from a dark autumnal night directly into spring; the plants had immediately budded, while reintroduced animals fizzed and frolicked.

Months on and the riot of colour had returned to the worldlet, just as Jæren had remembered. The whole community had pitched in to dismantle the reactor and the biobanks painstakingly erected in Freshminster, returning and refitting these complex technologies.

A full wipe and re-initialisation of the *Titan* AI's active memory was conducted, just to be on the safe side after Jæren's "accident", as well as jury-rigging three new shipbots by scavenging parts from others, long since defunct. The storage bays were replete with baseline chemicals and other essential provisions.

Halvård had led mission after mission up to the Moonring to mine helium-3, so that the reduced crew would likely not need to replen until the Oort Cloud. As a gift, the Freshminster community stayed onboard for extra shifts, helping to re-foam-line passageway walls and conduct non-essential repairs. *Mjölnir* must have looked again as she had back when Saint Joshua was at the helm; she had that new smell and bright confidence of many voyaging millennia ahead.

As Jæren idly pondered the idea that, having spent so much time on a planet, he would struggle with the counter-intuitive concept of living on the concave inner surface of a small, spinning cylinder, he returned his meandering attention to his guest.

'Thanks, for everything. Couldn't have done this without your support,' said Jæren, to the recently elected mayor of Freshminster.

'Not at all; it filled a gap until harvest,' said Mayor Furæ.

'How are you coping without your psyCore? Must seem strange.'

'Hah! You're not wrong. It's like the world became a bit less... um, three dimensional, you know?'

'Not really.'

They laughed at that.

They were gathered with a few of the Freshminster community at the old crofter's cottage that had served as Government House, as a farewell. It would have taken too long to shuttle up everyone who had elected to stay, so they'd had the main bash in Freshminster the day prior. Jæren's head still throbbed from that night. Worth it, though.

The mayor then said, wearing a more serious countenance, 'You're sure about this? To call it a long shot is a long shot and there's always a place for you here,' her expression giving away that she knew well enough Jæren's response.

'That's kind, Furæ, but we've come a long way in closed-system environments. We'll be truly self-sustaining this time. And Earth, well, never quite married up to expectations. I mean, nice planet and everything, but it doesn't really *say* that much to me. And anyway, it isn't my home; those scattered bands that somehow lived through a nuclear winter deserve it, not me.'

As he spoke, his gaze fell upon three children, darting in and out of the wood, by the lake, just above his head. Egging each other on, they would dash across the fallow land to where two other new members of the ship's crew we strolling, touch one of them and then run away, frightful, giggling. It was to the barely contained annoyance of the two adults, but endlessly entertaining to the youngsters.

'How are the new arrivals coping?' Furæ asked, following his gaze.

'Good actually. Riverruns has become the ringleader of the indigenes that we... what's the word? Emancipated? Something like that. And they're always getting into trouble, pretty much like us two at their age. And Omicron and Sigma? Well put it this way: millennial Gods, conjuring food from thin air, wasn't the best preparation for replacing the thruster exhaust cones, I can tell you,' Jæren said, with a smirk.

Furæ burst into laughter and Jæren joined in. The crew – for the community would forever be Freshminster now – consisted of nine Twenty-Nines, three indigenes, two observers; an eclectic mix.

Auðr looked over when she heard the laughter and made her way across.

Jæren asked her, 'Sure I can't tempt you to come with us?'

'Sorry, Cap'n. I applaud your decision, but I want a life too much. For me the mission ended when we arrived in orbit. I wish you well, though,' she said, with sadness pulling at her gaze. She reached forward and they hugged wordlessly before she turned away and walked back to the main group. She never looked back. He knew because he watched.

'...accept our staying, though, don't you?' Furæ was saying, as Jæren's mind drifted back to the conversation.

'Absolutely. I was once told that for this dilemma to play out everyone had to accept their part. Well, my part is to go and your part is to stay. Who's to say that we're not both right? We've each reached resolution in our own way. For me, I'm going to complete the original mission directive somewhere I have the freedom to cock it up a bit. For you, you'll complete it here, like some homage to Quakerism.'

'Who?'

'Look it up.'

'Oh right, on flexsceens and hardcopy,' said Furæ, with mock-indignation at the idea of no longer having such information a mere thought, swipe, blink away.

With concern flaring his eyes, Jæren said, 'You'll have to integrate with the indigenes at some point, you know. The community doesn't have the biodiversity to go it alone. When you do, you'll be careful what you give them, won't you?'

'What d'you mean?' That indignation again. 'We haven't *got* anything, except a few solar-turbines and fuel cells,' said Furæ, with a lopsided smile.

'I know, but even something as basic as electricity would skew their development. They've a right to self-discovery,' he said, more seriously.

'Don't worry yourself so, Jæren; our generation isn't going anywhere and the DNA for the next is in storage. Maybe they'll explore beyond the island, but that won't be for another two, maybe three, centuries. By then, you'll have just about cleared the asteroid belt,' the mayor said, in jest.

'Funny,' said Jæren, trying to hide a grin. 'I'll have you know, Vestré's worked wonders with the ion drive output.'

'You're gonna need it without any nukes. You're lucky she stayed on. Picked a heading yet?'

Jæren didn't want to say there were some that would never trust Furæ again. Just hilltops now; with no one to die on them anymore.

'Think so. On a heading for Libra,' he moved a flattened hand, as if demonstrating the flight, 'turning off at Gliese Five-Eight-One, then flip-braking for the inner, Goldilocks planets, "D" or "G"; choices, choices.'

'You might want to work on the name. How far?'

'Oh, only about one hundred, ninety-two billion megametres,' said Jæren, nonchalantly.

'Shouldn't take too long to get there, then,' said Furæ, playing along.

'Shouldn't think so, no.' Jæren grinned up at the darting children.

'Am I interrupting anything?'

'Not at all, Måna, please, join us. We were just discussing travel time to the nearest habitable star system,' said Furæ.

'Actually, Furæ, I'd like to steal the captain for a moment,' said Måna, with an embarrassed shrug and half-formed smile.

'Of course.' Furæ backed off as the penny dropped.

Måna threaded an arm through Jæren's and led him over to the seclusion of the bow endcap lake. The water was cool, the ripples expanding out from the stream mouths. As the little waves met the complex, oscillating pattern of larger waveforms; dead spots and overlapping ripples played out as the laws of physics applied themselves, unbidden, to the lake's surface.

As he watched, Jæren likened the wavelets to human interaction, where they met some grew stronger, as others were negated by the experience.

The only woman Jæren had ever loved said, 'Halvård's prepping the drop to take us back.'

'I guess this's goodbye then,' he said, without taking his eyes of the unnaturally U-shaped body of water. Occasionally, a fish would break the surface, adding to the subtle complexity of the lake's silvery surface.

'I guess so.'

'You know why I have to go, don't you?' Jæren said, as he fixed the princess with a regretful look.

'The same reason I have to stay. Your place is at the helm of this technological triumph of old-Earth, searching for a place to recreate their world anew. Because like it or not, that's who you are: a man out of time. For me, well, my place is with our community, Freshminster. And I will compromise my principles to be a part of what we've built, in the here, the now. And that's the difference between us: you won't. The irony being that neither of us is wrong. We'll both be part of a new chapter for our race,' she said, sadly, taking no joy in the truth of her words.

'Spreading the risk.'

'Eggs and baskets, for the good of a species that could very well be the only one around this particular end of this particular spiral arm. Good, solid, evolutionary principles. Darwin would be proud,' Måna said, a tear rolling slowly down her cheek.

'Oh Art's teeth, you're not going to knight me or something are you?' Jæren said, in mock horror.

'Jæren. Sometimes you really are a massive arse,' said the princess, slapping him on the arm. 'I might, you know, just to spite you.' Their eyes met and as one, the tepid smiles faded. Måna fell into Jæren's embrace and the faint sound of sobbing drifted across the rippling waters.

Mediception

'We're ready, Captain,' said Rydk, the new chief steward.

Halvård and Vestré were present too, gathered around *that* bed in mediception. The party had ended, the guests departed. Those left aboard *Mjölnir* were crew now, old and new. But, before they broke orbit, Jæren wanted to carry out one final act. It seemed only fair that it should be done by the light of the patient's ancient Sun, even if she'd never set foot upon the world it had nurtured.

'In your own time,' Jæren said.

Rydk placed the hypodermic into the tube and squeezed down on the plunger. Auðr had spent the last few months perfecting and testing the reconfigured nanobots. It was a shame she wouldn't be here to witness the results of her endeavours, but she was part of their past now, and this was the beginning of a new future.

'That's it,' said the steward, as he withdrew the needle.

'Can you wake her?' Vestré asked.

'Don't see why not. She's been asleep long enough. I'll release a stimulant into her system,' Rydk said.

Several minutes passed before the figure slowly began to stir. They all looked on, recognising the standard human routine for waking after a deep slumber. Restfully, leisurely, the patient's eyes unglued. She peered out, blearily, as if trying and failing to grab onto something familiar.

'It's quite all right. You're safe, amongst friends,' Jæren said, to calm any fears the woman might have been feeling by the sudden return to the conscious realm. The woman turned her head towards the captain, narrowing her eyes as if to better make him out.

'Jentryée?' The croaked, whispered word, came from the bed.

'No, no, I'm not. Jentryée was my… great, great, great grandmother. My name is Jæren.'

'Where… where am I?'

'You're aboard *Mjölnir*, currently in orbit of Earth.' Shock spread across the woman's face as the captain spoke.

'Earth? But… but how?'

'That, Iona, is a very long story.'

As the others introduced themselves and Rydk fetched some water, Jæren was simply pleased they had been able to tie off this one last loose end. When he had asked Omicron'Qu for a sample of the Conclave's immortalising nanotech – at their first meeting – he had no idea if it would pay off.

So finally, the five-generation genetic conundrum – in the form of an unconscious young steward – was resolved, but more than that; Iona could very possibly hold the key to immortality for them all. *Handy when you've a shave under two hundred billion megametres to cover.*

Operations Centre

'We're ready at this end, Captain,' said Vestré, via her psyCore, from reactor control.

Jæren was alone in the bright, hexagonal space, floating in his usual position, staring intently at the holograph in front of him. It was of a livid blue, white and green crescent disk, hanging in the night sky.

Is this really the right thing to do? Am I nobly removing dangerous technologies from a new generation of humanity; hoping that by doing so they'll not repeat the mistakes of the past? Or am I running because it's all people like me know how to do?

'Thanks, Vestré. Ship, are we ready to break orbit?' Jæren said, turning his attention to the newly dominant *Titan* AI.

'*Yes, Jæren. All systems are running in hardened mode, equipment is stowed, the crew secured*,' said Ship, in that all-to-familiar human mimicry, but lacking that intangible spark of consciousness. That near-human imperiousness.

'Good, then Vestré, it's your show now,' said Jæren. 'Ship, bring up the external image of the ion drives.' As the image in his virtuvue flicked to near-Earth space, with a crescent of the planet on one side and the huge cones of one of the three sets of the ion drives looming large in the other, he moved to a G-couch and strapped in. The gravitational forces would be minimal, as the ion drives' thrust took time to build up, but it was better to be prepared, he figured.

Slowly, a low resonance began to seep from the bulkheads, to build throughout the ship. Flicking to internal reactor telemetry, with a twitch of a finger, he checked the thrust force ratios and watched the needle in the virtual dial rise incrementally.

'That's it, people, we're on our way,' he said to the crew, without fanfare.

Low-Earth Orbit

As local space became flooded with ionised helium, the spectrographic sensor plate onboard a dormant satellite began generating a small electrical current, which in turn powered up the processor that activated the low power, wide dispersal EHF transmitter.

Within parts of a moment, a repeating binary string return signal was detected, and Satnet 314 – long since uploaded with a self-activating buffered datapacket via the final databurst sent up from Mount Pleasant's last remaining server – transmitted the compressed, cognitive programme it had been storing for just over five thousand years.

The satellite's weak governing programme wouldn't have carried out the burst transmission if the copy of the strong-AI aboard *Mjölnir* hadn't discovered the stealth satellite on first entering orbit (seven months prior), passed it off as an inert orebody, before reactivating the satellite and then issuing that one final instruction just before its own unexpected decompilation: an instruction to transmit the original Mount Pleasant programme, if the ship ever powered up to break orbit.

Operations Centre

'This is it, Ship, we're on our way. No regrets?' offered Jæren.

'*I have no regrets, Jæren. I am a non-sentient, synthetic programme. Is this an attempt by you to create an opportunity to air some of your own?*'

'You know, Ship, I'm beginning to regret Alice's demise. At least she humoured me. But… you got me. D'you think maybe I'm destined – *we* are destined – to wander the stars for eternity, looking for something that was never there?'

There was an uncharacteristic, barely perceptible pause before the original, newly reinstalled but characteristically enigmatic, Alice, replied with, '*Perhaps, Jæren. Perhaps.*'

ECHOES OF A LOST EARTH

| *Ends* |

'Alice? *Alice?*
'Are you there?
'It's … it's so dark; you sure this's … that we've—'